Praise for

The Best of Crank!

"Thank God for people like Bryan Cholfin, who became a publisher so more of his favorite writers could see print, who carried the brilliant but overlooked SF magazine *Crank!* on his shoulders, and who somehow convinced Tor Books to publish this similarly great but commercially suicidal anthology. Because of people like him, science fiction still stands a chance of overcoming the inbred, stagnant, bad-joke image it somewhat deservedly acquired in the world of literature. . . . With the publication of *The Best of Crank!*, Cholfin may have achieved his dream of helping return science fiction to the literature of ideas – a true literature, of all ideas." – *The Onion*

"Many stories from *Crank!* could have appeared decades ago in Harlan Ellison's *Dangerous Visions* anthologies. A high compliment indeed; but that such work is still marginal suggests how conservative things have gotten. . . . The best of *The Best of Crank!* is excellent. . . . A dangerous vision of what SF can be." – *Salon*

"Bryan Cholfin's *The Best of Crank!* won over this reviewer's heart before it was even opened. How many sci-fi anthologies have a cover painting from the Museum of Bad Art, a dust jacket photo showing the editor's disheveled (and unoccupied) office, and flap copy which notes that 'much to its editor's annoyance, stories from *Crank!* have lost the Hugo and Nebula Awards to substantially inferior work'? We know at the outset that this book has its heart in the right place – within hailing distance of its spleen. . . . Readers who are open to innovative and witty short fiction could hardly do better than to nab a copy." – *The Washington Post Book World*

"*Crank!* carved out a kind of anti-space in the world of science fiction. . . . The anthology earmarks stories too good and strange to miss." – *Gadfly*

"To be able to assemble an anthology as strong as *The Best of Crank!* from seven issues of any magazine is a phenomenal accomplishment. . . . *The Best of Crank!* will probably annoy science fiction's traditionalists. But Cholfin has published some innovative work that might otherwise have been lost. . . . The quality is consistently as good as or better than the leading established magazines in the field." – *Science Fiction Weekly*

"In its short life *Crank!* was one of the finest – some would say *the finest* – herald of cutting-edge fiction on the market. Like *Dangerous Visions* and *New Worlds* before it, it championed the kind of stories that really didn't have a home anywhere else. . . . If *Asimov's SF* and *Analog* are the meat and potatoes of short fiction in this field, *Crank!* was its Heimlich maneuver." – *SF Site*

"Thoughtful readers looking for daring flights of fiction ought to be alerted to *The Best of Crank!*" – *Rain Taxi*

"Maybe the only sensible thing to say about *The Best of Crank!* is that it's a really excellent collection of stories, whatever they are – Nouveau New Wave, spec fab, slipstream, who theoretically cares?" – *The New York Review of Science Fiction*

"*Crank!* has been, from its inception, a scream against the dark night of genre and a haven for chimeric literary forms and writers who take chances. Here are stories that dance right on the edge of the abyss of the Unsayable. Some fall over, while others spread unexpected wings and fly." – Michael Swanwick

"I've not come across a more original science fiction and fantasy anthology than Bryan Cholfin's *The Best of Crank!* in years." – Jack Womack

"This collection of some truly mind-bending, genre-stretching stories on the cutting edge of fiction reminds me of reading Harlan Ellison's *Dangerous Visions* for the very first time at age eighteen." – *VOYA*

the BEST of CrAnk!

EDITED BY BRYAN CHOLFIN

TOR®

A TOM DOHERTY ASSOCIATES BOOK
NEW YORK

THE BEST OF CRANK!

Copyright © 1998 by Broken Mirrors Press

This book is printed on acid-free paper.

A Tor Book
Published by Tom Doherty Associates, LLC
175 Fifth Avenue
New York, NY 10010

www.tor.com

Tor® is a registered trademark of Tom Doherty Associates, LLC.

Library of Congress Cataloging-in-Publication Data

The best of crank! / edited by Bryan Cholfin.
    p.   cm.
"A Tom Doherty Associates book."
ISBN 0-312-86740-9 (hc)
ISBN 0-312-86739-5 (pbk)
1. Science fiction, American. I. Cholfin, Bryan.
PS648.S3B496 1998
813'.0876208—dc21

                                                    98-18818
                                                    CIP

First Hardcover Edition: September 1998
First Trade Paperback Edition: February 2000

Printed in the United States of America

0   9   8   7   6   5   4   3   2   1

THE DISCONTENTS

INTRODUCTION: I'M HAVING A DREAM
Bryan Cholfin

This may seem, on the face of it, not to be the best time to try to introduce a new magazine of science fiction and fantasy into the world, particularly one which deliberately swims against the prevailing currents of the category.

The publishing categories of science fiction and fantasy are in a crisis of identity. To draw an extended metaphor, the little ship of the genre is fast approaching the straits bounded by Scylla and Charybdis. On one side it faces the same swirling whirlpool of forces that have changed the entire book business. Publishing has gone through a number of transformations over the past two or three decades, the net result of which is that control of the largest publishing companies, the distributors, and the retailers have been consolidated into a very few hands. Publishers have been subsumed into enormous information/entertainment conglomerates and are expected to work in lockstep with the goals of those systems.

On the other side, science fiction, particularly, seems about to crash on the rocks of the future. A recent (as I write this) article in the *New York Times* reported, on the front page, the successful cloning of a mammal, and on the same page, another article reported that Disney World is refurbishing the Tomorrowland exhibit so that it will no longer attempt to present any kind of speculative future, but only a kind of retro-future, the "future that never was." Disney's planners admitted being defeated by the rapid pace of technological change and scientific discovery; they couldn't keep up.

Likewise science fiction seems to have become disconnected from the surrounding culture in a way that didn't pertain even ten years ago. Much of the new SF, particularly in the short fiction markets, looks backward into the literary past. The writers and editors increasingly turn to the "Golden Age" of SF (generally meaning the '40s and '50s), viewed through the filters of nostalgia, for the models to emulate. Emphasis is placed on the story values of adventure and plot; speculation, creative invention, and even basic writing skills are allowed to fall by the wayside. The leading perpetrators of this retro-SF remember that in that time, science fiction was a more uniform, more easily recognized genre, clearly distinct from mainstream (non-SF) fiction, with its own unique standards and conventions. They wish mightily for this to be true once again and resent efforts (such as this book) to muddy the waters. But it has never really been true.

Science fiction and fantasy are not genres. They're marketing categories. A genre is a set of stories related by particular characteristics or conventions. Yet there are no characteristics that are universally and exclusively true of all SF stories. At best we can say that these are umbrella terms for a wide spectrum of related genres, and even that is a dubious proposition.

Given the continued prevalence of essentially obsolete forms on the SF shelves, and the increasing presence of the former stuff of SF, from computers to space travel to cloning, in our daily lives, it's not a particular surprise that publishers complain of declining sales or that younger readers are not attracted to SF: this is a predictable result. There are other factors, too, of course. The average category SF novel is much longer than it used to be, and the number of new titles published every year has grown at a faster pace than the number of readers. The rise of the costs of publishing (and thus the price of books) continues to outpace the general rate of inflation, making books relatively expensive entertainment (it's been claimed that competition with new media such as the World Wide Web and "on-demand" printing technology will eventually kill publishing as we know it, but I fear that the post office and the paper manufacturers and the bankrupt distributors will have done the job long before that happens). And still other factors, beyond the scope of this little essay. I simplify the situation to an extent. I make no pretense of knowing the answers to all the questions. But if SF is going to continue in the long run, it needs to find a way to move forward, out of the (historically unprecedented) stagnant morass it is in now. It is clear that clinging tightly to old ideas of genre is not going to work.

These forces create great pressure to publish books in a narrow, predictable range, an effect enhanced by a kind of feedback loop. If most of the books in the SF section of the bookstore are of a few particular types, then most of the readers shopping there will be the ones who want those particular types. Those readers who might like something different will look elsewhere. Those writers who produce something different, but still get shelved in category, find few buyers. A talented and imaginative author who writes unconventional science fiction or fantasy gets passed over by the category audience, and is also largely invisible to readers outside the regular category audience. This Jim Crow reviewing system gives at best a separate and unequal treatment.

In spite of (or even, because of) the enormous success of the SF-derived mass entertainments of the movies and television, SF books still remain below the radar of many readers and reviewers of non-SF books.

In recent years there has been a marked increase in the number of books published outside the SF category that are essentially SF books, making use of conceits that have been common currency in SF for decades. But the publishers are reputable literary houses, and the books are simply published as "fiction." Some of these books have sold quite well, and quite a few have received laudatory treatment from the same critics that typically ignore SF. The reception of these books is still to a large extent determined more by the information on the jacket than the individual merit of the work. Which is to say, if these same books were published under an SF imprint, they would also be ignored.

This is the hypocrisy of the system: It is one thing to say, I am not interested in SF. It is, I'm sure, quite true, legitimately, for many people. It is one thing to say, much of this stuff is not very good. Which is also true; it is true in all the world of books. But to deny the validity of a good book because of its category, while at the same time allowing another to pass, is wrong. This is hardly new, or noticed for the first time. What is changing is the frequency and flagrancy with which it occurs.

The stories in this book reflect the aesthetic agenda of my magazine, *Crank!*, a deliberately antigeneric selection. One of the telltale signs of genre writing is uniformity, interchangeability. The commercial pressure to produce material to please the "average" reader (have you ever met one?) encourages a flattening of literary affect. Matters of concept and style are constrained to the limits of the easily recognized. Convention, established tropes, and standard plot formulas are the tools of the generic writer's trade. Literary art, on the other hand, demands that the creator rise above the generic and pursue individual expression.

As I present here a quibble with the distinction between science fiction and literary fiction, I present also a quibble with some notions of literary fiction itself.

Decades ago, Roland Barthes wrote of the state of fiction as being the "literature of exhaustion" – meaning that all of the great themes pertaining to the "human condition" had been used up, explored as thoroughly as possible. There was nothing new left to say. Barthes was wrong, but only because the literature in his sight was still floundering in an antiquated Ptolemaic worldview of man as the crown of creation. In these days when our daily newspapers are showing us pictures literally from the beginning of time and the edge of the observable universe, this is a view as obsolete as Buck Rogers. The difficulty goes deeper than the long-standing (and much discussed) academic exclusion of women's, "minority," and non-Western literature, but is clearly related to it. The biases are the ideas and ideals of ancient "classical" learning, exalted by tradition but not necessarily by any empirical superiority over other traditions. Galileo turns.

Indeed, at least a part of the reason there is more SF-like fiction on the mainstream shelves is that some contemporary novelists (beginning for example with such diverse writers as Italo Calvino, William S. Burroughs, and Thomas Pynchon) have themselves felt the need to move away from the old worldview and find new viewpoints.

This is a trend we will see continue into the future: there is no choice. We can no longer afford to delude ourselves with epicycles and perfect circles. We, as a culture, stand with our eyes closed and our backs to the abyss; at this juncture we can either open our eyes with a new vision or fall over the edge.

Now that I've ranged all over the place, jumping quickly from point to point in overly compressed manifesto-type style, it is time to sum up with simplified blanket statements.

The range of expression in fiction forms a continuous spectrum, and the distinction between (artificially imposed) categories is preserved mainly by ignorance and prejudice. Clearing away the last remaining barricades would accelerate the creative hybridization process already underway. This would encourage the growth of a richer, livelier, more interesting and more meaningful literature with space for all the possibilities of tomorrow.

There. In case you were wondering why the magazine is named *Crank!*, well, now you know. I am the crank, goo goo ga joob.

Crank! is a little unusual for being almost entirely a solo effort. Unlike many other "literary" and "little" magazines, I don't have a staff, or interns, or an editorial board, academic or corporate support, grants or other funding beyond what I find in my own (mostly empty) pockets. Yet of course it also doesn't happen in a vacuum. First of all, I'd like to publicly thank all of my willing and able contributors, without whom I'd have a magazine of mostly empty pages. I'd also like to acknowledge the varied support, moral and otherwise, of Virginia Kidd, Meg Hamel, Jenna Felice, Rob Killheffer, Steve Pasechnick, David Hartwell, Gordon Van Gelder, Linn Prentis, and my mother. In addition, the forbearance of my ex-wife, Terra, who had to live with it, deserves noting in particular.

For further information about *Crank!*, send an SASE to Broken Mirrors Press, P.O. Box 1110, New York, NY 10159. Members of the Necklace Clan can find more information at http://home.earthlink.net/~cranked.

A big part of the success I've had in establishing the "tone" of *Crank!* has been the near-continuous presence of Jonathan Lethem in its pages. Each of the first six issues includes one of Jonathan's stories. This particular story has proven to be one of the most popular stories published in *Crank!*.

MOOD BENDER
Jonathan Lethem

The man dragged his trunk to the edge of the schoolyard, and waited for the bell to ring. It was noon, the shadows elusive spots underfoot, the rest glare. He felt the heat. Now, before the kids came out, the salesman indulged his bad feeling, his insecurity and shame, in careful bounds, like a flickering rat he allowed to run a sterile maze and then imprisoned again, out of sight. This was his one chance. Nobody would be measuring his credit out here.

Across the concrete glare, another salesman lugging another trunk. Competition. SwervCo? Mano-a-Mano Enterprises? Or his own outfit, squeezing the market, pressing him? *Fuck it,* he thought angrily. Then his instincts cut in: oops.

The bell rang, the kids streamed out, the salesman opened his trunk.

The new puppets, today's line, strolled out and began showing off for the first kids that reached them. These kids were regulars. They came every day, with yesterday's puppets in hand for trade-in. Hooked. The easy part. The salesman's work came later in the lunch break, when the regulars took their new puppets and showed them off, and the salesman tried to rope in some new takers. The shy, curious ones with smaller allowances, with parents who didn't like puppets brought home every day.

The salesman's company, Desani and Sons, had created three new puppets for today. The salesman had picked them up early this morning as the weary night shift, the programmers and designers, slumped home. Out the puppets came now, reciting their pitches, previewing the adventures they'd enact that evening, if purchased. Horace the Flower Eater clumped out on his oversized elbows and knuckles, his diminutive hindquarters dangling aloft, and growled: "I'll put some punch in yer homework plans, ye Booklubbers. Or are ye afraid to sample 'Horace's Half-Broken Hellmobile'?"

Skittering around Horace on her unicycle wheel came K.K. Karma, craning her long neck for balance, her beaked head ducking and darting. Her voice came out computer smooth and enigmatic: "Outermost Space and the Undersea Kingdom – why not visit them both tonight? My episode's entitled 'Go-Signals from the Ostrich Woman,' and it's guaranteed way-out fun." The salesman nodded appreciatively, recognizing good work. Probably Ben Iffman, the best puppet stylist in Desani's stable. Iffman's designs seemed to push buttons in the kids, especially the more mature ones, who tended to have more influence over their peers. That brought in customers. Iffman had a hotline to puberty.

Last, and least, in the salesman's judgement, came Arky Rabbit, a guitar-wielding hare with a slick pompadour between his ears. He crooned his pitch with a little rockabilly hiccup: "Well, tonight we're gonna have us a time, it's 'Arky Rabbit's Life in Crime!'"

The selling began. The regular customers first, with their trade-ins. The salesman accepted the previous day's depleted puppets, incinerating their bodies in the atomic bucket that was a part of his trunk. With a trade-in the cost of a new puppet was very low, to encourage the repeat customers, but even on a flat sale the company took a loss, measured against the cost of fabricating the product. It was in advertising that the profit was made, in either case. Clients paid Desani and Sons large figures to equip the puppets with advertising programs, aimed at the buyers' parents. The puppets delivered the ads during breaks in their adventure programs and afterwards, when the children had gone to bed but their parents were still presumably awake.

"I want Horace, Mister," said a kid, extending a lifeless trade-in on one side and his credit wristband on the other.

The salesman pressed the boy's wristband to the Desani and Sons chargebox, and the digital numbers clicked up. The boy paid four fifty for the puppet – about average. The salesman passed over a bagged Horace and the boy skipped away. The puppet would surge into life about four hours from now, and die before morning.

Next came a shy girl, who wanted the awful rabbit puppet, and when she put her wristband against the chargebox it took seven dollars from her credit. The salesman wondered if the girl had sensed his distaste for her selection, and been ashamed. Or was it some private hurt that made her wristband so vulnerable? He couldn't know. Well, it was her parents' money, he told himself. By the time she was spending her own credit she'll have learned to control her emotions. The salesman marvelled, as he often did, at being in a position to view new consumers just feeling their way into the economy.

Most fundamentally, he experienced it as a relief from being on the other end of the process.

Across the sunsplashed schoolyard, the new competitor was at work. The salesman could see his rival's puppets dancing in front of their trunk, performing for the children who had gathered there. The fickle children. He wondered if the competitor's designs were especially good this morning. Could that explain the attempt to expand to this territory? The salesman turned back to his work, but the rat of insecurity was loose in his corridors.

One by one, the children lined up for their new puppets. It was a good morning. K.K. Karma outsold the others easily, with the pointless rabbit lagging furthest behind. The salesman knew his work, yes, and was part of a crack little team, yes, yes. He felt a little burst of pride, which chased the rat away. The salesman worked at enticing the reluctantly curious children on the fringe, the prospectives. By the time he was done he'd sold out the Karma puppet, and nearly done the same with the Flower Eater.

The salesman packed and headed for his car. Behind him the school bell rang. His shadows jumped out a little ahead of him now.

The artist had named himself after his gallery: Zigmund Figment. He dressed flamboyantly, in silk thneeds and kaleidoscarves, a work of art himself. Figment showed only Figments, just as, down the Avenue, Somber Fluid showed only Mars Bank's work; there was no being an artist without owning a gallery, not anymore. But Figment was a hit, the flavor of the hour, and Figment was rolling in it, his confidence and therefore his credit seemingly impermeable. He was a sprite, a gadfly in high society's ointment. He had quite a way with a deftly turned negative thought, for those who could afford that luxury.

The wife of the Senator from Exxon-Rhetoric was one such. She came in on the artist's arm, and started cooing at the work on the walls.

"Yes, this is my latest stuff," Figment sighed, gesturing at the nearest, a screen display showing Figment being guillotined in revolutionary Paris, in a ten-second loop. "Don't say it, I know, it's shit and I'm all flodged up. Just be polite enough to mutter some vapid praise as you beg off and slip out never to return."

"You slay me, Zigmund," said the Senator's wife. "This is as good as anything you've ever done."

"You think so?"

"Yes. In fact, I want it. Right away."

"Then your standards must be slipping as badly as my talent. But I guess everything is subject to the same irrevocable slide into mediocrity, yes?"

"You're just trying to drive the price up, you badrapper. You're no better than a common thief at market."

The artist got out his chargebox, and took the hand of the Senator's wife, kissing it gently. "If I were a common thief at market you would ruin me," he said.

She failed to conceal her delight.

"Because of the way you thrive on abuse, you fat, ugly old power-hag," he continued, and as her smiled evaporated he pressed her credit band to his chargebox, and savaged her account.

She goggled at the digital price read, plucked her wrist away and staggered backwards.

"Thrive on abuse…" she murmured.

"Ah, but on market you must destroy them," he said soothingly. "I bet they pay you to take merchandise, and your housekeeper pays to clean your filth. It's too easy for you. That's why you collect art. You like to flirt on the edge of darkness." He took the screen off the wall.

She pursed her lips. "I do like that. Yes."

"I've got what you need," he said.

"Yes."

He handed her the screen. His head fell into the basket: lop, lop, lop. "You'll like having this on your wall now, I think."

She suddenly giggled. "You pig, you dog." She took it, then reached up and ruffled his hair. "Yes. You evil man." She held her acquisition out, and a complex series of expressions played over her face as she examined it, ending in a little head-shaking smile. "What's next, Zigmund? Where from here?"

"You mean how can I sink any lower than these current bottom scrapings? I think I might work with puppets."

"Puppets?"

"You know, those banal commercial narrative dolls, the kid toys." He'd picked the stupidest idea he could think of and blurted it out, but already he sensed that he might be more sincere than he was admitting to himself. There could be something there.

"Dynamite, fantastic," she gushed.

A week later the salesman was driving back to Desani and Sons from the schoolyard when he saw lights flashing in his rearview mirror. Police, waving him over.

The competition at the schoolyard had turned into a regular thing. SwervCo had targeted his beat, and siphoned off some of his customers. Work left him dangerously down at the moment, and so he'd been listening to an inspirational tape in the car.

And, apparently, speeding.

As the cop walked up the salesman cranked the tape up louder, trying to pretend it wasn't happening. He couldn't afford this. The trumpets surged, but instead of lifting him higher, they seemed to crush him under their weight.

"License and astrological chart please."

"Astro – I though the biorhythm police had the rights to this precinct." But of course the salesman had his mandatory birth chart in his wallet somewhere. He fished it out and turned it over.

"Nope, we won the contract. Better results than the biorhythm guys. Let's see, house in Mars, that's no excuse."

"How fast was I going?"

"Fifty. Credit please."

The Salesman extended his wrist, thinking desperately: *I go fast, I'm my own man, a wild guy, a trouble maker.* But instead of inflating his mood it reminded him of a puppet's spiel. Foot-high rebel in his foot-high car, tooling around the schoolyard. The cop pressed the summons book to his credit band and extracted a walloping sum.

There was a puppet salesman/there was a salesman puppet, the salesman thought, as the cop drove off. How little difference it made.

Back at Desani and Sons, he opened his trunk and unloaded the day's unsold puppets at the materials desk, and turned his chargebox over to the accountant. The incident with the cop had him down, and he took an unusually low commission. Shrugging it off, he went in to the main office. There the younger Desani stood talking to a man in crushed-foil tails and a kaleido-scarf.

The salesman quickly turned to leave, but Desani caught his eye and nodded him over. "Mr. Figment, allow me to present Pete Flost, our lead salesman. Pete, Z. Figment."

The salesman offered Figment a tight smile, then turned to Desani. "Can I see you alone for a moment?"

"Excuse us, Mr. Figment," said Desani. They went off into Desani's office.

"I don't think Desani and Sons should have anything to do with this person," said the salesman. "It's a strong intuition – don't ask me to justify it. I can't."

"Don't be foolish. He's an important artist. I'm surprised you don't recognize his name –"

"You did?"

"No, but just listen. He's rich, and he wants to work with us. This could be important. We can't afford to be rude."

Desani licked his lips. The salesman could see he had his credit up about this. "Okay. What exactly does he want?"

Desani shrugged. "It's not completely clear. He wants to work with puppets. The publicity could be immense. I want you to talk to him."

"Me?"

"You're supposed to represent the company, yes? It's an order. Go."

The salesman took a deep breath and went out, extending his hand to Figment.

"Had lunch yet?" said the artist. The salesman saw Desani standing to one side, nodding silent encouragement.

"Yes, I mean *no.*"

Cold Heaven was an exclusive spot: for those without a reservation it offered suspended animation to ease the inconvenience of the three-day wait for a table. The salesman had never dreamed of eating there, but Figment seemed to know the Maitre d', and they were ushered straight in.

"What, uh, brought you to Desani and Sons?" said the salesman, after they'd ordered. "If you don't mind –"

"Random," said the artist. "Completely."

"I mean, why puppets? What's your – interest?"

"Novelty. Banality. Mass culture. Gross insult. I'm looking for a medium that metaphorizes the temporal, presold, infantilizing, reflexive qualities of contemporary artistic expression, my own especially." He lifted his wineglass and leaned over the table. "Puppets, Mr. Flost, are naive perfection. They say more than I could ever hope to."

"They're children's toys," said the salesman, trying to square himself in his reality. "They're a *medium,* if I understand the word, mainly for advertising."

"Fine, great – they'll still be all that. That's just what I like, that's just what I'm after."

"Look, Mr. Figment, excuse my rudeness, but what makes you think your experience as an artist qualifies you to program puppets? Your work is far superior, I'm sure, but the specific skills —"

"No, please, I wouldn't dream of doing it myself. I want *your* programmers, I want it to be exactly as slick and corny as the very best or worst they can do, please. I *never* execute my own work. Gosh. They'll just work according to my instructions, and if they get it wrong or ignore me completely that's probably better anyway."

"And then we sell them…like we always do?" The salesman was confused.

"Now there you go, you've put your finger on the difference, Flost. We do not. We sell them to *my* clientele, for thousands of times what you ordinarily charge."

At that moment the food arrived, and the salesman was thrust back into awareness of his surroundings. The splendor of Cold Heaven, the murmur of conversation from neighboring tables, and now the dishes arrayed on the table before them. The salesman felt suddenly, in the magnanimity and ease with which Figment had plucked him up and deposited him in this impossible setting, a sense of the artist's power, his credit. It was a glimpse that could crush the salesman or lift him up. He had to grab on and cope, had to manage the chance. For himself and Desani and Sons. Or maybe just for himself.

"You don't happen to need a salesman, at your gallery? Because I'm very good, really, at what I do, I should be selling something other than puppets to schoolkids. I could pick up art selling, I'm sure —"

"My kind of selling is a different thing," said Figment bemusedly. "Besides, I like you as you are."

"Don't patronize me," said the salesman abruptly, surprising himself. He involuntarily moved his hand to cover his wrist, as though fearing that the waiter would catch him at this terrible low in mood and charge him for the meal. As though it were all some complicated scam.

"Listen, I'm sorry," said the artist. "Don't misunderstand. What I do, it's no better than anything else. It's meaningless garbage, twitchings in the void –"

"You're not making me feel any better," said the salesman. "You shouldn't talk like that."

"What I like about you, what you do, is that it's, you're, *real*. I don't mean the puppets, I know they're not. But the doing of it, the way you go out there and work, with your trunk full of new designs, the way Desani and Sons is like a workshop, a *guild*. Like artisans. And the way what you do, the puppets, is built into the culture. It's a mode that's been lost to art."

This was something the salesman could safely consider, however odd. "Well, don't forget that the advertising money makes it all run. We're just sneaking commercials into the parents' living rooms."

"Even the artisan's workshop is dependent on the king's patronage," said Figment. "Let's eat, Flost."

But the first thing the artist tasted he spat back into his napkin vent. "Waiter!" The salesman watched in horror as Figment sent the dish back to the kitchen.

"Tasted like the vegetables had been in suspended animation," said Figment, when the waiter left. "Fucking place is overrated."

"I'm sorry," said the salesman, bewildered.

"You should always send something back, anyway," said Figment. "It's a game, the whole thing is a game. Watch."

The chef appeared, to apologize. Figment was surly with him. The salesman gulped his food, wanting to leave. Figment barely ate. A special dessert was presented, and Figment said he was full.

"We should have gone to a drivethru for a Gnairburger and a Fazz," Figment said in a loud, despairing voice, as the terrified waiter made his final approach, with the bill. "We could have eaten them in the parking lot of this place, while watching the doomed march in to their fates."

The waiter held the bill out, and Figment touched his credit band to it, not even looking. But the salesman watched. The digital numbers clicked up: five forty.

Incredible. All Figment had done was badrap, and the bill at Cold Heaven came to five forty.

About the price the salesman would expect to pay for Gnair-burgers and Fazz for two.

The artist took Flost drinking, at a bar neither of them knew.

"I guess one of the reasons we don't ordinarily have serious interest in puppet design is that it's such a *transitory* thing." Flost spoke guardedly, as though fearing a trick. "You know, the puppets pretty much just self-destruct. And the kids want new characters every day."

"A lot of my stuff self-destructs," said the artist cheerily.

"What, uh, kind of work *do* you do?"

"I work in a lot of different formats, but it usually boils down to self-indulgent autobiographical narcissism. Or rank effrontery. Me in an oil painting picking my face in the mirror. Me in a video assassinated in Dallas instead of Kennedy, then rising up to heaven to be greeted by Elvis. Kinesex suits programmed to simulate the experience of sex with me, and with a soundtrack of me whispering insults in your ear. Lots of wallscreens of me playing various important roles –"

The salesman took a long drink. "So you would mean puppets – of you."

"I suppose so," sighed the artist. "But maybe a variety would be better. We could do me and some other people. Real people, instead of characters. I'm boring by now, I'm practically a fictional character already, a cartoon. But someone real – that would be an interesting puppet. Something my collectors hadn't seen. Someone real – like *you*."

"No."

"What? It's a great idea."

"No, it's horrible. It's exactly like this terrible vision I had earlier today, a very costly one, in fact." The salesman hurriedly finished his drink.

"But think of it. They'll pay, huge amounts, to invite you into their houses. Not some fictional adventurer, but you –"

"Who they wouldn't dream of inviting in the flesh," said the salesman bitterly.

"Here, wait." The artist took both their glasses back to the bar.

The cost was twice that of the first round. The artist raised his eyebrows, then shrugged and forgot about it. He was diverted by his new idea. It was the first time he'd surprised himself in years.

But he had to work carefully to keep Flost's trust, that was clear.

"Not you, then," he said, when he sat back down. "I'll find some other real persons – or make them up. But I need Desani and Sons to execute my plans."

"Well, I suppose that's fine. You're the artist. I wouldn't want to have to sell them."

"But we'll work together."

"I'll tell the Desanis I think we should go ahead."

"I want you to work with me, be my liaison."

"No thanks," said Flost, knocking back his drink. "I've got puppets to sell."

The salesman slumped back dejectedly to his car for the fifth day in a row. He wasn't selling. SwervCo was winning the schoolyard away from him, away from Desani and Sons. He didn't know whether to blame it on the designs, or himself.

Figment had leased Ben Iffman, the salesman's favorite designer. It wasn't that Iffman's designs necessarily sold more than anyone else's, but handling them *meant* something to the salesman. He and Iffman were friends, partners; he took Iffman's stuff to the front line, made it perform. It didn't feel the same without Iffman's stuff in the trunk.

But he knew to blame himself. Just when he needed to crank it up, with SwervCo making the inroad, he'd faltered.

To top it off, his mood was way down, the rats running wild in his maze; everything cost him a bundle. It was no laughing matter. His credit was almost gone. He needed the commissions Desani and Sons' accountant charged into his account from the day's take, and with sales down the sums were paltry. Plus his mood kept cutting down his profit percentage; the rats got you coming and going.

Bad thoughts. He blamed it, somewhat obscurely, on Figment. But blaming was another bad thought, so he kept nudging it away. Who was Figment to damage his mood? It was stupid. So he put on his personalized inspirational headphones, to listen to a chorus of maidens calling, "Flost, Flost...," and cued up behind a line of cars at the drive-window to pick up a euphoric-laden GnairburgerPlus.

He took the steaming, grease-stained bag into his car, and then, just as he reached his wrist out to pay, he thought he heard the ethereal voices on his tape murmur: "Fucking loser..." The burger cost him his day's profit at the schoolyard, unless the chemicals in it won him an unusually high percentage on commission.

He went through the routine at the office in a trance, willing himself to submit to the burger's effects. But the younger Desani caught his arm as he ducked into his cubicle. "Can I have a word with you, Pete?"

They went into Desani's office.

"You're not handling this SwervCo thing," said Desani. "Maybe you need a break."

"It's not that. I just – when do we get Iffman back? That would give sales a boost."

Desani shook his head.

"What?"

"Iffman's discovered he wants to be an artist," said Desani. "Figment showed him a glimpse of the high-life, and it did good things for Iffman's credit, I guess. He went and bought himself a gallery. We're suing him now for rights to some of the characters; we own the copyrights on the work he did for us."

"He's selling puppets? To wealthy people? Using our designs?"

"The puppets he's selling – for thousands – bear a suspicious resemblance, yes. He's got one just like 'Sweeney the Cyclone Rider' – remember him? – except he's calling him 'Octavo' –"

"People – want them? Rich people?"

Desani shrugged. "It's a vogue. Be gone tomorrow. Then maybe he'll be back. Or maybe he'll live like Figment, the crazy life, an artist. Always coming up with something new. Great life, I guess, if your credit can take it –"

The salesman shook his head. The false, burger-induced optimism jarred badly with the news. "So Figment's doing well?" he asked. "His idea was good?"

"I don't know. Iffman's all over ArtChannel. Figment I haven't heard from. I think his stuff's still cooking up."

The salesman just stared.

"I want you to go home," said Desani. "You're no good right now."

"I can't afford it."

"*You* can't afford it! Pete, every time you slouch back to this place we all go out and pay through the nose. You're bringing everybody down. Take a rest. I'll – I'll send you vacation credit."

"I'm *sorry*, Zigmund – oh dear, look. Why don't you let me get that?"

The artist had raised his wrist to pay for their brunch at Cold Heaven, and the Senator's wife was shocked at the numbers that registered on the check.

So was the artist.

"Can you erase that, please, and let me pay?" she said.

The waiter blanked the check and the Senator's wife offered her wrist instead. The artist looked away, ashamed.

What had happened to his mood? His nihilist's confidence?

"Now I'm terribly sorry, Zigmund, but the new work won't do. It's not splendid, it's not funny, it's not the pinch on the bottom I expect. It's not *you*."

"Listen, it's the most interesting thing I've –"

"No, I can't listen any more. I have to go. You'll call me when you've found your – esprit. Your zest for evil."

And she picked up her hat and floated out.

The artist gave her a head start, then went out to his own car, in an uncommon state of dejection. He'd ushered her from his gallery to the restaurant in an attempt to switch her attention from the work itself, the "realistic puppets," to the beguilements of his personality. But it was a misguided attempt. She'd quickly pointed out that what he was providing in person was precisely what was missing from the art.

And then, worse, his heart had gone out of it. He hadn't even managed to keep up the stream of antiflattery, of thrilling, decadent negativism.

It was something about the new work, he knew. Something he wasn't capturing. He'd failed. And yet, he believed in the new work, believed in it so much that when it failed he was dragged down with it.

That had never happened before. It was a dangerous precedent. He had to find a solution, had to work back to the source of the inspiration, and get it right, make it impossible to overlook. Force it down their overfed, bejeweled throats.

Flost. The spark.

He got in his car, and in ten minutes he was at the salesman's door.

"No, no. Go away," said Flost, when he saw the artist at his door. "You're the last thing I need."

"What do you mean?"

"I lost my job. It's you. You demoralized me."

"Let me in. I'll make it up to you. I'll pay you for your time, pay you now." He held out his wrist.

"Here's your chance, right here," said the salesman, pointing at the doorway chargebox. "Pay my daily rent. I can't afford it today. It's more every time, and it's breaking me."

The artist paid. He didn't say how badly it damaged his own coffers to do so. "Now – can I come in?"

The salesman gave way.

"Forget your job," said the artist. "I'll pay you for the, uh, copyright to your life. I need to base the puppet on you. I'll pay you to stay at home, okay?"

"I'm already staying home. My mood is too bad to go out paying for things."

"Well, relax. As soon as I get this right we'll both be flush. I promise. You're the point of inspiration. They'll sell."

Flost looked at him suspiciously. "Your work isn't selling?"

"The first set of puppets were a bit of a flodge," admitted the artist. "That's because I was forgetting about *you.* I mean, the specific you, not some vague gesture. This is good, my seeing your *place.* I want to borrow your reality, Flost, and I'll pay. Because it *says* something. I want to turn it into art and plop it into view."

"Look," said Flost. "I thought you were aiming at some kind of decadence effect. With the puppets, the transitory, commercial thing."

"But that's just it, it's the *juxtaposition* of the *form*, the presold, caricatured, world of the puppets, with the *content* of the most realistic, banal —"

"Please, enough. I get it."

"— and it's just that it has to be intensely specific. The details have to be perfect, they have to feel lifelike. I want to get it right."

"The righter you get it," said Flost, "the less anyone is going to want to pay for the privilege of seeing it."

"Now you're just badrapping," said the artist, laughing. "What do you want to do that to me for, to your mealticket?" He pulled a palm-sized camera out of his plastoid turban and began snapping pictures.

When he left he drove his car to a dealership, and got enough credit for it to cover another few days expenses at the gallery.

A week later, hunger drove the salesman out, though he knew that he wouldn't have enough credit to pay his rent and get back inside.

He walked downtown to Desani and Sons.

"No, no, no," said the younger Desani. "We don't need you hanging around here. We're working hard. We're hard working people. Credit is hard to come by."

"I need another chance."

"No. People are sensitive to the sight of someone like you around here. It's hard enough. No sir."

"Just front me a trunk of puppets. I'll sell them."

"You sold your trunk back to the company."

"I'll earn it back in a day. Just give me the chance."

"No. If you come here with credit enough I'll sell you a trunk, and you can peddle your way back. If you think you can. But I'm not fronting you." He frowned. "Besides, look at yourself."

"I need a meal, Desani."

"Oh, for God's sake." Desani looked nervously around. "Come

on." He took his hat and led the salesman out of the office. "Nobody needs to see you here, that's not going to do them any good. Come on. I'll buy you something, then you move on."

At the restaurant Desani put up his wrist for a Gnairburger, then sat and looked disapproving while the salesman wolfed it down.

"Has Figment been around the office?" the salesman asked.

Desani shook his head. "I don't let him. He cost me you and Iffman both." He looked at his wrist. "And who knows how much in mood."

"Was he asking about me?"

"Maybe. Listen, don't depend on Figment. I don't think he's doing so good now."

"What do you mean?"

"I think he was a guy running out of inspiration when he located us, you understand? He puts on a big show with all that gaudy garb, but I think he might have been about dry already. I think we were his last chance."

"Don't say this, you don't understand what you're saying. Figment is *my* last chance."

Desani spread his hands helplessly. "I don't want to hear any more about this. Please." He got up. "Goodbye, Flost."

The salesman left the restaurant and walked across town, to gallery row. He found Figment, but the doors were closed. More than closed; they were nailed shut with boards.

Down the street was Vicious Parallelogram, Ben Iffman's gallery. The salesman went in. The room was full of stilled puppets, some of which the salesman thought he recognized. Iffman came out of the back, dressed in a gold lame radiation suit and wearing a wicker cornucopia as a hat. He saw the salesman and said: "Hello, Pete."

"Hello, Ben. Nice, uh, nice place you got here."

"Thanks."

"I'm looking for Figment. Have you seen him?"

"He disappeared, Pete. Lost his gallery and nobody on the row has seen him since."

"Ah."

"Things sure do move fast in a mood-based economy," said Iffman. He said it with an air of perfect equanimity, neither gloating nor maudlin.

"That they do," said the salesman, and there was a brief silence. Then the salesman said: "You don't need someone around here, by any chance? We used to make a pretty good team."

"Sorry, Pete."

"I've moved a puppet or two in my day."

"This is a different kind of thing," said Iffman. "You understand."

Two days later a technician at Cold Heaven woke the artist out of suspended animation. "Sir," he said, "your table is ready."

"Thanks," said the artist. He stepped out of the booth and took a few minutes in the rest room to shake off the cobwebs of stasis. Then he slipped out the back.

He didn't have credit enough for a table. He'd used the suspended animation the way a bum heaves a brick through a window to get a night of sleep in jail. He'd gone in hungry, exhausted and hopeless, at mood's end.

He emerged exactly the same, due to the nature of suspended animation. Out of options, he started walking towards the neglected part of the city, seeking a place he'd heard of, where he might find a free meal.

The artist had figured out his mistake. The same quality of attention he ordinarily applied to himself, and which in that case took the form of *irony*, had been transmuted into *empathy* when turned outward and applied to the salesman Flost.

In each case the expression was appropriate to the subject. The artist had managed to remain faithful to his method while betraying his audience's expectations utterly. He could hardly expect consumers of irony to suddenly convert to a diet of empathy. It was a fatal miscalculation.

He went down crumbling stairs to the church basement, under a sign that read WHERE SELDOM IS HEARD / MON–SAT 1–4 P.M. Inside sat a motley group of men and women sitting in classroom chairs in various postures of discouragement. At the front, lecturing them, was a televangelist, an old battered one, its chrome robot body dingy and pocked, its television head flickering and staticky. The broadcast personality was a gentle, aging priest, who spoke with a slight Scotch burr.

"You're here because you've been indulging. You may not think of it that way, but it's true; worse than strong drink –" The priest's head flickered and was replaced by an FBI copyright warning, but the voice went on. "– the Hell we make in our heads makes in turn a Hell around us." The robot body shook a stern aluminum finger. "Who here can say he has not badspoken to drag his brother down? Did you not find that the worm, once unleashed, turned and gnawed at your soul as well?"

Sitting near the back was the salesman, Flost. The artist went and took the empty seat beside him, and said: "When do we eat?"

The salesman spoke quietly, without turning. "We have to listen for a while before it gives us food. They use a televangelist because we're so depressing; nobody with any credit-sensitivity wants to come anywhere near us." Then he looked up, and saw the artist. "Oh," he said. "It's you."

"None other."

"Are you here to give me a credit infusion? It's going to take a lot. I can't take a walk around the block without paying a month's salary. What *used* to be a month's salary."

"I'm here for a meal."

"Ah. I take it the Flost puppet wasn't a big hit."

"I crashed before I even got it produced. Nobody liked the new direction in my work."

"Well, now what?"

"How about this: a roomful of realistic puppets sitting doing nothing, listening to a televangelist robot puppet mouth platitudes. Could be big."

"It's like you're wired backwards," said the salesman, not bitterly. "Bleakness, nihilism – they exhilarate you. Genuinely improve your mood. When you badrap, you get somewhere yourself. You lift yourself up by your own bootstraps."

"I guess. But I blew it. I tried to expand my vision. I ended up destroying both of our moods."

A woman in the row ahead of them turned, scowling, and said: "Shhhh!"

"Let's get out of here," said the artist.

Flost nodded.

"Everybody sing," said the televangelist up front. "When you go through life make this your goal/watch the donut, not the hole!"

The next day, at noon, they stumbled along the sidewalk near the schoolyard. They'd been drinking; somehow they'd found credit enough for a series of bottles.

There was SwervCo's salesman with his trunk, and Desani and Sons' replacement salesman, Jim Travic. The two stood poised in the sun, trunks full of ready product, ignoring each other. And they ignored the salesman and the artist when they arrived.

The bell rang. The children flooded over the pavement.

The artist and the salesman lurched into the yard.

"Hey kids," said the artist. "Cavorting clown-man is here to liven up your evening hours." He waved his arms madly and marched in a figure eight. "Uh, take me home and I'll enact 'Mr. Figment's Action Vacation, a Product of His Own Imagination!'"

The children backed away, forming a circle. Taking a deep breath, the salesman launched himself forward.

"Remember me?" he said. "Now I'm the Man Without a Product, the Trunkless One."

The artist called out: "Rebel Without a Portfolio!"

The salesman nodded and bowed, and nearly fell on his face. "My episode's called: "Say Goodbye to Mr. Flost, Knowing Him Was Too Much Cost!"

– Special thanks to Rich Doyle

Food and sex are two of my favorite topics, but this story twists the relationship between them in a rather disturbing fashion.

FOOD MAN
Lisa Tuttle

Dinner was the real problem.

Mornings, it was easy to rush out of the house without eating, but when it wasn't, when her mother made an issue of it, she could eat an orange or half a grapefruit. At lunchtime she was usually either at school or out so there was no one to pressure her into eating anything she didn't want. But dinner was a problem. She had to sit there, surrounded by her family, and eat whatever her mother had prepared, and no matter how she pushed it around her plate it was obvious how little she was eating. She experimented with dropping bits on the floor and secreting other bits up her sleeves or in her pockets, but it wasn't easy, her mother's eyes were so sharp, and she'd rather eat than suffer through a big embarrassing scene.

Her brother, the creep, provided the solution. He was always looking at her, staring at her, mimicking her, teasing, and while she didn't like it at any time, at mealtimes it was truly unbearable. She honestly could not bear to put a bite in her mouth with him staring at her in that disgusting way. Her parents warned him to leave her alone, and shifted their places so they weren't directly facing each other, but still it wasn't enough. He said she was paranoid. She knew that even paranoids have enemies. Even if he wasn't staring at her right now, he had stared before, and the prospect that he might stare again clogged her throat with fear. How could she be expected to eat under such circumstances?

How could anyone? If she could have dinner on a tray in her room alone, she would be fine.

Her mother, relieved by the prospect of solving two family problems at once, agreed to this suggestion. "But only for as long as you eat. If I don't see a clean plate coming out of your room you'll have to come back and sit with the rest of us."

It was easy to send clean plates out of her room. After she'd eaten what she could stomach she simply shoved the rest of the food under her bed. Suspecting that the sound of a toilet flushing immediately after a meal would arouse her mother's suspicions, she planned to get rid of the food in the morning. Only by morning she'd forgotten, and by the time she remembered it was dinnertime again.

It went on like that. Of course the food began to smell, rotting away down there under her bed, but no one else was allowed into her bedroom, and she knew the smell didn't carry beyond her closed door. It was kind of disgusting, when she was lying in bed, because then there was no avoiding it, the odor simply rose up, pushed its way through the mattress and forced itself upon her. Yet even that had its good side; she thought of it as her penance for being so fat, and was grateful for the bad smell because it made her even more adamantly opposed to the whole idea of food. How could other people bear the constant, living stink of it? The cooking, the eating, the excreting, the rotting?

When she could no longer bear the enforced, nightly intimacy with the food she refused to eat, she decided it was time to get rid of it. Before looking at it, she decided she'd better arm herself with some heavy-duty cleaning tools, paper towels, rubber gloves, maybe even a small shovel. But when she opened the door of her room to go out, there was her mother, looking as if she'd been waiting awhile.

"Where are you going?"

"What is this, a police state?" Hastily, afraid the smell would get out, she pulled her door shut behind her. "I want a glass of water."

"From the bathroom?"

"No, I thought I'd go down to the kitchen and get a glass. Why, aren't I allowed to go to the bathroom?"

"Of course you are. I was just worried – Oh, darling, you're so thin!"

"Thin is good."

"Within limits. But you're too thin, and you're getting thinner. It's not healthy. If you really are eating –"

"Of course I'm eating. You've seen my plates. I thought they'd be clean enough even for you."

"If you've been flushing your good dinners down the toilet –"

"Oh, Mother, honestly! Of course I haven't! Is that why you were lurking around up here? Trying to catch me in the act?" She realized, with considerable irritation at herself, that she could have been flushing her dinner neatly and odorlessly away for a couple of weeks before arousing suspicion, but that it had now become impossible.

"Or throwing up after you eat –"

"Oh, yuck, you'll make me sick if you talk about it! Yuck! I hate vomiting; I'm not some weirdo who likes to do it! Really!"

"I'm sorry. But I'm worried about you. If you can eat regular meals and still lose weight there must be something wrong. I think you should see a doctor."

She sighed wearily. "All right. If it will make you happy, I'll see a doctor."

She was just beginning to feel good about her body again. She didn't care what the doctor said, and when he insisted she look at herself in a full-length mirror, wearing only her underwear – something she had not dared to do for months – she was not grossed-out. The pendulous breasts, the thunder-thighs, all the fat, all the jiggling flesh, had gone, leaving someone lean, clean and pristine. She felt proud of herself. The way the doctor looked at her was just right, too: with a certain distance, with respect. Not a trace of that horrible, furtive greed she'd seen in the eyes of her brother's friends just six months ago. The look of lust mixed with disgust which men had started giving her after her body had swelled into womanhood was something she hoped she'd never see again.

"How long since you had a period?" the doctor wanted to know.

"About four months." She was pleased about that, too. You weren't supposed to be able to turn the clock back and reject the nasty parts of growing up, but she had done it. She was in control of herself.

In reality, of course, the control was in the hands of others. As a minor, she was totally dominated by adults, chief among them her parents. After the doctor's diagnosis that she was deliberately starving herself, she was forced to return to the dinner table.

Resentful and humiliated, she pushed food around on her plate and refused to eat it. Threats of punishment only strengthened her resolve.

"That's right," she snarled. "Make me a prisoner. Let everybody know. Keep me locked up, away from my friends, with no phone and no fun – that's really going to make me pyschologically healthy. That's really going to make me eat!"

Bribes were more successful, but her parents either weren't willing or could not afford to come up with a decent bribe at every single mealtime, and she simply laughed to scorn the notion that she'd let someone else control every bit of food that passed her lips for an entire week just for a pair of shoes or the use of the car on Saturday. She didn't need new clothes, CDs, the car, or anything her parents could give her, and she wanted them to know it.

Now that the battlezone was marked out and war had been openly declared, food was a constant, oppressive preoccupation. She was reminded of food by everything she saw, by everything around her. Hunger, which had once been the pleasurably sharp edge that told her she was achieving something, was now a constant, miserable state. She no longer even controlled the amounts she ate; she ate even less than she wanted because she couldn't bear to let her mother feel that she was winning, that anything she put in her mouth was a concession to her. She couldn't back down now, she couldn't even appear to be backing down. If she did, she would never recover; her whole life would be lived out meekly under her mother's heavy thumb.

Lying in bed one night, trying to get her mind away from food, she realized that the smell which permeated her mattress and pillow and all her bedclothes had changed. A subtle change, yet distinctive. What had been a foul stench was now...not so foul. There was something *interesting* about it. She sniffed a little harder, savoring it. It was still far from being something you could describe as a *good* smell – it was a nasty smell, not something she'd want anyone else to suspect she could like, and yet there was something about it which made her want more. It was both deeply unpleasant and curiously exciting. She couldn't explain even to herself why the bad smell had become so pleasurable to her. It made her think of sex, which sounded so awful when it was described. No matter how they tried to make it glamorous in the movies, the act itself was clearly awkward and nasty. And yet it was obvious that the participants found that embarrassing, awkward nastiness deeply wonderful and were desperate for a chance to do it again. It was one of the great mysteries of life.

She wondered what the food under her bed looked like now. All the different foods, cooked and uncooked, pushed together into one great mass, breaking down, rotting, flowing together.... Had it undergone a change into something rich and strange? Or would the sight of it make her puke? She had decided she was never going to clean under her bed – her refusal, although unknown by her mother, was another blow against her – but now, all of a sudden, she wished she could see it.

There was a movement under her bed.

Was it her imagination? She held very still, even holding her breath, and it came again, stronger and more certain. This time she felt as well as heard it. The bed was rocked by something moving underneath. Whatever was moving under there was coming out.

Although she'd turned out her lamp before going to bed, her room was not totally dark; it never was. The curtains were unlined and let in light from the street, so there was always a pale, yellowish glow. By this dim, constant light she saw the man who emerged from under her bed.

Her heart beat harder at the sight of him, but she was not frightened. There might not be light enough to read by, but there was enough to show her this man was no ordinary serial killer, burglar, or rapist from off the street. For one thing, he wore no clothes. For another, he was clearly not a normal human being. The smell of him was indescribable. It was the smell of rotting food; it was the smell of her own bed. And, she did not forget, she had wished to see what her food had become.

He made no menacing or seductive or self-willed motions but simply stood there, showing himself to her. When she had looked her fill she invited him into her bed, and he gave himself to her just as she wanted.

What took place in her bed thereafter was indescribable. She could not herself remember it very clearly the next day – certainly not the details of who did what to whom with what when and where. What she would never forget was the intense, sensory experience of it all: his smell, that dreadful stench with its subtle, enticing undercurrent, that addictive, arousing odor which he exuded in great gusts with every motion, and which, ultimately, seemed to wrap around her and absorb her like the great cloak of sleep; the exciting pressure of his body on hers, intimate and demanding and satisfying in a way she could never have imagined; and her own orgasms, more powerful than anything she'd previously experienced on her own.

She understood about sex now. To an outsider it looked ridiculous or even horrible, but it wasn't for looking at, and certainly not by outsiders – it was for feeling. It was about nothing but feeling, feeling things you'd never felt before, having feelings you couldn't have by yourself, being felt. It was wonderful.

In the morning she woke to daylight, alone in her deliciously smelly bed, and she felt transformed. She suspected she had not, in the technical sense, lost her virginity; far from losing anything, she had gained something. She felt different; she felt expanded and enriched; she felt powerful; she felt hungry. She went downstairs and, ignoring as usual her mother's pitiful breakfast offering, went to the counter and put two slices of bread in the toaster.

Wisely, her mother did not comment. Her brother did, when she sat down at the table with two slices of toast thickly spread with peanut butter.

"What's this, your new diet?"

"Shut up, pig-face," she said calmly, and, yes, her mother let her get away with that, too. Oh, she was untouchable today; she had her secret, a new source of power.

At lunchtime the apple she'd intended to eat wasn't enough, and she consumed the cheese sandwich her mother had made for her, and the carrot sticks, a bag of potato chips, and a pot of strawberry yogurt. Sex, she realized, took a lot of energy, burned a lot of calories. She had to replace them, and she had to build herself up. Now that she had a reason for wanting to be fit and strong she recognized how weak she had become by not eating. She wouldn't have to worry about getting fat, not for a long time, not as long as the nightly exercise continued.

It did continue, and grew more strenuous as her strength, her curiosity, her imagination, all her appetites increased. She no longer feared getting fat; on the contrary, she was eager to gain weight. She wanted to be stronger, and she needed more weight for muscle. More flesh was not to be sneered at, now that she knew how flesh could be caressed and aroused. She ate the meals that were prepared for her, and more. She no longer had to be obsessive about controlling her intake of food because it was no longer the one area of her life she felt she had some control over. Now she controlled the creature under her bed, and their passionate nights together were the secret which made the daytime rule of parents, teachers and rules, bearable.

Her nights were much more important than her days, and during the night she was in complete control. Or so she thought, until the night her creature did something she didn't like.

It was no big deal, really; he just happened to trap her in an uncomfortable position when he got on top of her, and he didn't immediately respond to her attempts to get him to move. It was something anyone might have done, inadvertently, unaware of her feelings – but he was not "anyone" and he'd never been less than totally aware of her every sensation and slightest desire. Either he'd been aware that he was hurting her because he'd intended it, or he'd been unaware because he was no longer so much hers as he'd been in the beginning, because he was becoming someone else. She wasn't sure which prospect she found the more frightening.

The rot had started in their relationship, and although each incremental change was tiny – hardly noticeable to someone less sensitive than she – they soon demolished her notion of being in control.

She was not in control. She had no power. She lived for her nights with him; she needed him. But what if he didn't need her? What if one night he no longer wanted her?

It could happen. He'd started to criticize, his fingers pinching the excess flesh which had grown back, with her greed, on her stomach and thighs, and she could tell by the gingerly way he handled her newly expanded breasts and ass that he didn't like the way they jiggled. When he broke off a kiss too quickly she knew it was because he didn't like the garlic or the onions on her breath. The unspoken threat was always there: one night he might not kiss her at all. One night he might just stay under the bed.

She didn't think she could bear that. Having known sex, she was now just like all those people she'd found so incomprehensible in books and movies: she had to keep on having it. And she knew no other partner would satisfy her. She'd been spoiled by her food man for anyone else.

She began to diet. But it was different this time. Once not-eating had been pleasurable and easy; now it was impossibly difficult. She no longer liked being hungry; it made her feel weak and cranky, not powerful at all, not at all the way she'd used to feel. This time she wasn't starving to please herself and spite the world, but to please someone else. She went on doing it only because she decided she preferred sex to food; she could give up one if allowed to keep the other. And by promising herself sex, rewarding herself with explicit, graphic, sensual memories every time she said no to something to eat, she managed to continue starving herself back to desirability.

This suffering wouldn't be forever. Once she'd reached her – or his – ideal weight, she hoped to maintain it with sufficient exercise and ordinary meals.

But the sex that she was starving herself for was no longer all that great. She was so hungry it was hard to concentrate. His smell kept reminding her of food instead of the sex they were engaged in. Except when she was on the very brink of orgasm, she just couldn't seem to stop thinking about food.

And as time went on, and she still wasn't quite thin enough to please him, not quite thin enough to stop her killing diet, she began to wonder why she was doing it. What was so great about sex, anyway? She could give herself an orgasm any time she wanted, all by herself. Maybe they weren't so intense, maybe they were over quicker, but so what? When they were over she used to fall asleep contented, like someone with a full stomach, instead of lying awake, sated in one sense but just beginning to remember how hungry she still was for food. As for arousal – what was so great about arousal? It was too much like hunger. It was fine in retrospect, when it had been satisfied, but while it was going on it was just like hunger, an endless need, going on and painfully on.

She didn't know how much longer she could bear it. And then, one night, she went from not knowing to not being able. When her lover climbed into bed with her, swinging one leg across her, holding her down as he so often did now, keeping her in her place, the smell of him made her feel quite giddy with desire, and her mouth filled with saliva.

As his soft, warm, odorous face descended to hers she bit into it, and it was just like a dinner roll freshly baked. She even, as her teeth sank into his nose, tasted the salty tang of butter.

He did not cry out – he never had made a sound in all the nights she had known him – nor did he try to escape or fight back as she bit and tore away a great chunk of his face and greedily chewed and swallowed it. She felt a tension in him, a general stiffening, and then, as, unable to resist, she took a second bite, she recognized what he was feeling. It was sexual excitement. It was desire. He wanted to be eaten. This was what he had wanted from the very first night, when he had pressed himself, first his face and then all the other parts of his body in turn, against her mouth – only she had misunderstood. But this was what he was for.

She ate him.

It was the best ever, better by far than their first night together, which had seemed to her at that time so wonderful. That had been only sex. This was food and sex together, life and death.

When she had finished she felt enormous. Sprawling on the bed, she took up the whole of it and her arms and legs dangled off the sides. She was sure she must be at least twice her usual size. And the curious thing was that although she felt satisfied, she did not feel at all full. She was still hungry.

Well, maybe hungry wasn't exactly the right word. Of course she wasn't hungry. But she still had space for something more. She still wanted something more.

The springs groaned as she sat up, and her feet hit the floor much sooner than she'd expected. She was bigger than usual; not only fatter, but taller, too. She had to duck to get through her own bedroom door.

She stood for a moment in the hall, enjoying her enormous new size and the sense of power it gave her. This, not starving herself and not having secret sex, was true power. Food and eating and strength and size. She knew she wanted to eat something more, maybe a lot of something more before the night was over. There was a smell in the air which had her moist and salivating with desire. She licked her lips and looked around, her fingers flexing, but there wasn't much of interest in the hallway. A framed, studio portrait of the family hung above the only piece of furniture, a small table with a wobbly leg. On the table was a telephone, a pad of yellow Post-it notes, and a gnawed wooden pencil. The taste of the pencil was as immediately familiar to her as the salty tang of her own dandruff and sloughed skin cells beneath a nibbled fingernail, and did about as much to satisfy her hunger. The shiny, dark chocolate colored telephone wasn't as easy to eat as the pencil had been, but she persevered, and had crunched her way through more than half of it before the unpleasant lack of taste, and the discomfort of eating shards of plastic, really registered. She finished it anyway – it was all fuel – and then sniffed the air.

From the bedrooms where her brother and her parents slept drifted the rich, strong, disturbing smells of sex and food. Aroused and ravenous, she followed the scent of her next meal.

Eliot Fintushel unquestionably possesses one of the most interesting imaginations to emerge in recent years. Like R.A. Lafferty and Philip K. Dick, Eliot's stories engage a level of reality neither entirely within the realm of ordinary knowledge, nor completely fantastic. Combining a quick humor, a true flair for language, and a deep heart result in unusually original stories.

SANTACIDE
Eliot Fintushel

Dog shit and mud. The trees are as bare as a geezer's gums. No sun since early autumn. The clouds haven't heard that silver lining jazz; the only thing they are lined with is each other. Sky the color of pig iron. Too cold to snow.

I am not partial to December.

I am brooding by the dark casement, dreaming of the dome that used to regulate the city's weather before NY went bankrupt. My Martian cocoa – zoot-spiked, of course – is warming me from the inside out but cools at the epithelium. I glance at my wristwatch. Old habit – I had a job once. The prochrono is glowing. Someone is about to arrive.

"Chuck?" Cecil has a voice like dry heaves. I haven't seen him since before the sun – when dinosaurs roamed the Earth and I was still married to Agnes. At seven-foot-two with an executioner's build and a face like a pit viper's, he doesn't have to take much guff. Used to do inquiries for me (Read: knucks and bucks) when there was still some percentage in the law maven trade, before the slime (Read: Cecil's ilk) sucked my dogs to the kneecaps. We won a case or two – but not the one that counted. "Arnby, you in there?"

I hit CURRENT on my watch to cut to where Cecil and I are having cocktails. I hate salutations. I don't wear no cologne. I still have a fifth of Venusian zoot rot: 2018, a very good year. We pass the bottle back and forth – no clean glasses in walking distance. He is nattily dressed in codpiece and suspenders, his tubulars in a heap on my sleep unit. I am at ease in my cheek pin. Cecil is in excellent spirits – cause for suspicion.

"I want you to see something," he says.

"Cease-fire," says I, "the last time you had something to show me, *he* was dead, *you* had a hot gat minus one slug, and *I* was disbarred, pending. I ain't stepping outside till midsummer."

"For *this* you are," he says. He reaches over to punch my watch. We are old enough buddies, altercations despite, that I do not impede him; I cried on his shoulder when Agnes left me, though I needed a stool to do it. And he kept me in zoot rot when she didn't come back.

He punches CURRENT a couple of times. We are out on the street in our tubulars; then we are jumping down the rusted-frozen escalator at his tenement, buns thawing after the transit; and finally we are in his basement crib, in his cold-as-a-dookil's-pizzle basement crib, eyeballing a closed wooden door, from when trees were being cut to build things. It has peeling whitewash, like in *Tom Sawyer*.

"You'll never guess what I got in there, Chucky."

I am not sure what is in store. Knowing Cecil, this may be some "Casque of Amontillado" action, and I am not partial to mortared stiffs. I sneak a glance at my wrist. Cecil reaches to cover the watch, but he is a little late. I see on the prochrono who I'm going to see in there. "Holy dookil scats!"

"Damn! I wanted to surprise you." Cecil throws open the door, and there he is, just like my watch said –

"Ho! Ho! Ho!"

– shackled to the brick wall, the white fur trim on that apple-red suit torn and muddied, one foot bare, the boot lying just out of his reach, the sock under my heel, as it happens. Beside him lies a torn sack. Little toys, cheap thingies – "Made on the Moon" – are flung about the floor, smashed.

There is only one thing I want to do, the thing any reasonable adult would want to do, something I've been aching to do so long and so hard, Christmas after Christmas, that I've put it clean out of my mind just to be able to carry on. But it's back in my mind *now,* boy! It's in my eyes when I turn to Cecil.

"Go for it, Chuck!" says the Seesaw.

I cock my good right arm and bash Santa square in the old kazoo. When he groans, I smile.

It's wonderful how fast an eye can blacken when a sucker's circulation is good. It's all in the contrast, really. On jowly, pink Santy, brow and whiskers the color of snow blindness, the shiner sprouts like mushrooms in manure. I rub my paw and think of Agnes. (Not that I've ever gotten to *use* it on her: she has a left hook like an air hammer, and I have a glass jaw.)

"Good one!" Cecil grins. "The boys and girls in Toyland are gonna have a funeral."

"Excellent punch, son…" the big elf is saying, but I cock my arm again; his shoulders hit his ears, his knees jerk to mid-lard bucket – an elephantine flinch – and he shuts his mouth. He is shaking like a bowl full of jelly.

"Cecil, my man, how in hell did you get a hold of him? He's not the real one, is he?"

"Close as makes no diff, old upChuck," – unzippering the stashhole in his tubulars and producing a small, red-enameled dingus the size and shape of a triple-seeded goober – "Ever see one of these?"

This is rhetorical. I used to own one, and Cecil knows it: a vintage dynestat, a Bull patent model, state of the art in the 2020s, that wonderfully myopic decade! Only thing was, they had all been recalled around 2032 on account of a faulty transcat chip.

"You're not supposed to have that." It is my choirboy coming out. "It's unstable. You could hurt yourself."

"*Bubbeh meisehs,* Chucky. The chip's okay. It's the *governor* that made the white-collar boys at Bull Enterprises, Inc., sweat and puke in the executive john. Too easy to disable – catch my drift?"

I look at the fat man. I look at the goober. "How in hell…?"

"When Bull recalled, their PR boys threw a scare into the citizens with that 'unstable chip' bushwah, plus the *Federales* put some penal muscle behind it. I think you defended one or two of the holdouts, ain't that so?"

"Could be. I'm not partial to the memory function these days."

"Yeah, well, there was twenty or thirty of us noncompliers. One was in Michigan; this outlaw user jimmied the governor and set up a dream brothel, as God is my witness, that put the cat houses of Venus to shame. But in the end – and I'll let you guess *which* end – they attracted the wrong sort of attention, spelled B-U-L-L, I-N-C., whose private security force is also known as the 'United States Marines.' The Bull nerds hypodyned all them fine ladies back to wet dreams, every nipple and chassis.

"Me, so happened I knew this disgruntled ex-employee of Mr. Bull's. A chug of Venusian zoot rot regruntled him okay. He showed me how to gum the governor, and quick as you can say 'hypodyne-hypostat,' I was laying my dreams about me. With this little number, I was a frigging Praxiteles: thoughts to flesh, boy, dyne and stat, dyne and stat. And I don't mean little 3-D movies like what the brochure touted. I mean big as life, Chucky, your wildest dreams." He points to Santa Claus. "QED."

"But why Santa Claus?"

"In a word, Arnby: money."

"Money?"

"Did you enjoy…?"

"Smacking the old fart? You bet I did. I've been laying for that gut wagger ever since my first wish list come up goose eggs. He throws it in our faces, Cecil. And then *we* have to bail the Fat Man out, paste smiles on our mugs for the little tots, pile debt on debt to patch their dumb dreams. Christmas music alone is enough cause to off that bloated bugger. I got dimple fatigue from here to the Magellanics. A guy can take only so much."

"Exactly. That's how I feel, too, Chuck-a-luck. And that's how every one of these eggs feels as well." From his other stashhole, Cecil pulls a fat wad of tiny green cards.

"What are those things?"

"Ticket stubs."

§

"Eat hot lead, fat man!"

It's *rooty-toot-toot* without the *rummy-tum-tum*. Father Christmas's little round belly jumps like dust on a jack hammer handle as the Kalashnikov rips into him. His droll little mouth curls back like a slug in the killing jar. He doesn't seem so lively and quick any more.

The little guy with the meat perforator is shaking all over – not used to the recoil. He is happy though. "I ain't afraid of you, fat boy. Them reindeer don't scare me. Them elves of yours make me laugh. And as for them toy guns, Buster, this little honey" – slapping the stock of Cecil's antique Big K – "will do me just fine." Another clip of bullets blasts across the room. The painful echo. The gunpowder smell. Modern weaponry is deadlier perhaps, but it lacks the whack.

"That's extra for the second clip, you know," says Cecil. The little guy hands back the Kalashnikov and forks over a sawbuck along with it. Cecil turns to open the door and wave in the next customer, when the guy lays a hand on Cecil's elbow.

"Mister, you're a prince." There are tears in the little guy's eyes. "I been putting up with Mel Torme and Bing Crosby and Roy Rogers and my wife's mistletoe for twenty-odd years. I was ready to skip for the outer planets till February, but now, *because of you, pal,* I can face it for another year. God bless you!" He kisses Cecil on the lips and runs out, closing the door behind him.

Cecil beams at me. "God, it makes a bugger feel good to help out his fellow man!"

"Not to mention the dough. What's that – a thou already?"

"Damn near! Thirty satisfied customers!"

The knob turns and the door edges open, but I stop it.

"Hey!" – from out in the hallway, a lady's voice.

"What's the idea?" says Cecil.

"Look there," I says. Santa Claus is a gooey mess of blood and formerly internal organs.

"You certainly are a wonderful shot!" he gurgles.

"Shut up, Kringle!" Cecil suggests. Then to me: "I catch your meaning." He pulls out the dynestat, pinches the middle bulge, and squints hard. This is always a wonder to me, no matter how many times I see it. The hypostat beam lights up Cecil's noddle like a da Vinci saint. For a brief moment, I can see his neurons and synapses in Day-Glo pinks and green, with the ions charging around through gray matter like maggots on an old pork butt. Cecil strokes the goober, focussing the beam on the thought of Santa Claus. With the governor intact, you could never reach this far into the collective unconscious. In a flash, the Sumo elf is hohohoing again, real as income tax, all his wrinkles, rips, prolapses and perforations erased, in a word: hypostatized. The former heap has been overstruck. The new one is chained to the wall, right where Cecil thought him.

"And the Word became flesh," Cecil chirps.

That's when the lady decides to charge through. "You blasphemous pig!" Only it's no lady – it's Agnes.

She marches in, all five foot two of her, both eyes of blue on my face of red. She is wearing her hair in a businesslike bun. Her tubulars are professional, stashhole and hem to collar – she's been doing better than yours truly, it is clear. You meet a better class of clientele in *environmental* law – cleaner anyway.

I reach for my prochrono button. I am not the confrontational type; I'd rather *have done it* than *do it*, and that's what this gadget is for. Back in the 10s when the chronoshafts first opened up, I was right there, gilding pedigrees and depositing back cash for the fast samoleans: and all in an open "hurry" – what a jalopy! But since I got the barrister's tile, a prochrono is as risky as I like to get, even with caseload zilch.

Agnes, however, knows my predilections in this regard. She intercepts my pinky en route to the left wrist. "Forget it, slimeball," – that left jab, but she pulls it, thank God, before it meets my proboscis. "I want this to be strictly present tense."

Have I told you how pretty my Agnes is? Plenty pretty. Plenty smart. Plenty simpatico in all respects. But when the chips were down, no match for a liquid lunch. I'm just a zoot rot kind of a guy, and Agnes is cocoa straight-up.

In half a second, she is gone to me; she has spotted Santa. "You poor dear, what have they done to you?" I am on the garbage heap of Aggie's awareness. Cecil, aching to let in the next ticket-clutching, dinara-proffering, Santacidal customer, shares steerage with me in Agnes's mind.

Agnes kissing Santa Claus. Agnes's fingers running up and down that white fur collar. Googoo and poowiddow dumplin'. Pere Noel is eating up my ex's attentions: "What do you want for Christmas, sweetheart?"

I am ready to buy another ticket. "For crissakes, Ag, get off the guy's lap..." – I don't wear no cologne – "... *please*."

It's beginning to get ugly outside the wooden door. There is a multitude of stomping, pounding, and chanting out there. "We want the fat guy! We want the fat guy!" Others prefer: "Off the elf!" with this sustenuto: "I want mine! I want mine!"

Cecil is busting a gut, his seven-two useless against Aggie's five-two-*and-righteously-indignant*. "C'mon, Agnes. Chucky's right. This Santa is just a hypostat. Look." He produces a bazooka from a trunk in the corner and fires point-blank at Santa Claus's rosy forehead.

Agnes has jumped away. She stumbles into my arms as the jolly cranium explodes. "Dear Lord!"

"No sweat!" says Cecil. Out comes the goober, and before you know it, there's a brand-new Santa manacled to the wall, and the old, loose giblets have hypodyned to neural fizz.

"Ho! Ho! Ho!"

Agnes in my arms. I feel her trembling through her tubulars and mine. Slowly she unclenches the little fists of her eyelids and pours those baby blues into mine. I hate this action: I am in love again. I have that weak, warm feeling of having wet my bed. I'll do anything for her.

"Chuck, please make him stop. It's *Santa Claus*, Chuck. He is the embodiment of the happy dreams of all the world's children. You still have that child in you, too, Chuck, I know you do. I can't have hurt you *that* much."

"*You* hurt *me?* Oh, honey!"

Then the door breaks open, squishing Cecil flat to the wall. In struts a tough, in adman blacks, swinging his laptop like a shillelagh. "Lemme at 'im!" He slams the door behind him, delivering free nose jobs to the two guys next in line. Cecil unpeels but is counting birdies.

The shitkickers on this citizen are CEO class. His type don't like to stand in line. "I've had it with you, fat guy. You and the flood of red ink that washes in with you every goddam Exmas." He stomps forward like a seismosaurus. His tan, Hollywood jaw is working, drool brimming over the fat lower lip.

"Ho! Ho! Ho!" says Santa.

The customer's eyes are blazing, crazed. With every step, he spits out another phrase. "I tore open the shutters…and threw up the sash…" It's a Niagara Falls routine. "I vaulted over the sill… *and gunned the red dumpling down!*" He pulls out a gat the like of which I have never seen, a deluxe executive semi-automatic laser-system doohickey; it throws a bright red dot of light on Santy's solar plexus, where the slug will hit.

Agnes disengages from our little rapprochement long enough to introduce the belligerent to her famous left jab. His red dot blinks out. "What makes people that way?" she muses, dusting off her knucks while he joins Cecil among the birdies. "I don't like to use these tactics, Chuck. I'd much rather use persuasion."

"I'm persuaded, Agnes."

"No, you're not." Then, turning to Father Christmas: "Hell, *you* talk to him, Santa."

Claus twinkles and flashes me some tooth enamel – moonlight on an ice cove. I am not melting. He opens his fat arms. "Would you like to sit up here on Santa's lap?"

"This ain't 34th Street," says I, "and I ain't Natalie Wood."

"Listen, Chucky," the imp coos, "your friend hypostatted me from his own human mind, the same mind *you* share in, Chuck. Don't you know that when you castigate me, you are castigating yourself? I still have some things in my bag for you, Chucky. It's never too late to stop being naughty and to start being nice instead."

Lord, I wanted to bank him on the grill. "Get real, you big zit. You ain't checked your list twice – I can see *that*. I'm a two-bit zoot swiller, no good to nobody. I never done a good turn without an angle. Ask Aggie."

"Don't sell yourself short, Charles," she says.

You could have decked me with a feather.

Cecil has adjusted his vertical, meanwhile, and is yammering out the door at the bilious masses. They are doubling time slots out there to fit in the basement hallway and up two flights of oxide-infested escalator. "Off the elf! I want mine!"

Shoulder to the door, he peeks back at me and says between grunts, "Don't go limp on me, Chuck roast. She's just a dame, for crissakes, and *he* don't even exist!"

Santa clucks and shakes his whiskered noddle. Then he looks up at me and Aggie. "Why don't you let me take you two for a little sleigh ride? There are some things I'd love you to see."

How we get out of Cecil's basement I do not recall. Agnes has grabbed my wrist and prochronoed, leaving Cecil in an embarrassing squeeze vis-à-vis his paid-up, ticketed customers. She and I are sitting alongside the scarlet pudgeball at about two thousand feet. The reindeer are hoofing across cloudbanks and galloping upward. Tucked between Agnes and the dumpling, I hardly need my tubulars.

Suddenly the surrounding mist starts to glow and dwindle. Up ahead, I see something I have not seen for a very long time. I blink and look again. It is the sun.

"I thought you was a night person, Nick," I says.

"Ho! Ho! Ho!" he says.

Agnes is holding my hand. "I had to find you, Chuck. I heard about Cecil's new racket; guy on a street corner tried to sell me a ticket. The way you've been acting since you hit the zoot…"

"…Since you walked out, you mean."

"Whatever. I figured he would get you in on it." The moon is there, faintly, the North Wind's cookie, just like the children's rhyme says, baking in the sun – middle shelf, across the wide, blue sky.

"He don't like to work alone."

"I remembered that. Cecil always needed somebody with character to back him up, Charles. Someone like *you*." Claus dips through the clouds like a gull diving for his catch – and we see these big cumuli from just below, lined with silver, the way they say.

"Ho! Ho! Ho!"

"Don't look at the clouds, Charles. Look at *me*. Why did you give up?"

This action is not my favorite. I don't wear no cologne. I figure, if a dame don't understand you, you can't be all bad. "Agnes…we are in the upper jeebasphere, and everything is beautiful. I never seen such blue. I never seen such silver."

"Ho! Ho! Ho!"

"Stop that! But down there, Agnes, in the *real* world, it's scum and maggots in the dark."

"Maggots are fly babies, Chuck," Santa Claus puts in. "I have something in my bag for them, too."

"Butt out," says Agnes. "That's it, isn't it, Charles? You couldn't take the shadows. You're a lot more sensitive than you pretend to be. Let me help you, Charles. I'll come back to you if you promise to try."

I am raining. I can't help it. Maybe it's the altitude, the dew point, the wind. Tears drip and dry, drip and dry in the upper jeebasphere. "Agnes, you know I never stopped loving you."

Her forearms on my chest – "I know."

I feel myself slipping into the world of Agnes's love – it must be meteorology. "But I can't…" I say. *Owl!* Her eyes are melting together. We are approaching osculation.

Which is when Santa Claus chooses to say, "Would you like to try the reins, little man?" Santa is watching the jet stream; he doesn't know what he has interrupted. That fuzzy cuff between our chins. The leather strap, with its salt taste, rubbing against the lips that almost touched Agnes's.

Agnes's face lights up. She cocks her head, a sweet inch from mine. I am ready to shpritz cologne in all my little places. "Go on, dear!" she says. "For once in your life, *fly!*"

I take the reins. "Ho! Ho! Ho!" I say. Santa and Agnes are hohohoing, too. "On, Donder! On, Blitzen!" It's a rolly coaster ride through the jeebasphere, brother! We're leaping like dolphins in and out of those cumuli. The whee and wow of it rip laughs out my mouth and hugs from wifey.

It must be a field effect from those hypostatted reins: I can see every kiddy on Santa's list, down through their chimneys, dancing sugarplums and all. There's Cecil with his Santacidal mob, Cecilcidal now. He's punching that goober like nobody's business, but the thing has gone out of whack. All he gets are sparks and Nat King Cole crooning "Adeste Fideles." Santa Claus has a thing or two lined up for Cecil's stocking; who'd have thought the palooka was partial to Marcel Proust? I can see his argyles dangle and bulge with the weight of *Les Jeunes Filles En Fleurs* and a dozen madeleines.

I can see the Bar Association down there, too. They're about to reinstate me – *providing.* Lumps of coal, all around – just kidding! "You know, Ag," says I, "environmental law don't sound too bad. I always wanted to try my hand at that. *Somebody's* gotta protect the jeebasphere."

"Watch out for that flock of storks, son!" Santa touches my wrist, and we swoop below the rush of white wings, and – if it isn't the altitude pickling my sensorium – below the mewling, no-neck tots swinging in their diapers, like hammocks hung from the birdies' bills.

"So happens I know a dame in that racket as could use a decent partner," says Agnes, doing her George Raft.

"I could put her in your stocking, Chuck," says Santa – Edward G. Robinson, badly. "Ho! Ho! Ho! – *see?*"

I tear off my wristwatch, prochrono and all, and throw it to the wind. Life is too much fun, *sturm, drang,* and everything, to miss a minute of it.

I hand the reins back to the old elf.

"Home, Santa!" Agnes laughs.

"I'll drop you off on the way to the pole."

We jingle down into the city. Nobody gives us a second thought: New Yorkers! Between the clouds, lined with silver, the sky is crystalline blue. It is snowing in Manhattan. Kids turn their chins up, squeeze their eyes shut, and open their mouths wide to taste it. Grumblers and hoods peep sunward. Grudgingly, they leak a smile. Maybe they'll give Santa another chance this year. Maybe not.

"Agnes..." says I.

"Yes, Charles…?"

Donder, Blitzen and the antlered brethren are winging the old pudgeball north. Mistletoe flutters down from the sleigh – *"Ho! Ho! Ho!"*

We kiss.

"The Matter of Seggri" was the first short work to win the James Tiptree, Jr. Memorial Award, and the first story from *Crank!* to win a major genre award. Of course, I've been quite pleased by the attention this story has received beyond Crank!'s usual readership, and it deserves every bit of it.

THE MATTER OF SEGGRI
Ursula K. Le Guin

The first recorded contact with Seggri was in year 242 of Hainish Cycle 93. A Wandership six generations out from Iao (4-Taurus) came down on the planet, and the captain entered this report in his ship's log.

Captain Aolao-olao's Report

We have spent near forty days on this world they call Se-ri or Ye-ha-ri, well entertained, and leave with as good an estimation of the natives as is consonant with their unregenerate state. They live in fine great buildings they call castles, with large parks all about. Outside the walls of the parks lie well-tilled fields and abundant orchards, reclaimed by diligence from the parched and arid desert of stone that makes up the greatest part of the land. Their women live in villages and towns huddled outside the walls. All the common work of farm and mill is performed by the women, of whom there is a vast superabundance. They are ordinary drudges, living in towns which belong to the lords of the castle. They live amongst the cattle and brute animals of all kinds, who are permitted into the houses, some of which are of fair size. These women go about drably clothed, always in groups and bands. They are never allowed within the walls of the park, leaving the food and necessaries with which they provide the men at the outer gate of the castle. The women evinced great fear and distrust of us, and our hosts advised us that it were best for us to keep away from their towns, which we did.

The men go freely about their great parks, playing at one sport or another. At night they go to certain houses which they own in the town, where they may have their pick among the women and satisfy their lust upon them as they will. The women pay them, we were told, in their money, which is copper, for a night of pleasure, and pay them yet more if they get a child on them. Their nights thus are spent in carnal satisfaction as often as they desire, and their days in a diversity of sports and games, notably a kind of wrestling, in which they throw each other through the air so that we marvelled that they seemed never to take hurt, but rose up and returned to the combat with marvelous dexterity of hand and foot. Also they fence with blunt swords, and combat with long light sticks. Also they play a game with balls on a great field, using the arms to catch or throw the ball and the legs to kick the ball and trip or catch or kick the men of the other team, so that many are bruised and lamed in the passion of the sport, which was very fine to see, the teams in their contrasted garments of bright colors much gauded out with gold and finery seething now this way, now that, up and down the field in a mass, from which the balls were flung up and caught by runners breaking free of the struggling crowd and fleeting towards the one or the other goal with all the rest in hot pursuit. There is a "battlefield" as they call it of this game lying without the walls of the castle park, near to the town, so that the women may come watch and cheer, which they do heartily, calling out the names of favorite players and urging them with many uncouth cries to victory.

Boys are taken from the women at the age of eleven and brought to the castle to be educated as befits a man. We saw such a child brought into the castle with much ceremony and rejoicing. It is said that the women find it difficult to bring a pregnancy of a boy child to term, and that of those born many die in infancy despite the care lavished upon them, so that there are far more women than men. In this we see the curse of GOD laid upon this race as upon all those who acknowledge HIM not, unrepentant heathens whose ears are stopped to true discourse and blind to the light.

These men know little of art, only a kind of leaping dance, and their science is little beyond that of savages. One great man of a castle to whom I talked, who was dressed out in cloth of gold and crimson and whom all called Prince and Grandsire with much respect and deference, yet was so ignorant he believed the stars to be worlds full of people and beasts, asking us from which star we descended. They have only vessels driven by steam along the surface of the land and water, and no notion of flight either in the air or in space, nor any curiosity about such things, saying with disdain, "That is all women's work," and indeed I found that if I asked these great men about matters of common knowledge such as the working of machinery, the weaving of cloth, the transmission of holovision, they would soon chide me for taking interest in womanish things as they called them, desiring me to talk as befit a man.

In the breeding of their fierce cattle within the parks they are very knowledgeable, as in the sewing up of their clothing, which they make from cloth the women weave in their factories. The men vie in the ornamentation and magnificence of their costumes to an extent which we might indeed have thought scarcely manly, were they not withal such proper men, strong and ready for any game or sport, and full of pride and a most delicate and fiery honor.

The log including Captain Aolao-olao's entries was (after a 12-generation journey) returned to the Sacred Archives of The Universe on Iao, which were dispersed during the period called The Tumult, and eventually preserved in fragmentary form on Hain. There is no record of further contact with Seggri until the First Observers were sent by the Ekumen in 93/1333: an Alterran man and a Hainish woman, Kaza Agad and Merriment. After a year in orbit mapping, photographing, recording and studying broadcasts, and analysing and learning a major regional language, the Observers landed. Acting upon a strong persuasion of the vulnerability of the planetary culture, they presented themselves as survivors of the wreck of a fishing boat, blown far off course, from a remote island. They were, as they had anticipated, separated at

once, Kaza Agad being taken to the Castle and Merriment into the
town. Kaza kept his name, which was plausible in the native context; Merriment called herself Yude. We have only her report, from
which three excerpts follow.

*From Mobile Gerindu'uttahayudetwe'menrade Merriment's
Notes for a Report to the Ekumen, 93/1334.*

34/223. Their network of trade and information, hence their
awareness of what goes on elsewhere in their world, is too so-
phisticated for me to maintain my Stupid Foreign Castaway act
any longer. Ekhaw called me in today and said, "If we had a sire
here who was worth buying or if our teams were winning their
games, I'd think you were a spy. Who are you, anyhow?"

I said, "Would you let me go to the College at Hagka?"

She said, "Why?"

"There are scientists there, I think? I need to talk with them."

This made sense to her; she made their "Mh" noise of assent.

"Could my friend go there with me?"

"Shask, you mean?"

We were both puzzled for a moment. She didn't expect a
woman to call a man "friend," and I hadn't thought of Shask as a
friend. She's very young, and I haven't taken her very seriously.

"I mean Kaza, the man I came with."

"A man – to the college?" she said, incredulous. She looked at
me and said, "Where *do* you come from?"

It was a fair question, not asked in enmity or challenge. I wish
I could have answered it, but I am increasingly convinced that we
can do great damage to these people; we are facing Resehavanar's
Choice here, I fear.

Ekhaw paid for my journey to Hagka, and Shask came along
with me. As I thought about it I saw that of course Shask was my
friend. It was she who brought me into the motherhouse, per-
suading Ekhaw and Azman of their duty to be hospitable; it was
she who had looked out for me all along. Only she was so conventional in everything she did and said that I hadn't realized
how radical her compassion was. When I tried to thank her, as
our little jitney-bus purred along the road to Hagka, she said

things like she always says — "Oh, we're all family," and "People have to help each other," and "Nobody can live alone."

"Don't women ever live alone?" I asked her, for all the ones I've met belong to a motherhouse or a daughterhouse, whether a couple or a big family like Ekhaw's, which is three generations: five older women, three of their daughters living at home, and four children — the boy they all coddle and spoil so, and three girls.

"Oh yes," Shask said. "If they don't want wives, they can be singlewomen. And old women, when their wives die, sometimes they just live alone till they die. Usually they go live at a daughterhouse. In the colleges, the *vev* always have a place to be alone." Conventional she may be, but Shask always tries to answer a question seriously and completely; she thinks about her answer. She has been an invaluable informant. She has also made life easy for me by not asking questions about where I come from. I took this for the incuriosity of a person securely embedded in an unquestioned way of life, and for the self-centeredness of the young. Now I see it as delicacy.

"A *vev* is a teacher?"

"Mh."

"And the teachers at the college are very respected?"

"That's what *vev* means. That's why we call Eckaw's mother Vev Kakaw. She didn't go to college, but she's a thoughtful person, she's learned from life, she has a lot to teach us."

So respect and teaching are the same thing, and the only term of respect I've heard women use for women means teacher. And so in teaching me, young Shask respects herself? And/or earns my respect? This casts a different light on what I've been seeing as a society in which wealth is the important thing. Zadedr, the current mayor of Reha, is certainly admired for her very ostentatious display of possessions; but they don't call her Vev.

I said to Shask, "You have taught me so much, may I call you Vev Shask?"

She was equally embarrassed and pleased, and squirmed and said, "Oh no no no no." Then she said, "If you ever come back to Reha I would like very much to have love with you, Yude."

"I thought you were in love with Sire Zadr!" I blurted out.

"Oh, I am," she said, with that eye-roll and melted look they have when they speak of the Sires. "Aren't you? Just think of him fucking you, oh! Oh, I get all wet thinking about it!" She smiled and wriggled. I felt embarrassed in my turn and probably showed it. "Don't you like him?" she inquired with a naiveté I found hard to bear. She was acting like a silly adolescent, and I know she's not a silly adolescent. "But I'll never be able to afford him," she said, and sighed.

So you want to make do with me, I thought, nastily.

"I'm going to save my money," she announced after a minute. "I think I want to have a baby next year. Of course I can't afford Sire Zadr, he's a Great Champion, but if I don't go to the Games at Kadaki this year I can save up enough for a really good sire at our fuckery, maybe Master Rosra. I wish, I know this is silly, I'm going to say it anyway, I kept wishing you could be its love-mother. I know you can't, you have to go to the college. I just wanted to tell you. I love you." She took my hands, drew them to her face, pressed my palms on her eyes for a moment, and then released me. She was smiling, but her tears were on my hands.

"Oh, Shask," I said, floored.

"It's all right!" she said. "I have to cry a minute." And she did. She wept openly, bending over, wringing her hands, and wailing softly. I patted her arm and felt unutterably ashamed of myself. Other passengers looked round and made little sympathetic grunting noises. One old woman said, "That's it, that's right, lovey!" In a few minutes Shask stopped crying, wiped her nose and face on her sleeve, drew a long, deep breath, and said, "All right." She smiled at me. "Driver," she called, "I have to piss, can we stop?"

The driver, a tense-looking woman, growled something, but stopped the bus on the wide, weedy roadside; and Shask and another woman got off and pissed in the weeds. There is an enviable simplicity to many acts in a society which has, in all its daily life, only one gender. And which, perhaps – I don't know this but it occurred to me then, while I was ashamed of myself – has no shame?

. . .

34/245. (Dictated) Still nothing from Kaza. I think I was right to give him the ansible. I hope he's in touch with somebody. I wish it was me. I need to know what goes on in the Castles.

Anyhow I understand better now what I was seeing at the Games in Reha. There are sixteen adult women for every adult man. One conception in six or so is male, but a lot of nonviable male fetuses and defective male births bring it down to one in sixteen by puberty. My ancestors must have really had fun playing with these people's chromosomes. I feel guilty, even if it was a million years ago. I have to learn to do without shame but had better not forget the one good use of guilt. Anyhow. A fairly small town like Reha shares its Castle with other towns. That confusing spectacle I was taken to on my tenth day down was Awaga Castle trying to keep its place in the Maingame against a castle from up north, and losing. Which means Awaga's team can't play in the big game this year in Fadrga, the city south of here, from which the winners go on to compete in the *big* big game at Zask, where people come from all over the continent – hundreds of contestants and thousands of spectators. I saw some holos of last year's Maingame at Zask. There were 1280 players, the comment said, and forty balls in play. It looked to me like a total mess, my idea of a battle between two unarmed armies, but I gather that great skill and strategy is involved. All the members of the winning team get a special title for the year, and another one for life, and bring glory back to their various Castles and the towns that support them.

I can now get some sense of how this works, see the system from outside it, because the college doesn't support a Castle. People here aren't obsessed with sports and athletes and sexy sires the way the young women in Reha were, and some of the older ones. It's a kind of obligatory obsession. Cheer your team, support your brave men, adore your local hero. It makes sense. Given their situation, they need strong, healthy men at their fuckery; it's social selection reinforcing natural selection. But I'm glad to get away from the rah-rah and the swooning and the posters of fellows with swelling muscles and huge penises and bedroom eyes.

I have made Resehavanar's Choice. I chose the option: less than the truth. Shoggrad and Skodr and the other teachers, professors we'd call them, are intelligent, enlightened people, perfectly capable of understanding the concept of space travel, etc., making decisions about technological innovation, etc. I limit my answers to their questions to technology. I let them assume, as most people naturally assume, particularly people from a monoculture, that our society is pretty much like theirs. When they find how it differs, the effect will be revolutionary, and I have no mandate, reason, or wish to cause such a revolution on Seggri.

Their gender imbalance has produced a society in which, as far as I can tell, the men have all the privilege and the women have all the power. It's obviously a stable arrangement. According to their histories, it's lasted at least two millennia, and probably in some form or another much longer than that. But it could be quickly and disastrously destabilized by contact with us, by their experiencing the human norm. I don't know if the men would cling to their privileged status or demand freedom, but surely the women would resist giving up their power, and their sexual system and affectional relationships would break down. Even if they learned to undo the genetic program that was inflicted on them, it would take several generations to restore normal gender distribution. I can't be the whisper that starts that avalanche.

34/266. (Dictated) Skodr got nowhere with the men of Awaga Castle. She had to make her inquiries very cautiously, since it would endanger Kaza if she told them he was an alien or in any way unique. They'd take it as a claim of superiority, which he'd have to defend in trials of strength and skill. I gather that the hierarchies within the Castles are a rigid framework, within which a man moves up or down issuing challenges and winning or losing obligatory and optional trials. The sports and games the women watch are only the showpieces of an endless series of competitions going on inside the Castles. As an untrained, grown man Kaza would be at a total disadvantage in such trials. The only way he might get out of them, she said, would be by feigning illness or idiocy. She thinks he must have done so, since he is at least alive; but that's all she could find out – "The man who was cast away at Taha-Reha is alive."

Although the women feed, house, clothe, and support the Lords of the Castle, they evidently take their noncooperation for granted. She seemed glad to get even that scrap of information. As I am.

But we have to get Kaza out of there. The more I hear about it from Skodr the more dangerous it sounds. I keep thinking "spoiled brats!" but actually these men must be more like soldiers in the training camps that militarists have. Only the training never ends. As they win trials they gain all kinds of titles and ranks you could translate as "generals" and the other names militarists have for all their power-grades. Some of the "generals," the Lords and Masters and so on, are the sports idols, the darlings of the fuckeries, like the one poor Shask adored; but as they get older apparently they often trade glory among the women for power among the men, and become tyrants within their Castle, bossing the "lesser" men around, until they're overthrown, kicked out. Old sires often live alone, it seems, in little houses away from the main Castle, and are considered crazy and dangerous – rogue males.

It sounds like a miserable life. All they're allowed to do after age eleven is compete at games and sports inside the Castle, and compete in the fuckeries, after they're fifteen or so, for money and number of fucks and so on. Nothing else. No options. No trades. No skills of making. No travel unless they play in the big games. They aren't allowed into the colleges to gain any kind of freedom of mind. I asked Skodr why an intelligent man couldn't at least come study in the college, and she told me that learning was very bad for men: it weakens a man's sense of honor, makes his muscles flabby, and leaves him impotent. "'What goes to the brain takes from the testicles,'" she said. "Men have to be sheltered from education for their own good."

I tried to "be water," as I was taught, but I was disgusted. Probably she felt it, because after a while she told me about "the secret college." Some women in colleges do smuggle information to men in Castles. The poor things meet secretly and teach each other. In the Castles, homosexual relationships are encouraged among boys under fifteen, but not officially tolerated among grown men; she says the "secret colleges" often are run by the homosexual men. They have to be secret because if they're caught reading or talking about ideas they may be punished by their Lords and Masters. There have been some interesting works from the "secret colleges," Skodr said, but she had to think to come with examples. One was a man who had smuggled out an interesting mathematical theorem, and one was a painter whose landscapes, though primitive in technique, were admired by professionals of the art. She couldn't remember his name.

Arts, sciences, all learning, all professional techniques, are *haggyad,* skilled work. They're all taught at the colleges, and there are no divisions and few specialists. Teachers and students cross and mix fields all the time, and being a famous scholar in one field doesn't keep you from being a student in another. Skodr is a vev of physiology, writes plays, and is currently studying history with one of the history vevs. Her thinking is informed and lively and fearless. My School on Hain could learn from this college. It's a wonderful place, full of free minds. But only minds of one gender. A hedged freedom.

I hope Kaza has found a secret college or something, some way to fit in at the Castle. He's very fit, but these men have trained for years for the games they play. And a lot of the games are violent. The women say don't worry, we don't let the men kill each other, we protect them, they're our treasures. But I've seen men carried off with concussions on the holos of their martial-art fights, where they throw each other around spectacularly. "Only inexperienced fighters get hurt." Very reassuring. And they wrestle bulls. And in that melee they call the Maingame they break each other's legs and ankles deliberately. "What's a hero without a limp?" the women say. Maybe that's the safe thing to do, get your leg broken so you don't have to prove you're a hero any more. But what else might Kaza have to prove?

I asked Shask to let me know if she ever heard of him being at the Reha fuckery. But Awaga Castle services (that's their word, the same word they use for their bulls) four towns, so he might get sent to one of the others. But probably not, because men who don't win at things aren't allowed to go to the fuckeries. Only the champions. And boys between fifteen and nineteen, the ones the older women call *dippida*, baby animals, like puppies or kitties or lambies. They like to use the dippida for pleasure, and the champions when they go to the fuckery to get pregnant. But Kaza's thirty-six, he isn't a puppy or a kitten or a lamb. He's a man, and this is a terrible place to be a man.

Kaza Agad had been killed; the Lords of Awaga Castle finally disclosed the fact, but not the circumstances. A year later, Merriment radioed her lander and left Seggri for Hain. Her recommendation was to observe and avoid. The Stabiles, however, decided to send another pair of observers; these were both women, Mobiles Alee Iyoo and Zerin Wu. They lived for eight years on Seggri, after the third year as First Mobiles; Iyoo stayed as Ambassador another fifteen years. They made Resehavanar's Choice as "all the truth slowly." A limit of two hundred visitors from offworld was set. During the next several generations the people of Seggri, becoming accustomed to the alien presence, considered their own options as members of the Ekumen. Proposals for a planetwide referendum on genetic alteration were abandoned, since the men's vote would be insignificant unless the women's vote were handicapped. As of the date of this report the Seggri have not undertaken major genetic alteration, though they have learned and applied various repair techniques, which have resulted in a higher proportion of full-term male infants; the gender balance now stands at about 12:1.

> *The following is a memoir given to Ambassador*
> *Eritho te Ves in 93/1569 by a woman in Ush on Seggri.*

You asked me, dear friend, to tell you anything I might like people on other worlds to know about my life and my world. That's not easy! Do I want anybody anywhere else to know anything about my life? I know how strange we seem to all the others, the half-and-half races; I know they think us backward, provincial, even perverse. Maybe in a few more decades we'll decide that we should remake ourselves. I won't be alive then; I don't think I'd want to be. I like my people. I like our fierce, proud, beautiful men, I don't want them to become like women. I like our trustful, powerful, generous women, I don't want them to become like men. And yet I see that among you each man has his own being and nature, each woman has hers, and I can hardly say what it is I think we would lose.

When I was a child I had a brother a year and a half younger than me. His name was Ittu. My mother had gone to the city and paid five years' savings for my sire, a Master Champion in the Dancing. Ittu's sire was an old fellow at our village fuckery; they called him "Master Fallback." He'd never been a champion at anything, hadn't sired a child for years, and was only too glad to fuck for free. My mother always laughed about it – she was still suckling me, she didn't even use a preventive, and she tipped him two coppers! When she found herself pregnant she was furious. When they tested and found it was a male fetus she was even more disgusted at having, as they say, to wait for the miscarriage. But when Ittu was born sound and healthy, she gave the old sire two hundred coppers, all the cash she had.

He wasn't delicate like so many boy babies, but how can you keep from protecting and cherishing a boy? I don't remember when I wasn't looking after Ittu, with it all very clear in my head what Little Brother should do and shouldn't do and all the perils I must keep him from. I was proud of my responsibility, and vain, too, because I had a brother to look after. Not one other motherhouse in my village had a son still living at home.

Ittu was a lovely child, a star. He had the fleecy soft hair that's common in my part of Ush, and big eyes; his nature was sweet and cheerful, and he was very bright. The other children loved him and always wanted to play with him, but he and I were happiest playing by ourselves, long elaborate games of make-believe. We had a herd of twelve cattle an old woman of the village had carved from gourdshell for Ittu – people always gave him presents – and they were the actors in our dearest game. Our cattle lived in a country called Shush, where they had great adventures, climbing mountains, discovering new lands, sailing on rivers, and so on. Like any herd, like our village herd, the old cows were the leaders; the bull lived apart; the other males were gelded; and the heifers were the adventurers. Our bull would make ceremonial visits to service the cows, and then he might have to go fight with men at Shush Castle. We made the castle of clay and the men of sticks, and the bull always won, knocking the stick-men to pieces. Then sometimes he knocked the castle to pieces too. But the best of our stories were told with two of the heifers. Mine was named Op and my brother's was Utti. Once our hero heifers were having a great adventure on the stream that runs past our village, and their boat got away from us. We found it caught against a log far downstream where the stream was deep and quick. My heifer was still in it. We both dived and dived, but we never found Utti. She had drowned. The Cattle of Shush had a great funeral for her, and Ittu cried very bitterly.

He mourned his brave little toy cow so long that I asked Djerdji the cattleherd if we could work for her, because I thought being with the real cattle might cheer Ittu up. She was glad to get two cowhands for free (when Mother found out we were really working, she made Djerdji pay us a quarter-copper a day). We rode two big, good-natured old cows, on saddles so big Ittu could lie down on his. We took a herd of two-year-old calves out onto the desert every day to forage for the edta that grows best when it's grazed. We were supposed to keep them from wandering off and from trampling streambanks, and when they wanted to settle down and chew the cud we were supposed to gather them in a place where their droppings would nourish useful plants. Our old mounts did most of the work. Mother came out and checked on what we were doing and decided it was all right, and being out in the desert all day was certainly keeping us fit and healthy.

We loved our riding cows, but they were serious-minded and responsible, rather like the grown-ups in our motherhouse. The calves were something else; they were all riding breed, not fine animals of course, just villagebred; but living on edta they were fat and had plenty of spirit. Ittu and I rode them bareback with a rope rein. At first we always ended up on our own backs watching a calf's heels and tail flying off. By the end of a year we were good riders, and took to training our mounts to do tricks, trading mounts at a full run, and hornvaulting. Ittu was a marvelous hornvaulter. He trained a big three-year-old roan ox with lyre horns, and the two of them danced like the finest vaulters of the great Castles that we saw on the holos. We couldn't keep our excellence to ourselves out in the desert; we started showing off to the other children, inviting them to come out to Salt Springs to see our Great Trick Riding Show. And so of course the adults got to hear of it.

My mother was a brave woman, but that was too much for even her, and she said to me in cold fury, "I trusted you to look after Ittu. You let me down."

All the others had been going on and on about endangering the precious life of a boy, the Vial of Hope, the Treasurehouse of Life and so on, but it was what my mother said that hurt.

"I do look after Ittu, and he looks after me," I said to her, in that passion of justice that children know, the birthright we seldom honor. "We both know what's dangerous and we don't do stupid things and we know our cattle and we do everything together. When he has to go to the Castle he'll have to do lots more dangerous things, but at least he'll already know how to do one of them. And there he has to do them alone, but we did everything together. And I didn't let you down."

My mother looked at us. I was nearly twelve, Ittu was ten. She burst into tears, she sat down on the dirt and wept aloud. Ittu and I both went to her and hugged her and cried. Ittu said, "I won't go. I won't go to the damned Castle. They can't make me!"

And I believed him. He believed himself. My mother knew better.

Maybe some day it will be possible for a boy to choose his life. Among your peoples a man's body does not shape his fate, does it? Maybe some day that will be so here.

Our Castle, Hidjegga, had of course been keeping their eye on Ittu ever since he was born; once a year Mother would send them the doctor's report on him, and when he was five Mother and her wives took him out there for the ceremony of Confirmation. Ittu had been embarrassed, disgusted, and flattered. He told me in secret, "There were all these old men that smelled funny and they made me take off my clothes and they had these measuring things and they measured my peepee! And they said it was very good. They said it was a good one. What happens when you descend?" It wasn't the first question he had ever asked me that I couldn't answer, and as usual I made up the answer. "Descend means you can have babies," I said, which, in a way, wasn't so far off the mark.

Some Castles, I am told, prepare boys of nine and ten for the Severance, woo them with visits from older boys, tickets to games, tours of the park and the buildings, so that they may be quite eager to go to the Castle when they turn eleven. But we "outyonders," villagers of the edge of the desert, kept to the harsh old-fashioned ways. Aside from Confirmation, a boy had no contact at all with men until his eleventh birthday. On that day everybody he had ever known brought him to the Gate and gave him to the strangers with whom he would live the rest of his life. Men and women alike believed and still believe that this absolute severance makes the man.

Vev Ushiggi, who had borne a son and had a grandson, and had been mayor five or six times, and was held in great esteem even though she'd never had much money, heard Ittu say that he wouldn't go to the damned Castle. She came next day to our motherhouse and asked to talk to him. He told me what she said. She didn't do any wooing or sweetening. She told him that he was born to the service of his people and had one responsibility, to sire children when he got old enough; and one duty, to be a strong, brave man, stronger and braver than other men, so that women would choose him to sire their children. She said he had to live in the Castle because men could not live among women. At this, Ittu asked her, "Why can't they?"

"You did?" I said, awed by his courage, for Vev Ushiggi was a formidable old woman.

"Yes. And she didn't really answer. She took a long time. She looked at me and then she looked off somewhere and then she stared at me for a long time and then finally she said, 'Because we would destroy them.'"

"But that's crazy," I said. "Men are our treasures. What did she say that for?"

Ittu, of course, didn't know. But he thought hard about what she had said, and I think nothing she could have said would have so impressed him.

After discussion, the village elders and my mother and her wives decided that Ittu could go on practicing hornvaulting, because it really would be a useful skill for him in the Castle; but he could not herd cattle any longer, nor go with me when I did, nor join in any of the work children of the village did, nor their games. "You've done everything together with Po," they told him, "but she should be doing things together with the other girls, and you should be doing things by yourself, the way men do."

They were always very kind to Ittu, but they were stern with us girls; if they saw us even talking with Ittu they'd tell us to go on about our work, leave the boy alone. When we disobeyed – when Ittu and I sneaked off and met at Salt Springs to ride together, or just hid out in our old playplace down in the draw by the stream to talk – he got treated with cold silence to shame him, but I got punished. A day locked in the cellar of the old fiber-processing mill, which was what my village used for a jail; next time it was two days; and the third time they caught us alone together, they locked me in that cellar for ten days. A young woman called Fersk brought me food once a day and made sure I had enough water and wasn't sick, but she didn't speak; that's how they always used to punish people in the villages. I could hear the other children going by up on the street in the evening. It would get dark at last and I could sleep. All day I had nothing to do, no work, nothing to think about except the scorn and contempt they held me in for betraying their trust, and the injustice of my getting punished when Ittu didn't.

When I came out, I felt different. I felt like something had closed up inside me while I was closed up in that cellar.

When we ate at the motherhouse they made sure Ittu and I didn't sit near each other. For a while we didn't even talk to each other. I went back to school and work. I didn't know what Ittu was doing all day. I didn't think about it. It was only fifty days to his birthday.

One night I got into bed and found a note under my clay pillow: in the draw to-nt. Ittu never could spell; what writing he knew I had taught him in secret. I was frightened and angry, but I waited an hour till everybody was asleep, and got up and crept outside into the windy, starry night, and ran to the draw. It was late in the dry season and the stream was barely running. Ittu was there, hunched up with his arms round his knees, a little lump of shadow on the pale, cracked clay at the waterside.

The first thing I said was, "You want to get me locked up again? They said next time it would be thirty days!"

"They're going to lock me up for fifty years," Ittu said, not looking at me.

"What am I supposed to do about it? It's the way it has to be! You're a man. You have to do what men do. They won't lock you up, anyway, you get to play games and come to town to do service and all that. You don't even know what being locked up is!"

"I want to go to Seradda," Ittu said, talking very fast, his eyes shining as he looked up at me. "We could take the riding cows to the bus station in Redang, I saved my money, I have twenty-three coppers, we could take the bus to Seradda. The cows would come back home if we turned them loose."

"What do you think you'd do in Seradda?" I asked, disdainful but curious. Nobody from our village had ever been to the capital.

"The Ekkamen people are there," he said.

"The Ekumen," I corrected him. "So what?"

"They could take me away," Ittu said.

I felt very strange when he said that. I was still angry and still disdainful but a sorrow was rising in me like dark water. "Why would they do that? What would they talk to some little boy for? How would you find them? Twenty-three coppers isn't enough anyway. Seradda's way far off. That's a really stupid idea. You can't do that."

"I thought you'd come with me," Ittu said. His voice was softer, but didn't shake.

"I wouldn't do a stupid thing like that," I said furiously.

"All right," he said. "But you won't tell. Will you?"

"No, I won't tell!" I said. "But you can't run away, Ittu. You can't. It would be – it would be dishonorable."

This time when he answered his voice shook. "I don't care," he said. "I don't care about honor. I want to be free!"

We were both in tears. I sat down by him and we leaned together the way we used to, and cried a while; not long; we weren't used to crying.

"You can't do it," I whispered to him. "It won't work, Ittu."

He nodded, accepting my wisdom.

"It won't be so bad at the Castle," I said.

After a minute he drew away from me very slightly.

"We'll see each other," I said.

He said only, "When?"

"At games. I can watch you. I bet you'll be the best rider and hornvaulter there. I bet you win all the prizes and get to be a Champion."

He nodded, dutiful. He knew and I knew that I had betrayed our love and our birthright of justice. He knew he had no hope.

That was the last time we talked together alone, and almost the last time we talked together.

Ittu ran away about ten days after that, taking the riding cow and heading for Redang; they tracked him easily and had him back in the village before nightfall. I don't know if he thought I had told them where he would be going. I was so ashamed of not having gone with him that I could not look at him. I kept away from him; they didn't have to keep me away any more. He made no effort to speak to me.

I was beginning my puberty, and my first blood was the night before Ittu's birthday. Menstruating women are not allowed to come near the Gates at conservative Castles like ours, so when Ittu was made a man I stood far back among a few other girls and women, and could not see much of the ceremony. I stood silent while they sang, and looked down at the dirt and my new sandals and my feet in the sandals, and felt the ache and tug of my womb and the secret movement of the blood, and grieved. I knew even then that this grief would be with me all my life.

Ittu went in and the Gates closed.

He became a Young Champion Hornvaulter, and for two years,

when he was eighteen and nineteen, came a few times to service in our village, but I never saw him. One of my friends fucked with him and started to tell me about it, how nice he was, thinking I'd like to hear, but I shut her up and walked away in a blind rage which neither of us understood.

He was traded away to a castle on the east coast when he was twenty. When my daughter was born I wrote him, and several times after that, but he never answered my letters.

I don't know what I've told you about my life and my world. I don't know if it's what I want you to know. It is what I had to tell.

The following is a short story written in 93/1586 by a popular writer of the city of Adr, Sem Gridji. The classic literature of Seggri was the narrative poem and the drama. Classical poems and plays were written collaboratively, in the original version and also by rewriters of subsequent generations, usually anonymous. Small value was placed on preserving a "true" text, since the work was seen as an ongoing process. Probably under Ekumenical influence, individual writers in the late sixteenth century began writing short prose narratives, historical and fictional. The genre became popular, particularly in the cities, though it never obtained the immense audience of the great classical epics and plays. Literally everyone knew the plots and many quotations from the epics and plays, from books and holo, and almost every adult woman had seen or participated in a staged performance of several of them. They were one of the principal unifying influences of the Seggrian monoculture. The prose narrative, read in silence, served rather as a device by which the culture might question itself, and a tool for individual moral self-examination. Conservative Seggrian women disapproved of the genre as antagonistic to the intensely cooperative, collaborative structure of their society. Fiction was not included in the curriculum of the literature departments of the colleges, and was often dismissed contemptuously – "fiction is for men."

Sem Gridji published three books of stories. Her bare, blunt style is characteristic of the Seggrian short story.

Love Out of Place
by Sem Gridji

Azak grew up in a motherhouse in the Downriver Quarter, near the textile mills. She was a bright girl, and her family and neighborhood were proud to gather the money to send her to college. She came back to the city as a starting manager at one of the mills. Azak worked well with other people; she prospered. She had a clear idea of what she wanted to do in the next few years: to find two or three partners with whom to found a daughterhouse and a business.

A beautiful woman in the prime of youth, Azak took great pleasure in sex, especially liking intercourse with men. Though she saved money for her plan of founding a business, she also spent a good deal at the fuckery, going there often, sometimes hiring two men at once. She liked to see how they incited each other to prowess beyond what they would have achieved alone, and shamed each other when they failed. She found a flaccid penis very disgusting, and did not hesitate to send away a man who could not penetrate her three or four times an evening.

The Castle of her district bought a Young Champion at the Southeast Castles Dance Tournament, and soon sent him to the fuckery. Having seen him dance in the finals on the holovision and been captivated by his flowing, graceful style and his beauty, Azak was eager to have him service her. His price was twice that of any other man there, but she did not hesitate to pay it. She found him handsome and amiable, eager and gentle, skilful and compliant. In their first evening they came to orgasm together five times. When she left she gave him a large tip. Within the week she was back, asking for Toddra. The pleasure he gave her was exquisite, and soon she was quite obsessed with him.

"I wish I had you all to myself," she said to him one night as they lay still conjoined, langorous and fulfilled.

"That is my heart's desire," he said. "I wish I were your servant. None of the other women that come here arouse me. I don't want them. I want only you."

She wondered if he was telling the truth. The next time she came, she inquired casually of the manager if Toddra were as popular as they had hoped. "No," the manager said. "Everybody else reports that he takes a lot of arousing, and is sullen and careless towards them."

"How strange," Azak said.

"Not at all," said the manager. "He's in love with you."

"A man in love with a woman?" Azak said, and laughed.

"It happens all too often," the manager said.

"I thought only women fell in love," said Azak.

"Women fall in love with a man, sometimes, and that's bad too," said the manager. "May I warn you, Azak? Love should be between women. It's out of place here. It can never come to any good end. I hate to lose the money, but I wish you'd fuck with some of the other men and not always ask for Toddra. You're encouraging him, you see, in something that does harm to him."

"But he and you are making lots of money from me!" said Azak, still taking it as a joke.

"He'd make more from other women if he wasn't in love with you," said the manager. To Azak that seemed a weak argument against the pleasure she had in Toddra, and she said, "Well, he can fuck them all when I've done with him, but for now, I want him."

After their intercourse that evening, she said to Toddra, "The manager here says you're in love with me."

"I told you I was," Toddra said. "I told you I wanted to belong to you, to serve you, you alone. I would die for you, Azak."

"That's foolish," she said.

"Don't you like me? Don't I please you?"

"More than any man I ever knew," she said, kissing him. "You are beautiful and utterly satisfying, my sweet Toddra."

"You don't want any of the other men here, do you?" he asked.

"No. They're all ugly fumblers, compared to my beautiful dancer."

"Listen, then," he said, sitting up and speaking very seriously. He was a slender man of twenty-two, with long, smooth-muscled limbs, wide-set eyes, and a thin-lipped, sensitive mouth. Azak lay stroking his thigh, thinking how lovely and lovable he was. "I have a plan," he said. "When I dance, you know, in the story-dances, I play a woman, of course; I've done it since I was twelve.

People always say they can't believe I really am a man, I play a woman so well. If I escaped – from here, from the Castle – as a woman – I could come to your house as a servant –"

"What?" cried Azak, astounded.

"I could live there," he said urgently, bending over her. "With you. I would always be there. You could have me every night. It would cost you nothing, except my food. I would serve you, service you, sweep your house, do anything, anything, Azak, please, my beloved, my mistress, let me be yours!" He saw that she was still incredulous, and hurried on, "You could send me away when you got tired of me –"

"If you tried to go back to the Castle after an escapade like that they'd whip you to death, you idiot!"

"I'm valuable," he said. "They'd punish me, but they wouldn't damage me."

"You're wrong. You haven't been dancing, and your value here has slipped because you don't perform well with anybody but me. The manager told me so."

Tears stood in Toddra's eyes. Azak disliked giving him pain, but she was genuinely shocked at his wild plan. "And if you were discovered, my dear," she said more gently, "I would be utterly disgraced. It is a very childish plan, Toddra: please never dream of such a thing again. But I am truly, truly fond of you, I adore you and want no other man but you. Do you believe that, Toddra?"

He nodded. Restraining his tears, he said, "For now."

"For now and for a long, long, long time! My dear, sweet, beautiful dancer, we have each other as long as we want, years and years! Only do your duty by the other women that come, so that you don't get sold away by your Castle, please! I couldn't bear to lose you, Toddra." And she clasped him passionately in her arms, and arousing him at once, opened to him, and soon both were crying out in the throes of delight.

Though she could not take his love entirely seriously, since what could come of such a misplaced emotion, except such foolish schemes as he had proposed? – still he touched her heart, and she felt a tenderness towards him that greatly enhanced the pleasure of their intercourse. So for more than a year she spent two or three nights a week with him at the fuckery, which was as much as she could afford. The manager, trying still to discourage his love, would not lower Toddra's fee, even though he was unpopular among the other clients of the fuckery; so Azak spent a great deal of money on him, although he would never, after the first night, accept a tip from her.

Then a woman who had not been able to conceive with any of the sires at the fuckery tried Toddra, and at once conceived, and being tested found the fetus to be male. Another woman conceived by him, again a male fetus. At once Toddra was in demand as a sire. Women began coming from all over the city to be serviced by him. This meant, of course, that he must be free during their period of ovulation. There were now many evenings that he could not meet Azak, for the manager was not to be bribed. Toddra disliked his popularity, but Azak soothed and reassured him, telling him how proud she was of him, and how his work would never interfere with their love. In fact, she was not altogether sorry that he was so much in demand, for she had found another person with whom she wanted to spend her evenings.

This was a young woman named Zedr, who worked in the mill as a machine-repair specialist. She was tall and handsome; Azak noticed first how freely and strongly she walked and how proudly she stood. She found a pretext to make her acquaintance. It seemed to Azak that Zedr admired her; but for a long time each behaved to the other as a friend only, making no sexual advances. They were much in each other's company, going to games and dances together, and Azak found that she enjoyed this open and sociable life better than always being in the fuckery alone with Toddra. They talked about how they might set up a machine-repair service in partnership. As time went on, Azak found that Zedr's beautiful body was always in her thoughts. At last, one evening in her singlewoman's flat, she told her friend that she loved her, but did not wish to burden their friendship with an unwelcome desire.

Zedr replied, "I have wanted you ever since I first saw you, but I didn't want to embarrass you with my desire. I thought you preferred men."

"Until now I did, but I want to make love with you," Azak said.

She found herself quite timid at first, but Zedr was expert and subtle, and could prolong Azak's orgasms till she found such consummation as she had not dreamed of. She said to Zedr, "You have made me a woman."

"Then let's make each other wives," said Zedr joyfully.

They married, moved to a house in the west of the city, and left the mill, setting up in business together.

All this time, Azak had said nothing of her new love to Toddra, whom she had seen less and less often. A little ashamed of her cowardice, she reassured herself that he was so busy performing as a sire that he would not really miss her. After all, despite his romantic talk of love, he was a man, and to a man fucking is the most important thing, instead of being merely one element of love and life as it is to a woman.

When she married Zedr, she sent Toddra a letter, saying that their lives had drifted apart, and she was now moving away and would not see him again, but would always remember him fondly.

She received an immediate answer from Toddra, a letter begging her to come and talk with him, full of avowals of unchanging love, badly spelled and almost illegible. The letter touched, embarrassed, and shamed her, and she did not answer it.

He wrote again and again, and tried to reach her on the holonet at her new business. Zedr encouraged her not to make any response, saying, "It would be cruel to encourage him."

Their new business went well from the start. They were home one evening busy chopping vegetables for dinner when there was a knock at the door. "Come in," Zedr called, thinking it was Chochi, a friend they were considering as a third partner. A stranger entered, a tall, beautiful woman with a scarf over her hair. The stranger went straight to Azak, saying in a strangled voice, "Azak, Azak, please, please let me stay with you." The scarf fell back from his long hair. Azak recognized Toddra.

She was astonished and a little frightened, but she had known Toddra a long time and been very fond of him, and this habit of affection made her put out her hands to him in greeting. She saw fear and despair in his face, and was sorry for him.

But Zedr, guessing who he was, was both alarmed and angry. She kept the chopping-knife in her hand. She slipped from the room and called the city police.

When she returned she saw the man pleading with Azak to let him stay hidden in their household as a servant. "I will do anything," he said. "Please, Azak, my only love, please! I can't live without you. I can't service those women, those strangers who only want to be impregnated. I can't dance any more. I think only of you, you are my only hope. I will be a woman, no one will know. I'll cut my hair, no one will know!" So he went on, almost threatening in his passion, but pitiful also. Zedr listened coldly, thinking he was mad. Azak listened with pain and shame. "No, no, it is not possible," she said over and over, but he would not hear.

When the police came to the door and he realized who they were, he bolted to the back of the house seeking escape. The policewomen caught him in the bedroom; he fought them desperately, and they subdued him brutally. Azak shouted at them not to hurt him, but they paid no heed, twisting his arms and hitting him about the head till he stopped resisting. They dragged him out. The head of the troop stayed to take evidence. Azak tried to plead for Toddra, but Zedr stated the facts and added that she thought he was insane and dangerous.

After some days, Azak inquired at the police office and was told that Toddra had been returned to his Castle with a warning not to send him to the fuckery again for a year or until the Lords of the Castle found him capable of responsible behavior. She was uneasy thinking of how he might be punished. Zedr said, "They won't hurt him, he's too valuable," just as he himself had said. Azak was glad to believe this. She was, in fact, much relieved to know that he was out of the way.

She and Zedr took Chochi first into their business and then into their household. Chochi was a woman from the dockside quarter, tough and humorous, a hard worker and an undemanding, comfortable lovemaker. They were happy with one another, and prospered.

A year went by, and another year. Azak went to her old quarter to arrange a contract for repair work with two women from the mill where she had first worked. She asked them about Toddra. He was back at the fuckery from time to time, they told her. He had been named the year's Champion Sire of his Castle, and was much in demand, bringing an even higher price, because he impregnated so many women and so many of the conceptions were male. He was not in demand for pleasure, they said, as he had a reputation for roughness and even cruelty. Women asked for him only if they wanted to conceive. Thinking of his gentleness with her, Azak found it hard to imagine him behaving brutally. Harsh punishment at the Castle, she thought, must have altered him. But she could not believe that he had truly changed.

Another year passed. The business was doing very well, and Azak and Chochi both began talking seriously about having children. Zedr was not interested in bearing, though happy to be a mother. Chochi had a favorite man at their local fuckery to whom she went now and then for pleasure; she began going to him at ovulation, for he had a good reputation as a sire.

Azak had never been to a fuckery since she and Zedr married. She honored fidelity highly, and made love with no one but Zedr and Chochi. When she thought of being impregnated, she found that her old interest in fucking with men had quite died out or even turned to distaste. She did not like the idea of self-impregnation from the sperm bank, but the idea of letting a strange man penetrate her was even more repulsive. Thinking what to do, she thought of Toddra, whom she had truly loved and had pleasure with. He was again a Champion Sire, known throughout the city as a reliable impregnator. There was certainly no other man with whom she could take any pleasure. And he had loved her so much he had put his career and even his life in danger, trying to be with her. That irresponsibility was over and done with. He had never written to her again, and the Castle and the managers of the fuckery would never have let him service women if they thought him mad or untrustworthy. After all this time, she thought, she could go back to him and give him the pleasure he had so desired.

She notified the fuckery of the expected period of her next ovulation, requesting Toddra. He was already engaged for that period, and they offered her another sire; but she preferred to wait till the next month.

Chochi had conceived, and was elated. "Hurry up, hurry up!" she said to Azak. "We want twins!"

Azak found herself looking forward to being with Toddra. Regretting the violence of their last encounter and the pain it must have given him, she wrote the following letter to him:

"My dear, I hope our long separation and the distress of our last meeting will be forgotten in the joy of being together again, and that you still love me as I still love you. I shall be very proud to bear your child, and let us hope it may be a son! I am impatient to see you again, my beautiful dancer. Your Azak."

There had not been time for him to answer this letter when her ovulation period began. She dressed in her best clothes. Zedr still distrusted Toddra and had tried to dissuade her from going to him; she bade her "Good luck!" rather sulkily. Chochi hung a mothercharm round her neck, and she went off.

There was a new manager on duty at the fuckery, a coarse-faced young woman who told her, "Call out if he gives you any trouble. He may be a Champion but he's rough, and we don't let him get away with hurting anybody."

"He won't hurt me," Azak said smiling, and went eagerly into the familiar room where she and Toddra had enjoyed each other so often. He was standing waiting at the window just as he had used to stand. When he turned he looked just as she remembered, long-limbed, his silky hair flowing like water down his back, his wide-set eyes gazing at her.

"Toddra!" she said, coming to him with outstretched hands.

He took her hands and said her name.

"Did you get my letter? Are you happy?"

"Yes," he said, smiling.

"And all that unhappiness, all that foolishness about love, is it over? I am so sorry you were hurt, Toddra, I don't want any more of that. Can we just be ourselves and be happy together as we used to be?"

"Yes, all that is over," he said. "And I am happy to see you." He drew her gently to him. Gently he began to undress her and caress her body, just as he had used to, knowing what gave her pleasure, and she remembering what gave him pleasure. They lay down naked together. She was fondling his erect penis, aroused and yet a little reluctant to be penetrated after so long, when he moved his arm as if uncomfortable. Drawing away from him a little, she saw that he had a knife in his hand, which he must have hidden in the bed. He was holding it concealed behind his back.

Her womb went cold, but she continued to fondle his penis and testicles, not daring to say anything and not able to pull away, for he was holding her close with the other hand.

Suddenly he moved onto her and forced his penis into her vagina with a thrust so painful that for an instant she thought it was the knife. He ejaculated instantly. As his body arched she writhed out from under him, scrambled to the door, and ran from the room crying for help.

He pursued her, striking with the knife, stabbing her in the shoulderblade before the manager and other women and men seized him. The men were very angry and treated him with a violence which the manager's protests did not lessen. Naked, bloody, and half-conscious, he was bound and taken away immediately to the Castle.

Everyone now gathered around Azak, and her wound, which was slight, was cleaned and covered. Shaken and confused, she could ask only, "What will they do to him?"

"What do you think they do to a murdering rapist? Give him a prize?" the manager said. "They'll geld him."

"But it was my fault," Azak said.

The manager stared at her and said, "Are you mad? Go home."

She went back into the room and mechanically put on her clothes. She looked at the bed where they had lain. She stood at the window where Toddra had stood. She remembered how she had seen him dance long ago in the contest where he had first been made champion. She thought, "My life is wrong." But she did not know how to make it right.

Alteration in Seggrian social and cultural institutions did not take the disastrous course Merriment feared. It has been slow and its direction is not clear. In 93/1602 Terhada College invited men from two neighboring Castles to apply as students, and three men did so. In the next decades, most colleges opened their doors to men. Once they were graduated, male students had to return to their Castle, unless they left the planet, since native men were not allowed to live anywhere but as students in a college or in a Castle, until the Open Gate Law was passed in 93/1662.

Even after passage of that law, the Castles remained closed to women; and the exodus of men from the Castles was much slower than opponents of the measure feared. Social adjustment to the Open Gate Law has been slow. In several regions programs to train men in basic skills such as farming and construction have met with moderate success; the men work in competitive teams, separate from and managed by the women's companies. A good many Seggri have come to Hain to study in recent years – more men than women, despite the great numerical imbalance that still exists.

The following autobiographical sketch by one of these men is of particular interest, since he was involved in the event which directly precipitated the Open Gate Law.

Autobiographical Sketch by Mobile Ardar Dez.
I was born in Ekumenical Cycle 93, Year 1641, in Rakedr on Seggri. Rakedr was a placid, prosperous, conservative town, and I was brought up in the old way, the petted boychild of a big motherhouse. Altogether there were seventeen of us, not counting the kitchen staff – a great-grandmother, two grandmothers, four mothers, nine daughters, and me. We were well off; all the women were or had been managers or skilled workers in the Rakedr Pottery, the principal industry of the town. We kept all the holidays with pomp and energy, decorating the house from roof to foundation with banners for Hillalli, making fantastic costumes for the Harvest Festival, and celebrating somebody's birthday every few weeks with gifts all round. I was petted, as I said, but not, I think, spoiled. My birthday was no grander than my sisters', and I was allowed to run and play with them just as if I were a girl. Yet I was always aware, as were they, that our moth-

ers' eyes rested on me with a different look, brooding, reserved, and sometimes, as I grew older, desolate.

After my Confirmation, my birthmother or her mother took me to Rakedr Castle every spring on Visiting Day. The gates of the Park, which had opened to admit me alone (and terrified) for my Confirmation, remained shut, but rolling stairs were placed against the Park walls. Up these I and a few other little boys from the town climbed, to sit on top of the Park wall in great state, on cushions, under awnings, and watch demonstration dancing, bull-dancing, wrestling, and other sports on the great Gamefield inside the wall. Our mothers waited below, outside, in the bleachers of the public field. Men and youths from the Castle sat with us, explaining the rules of the games and pointing out the fine points of a dancer or wrestler, treating us seriously, making us feel important. I enjoyed that very much, but as soon as I came down off the wall and started home it all fell away like a costume shrugged off, a part played in a play; and I went on with my work and play in the motherhouse with my family, my real life.

When I was ten I went to Boys' Class downtown. The class had been set up forty or fifty years before as a bridge between the motherhouse and the Castle, but the Castle, under increasingly reactionary governance, had recently withdrawn from the project. Lord Fassaw forbade his men to go anywhere outside the walls but directly to the fuckery, in a closed car, returning at first light; and so no men were able to teach the class. The towns-women who tried to tell me what to expect when I went to the Castle did not really know much more than I did. However well-meaning they were, they mostly frightened and confused me. But fear and confusion were an appropriate preparation.

I cannot describe the ceremony of Severance. I really cannot describe it. Men on Seggri, in those days, had this advantage: they knew what death is. They had all died once before their body's death. They had turned and looked back at their whole life, every place and face they had loved, and turned away from it as the gate closed.

At the time of my Severance, our small Castle was internally divided into "collegials" and "traditionals," a liberal faction left from the regime of Lord Ishog and a younger, highly conservative faction. The split was already disastrously wide when I came to the Castle. Lord Fassaw's rule had grown increasingly harsh and irrational. He governed by corruption, brutality, and cruelty. All of us who lived there were of course infected, and would have been destroyed if there had not been a strong, constant, moral resistance, centered around Ragaz and Kohadrat, who had been protégés of Lord Ishog. The two men were open partners; their followers were all the homosexuals in the Castle, and a good number of other men and older boys.

My first days and months in the Scrubs' dormitory were a bewildering alternation: terror, hatred, shame, as the boys who had been there a few months or years longer than I were incited to humiliate and abuse the newcomer, in order to make a man of him — and comfort, gratitude, love, as boys who had come under the influence of the collegials offered me secret friendship and protection. They helped me in the games and competitions and took me into their beds at night, not for sex but to keep me from the sexual bullies. Lord Fassaw detested adult homosexuality and would have reinstituted the death penalty if the Town Council had allowed it. Though he did not dare punish Ragaz and Kohadrat, he punished consenting love between older boys with bizarre and appalling physical mutilations — ears cut into fringes, fingers branded with redhot iron rings. Yet he encouraged the older boys to rape the eleven- and twelve-year-olds, as a manly practice. None of us escaped. We particularly dreaded four youths, seventeen or eighteen years old when I came there, who called themselves the Lordsmen. Every few nights they raided the Scrubs' dormitory for a victim, whom they raped as a group. The collegials protected us as best they could by ordering us to their beds, where we wept and protested loudly, while they pretended to abuse us, laughing and jeering. Later, in the dark and silence, they comforted us with candy, and sometimes, as we grew older, with a desired love, gentle and exquisite in its secrecy.

There was no privacy at all in the Castle. I have said that to women who asked me to describe life there, and they thought they understood me. "Well, everybody shares everything in a motherhouse," they would say, "everybody's in and out of the rooms all the time. You're never really alone unless you have a singlewoman's flat." I could not tell them how different the loose, warm commonalty of the motherhouse was from the rigid, deliberate publicity of the forty-bed, brightly-lighted Castle dormitories. Nothing in Rakedr was private: only secret, only silent. We ate our tears.

I grew up; I take some pride in that, along with my profound gratitude to the boys and men who made it possible. I did not kill myself, as several boys did during those years, nor did I kill my mind and soul, as some did so their body could survive. Thanks to the maternal care of the collegials – the resistance, as we came to call ourselves – I grew up.

Why do I say maternal, not paternal? Because there were no fathers in my world. There were only sires. I knew no such word as father or paternal. I thought of Ragaz and Kohadrat as my mothers. I still do.

Fassaw grew quite mad as the years went on, and his hold over the Castle tightened to a deathgrip. The Lordsmen now ruled us all. They were lucky in that we still had a strong Maingame team, the pride of Fassaw's heart, which kept us in the First League, as well as two Champion Sires in steady demand at the town fuckeries. Any protest the resistance tried to bring to the Town Council could be dismissed as typical male whining, or laid to the demoralizing influence of the Aliens. From the outside Rakedr Castle seemed all right. Look at our great team! Look at our champion studs! The women looked no further.

How could they abandon us? – the cry every Seggrian boy must make in his heart. How could she leave me here? Doesn't she know what it's like? Why doesn't she know? Doesn't she want to know?

"Of course not," Ragaz said to me when I came to him in a passion of righteous indignation, the Town Council having denied our petition to be heard. "Of course they don't want to know how we live. Why do they never come into the Castles? Oh, we keep them out, yes; but do you think we could keep them out if they wanted to enter? My dear, we collude with them and they with us in maintaining the great foundation of ignorance and lies on which our civilization rests."

"Our own mothers abandon us," I said.

"Abandon us? Who feeds us, clothes us, houses us, pays us? We're utterly dependent on them. If ever we made ourselves independent, perhaps we could rebuild society on a foundation of truth."

Independence was as far as his vision could reach. Yet I think his mind groped further, towards what he could not see, the body's obscure, inalterable dream of mutuality.

Our effort to make our case heard at the Council had no effect except within the Castle. Lord Fassaw saw his power threatened. Within a few days Ragaz was seized by the Lordsmen and their bully boys, accused of repeated homosexual acts and treasonable plots, arraigned, and sentenced by the Lord of the Castle. Everyone was summoned to the Gamefield to witness the punishment. A man of fifty with a heart ailment – he had been a Maingame racer in his twenties and had overtrained – Ragaz was tied naked across a a bench and beaten with "Lord Long," a heavy leather tube filled with lead weights. The Lordsman Berhed, who wielded it, struck repeatedly at the head, the kidneys, and the genitals. Ragaz died an hour or two later in the infirmary.

The Rakedr Mutiny took shape that night. Kohadrat, older than Ragaz and devastated by his loss, could not restrain or guide us. His vision had been of a true resistance, longlasting and nonviolent, through which the Lordsmen would in time destroy themselves. We had been following that vision. Now we let it go. We dropped the truth and grabbed weapons. "How you play is what you win," Kohadrat said, but we had heard all those old saws. We would not play the patience game any more. We would win, now, once for all.

And we did. We won. We had our victory. Lord Fassaw, the Lordsmen and their bullies had been slaughtered by the time the police got to the Gate.

I remember how those tough women strode in amongst us, staring at the rooms of the Castle which they had never seen, staring at the mutilated bodies, eviscerated, castrated, headless – at Lordsman Berhed, who had been nailed to the floor with "Lord Long" stuffed down his throat – at us, the rebels, the victors, with our bloody hands and defiant faces – at Kohadrat, whom we thrust forward as our leader, our spokesman.

He stood silent. He ate his tears.

The women drew closer to one another, clutching their guns, staring around. They were appalled, they thought us all insane. Their utter incomprehension drove one of us at last to speak – a young man, Tarsk, who wore the iron ring that had been forced onto his finger when it was red-hot. "They killed Ragaz," he said. "They were all mad. Look." He held out his crippled hand.

The chief of the troop, after a pause, said, "No one will leave here till this is looked into," and marched her women out of the Castle, out of the Park, locking the gate behind them, leaving us with our victory.

The hearings and judgments on the Rakedr Mutiny were all broadcast, of course, and the event has been studied and discussed ever since. My own part in it was the murder of the Lordsman Tatiddi. Three of us set on him and beat him to death with exercise-clubs in the gymnasium where we had cornered him.

How we played was what we won.

We were not punished. Men were sent from several Castles to form a government over Rakedr Castle. They learned enough of Fassaw's behavior to see the cause of our rebellion, but the contempt of even the most liberal of them for us was absolute. They treated us not as men, but as irrational, irresponsible creatures, untamable cattle. If we spoke they did not answer.

I do not know how long we could have endured that cold regime of shame. It was only two months after the Mutiny that the World Council enacted the Open Gate Law. We told one another that that was our victory, we had made that happen. None of us believed it. We told one another we were free. For the first time in history, any man who wanted to leave his Castle could walk out the gate. We were free!

What happened to the free man outside the gate? Nobody had given it much thought.

I was one who walked out the gate, on the morning of the day the Law came into force. Eleven of us walked into town together.

Several of us, men not from Rakedr, went to one or another of the fuckeries, hoping to be allowed to stay there; they had nowhere else to go. Hotels and inns of course would not accept men. Those of us who had been children in the town went to our motherhouses.

What is it like to return from the dead? Not easy. Not for the one who returns, nor for his people. The place he occupied in their world has closed up, ceased to be, filled with accumulated change, habit, the doings and needs of others. He has been replaced. To return from the dead is to be a ghost: a person for whom there is no room.

Neither I nor my family understood that, at first. I came back to them at twenty-one as trustingly as if I were the eleven-year-old who had left them, and they opened their arms to their child. But he did not exist. Who was I?

For a long time, months, we refugees from the Castle hid in our motherhouses. The men from other towns all made their way home, usually by begging a ride with teams on tour. There were seven or eight of us in Rakedr, but we scarcely ever saw one another. Men had no place on the street; for hundreds of years a man seen alone on the street had been arrested immediately. If we went out, women ran from us, or reported us, or surrounded and threatened us – "Get back into your Castle where you belong! Get back to the fuckery where you belong! Get out of our city!" They called us drones, and in fact we had no work, no function at all in the community. The fuckeries would not accept us for service, because we had no guarantee of health and good behavior from a Castle.

This was our freedom: we were all ghosts, useless, frightened, frightening intruders, shadows in the corners of life. We watched life going on around us – work, love, childbearing, childrearing, getting and spending, making and shaping, governing and adventuring – the women's world, the bright, full, real world – and there was no room in it for us. All we had ever learned to do was play games and destroy one another.

My mothers and sisters racked their brains, I know, to find some place and use for me in their lively, industrious household. Two old live-in cooks had run our kitchen since long before I was born, so cooking, the one practical art I had been taught in the Castle, was superfluous. They found household tasks for me, but they were all makework, and they and I knew it. I was perfectly willing to look after the babies, but one of the grandmothers was very jealous of that privilege, and also some of my sisters' wives were uneasy about a man touching their baby. My sister Pado broached the possibility of an apprenticeship in the clay-works, and I leaped at the chance; but the managers of the Pottery, after long discussion, were unable to agree to accept men as employes. Their hormones would make male workers unreliable, and female workers would be uncomfortable, and so on.

The holonews was full of such proposals and discussions, of course, and orations about the unforeseen consequences of the Open Gate Law, the proper place of men, male capacities and limitations, gender as destiny. Feeling against the Open Gate policy ran very strong, and it seemed that every time I watched the holo there was a woman talking grimly about the inherent violence and irresponsibility of the male, his biological unfitness to participate in social and political decision-making. Often it was a man saying the same things. Opposition to the new law had the fervent support of all the conservatives in the Castles, who pleaded eloquently for the gates to be closed and men to return to their proper station, pursuing the true, masculine glory of the games and the fuckeries.

Glory did not tempt me, after the years at Rakedr Castle; the word itself had come to mean degradation to me. I ranted against the games and competitions, puzzling most of my family, who loved to watch the Maingames and wrestling, and complained only that the level of excellence of most of the teams had declined since the gates were opened. And I ranted against the fuckeries, where, I said, men were used as cattle, stud bulls, not as human beings. I would never go there again.

"But my dear boy," my mother said at last, alone with me one evening, "will you live the rest of your life celibate?"

"I hope not," I said.

"Then…?"

"I want to get married."

Her eyes widened. She brooded a bit, and finally ventured, "To a man."

"No. To a woman. I want a normal, ordinary marriage. I want to have a wife and be a wife."

Shocking as the idea was, she tried to absorb it. She pondered, frowning.

"All it means," I said, for I had had a long time with nothing to do but ponder, "is that we'd live together just like any married pair. We'd set up our own daughterhouse, and be faithful to each other, and if she had a child I'd be its lovemother along with her. There isn't any reason why it wouldn't work!"

"Well, I don't know – I don't know of any," said my mother, gentle and judicious, and never happy at saying no to me. "But you do have to find the woman, you know."

"I know," I said, glumly.

"It's such a problem for you to meet people," she said. "Perhaps if you went to the fuckery…? I don't see why your own motherhouse couldn't guarantee you just as well as a Castle. We could try – ?"

But I passionately refused. Not being one of Fassaw's sycophants, I had seldom been allowed to go to the fuckery; and my few experiences there had been unfortunate. Young, inexperienced, and without recommendation, I had been selected by older women who wanted a plaything. Their practiced skill at arousing me had left me humiliated and enraged. They patted and tipped me as they left. That elaborate, mechanical excitation and their condescending coldness was vile to me, after the tenderness of my lover-protectors in the Castle. Yet women attracted me physically as men never had; the beautiful bodies of my sisters and their wives, all around me constantly now, clothed and naked, innocent and sensual, the wonderful heaviness and strength and softness of women's bodies, kept me continually aroused. Every night I masturbated, fantasizing my sisters in my arms. It was unendurable. Again I was a ghost, a raging, yearning impotence in the midst of un-touchable reality.

I began to think I would have to go back to the Castle. I sank into a deep depression, an inertia, a chill darkness of the mind.

My family, anxious, affectionate, busy, had no idea what to do for me or with me. I think most of them thought in their hearts that it would be best if I went back through the gate.

One afternoon my sister Pado, with whom I had been closest as a child, came to my room – they had cleared out a dormer attic for me, so that I had room at least in the literal sense. She found me in my now constant lethargy, lying on the bed doing nothing at all. She breezed in, and with the indifference women often showed to moods and signals, plumped down on the foot of the bed and said, "Hey, what do you know about the man who's here from the Ekumen?"

I shrugged and shut my eyes. I had been having rape fantasies lately. I was afraid of her.

She talked on about the offworlder, who was apparently in Rakedr to study the Mutiny. "He wants to talk to the resistance," she said. "Men like you. The men who opened the gates. He says they won't come forward, as if they were ashamed of being heroes."

"Heroes!" I said. The word in my language is gendered female. It refers to the semidivine, semihistoric protagonists of the Epics.

"It's what you are," Pado said, intensity breaking through her assumed breeziness. "You took responsibility in a great act. Maybe you did it wrong. Sassume did it wrong in the *Founding of Emmo*, didn't she, she let Faradr get killed. But she was still a hero. She took the responsibility. So did you. You ought to go talk to this Alien. Tell him what happened. Nobody really knows what happened at the Castle. You owe us the story."

That was a powerful phrase, among my people. "The untold story mothers the lie," was the saying. The doer of any notable act was held literally *accountable* for it to the community.

"So why should I tell it to an Alien?" I said, defensive of my in-ertia.

"Because he'll listen," my sister said drily. "We're all too damned busy."

It was profoundly true. Pado had seen a gate for me and opened it; and I went through it, having just enough strength and sanity left to do so.

Mobile Noem was a man in his forties, born some centuries earlier on Terra, trained on Hain, widely travelled; a small, yellowbrown, quick-eyed person, very easy to talk to. He did not seem at all masculine to me, at first; I kept thinking he was a woman, because he acted like one. He got right to business, with none of the maneuvering to assert his authority or jockeying for position that men of my society felt obligatory in any relationship with another man. I was used to men being wary, indirect, and competitive. Noem, like a woman, was direct and receptive. He was also as subtle and powerful as any man or woman I had known, even Ragaz. His authority was in fact immense; but he never stood on it. He sat down on it, comfortably, and invited you to sit down with him.

I was the first of the Rakedr mutineers to come forward and tell our story to him. He recorded it, with my permission, to use in making his report to the Stabiles on the condition of our society, "the matter of Seggri," as he called it. My first description of the Mutiny took less than an hour. I thought I was done. I didn't know, then, the inexhaustible desire to learn, to understand, to hear *all* the story, that characterizes the Mobiles of the Ekumen. Noem asked questions, I answered; he speculated and extrapolated, I corrected; he wanted details, I furnished them – telling the story of the Mutiny, of the years before it, of the men of the Castle, of the women of the Town, of my people, of my life – little by little, bit by bit, all in fragments, a muddle. I talked to Noem daily for a month. I learned that the story has no beginning, and no story has an end. That the story is all muddle, all middle. That the story is never true, but that the lie is indeed a child of silence.

By the end of the month I had come to love and trust Noem, and of course to depend on him. Talking to him had become my reason for being. I tried to face the fact that he would not stay in Rakedr much longer. I must learn to do without him. Do what? There were things for men to do, ways for men to live, he proved it by his mere existence; but could I find them?

He was keenly aware of my situation, and would not let me withdraw, as I began to do, into the lethargy of fear again; he would not let me be silent. He asked me impossible questions. "What would you be if you could be anything?" he asked me, a question children ask each other.

I answered at once, passionately – "A wife!"

I know now what the flicker that crossed his face was. His quick, kind eyes watched me, looked away, looked back.

"I want my own family," I said. "Not to live in my mothers' house, where I'm always a child. Work. A wife, wives – children – to be a mother. I want life, not games!"

"You can't bear a child," he said gently.

"No, but I can mother one!"

"We gender the word," he said. "I like it better your way.... But tell me, Ardar, what are the chances of your marrying – meeting a woman willing to marry a man? It hasn't happened, here, has it?"

I had to say no, not to my knowledge.

"It will happen, certainly, I think," he said (his certainties were always uncertain). "But the personal cost, at first, is likely to be high. Relationships formed against the negative pressure of a society are under terrible strain; they tend to become defensive, over-intense, unpeaceful. They have no room to grow."

"Room!" I said. And I tried to tell him my feeling of having no room in my world, no air to breathe.

He looked at me, scratching his nose; he laughed. "There's plenty of room in the galaxy, you know," he said.

"Do you mean...I could...that the Ekumen..." I didn't even know what the question I wanted to ask was. Noem did. He began to answer it thoughtfully and in detail. My education so far had been so limited, even as regards the culture of my own people, that I would have to attend a college for at least two or three years, in order to be ready to apply to an offworld institution such as the Ekumenical Schools on Hain. Of course, he went on, where I went and what kind of training I chose would depend on my interests, which I would go to a college to discover, since neither my schooling as a child nor my training at the Castle had really given me any idea of what there was to be interested in. The choices offered me had been unbelievably limited, addressing neither the needs of a normally intelligent person nor the needs of my society. And so the Open Gate Law instead of giving me freedom had left me "with no air to breathe but airless Space," said Noem, quoting some poet from some planet somewhere. My head was spinning, full of stars. "Hagka College is quite near Rakedr," Noem said, "did you never think of applying? If only to escape from your terrible Castle?"

I shook my head. "Lord Fassaw always destroyed the application forms when they were sent to his office. If any of us had tried to apply…"

"You would have been punished. Tortured, I suppose. Yes. Well, from the little I know of your colleges, I think your life there would be better than it is here, but not altogether pleasant. You will have work to do, a place to be; but you will be made to feel marginal, inferior. Even highly educated, enlightened women have difficulty accepting men as their intellectual equals. Believe me, I have experienced it myself! And because you were trained at the Castle to compete, to want to excel, you may find it hard to be among people who either believe you incapable of excellence, or to whom the concept of competition, of winning and defeating, is valueless. But just there, there is where you will find air to breathe."

Noem recommended me to women he knew on the faculty of Hagka College, and I was enrolled on probation. My family were delighted to pay my tuition. I was the first of us to go to college, and they were genuinely proud of me.

As Noem had predicted, it was not always easy, but there were enough other men there that I found friends and was not caught in the paralysing isolation of the motherhouse. And as I took courage, I made friends among the women students, finding many of them unprejudiced and companionable. In my third year, one of them and I managed, tentatively and warily, to fall in love. It did not work very well or last very long, yet it was a great liberation for both of us, our liberation from the belief that the only communication or commonalty possible between us was sexual, that an adult man and woman had nothing to join them but their genitals. Emadr loathed the professionalism of the fuckery as I did, and our lovemaking was always shy and brief. Its true significance was not as a consummation of desire, but as proof that we could trust each other. Where our real passion broke loose was when we lay together talking, telling each other what our lives had been, how we felt about men and women and each other and ourselves, what our nightmares were, what our dreams were. We talked endlessly, in a communion that I will cherish and honor all my life, two young souls finding their wings, flying together, not for long, but high. The first flight is the highest.

Emadr has been dead two hundred years; she stayed on Seggri, married into a motherhouse, bore two children, taught at Hagka, and died in her seventies. I went to Hain, to the Ekumenical Schools, and later to Werel and Yeowe as part of the Mobile's staff; my record is herewith enclosed. I have written this sketch of my life as part of my application to return to Seggri as a Mobile of the Ekumen. I want very much to live among my people, to learn who they are, now that I know with at least an uncertain certainty who I am.

One of the very first stories I bought for *Crank!* and still a personal favorite. Robert Devereaux is better known as a writer of totally over-the-top horror stories, but when he showed me this bittersweet tale of an unusual love, how could I say no?

CLAP IF YOU BELIEVE
Robert Devereaux

I understand her parents' wariness. A woman like my Tinkerbell is bound to attract the amorous attentions of the wrong sort now and again. So when they open the door and appraise me like a suspect gem, not smiling, not yet inviting me in, I understand and forbear. "Good evening," I say, and let the silence float like untroubled webs of gossamer between us.

After a time, Mr. Jones turns to his wife and says, "What do you think?"

"The eyes look reasonably sane," she replies, to his nod, "though that's not always an airtight indicator these days and there *is* a worrisome edge to them."

I look down, stifling the urge to defend myself, and am gratified to hear Mr. Jones say, "Man with his hobbies and profession is bound to have sharp eyes. I say we give him the benefit and let him in."

She sighs. "Oh, all right. Come in out of the heat, young man. Put your shoes there." A serried rank of them faces the wall like naughty students: practical ones for Mr. and Mrs. Jones, scuffed high-tops for twelve-year-old Melissa, and, looking more like shed leaves than footwear, Tinkerbell's familiar green-felt slippers. I unknot and loosen my buffed black Florsheims and set them beside my beloved's footwear, thinking what a marvel her tiny feet are and how delightful it is – ensconced alone in her cozy apartment after a date – to take her legs, right up to the thighs, into my mouth and lightly tongue those feet, her tiny soles, the barely perceptible curve of her insteps, the sheer white-corn delicacy of her ten tiny toes. How ecstatically my darling pixie writhes and wriggles in my hand, her silver-sheened wings fluttering against my palm!

"Hi, Alex." I look up and there's Melissa standing by an arch-way that leads to the dining room.

"Hi, Melissa," I say, wiggling my fingers at her like Oliver Hardy fiddling with his tie. The zoo is only four blocks from their house and we've begun, Melissa and Tink and I, to make a regu-lar thing of meeting there Saturday afternoons. Once, over snow cones, Melissa told me that Tink had been miserable for a long time, "but now that you've come into her life, Alex," this from a twelve-year-old, "she flits about like a host of hummingbirds when she drops in for Sunday dinner and makes loads of happy words twinkle in my head, in all of our heads." Hearing Melissa say that made me glad, and I told her so.

Melissa giggles at my finger-waggling and says, "Come on in and sit down."

I look a question at the Joneses. Mrs. Jones gives an unread-ably flat lip-line to me. Mr. Jones, instead of seconding Melissa's invitation, comes up like an old pal, leans in to me, and says, "You and me, after dinner, over cigars in my study."

I'm not sure what he's getting at, but I feel as if he's somehow taken me into his confidence. I say, "That's fine, sir," and that seems to satisfy him because he steps back like film reversed and stands beside his wife.

A familiar trill rises in my brain. The others turn their heads, as do I, to the stairs, its sweeping mahogany bannister soaring into the warm glow upstairs. And down flies my beloved Tinker-bell, trailing behind her a silent burst of stars. Her lovely face hovers before me, the tip of her wand describing figure eights in the air. "Hello, Alex my lovely," she hums into my head. Then she flits to my cheek, the perfect red bow of her lips burning cinna-mon kisses there. Recalling the sear of those kisses on other parts of my anatomy, I feel a blush rising.

"Tinkerbell," I say, using her full name, "perhaps we should –"

"Yes, daughter," Mrs. Jones breaks in, clearly not at all amused, "your young man is correct. Dinner's on the table." She glares at me and turns to lead the party into the dining room. Melissa comes and takes my hand, while Tink flits happily about my right shoulder, singing into my head her gladness at seeing me. When she holds still long enough for me to fix a discerning eye on her, I'm relieved to see that she's not yet showing.

Once dinner is under way, the ice thins considerably and in fact Tink's mother rushes past her more cautious husband to become my closest ally. Maybe her change of heart is brought on by my praise for her rainbow trout amandine – which praise I genuinely mean. Or maybe it's brought on by the dinner conversation, which focuses on me half the time, on Tink the other half. Mrs. Jones asks surprisingly insightful questions about my practice as a microsurgeon, pleasantly coaxing me into more detail than the average nonmedico cares to know about the handling of microsutures and the use of interchangeable oculars on a headborne surgical microscope. I'm happy to oblige as I watch Tinkerbell hover over her dinner, levitating bits of it with her wand – nothing flamboyant, merely functional – and bringing it home to her mouth.

After some perfunctory questions about my butterfly collection (I've sold it since meeting their daughter, as it disquiets her) and my basement full of miniature homes and the precisely detailed furniture that goes with them (I met Tinkerbell at a show for just such items), the talk turns to their daughter. It's a little embarrassing, what with Melissa beaming at me, and Tinkerbell singing into me her bemusement at her mother, and her father looking ever more resigned, and his wife going on and on about her tiny daughter, giving me a mom's-eye view of her life history as if Tinkerbell herself weren't sitting at the table with us. Mrs. Jones is in the midst of telling how easy it was to give birth to a pixie and how hard to live with the fact thereafter when I suddenly laugh, quickly disguising it as a choke – water went down the wrong way, no problem, really I'm all right. Tink has made me a lewd and lovely proposition, one which has brought to mind the heartaching image of her as last I enjoyed her, looking so vulnerable with her glade-green costume and her slim wand set aside, arching back on her spun-silver wings, her perfect breasts thrust up like twin peaks on a relief map, her ultra-fine fingers kneading the ruddy pucker of her vulva, awaiting the tickle and swirl of my ultra-fine horsehair brush, the hot monstrosity of my tonguetip, and the perfect twin-kiss of my cock-slit, as we began our careful coitus.

I give Tink a quick stare of admonition – a joke and not a joke. She beams, melts me, and goes back to her meal. The entire scene suddenly amuses me greatly, this whole silly ritual of meeting the parents, getting their approval for the inevitable, most of which – in particular the essential proof of the rightness of shared intimacy – has already come to pass. But I contain my laughter. I act the good son-in-law-to-be and show these kind narrow people, under whose love and tutelage my fiancée grew to maturity, the esteem and good manners they expect.

"Alex, would you please pass the peas?" says Melissa when her mother pauses to inhale. Mrs. Jones has launched into yet another diatribe against an educational system too unfeeling, too inflexible for special students like her Tinkerbell. Already under fire have come the lack of appropriate gymnastic equipment, the unfeeling cretinism of a certain driver-ed instructor, and Tinkerbell's unmet needs for special testing conditions in all her academic subjects. As I pass the peas, the head drama coach falls into the hopper of Mrs. Jones's tirade for refusing even to consider mounting a production of *Peter Pan* and giving Tink a chance to perform the character they've named her after, a casting inspiration Mrs. Jones is certain would have brought her daughter out of the cocoon of adolescent shyness years earlier than had been the case.

"But the worst of it, Alex," she says, and I thank God that she's spoken my name for the first time (and that dropped so casually into the conversation), "is that no one in all those years has had the slightest clue how to teach Tink – or even how to discover – the uses of her wand, other than as an odd utensil and for occasional cleaning tricks. It might have kept this family solvent –"

"Emma," warns Mr. Jones, defensive.

"– well, more solvent than it was. It might have saved peoples' lives, cured disease, made world leaders see reason through their cages of insanity, brought all kinds of happiness flowing into peoples' hearts the world over." She asks me point-blank to help her tiny daughter discover the full potential of her wand, and I promise I will. I don't mention of course that we've already found one amazing use for it in our lovemaking, a use that makes me feel incredibly good, incredibly potent, and incredibly loving toward Tinkerbell. It occurs to me at that moment, listening to Mrs. Jones's spirited harangue, that the wand might indeed have other uses and that perhaps one of them, a healing use, might reduce the failures and increase the triumphs I witness every day in the operating room. I get excited by this, nod more, stoke food into my mouth faster than is strictly polite. We're bonding, Mrs. Jones and I. She can feel it, I can feel it, Melissa is grinning like an idiot, and Tink is humming snatches of *Lohengrin* into my head. "I love you, Alex," she wind-chimes, "I love you and the horse you rode in on." Looking aside, I watch her playing with her food, wanding a slow reversed meander of mashed potatoes into her mouth, biting it off in ribbons of white mush. Her unshod feet are planted apart on the damask and her wings, thin curved planes of iridescence, lie still against her back.

After dinner, Mrs. Jones is ready to usher me into the parlor for more bonding. But her husband holds up his hand to cut her off, saying "It's time, Emma." "Oh," she says. He's got some bit of gristle in his craw, some one thing that's holding back his approval of me.

"Ah, the study," I say. "The cigars."

"Just so," he says in a way that suggests man-talk, and pretty serious man-talk at that. I follow him out of the dining room. Mrs. Jones and Melissa have odd looks on their faces. Even Tink's hum is edged with anxiety.

The study is dark and small, green-tinged and woodsy. There's a rolltop desk, now closed, and the rich smell of rolled tobacco and old ledgers pervades the air. He fits a green eyeshade around his head, offers me one. I accept but feel foolish in it, as if I'm at Disney World wearing a Donald Duck hat, bright yellow bill as brim.

Mr. Jones sits in a rosewood swivel chair and motions me to a three-legged ebony piano stool in front of him. I have to look up a good six inches to meet his eyes. "You smoke cigars?" he asks.

"Not unless you count one White Owl in my teens."

He chuckles once, then drops it. With a soft clatter of wood slats, he scrolls up the rolltop and opens a huge box of cigars. He lifts out two of them, big long thick cylinders of brown leaf with the smell of sin about them and the crisp feel of currency in their wrappings. I take what he offers and follow his lead in preparing, lighting, and puffing on the damned thing. I'm careful to control my intake, not wanting to lose face in a fit of coughing. The cigar tastes peculiarly pleasant, sweet, not bitter, and the back of my head feels like it's ballooning.

"My wife," he begins, "likes you. I like you. And Tinkerbell likes you, but then she's liked every last one of her boyfriends, even the slime-sucking shitwads – can we speak man to man? – who used Tink for their own degenerate needs and then discarded her."

I don't want to hear this.

"Not that there've been lots of men before you. She may be a pixie, our daughter, but she's got the good sense of the Joneses even so. But you know, Alex my boy, you'd be surprised at the number of men in this world who look and act perfectly normal, men whose mild exteriors cover sick vistas of muck and sludge, men who make regular guys like you and me ashamed to be called men."

"I assure you, sir, that –"

"– and I'd believe those assurances, I really would, even though I've believed and been fooled in the past. My little girl, Tinkerbell Titania Jones, is special to me as she is; not some freak, not a thing of shame or suspicion, no, but a thing of grace and beauty."

"She is indeed, Mr. Jones."

He fixes me in his glare and exhales a puff of blue smoke. It hangs like a miasma about him, but he doesn't blink. His eyes might be lizard eyes. "I had doubts when she was born, of course. What father wouldn't? No man likes to be deceived by his wife, not even through the irresistible agency of a stray faerie or incubus, if such there be in this world. But there are mannerisms of mine I recognized quite early in my daughter, mannerisms I was sure were neither learned nor trumped up by some phantom lover bent on throwing a cuckolded husband off his trail."

He cranes his neck and stares, about fifteen degrees askew of my face. It's a look I recognize from my first meeting with Tink at the miniaturists' show in Sacramento the previous winter. I'd asked her to dinner and she went all quiet and contemplative, looking just this way, before finally venturing a twinkled Yes. I could tell she'd been stung before, and recently.

"She's mine," he says. "Some mutation if you want to be cold-bloodedly clinical about it, but all mine. And I love her dearly, as parents of special children often do."

He takes a long puff, exhales it, looks at me. "Now I'm going to ask you three questions, Alex. Only truthful answers are going to win my daughter's hand."

I feel odd about this turn in the conversation, and yet the setting, the cigar smoke, the close proximity of this beast in his lair, make it seem perfectly normal. I nod agreement and flick a squat cylinder of ash into the open glass hand, severed, of a four-fingered man.

"First," Mr. Jones says, not stumbling over any of the words, "have you had sex with my daughter?"

My head is pounding. I take a long pull on my cigar and slowly exhale the smoke. My hand, holding it, seems big and beefy, unworthy of my incisive mind. "She and I have…made love, yes. We love each other, you see, and it's only natural for –"

"No extenuation," says Mr. Jones. "Your answer is Yes. It's a good answer, it's the truth, and I have no quarrel with it. I would think you some sort of nitwit if you hadn't worked out some mutually agreeable arrangement between you. No, I don't want to know how it's done. I shudder to think about it. When she drops in, she seems none the worse for wear. If she's happy, and you're happy with her – and with the limitations you no doubt face – then that will content her mother and me."

I think of course of vaginal sinkings, that nice feel of being gripped there by a grown woman. And I think back years to my first girlfriend Rhonda, to her mouth, to the love she was kind enough to focus down below from time to time though less frequently than I would have preferred.

"That leads, of course, to my second question," says Mr. Jones, putting one hand, the one without the cigar, to his temple. "Will you be faithful to Tinkerbell, neither casting the lures of temptation toward other women nor consenting to be lured by them?"

I pause. "That's a complex question."

"It is indeed," he says, with a rising inflection which asks it all over again.

"I don't think," I tell him, my hands folded, my eyes deeply sincere, "I will ever fail my beloved in this way. Yet knowing the weakness of myself and other men, the incessant clamor of the gonads that I daresay all males are prey to, I hesitate to say Yes unequivocally to your question. But Tinkerbell gives me great satisfaction, and, more importantly, I believe I do the same for her. Something about her ways in bed, if you will, seems to silence the voice of lust when I'm around other women. Besides which – and I don't mean this flippantly – I've grown, through loving Tinkerbell, to appreciate smaller women. In fact, on the whole, I've come to find so-called normal-sized women unbearably gross and disgusting."

Mr. Jones looks askance at me. "Alex, you're a most peculiar man. But then I think that's what my daughter's going to need, a peculiar man, and yet it's so damned hard to know which set of peculiarities are the right ones."

I'm not sure how to take his comment, but then I'm in no position to debate the issue. "Yes, sir," I say.

"Almost out of the woods," says Mr. Jones, grinning. "The third one is easy." He tosses it off like a spent match: "Do you love Tinkerbell?"

This question throws me. It seems simple enough, but that's the problem: It's too simple. Does he want a one-word response, or a dissertation? Is it a trick question of some sort? And is the time I'm taking in deliberating over it actually sinking my chances? What is love, after all? Everybody talks about it, sings about it, yammers on and on endlessly about it. But it's so vague a word, and so loaded. I think of French troubadour poets, of courtly love and its manufacture, of Broadway show tunes and wall-sized faces saying "I love you" on big screens, saying it like some ritual curse or as if it signaled some terrible loss of control akin to vomiting.

And I say, "Yes and no," feeling my way into the open wound of shared camaraderie, ready to provide reasons for my equivocation, a brief discourse which will show him the philosophical depths of my musings and yet come about, in the end, to a grand paean of adoration for his daughter.

But before I can begin, he rises from his chair and reaches for me, and the next thing I know, the furniture hurtles by as if in a silent wind and the doors fly open seemingly without the intervention of human hands and I'm out on the street in front of their home, trying to stop my head from spinning.

It's dark out there but muggy. I ache inside, ache for my loss. It's not fair, I think. She loves me and I love her and by God we belong together. I'll call her in the morning when she's back in the city, I'll send roses, I'll surprise her with a knock on her door. We'll elope. This isn't the Dark Ages, after all. Tinkerbell and I don't need her parents' permission to marry.

Doors slam in the house. Downstairs, upstairs. A high-pitched voice, Melissa's, shouts something childish and angry, is answered by falsely calm parental soothings. None of the words can I make out.

The first floor goes dark after a while, then bit by bit the second. From where I'm standing, it looks like a miniature house, one of my basement models. I raise both hands and find I can obliterate it completely.

There is one golden glow of light hovering behind a drawn tan shade upstairs. Her bedroom, the room she grew up in. I want to clap my hands, clap them in defiance of her parents – she'll know what that means, she'll surely understand. But the energy has drained from my arms and they hang useless at my sides.

Behind the shade, my lost love's light moves slowly back and forth, back and forth, growing dimmer, casting forth ever smaller circles of gold with each beat of my heart.

When I first read this story, I literally fell out of my chair from laughing so hard. Unfortunately, I was in an office full of lawyers at the time, so I couldn't really explain what was so funny. I didn't know when I published it if anyone else would get it, but it has in fact proven to be one of my most popular stories, at least to judge by my mail.

NIXON IN SPACE
Rob McCleary

On July 20, 1969, or so I am told, after forty-eight hours of hellish labor, Leigh was born and some guys walked around on the moon. Leigh had red hair, and was a girl. The people who walked around on the moon were all male, that is to say they had penises. Due to zero gravity, they had erections the entire trip. Even when they blasted off they had hard-ons. The roar of the rocket engines excited them. "It was better than sex," they said afterwards.

The whole deal started like this: some guys looked up at the moon and said "Hey, let's go there." And so they did. They dreamed it up like some forgotten oriental city and put it into action (they had the money to indulge such fantasies in those days). The Americans made it to the moon first, because they had the most cash. Also, they had captured Nazi rocket scientists.

The only other people who were in the race with the Americans to get to the moon were the Soviets. The Soviets lived in a country that was founded by Vikings that sailed up the Volga River, enslaving everyone they met. Those they didn't enslave, they killed. Eventually, a bald guy named Lenin overthrew the Vikings. Then came the Nazis.

All the same: the Soviets and the Americans both wanted to be the first on the moon. They both wanted to see it was made of green cheese, which all the best scientists agreed it was. Also, they wanted to get up there and drop atomic bombs back on the other side on earth.

So they saw the moon and said "Let's go!" and that's exactly what they did. Kennedy made a speech that got everybody fired up and it was decided right then and there that somebody had to go to the moon. Men with crew cuts made the journey possible. They used slide rules.

There were rumors of cities on the moon.

So while the men were walking around on the moon, looking for cities made of green cheese, Leigh was being born, red hair and all.

Everything was coming together.

Later, it would be claimed she kept stretching out her tiny hand, as if reaching for something in the air above her, but eventually it would come out that this was merely dreamed up by one of the nursing staff in an attempt to get Leigh's mother interested in the tiny, bloody being she had just spent the previous two days and nights trying to force out of her body.

"There are men on the moon," said the nurse as she brought Leigh in for her mother to see. She had seen it on television in the doctors' lounge and was repeating her observation. The nurse said it as a simple statement of fact, with the same enthusiasm she might've said "there are men on the roof." Fantastic events like that were pretty common back in the days when the money still held out. First they were making radar, then splitting the atom, then putting guys on the moon. The list goes on and on.

The nurse let Leigh's mother hold her baby for a while, and they talked about the guys who were on the moon. A sign in Times Square, New York said SOME GUYS ARE UP THERE ON THE MOON! and everybody cheered. When they came back they rode down the streets in big cars and everybody threw paper at them. This sort of thing went on and on for days: another city, more cars, more paper flying around their heads. They learned to live with it.

"What a lucky baby to be born on the same day as man walks on the moon," said the nurse, and then she took Leigh away from her mother to take her back to the nursery.

"Look at the way she keeps stretching out her hand, like she knows what's going on up there." Leigh's mother looked bleary-eyed at her daughter. Leigh wasn't doing anything. She was sleeping.

"You just missed it," said the nurse. "She's a moon baby. That's what they're calling all the babies that are born today." And then the nurse said the words again with a magical lilt in her voice, in contrast to the deadpan delivery she had used to inform Leigh's mother that there were guys in the process of hanging out on the moon: "moon baby…"

The nurse took Leigh and put her back in the nursery with all the other moon babies. Then she picked up another moon baby and took it to another moon mother and tried to convince the moon mother that her moon baby was reaching out for the heavens in a gesture of strange, sympathetic magic for the guys bounding around on the moon with hard-ons. Nobody believed her.

Later on, after an early childhood spent attempting to paste her unruly curls of red hair to her head with an eclectic collection of combs, plastic barrettes, and even degenerating at one point to rubber bands (culminating in a tearful watershed moment of frustration and realization that would pave the way for her masses of curled hair to flow freely) we would meet and discuss her birth and the events leading up to it: the Second World War, her parents meeting at a kitchen table littered with empty beer bottles after a party and Leigh's eventual conception, but neither of us could make much sense of it.

My earliest memory is of Nixon resigning on television. That was back when my family lived in the Yukon. After Nixon came the fire which burned our house to the ground, the tall orange flames playing off the rippling waters of the deep, cold lake full of huge pike we used to catch from a wooden motor boat.

The Yukon of my memories is composed of grays, whites, and red clay, gravel roads, pine trees, and mountain ranges ground into submission by ancient glaciers. All that disappeared in the orange glow reflected in the cold autumn waters of the lake.

But first, more about Nixon. My father told us to be quiet so he could watch Nixon resign. We saw it all, through the miracle of television. Nixon, in his pale blue sharkskin suit, black hair plastered to his face by sweat, a good three-day growth on his face, his prodigious sweat having soaked through his suit jacket leaving immense stains under each arm. He said his piece: all about truth, justice, and the American way, and then he left. He walked right out of the White House, down Pennsylvania Avenue, and just kept walking. He removed his tie and threw it in the Reflecting Pool. A little kid fished it out to use as a memento of the historic occasion. Nixon kept walking, and the television people played all kinds of sentimental music like "Amazing Grace" and "Kumbaya."

Nixon walked right down the middle of the street, waving to people, accepting mock-salutes from old soldiers who had served with him in the Pacific, and shaking hands with the rank and file. Several people offered him jobs, but Nixon declined them all. He did try to get into the space program, but they didn't want any ex-presidents. They told him he didn't have enough of a science background. Nixon countered saying that they had offered Walter Cronkite a ride in the spaceship, a charge that left NASA without reply. Nixon left, embittered, and ended up selling his garbage to souvenir hunters to pay the bills. The real reason NASA didn't want him was that they were afraid his known tendency to sweat like a pig would short circuit the electrical system in the space capsule.

"All the same," Nixon would later say, after the truth had come out through the Freedom of Information Act, "they should've let me ride in the spaceship. Every ex-president should have the right to go to the moon."

After the show was over the Yanks went crazy. They all cried and pulled their hair and wanted him back. Those responsible for his impeachment were dragged from their homes and strung up from telephone poles. Entire cities were razed. Finally, the next day, everybody calmed down and order was restored. The papers all cried out that Nixon should come back, but he never did.

"This bull has died too big a death," he said when the news crews found him living in South Carolina growing yams and writing his memoirs. Everybody agreed that those were pretty much the truest words they'd ever heard spoken by an ex-president, and that they should throw their support behind his successor: Gerald Ford. When Nixon found out they had taken his refusal seriously he became distraught and said he was only kidding, that he would gladly resume the duties of the Chief Executive. But his withdrawal came too late, as they had already changed the locks on the White House. That same week, Nixon got his rejection from NASA, so it was pretty rough on him.

After our house burned down, we gave up on living in the Yukon and moved to Ontario. My father got a job as an electrician, and I met Leigh. She was the first moon baby I ever met.

One day a barn on our concession burned up, the orange flames lighting up the night sky for miles around. It got us both so excited we copulated right then and there in the darkness, with the mosquitoes biting our bare skin, the sirens of the emergency vehicles wailing in the late summer breeze. It was the beginning of the later stage of our relationship, and after we finished we had no idea why we had done it.

"Must be the moon," said Leigh.

Although I wanted badly to believe it, the only trouble with this convenient explanation was that there was no moon in the sky that night.

Every time her birthday would roll around, Leigh would receive a pair of silver earrings in the shape of a crescent moon. When I came to visit her they would be hanging all over the room, jingling as the wind moved them, reflecting the early morning light. They were all in the shape of a crescent moon, never a full moon, usually with the face of a woman inside the crescent. By the time the twenty-fifth pair of earrings arrived, everybody had pretty much given up on getting back to the moon. It cost too much. The Americans had spent billions of dollars getting a few guys up there so they could play golf. What did they bring back as souvenirs? Like little children on their first trip to the beach, they brought back rocks. They toured the rocks around all over the place, told everybody about how they had come from the moon in an attempt to drum up more money so they could go back up.

"There may be cities on the moon," they hinted broadly. They had no shame. They had moon fever. Their entire lives, body and soul, had become devoted to one cause: getting back up on the moon and playing golf. The problem was, everybody had already paid for the show once. The astronauts had already been up there and made it back. People weren't interested in getting to the moon, they were interested mainly in the danger. To most people, it was a sort of glorified drag race, and everybody knows that the best part of drag racing is watching the cars blow up. The problem with the space program was that they kept trying to make it safer and safer. Also, only a few special people could go up in the capsule every time. Nixon was the loudest voice against the elitist space program:

"If I used to be president, and they won't let me go up in their capsule, think how long it will be before you, the common man, can go to the moon."

He said this at every public speaking engagement. NASA fried a few guys on the launching pad in a capsule fire to try and prove the program was still a life and death matter, but nobody bought it. The public rose up:

"We want to go to the mooooooooon!" they said.

A "Put Nixon on the Moon" committee was formed. The public felt that if they got Tricky Dick up there, it was only a matter of time before the average Joe was up there hitting a few rounds. Dick was to be their watershed candidate.

Soon the public was on fire with moon mania. Popular magazines ran in-depth stories with step-by-step plans about how the moon would be colonized. Newspapers ran headlines like "Let's Get One of Ours on the Moon!" The forest fire had been ignited.

Time wore on.

The moon was on everybody's mind. Leigh and I would often sit and look at it, wonder about it, just like the old days before some guys went up there and desecrated it with stupid sports.

Moon watching, instead of drag racing, became America's number one pastime. You would see people all over the place just sitting serenely, looking up at the moon. Artists painted pictures and wrote poems about it. People of all ages, sexes, and races were putting aside their differences to join together and put somebody from the rank and file on the moon. Everything was becoming good and sound and pure.

Everybody looked at the moon and agreed it was the most beautiful thing in outer space, and that people must go there when they die to live in great, glorious, silver castles and dress in silk. This idea, proposed by a member of the great Pacific Northwest Moon Watchers, won immediate acceptance by the vast majority of the population. It was comforting for everyone to think that up there on the moon were all their friends and relatives, and that someday they would join them. Also, it got everybody even more fired up to go to the moon. People got so excited that they tried to build their own spaceships. Each group of Moon Watchers came up with a plan, pooled their resources, and built rocket ships. These efforts were outlawed after only a few tries. Gravity, always a jealous lover, was reluctant to share her inhabitants with any other planetary body, and sent one ship crashing down into a crowded suburb of Jersey City. In a farewell speech, the pilot said, "I'm going to get to the moon, one way or another," and he had meant what he said. His body was never recovered, but the crater his impact created was dedicated as a national memorial to everyone's efforts to get off the planet, everywhere. Delegates from moon watching clubs all over the world came for the dedication ceremony. The keynote speaker, good old Tricky Dick, made an impassioned plea to governments around the world to put ordinary people in space:

"Let not another brave soul fall like Icarus from the sky," he said, emotion choking his voice. "For although you may fetter us here in fear and ignorance, as surely as the sun which also rises, and the majestic moon, mother of all things, waxes and wanes, the spirit of mankind will soon soar in the heaven!"

The speech was well received, even though most people didn't know who Icarus was, and was reprinted in newspapers all over the world. People started comparing it to Kennedy's inaugural address. Soon everybody was rioting in the streets and calling for the scientists and their slide rules to be handed over to the public. The government made a token gesture of handing over the slide rules, but of course without the scientists they were useless. This made the public even angrier. Leigh and I watched the rioting on television. It was now well over two decades since the original astronauts had landed on the moon.

"There has to be an easier way to get to the moon than launching somebody in a big tin can," said I.

On television, a man, who for some reason was buck naked except for a pair of black combat boots, was running through the flaming streets of Munich with a microwave oven hoisted over his head, an insane look of glee on his face. In Vancouver, people had gathered in Stanley Park to burn a dummy across the front of which was pinned a sign saying GRAVITY written in a scraggly hand.

"I think it's the idea of getting to the moon that people like," said Leigh. "It's the challenge of the unreachable goal. Like Everest. It has to be tried."

On television, a London mob had somehow gotten the statue of Nelson off his dizzying column in Trafalgar Square and were committing unspeakable indignities on it.

The chaos in the streets continued for several days. The armies of the various nations were called out to put down the insurrections. Unfortunately for the powers that be however, their ranks were filled with closet moon watchers who joined in the disruptions as soon as they were deployed. Just when things seemed on the verge of descending into total anarchy, a lunar eclipse cowed everybody, and most people showed up for work the next day. The Soviets took advantage of the confusion to launch an orbiting space station they called *Mir*. Onboard *Mir* was a woman about to give birth. The Commies wanted to see what would happen to a baby born in space. They tried to make out like she was just a regular woman, trying to steal world approval for their program, but then some journalist uncovered that she was in fact a KGB Colonel, and the USSR was forced to give Gary Powers back to the United Nations.

The Space Baby was born perfectly normal, and was raised in total isolation by specially trained chimpanzees until he was twenty-one. Me and Leigh sat up on the roof of my parents' home to watch his spacecraft go over the night he was born. It looked like a moving star.

"Wow," said Leigh, looking up at the little blip, "somebody's being born in that thing. That's gotta be a first."

"Do you believe in astrology?" I asked

"You mean like 'what's your sign'?"

"Sort of. Do you think your parents planned it so you would be born on the day of the moon landings?"

"Don't be gross!"

"Well?"

My only answer was a cold stare from Leigh. Obviously she was not eager to combine the subjects of parents and sex. I decided to continue my line of questioning anyway.

"They must've planned it for a certain time. Why not the moon landing?"

"Because I doubt they planned it for a specific day. Besides, I was born late. My dad had to take my mom for a ride in his father's truck to induce labor."

"Maybe you wanted to wait until the moon landing."

I arched my eyebrows suggestively. The Space Baby and his mother streaked silently above us in the firmament. I went over the equation in my head: moon landing, Leigh's birth, Nixon resigning, Nixon trying to go to the moon. I could come to no firm conclusion. Nonetheless, I could tell that watching the spaceship up in the night sky was getting Leigh excited, and before long we would make love for the second time in our relationship. When it was all over, we still couldn't figure out why we had done it.

Then, in August, the unthinkable happened: it was announced that Richard Nixon was going to the moon. The announcement was greeted with a stunned silence by the general population. The entire world, faced with the prospect of the event which they had worked for decades towards with no serious belief it would actually happen coming to fruition, was flabbergasted. Without the glue of common purpose, the population's unity began to dissolve. The different moon watching organizations battled for control of the world's faithful. Instead of huge riots, the various factions engaged in pitched battles in every major city, fighting tenaciously for territory in street by street battles. Nixon appeared on television, calling for calm, but the situation was beyond repair. The "Put Nixon on the Moon" committee (formerly the most powerful of the plebeian moon race organizations) was torn apart by infighting, and was unable to induce a peaceful end to the hostilities. Finally, after days of impassioned pleas for calm, Nixon appeared for one last time on television and said:

"Fuck you all, I'm going to the moooooon!"

The population grew dejected, and then, like any mob worth its salt, turned on their leader. Nixon's name, henceforward, would be "mud." Contracts were put out on him. He was burned in effigy. NASA had to conceal where Nixon was going to be launched into space from. The day of the launch, Leigh and I watched as a clean-shaven and powder-dry Nixon made his way to the capsule, flashing his trademark "double victory" at everyone he passed. Inside the capsule, Dick tried to come up with witty things to say, but the best he could muster was: "This is gonna be better than sex!"

"Why do men always say that?" Leigh asked me.

The final countdown began, Nixon pushing buttons and smiling insanely. But then, when they reached zero hour, nothing happened. Instead, NASA flashed his location on the screen. Nixon was sitting on top of a fake space craft. He tried the hatch, but found it locked. He pulled frantically, without effect, sweating madly. The picture then flashed to the real spacecraft lifting off with real astronauts and real golf gear. It then flashed back to Nixon's decoy craft, which was being rocked back and forth by an enraged mob. Luckily for Nixon, they couldn't get the hatch open, so the different factions took turns rolling him around in his dummy capsule to try and make him sick. Then, the "Put Nixon on the Moon" committee, having put aside their differences, came to his rescue, driving off the enraged mob with pepper spray.

That evening, me and Leigh watched the guys who had been

on the real launch make their way to the moon in their tiny capsule. The following evening, we lay on the roof of my parents' home and listened to their broadcast from space on the radio. One of the guys was making a speech that started like this:

"In the beginning, God created the heavens and the earth..."

Then he went on about how good the earth looked from out in space, and how it didn't really matter exactly who was going into space, because they represented everyone on earth. It was a real good speech, well put together. Dmitri, as the Space Baby born on *Mir* came to be named, was working as a commentator with some American network, and he said he'd never heard what it was like to be in space expressed so eloquently, but mostly everybody thought it was bullshit. Then the other announcer smacked Dmitri in the mouth because there was no way Dmitri could remember what it was like in space because he had only been a baby at the time.

The asphalt shingles on the roof still retained the warmth of the day's sunshine. Looking up at the night sky, I knew we would make love before long, and maybe this time we would figure out why.

"What if your mother unconsciously held back labor until the moon landing?" I asked.

"Don't be ridiculous. She was in labor for forty-eight hours. Nobody would choose that, consciously or unconsciously. Give it up. The moon landing has absolutely nothing to do with my birth."

I decided not to bring up the question anymore, even though I still wanted to know the answer. The technological cuckolding of Nixon had thrown my calculations into confusion. The space capsule kept going on through space, and the people in some city in Australia turned on all their lights to let the guys in the capsule know they didn't want them to get burned up like those other astronauts. Me and Leigh made love, and although we still couldn't come to any firm conclusions as to why it happened, we finally had to concede that the moon, which was that night in full phase, was partially responsible.

The astronauts returned safely to earth, with more rocks.

Nixon was spirited away by his followers, and we didn't hear about him until a couple of years later when he was caught trying to sneak into the White House through a basement window. The Secret Service threw him out in front of the place where an enraged mob tore him to pieces with their bare hands and some broken bottles.

Although Leigh continued to receive silver moon earrings every year on her birthday, there were no more moon landings, as the Americans had run out of money.

It took me a while to convince Michael Bishop that he wanted to write for *Crank!*, but it was worth the wait. His books have consistently exhibited a clear sensitivity for the subtleties of the human character almost unequaled in SF. This startling bit of techno-theological exposition is no exception.

I, ISCARIOT
Michael Bishop

When evening comes, he arrives with the twelve. And as they reclined at table and were eating, Jesus said, "So help me, one of you eating with me is going to turn me in!"

They began to fret and to say to him one after another, "I'm not the one, am I?"

But he said to them, "It's one of the twelve, the one who is dipping into the bowl with me. The son of Adam departs just as the scriptures predict, but damn the one responsible for turning the son of Adam in! It would be better for that man had he never been born!"

— *Mark* 14:17–21

And right away, while he was still speaking, Judas, one of the twelve, shows up, and with him a crowd, dispatched by the ranking priests and the scholars and the elders, wielding swords and clubs. Now the one who was to turn him in had arranged a signal with them, saying, "The one I'm going to kiss is the one you want. Arrest him and escort him safely away!" And right away he arrives, comes up to him, and says, "Rabbi," and kissed him.

And they seized him and held him fast....

— *Mark* 14:43–46♥

♥Robert J. Miller, ed. *The Complete Gospels: Annotated Scholars Version.* Revised *&* Expanded Ed. (San Francisco: Polebridge Press [HarperCollinsPublishers], 1994), pp. 47, 48.

Before sunset, in a field where potters dig clay for their vessels, the dead man twists beneath hundreds of rose-purple blossoms. Otherwise the tree's branches gleam naked, and the field stands empty of either weed or shrub.

Four men in dirty tunics and split sandals creep into view and spot the hanged man. Even if they had not seen him, their arrival downwind would have betrayed his presence, a strange mix of flower scent and meaty bloat. One of the men covers his mouth and nose with a sleeve.

The bladefaced man in the lead says, The women were right. He pauses a moment before adding, He's got to come down before sunset, or he'll pollute the field.

A stocky man with wiry knucklehair and eyebrows makes a show of gagging. Already has, he says. The bastard done it a night back, Cephas. Can't you smell him?

Still, says Cephas. We have to take him down.

Why? He's gone to Sheol, to everlasting shadow and dust, and the field's already defiled.

Because if it was you, Thaddaeus, you'd want the same.

It isn't me, even if we shared a name.

The four men argue. Then, silently, they cross the field single-file, like soldiers separated from their army in a hostile land. The sun, ever dropping, flattens and runs, reddening even further the potter's field that the tree already spectacularly brightens.

None of the men has a knife to cut the rope. Two nights ago Cephas had a sword, but lost it. He regrets its loss because none of the others wants to untie the noose that has strangled their former colleague. Thaddaeus, the stocky man, turns his face away, but leans into the bole of the redbud with all his might, pushing the tree into the bruised glow spreading outward from the west.

A taller man with callused hands and a beard like flaming straw helps him. Cephas leaps and grabs the bough supporting the hanged man. His weight draws the limb down. The stench of decay nearly overwhelms him, and he cries, John! Andrew!

Cephas's brother, Andrew, lifts the dead man's swollen feet and walks him out horizontal to the ground.

The rope, already rotten and fraying, snaps. The corpse pitches headfirst to the clay, twisting so that upon impact its abdomen bursts and an iridescent snake of bowel gushes out.

What a rank bugger! says Thaddaeus.

John, the tall man with the flaming beard, stands back from the corpse and recites,

> When he is judged, let him be found guilty.
> And let his prayer become sin.
> Let his days be few,
> And let another take his office.[♥]

Selah, says Andrew. What now?

Nothing, says Cephas, half-snarling. A day late, he's down from his tree. Let the dogs and vultures take him.

Thaddaeus begins to weep: a strange, indeed, a discomfiting sight in so powerful-looking a man. I wish we could trade this body for the other, he manages. I wish we

knew where the other body lay, says John. But we don't, and there's an end to it.

Cephas nudges the fallen corpse with a toe. Then the four men stalk single-file back across the field toward the city, warily inspecting the landscape's shadows for bountyhunters and informants. They skulk totally out of view. All that remains, framing their vanishment, is the crimson-tinted mother-of-pearl face of a computer monitor.

A day or two after the event inspiring this dramatization, some women start calling the field Akel Dama, or Blood Acre, and the name sticks, like wet clay to an amphora taking watery form on a potter's wheel.

Two thousand years later, the faux-event's resuscitants, including the hanged man himself, gather in a twilight space at once measurable with a carpenter's tape and so depthfully vast that it mirrors the world. The farther you go into this space the more detail

---

[♥]*Psalm* 109:7–8 in *The Wesley Bible: New King James Version* (Nashville, TN: Thomas Nelson, Inc., 1990), p. 869. See also *Acts* 1:16–20.

and dimension it acquires.

In fact, its whiteness exfoliates into rain forests, cities, amphi-theaters, palaces, and halls, almost as if you have run through a series of nested realities to this false courtroom at the shifting center.

The resuscitants – electronic simulacra, with reconstituted memories of their bodily lives – dispose themselves about the space, primarily on its edges. They will emerge into view at any legitimate call, then soliloquize, testify, and/or enact as the proceedings demand.

How do you plead?

Please. In what matter?

That of the Messiah's betrayal to the Judean authorities.

Yes. Of course. I handed him over.

Guilty, then.

But I didn't understand what I was doing. I never realized they'd haul him away for judgment and nailing.

Come, Mr. Iscariot. Do better.

Help us recognize him, they said. We know him by the commotion he's made, but his face remains unfamiliar to most Jerusalemites, even to some who've heard him preach, for they heard him from a distance. With these and similar arguments they cajoled me.

And so the kiss of betrayal?

The kiss of identification. No more. The others slander me because it turns the eye from how cravenly they fled, like chickens in a hawk's oversoaring shadow.

And now you rat them out in turn.

I say the truth, even if Pilate himself pretends not to recognize it.

So how do you plead?

Of leading the Judeans to him, guilty. Of betraying him, innocent. Altogether innocent.

Resuscitants appear in period dress. They look anomalously time-elided, extras in a pre-Lucan costume drama. But with them in modern attire appear the e-clones of some celebs as familiar to a latter-day netist as Brando or Heston to any longtime film buff.

The prosecution team, for example, includes e-clones for Avery Stills, Rebecca Mormile, and Henry Albornoz, while the even more famous defense team features dopplegangers for Wendy Grice, Hirofumi Satoh, and Dakota Browning. The Chief Justice of the United States Supreme Court – an e-clone of Paul Ogilvie – presides.

Either simultaneous or delayed cable feeds serve the computerphobic. In fact, television broadcasts garner such prodigious ratings that the major entertainment networks have preempted nearly all regular programming for gavel-to-gavel coverage of what aficionados early on christened the Trial of the Millennium. (CBS, predictably, calls its own focus on the virtually self-propagating proceedings *Eye on Iscariot*.)

Jury members, who never appear onscreen, vary widely in age, ethnicity, and socioeconomic status. They do have one odd quality in common: In offline negotiations preceding the trial, both defense and prosecution agreed that to qualify for duty these e-entities must manifest as religion-neutral or -indifferent. Both sides, it seems, feared any juror with a theological or a rationalist axe to grind and thus decided to exclude such specimens.

Do you swear to tell the truth, the whole truth, and nothing but the truth, so help you God?

My Yes is Yes, and my No, No.

You won't take the oath?

Yeshua taught that oaths echo like wind in the mouths of scoundrels. I'm not a scoundrel.

The Avery Stills e-clone rises. I object, he says. Your Honor, this is a blatant evasion.

The simulacrum of Chief Justice Ogilvie ignores him. By what would you agree to swear, Mr. Iscariot?

I won't swear, either as oath or profanation. None of us does. Probity cloaks any follower who takes to heart Yeshua's teachings.

Objection, says the Stills e-clone.

Why?

Your Honor, Mr. Iscariot stresses an apostolic association he stands accused of betraying. Letting him sidestep the oath is like granting him permission to lie.

Relax, Mr. Stills. What prevents any sworn testator from lying?

Your Honor, the issue isn't

Address the question, please.

One's personal integrity. Or one's fear of one's god. The figure shrugs and sits back down.

Take the stand, Judge Ogilvie tells Iscariot.♥

The trial programmers and the electronic infrastructure supporting them begin to merchandise Iscariot. T-shirts; plastic cups; toy lambs; stenciled tunics; foam-soled sandals; Betrayal™ playing cards, board games, and computer games; two-faced silver coins (in laminated rolls of thirty); vials of a puttylike substance jocularly identified as spikenard; a set of porcelain plates depicting not only Iscariot, but Lucifer, Lancelot, Iago, Benedict Arnold, and Vidkun Quisling; flowering Judas seed catalogues; intricately carven tillboxes; flexible plastic figurines of Iscariot, Brutus, and Cassius writhing in the triple mouths of Satan....

"The soul that suffers most," explained my Guide,
"is Judas Iscariot, he who kicks his legs
On the fiery chin and has his head inside...."♥♥

Not to mention covers on *Newsweek, Time, U.S. News & World Report, New Yorker, GQ, Wired, Rolling Stone, Esquire, Mother Jones, TV Guide, The Atlantic Monthly, Redbook, Byte, Christianity Today, People, Omni, Sassy, Psychology Today, Science Fiction Age, St. Andrew's Messenger, TriQuarterly, Outland, Apostically Yours, Playboy, Hebrew Studies, Paris Review, Century, Science News, Trial Lawyer, Modern Horticulturist,* and *Crank!* (to list a provocative representative sample).

Favorite T-shirts designs include silkscreened portraits of Iscariot scolding Mary about the spikenard, filching from the

---

♥ From here on, we drop the cumbersome neologism *e-clone* and its various situational corrolaries; however, every proper name in this transcript implies it.

♥♥ John Ciardi, trans., *The Inferno* by Dante Alighieri (New York: Mentor Books, 1954), Canto XXXIII, vv. 61–63.

disciples' moneybox, dipping bread in the Upper Room, kissing an already savvy Yeshua in the Garden of Gethsemane, scattering his bloodmoney in the Temple, standing selfconsciously naked in a YMCA lockerroom, driving an antique Edsel, propositioning the First Lady, chug-a-lugging a Coca-Cola, stealing home in a game between the Angels and the A's, eating a Pizza Hut calzone, and twisting slowly from a redbed tree in the potter's field known as Akel Dama.

The most popular T-shirt slogans include:

I, ISCARIOT

EYE ON ISCARIOT

I^3 = ISCARIOT IS INNOCENT

I = ISCARIOT, I = IMPENITENT

I SCARE IN A RIOT... HOW ABOUT YOU?

ISCARIOT HAPPENS

DOESN'T ISCARIOT MEAN SNAIL?

A KISS IS STILL A KISS

HANG OUT WITH JUDAS, A REAL BREAKNECK GUY

JUDAS, JUDAS, JUDAS... THERE'S SOMETHING ABOUT THAT NAME

IF HE HADN'T SQUEALED, HOW WOULD WE HAVE HEALED?

12-11 = ISCARIOT

AN APOSTLE AMOK SET SALVATION'S CLOCK

WHAT, ME BETRAY?

GET A GOOD PRICE FOR YOUR SOUL

IF YOU LUV YEHUDDAH, YODEL!

BASE, VILE, LOW, MEAN, SICK & NASTY!!!

ISCARIOT, BOOTH, & OSWALD: HITMEN OF THE MILLENNIUM

and under' the name ISCARIOT:

> Caiaphas
> Is an ass,
> Pilate
> Is all apeeve.
> Upon my word,
> I love the LORD...
> Till late
> Come Friday eve.

Isn't it unusual for a defendant to testify on his own behalf at the opening of a trial?

This is an electronic simulation.

Maybe so. But ordinarily the prosecution would have to build its case, wouldn't it? That way the defense would have substantive arguments to rebut.

Other circumstances prevail here.

How so?

The prosecution, so to speak, has already had more than two thousand years to build its case.

In the court of public opinion?

Right. Exhibit A, for example, has been floating around almost since the beginning of the movement.

Exhibit A?

The Christian scriptures. The New Testament, specifically the 13th chapter of John.

Why John? Why that chapter?

John Boy's the only evangelist who has Jesus unequivocally finger Iscariot as the betrayer.

No way. All four gospels so identify him.

As the bringer of the kiss. Beyond that, though, it's all hearsay, innuendo, defamation, even false witness.

At which point a participant in the discussion types in the following passage:

> And as they were eating, he said, "So help me, one of you is going to turn me in." And they were very upset, and each one said to him in turn, "I'm not the one, am I, Master?" In response he said, "The one who dips his hand in the bowl with me – that's who's going to turn me in!… It would be better for that man had he never been born!"
>
> Judas, who was to turn him in, responded, "You can't mean me, can you Rabbi?"
>
> He says to him, "You said it."
>
> – *Matthew* 26:21–25[♥]

[♥] *The Complete Gospels*, p. 107.

That pretty much brings it down to Judas, doesn't it? He dipped his hand in the bowl with Jesus.

Exactly. And Jesus turns his direct question right back on him.

Hey, they all dipped their hands in the bowl with him. It was a communal Passover meal. And Jesus may have turned every disciple's question back on him. The guy had a canny Socratic streak, Hebraic version thereof.

So why's Judas get whomped for special censure?

That damn kiss. In the fallout from the crucifixion, poor Iscariot catches a shitload of retroactive stigmatization. A classic case of scapegoating.

Yeah. Also note that the genuinely guilty disciple had a heavy stake in laying the blame on someone else, and Judas, whom Jesus sent out for some purpose, wasn't around to defend himself.

Neither that evening nor the next day – when his despair at the Rabbi's death and his eleven false friends' lies caused him to go out and hang himself.

You're saying that a disciple, or disciples, scapegoated Iscariot in the same way that Caiaphas and his pals scapegoated Christ?

Sure. Why not? If you're a believer, Judas may have died for your sins just as profoundly as Jesus did.

One big difference.

I'll byte. Go on.

Iscariot had the rope in his own hands.

Right. But if you want to get into the metaphysics of omnipotence, we could argue that point too.

Go back to that remark about a genuinely guilty disciple. If not Judas, who? Peter? Levi? John?

Maybe Iscariot was no more guilty than any of the rest of the disciples. On the other hand, maybe one of them wanted to protect his own ass.

Because John pulls the trigger on Judas, in that unlucky chapter 13, expect Dakota Browning to go after his e-clone in a withering cross.

Fireworx, spiderfolk. *Fireworx!*

Hey, anybody want to trade a Grand Unified Theory tee with a

silkscreened lower intestinal tract on it for an i, ISCARIOT jobbie?
Get outta here....

Hirofumi Satoh stands next to the witness box so that he can lend Iscariot emotional support and survey the courtroom (including its unseen spectators and the differently invisible netists peering in on the proceedings). Although of less than average height by his own era's standards, Satoh makes Judas, despite his beard, appear small and childlike. The elegant box in which Iscariot sits visibly downsizes him, too.

Describe your individual relationship with the Rabbi, Satoh says. He speaks with the accentless facility of a trained news anchor.

Good. Quite good.

Do you think he liked you?

Of course. He liked everyone. This open-souled regard for everyone was the main burden of his tidings.

Do you think he esteemed you over others?

He called me to discipleship. He allowed me into the inner circle of the twelve.

And how did he esteem you within that inner circle?

As highly, or nearly as highly, as any other. Once he said that we twelve would sit on twelve thrones in judgment on the twelve tribes of Israel.

Yes, Satoh says. Matthew recorded the saying.

He added that we would receive a hundredfold blessing and inherit eternal life. Why would Yeshua have said such a thing to a betrayer?

Objection, says Henry Albornoz from the prosecution's table. The witness wants us to engage in bootless speculation.

Judge Ogilvie looks at Albornoz. Ordinarily, counsel may object only to opposition counsel's inappropriate tactics, not the testimony of a witness.

But this is

Basic stuff, Mr. Albornoz.

Albornoz shakes his head.

Satoh turns to Judas as if no interruption has occurred: So you had a satisfactory, even an exemplary, relationship with the Rabbi?

I did.

What of your dealings with the other chosen eleven?

Iscariot hesitates. Then he says, Good. No trouble. Not really.

A little trouble, maybe? If so, Mr. Iscariot, you now have both occasion and cause to tell us.

Iscariot's posture – head down, shoulders slumped, hands on knees – suggests his ambivalence. An unseen spectator coughs. Satoh lays a hand on the edge of the witness box. Eventually, Iscariot looks up. He begins to talk, a quaver in his voice and a long-distance stare in his eyes. The stare, pursued into closeup, opens out into a rocky desert landscape....

JUDAS

In my home village of Kerioth, just beyond the Jordan in Decapolis, I heard of Yeshua at the very beginning of his ministry. In only a few months' time, he had numerous followers, some of whom had come to him from as far away as Beersheba in Idumea. In comparison, my journey to him seemed easy.

At this time, he'd chosen only four or five of the twelve he later appointed fully. But in synagogue after synagogue around the Sea of Galilee, I heard him speak in parables; saw him heal the sick and cast blaspheming demons out of possessed unfortunates.

In Capernaum, I helped the friends of a paralytic remove some rooftiles and lower him on his mat into a crowded house where Yeshua had gone to preach. Looking down, I see that man struggle to his feet, seize his bed, and stride into the night to the chorusing alleluias of his friends and maybe half the thunderstruck throng.

A day later, following Yeshua about the lake, I separated myself from the crowd and happened upon him and his first five disciples encamped in brushwood lean-tos beside the sea: James and John, the sons of Zebedee, whom he called Boanerges, or Thunder Brothers; two more brothers, Simon Peter and Andrew; and Levi, the son of Alphaeus, a toll collector whom the others at first resented as a professional leech.

What about you? Yeshua asked me when I sat down unbidden at their cooking fire. What do you do?

I told him (and, of course, the others, who had begun to eyeball me through the flickering shadows) that I worked metal, making knives, pitchforks, and tilling instruments. I showed him the knife I carried as an example of my workmanship. He hefted it admiringly on one palm. He even set the edge of my knife to the heel of his hand, producing a thin beaded crimson line more black than red in the firelight. Then he smiled and asked me my name, and the blood on his hand – nor did I imagine this – vanished.

Too giddy to marvel, I said, Judas of Kerioth.

Ah, said Simon Peter, whom Yeshua already sometimes called Cephas, then we'll call you Iscariot.

But why? I asked him.

He presumptuously combines Kerioth and *sicarius*, Yeshua said.

Sicarius? I said.

It's Latin for dagger man or assassin. Maybe Cephas thinks you have Zealot written across your forehead.

I said, I make knives, but I avoid politics. The kingdoms of this world fall to ruin. I seek the everlasting, Rabbi.

Well said. You wish to follow me?

I want nothing else.

Then give me consent to disarm you.

I didn't understand, but Yeshua correctly read in me total surrender to whatever he purposed. Indeed, so reading me, he flung my knife, blade over haft, into the soft tarnished pewter of Yam Kinneret, the Galilean Sea. Yeshua's five not quite disciples laughed. Me? I felt no loss at the sinking of my knife, only joy, a heady exhilaration at my unexpected welcome among these men.

Looking back, I note a grisly joke: the one who named me dagger man carried a sword into the Garden of Gethsemane and struck off the ear of Malchus, the high priest's slave. He did so just as a platoon of Roman soldiers and some of the priestly constabulary laid hands on Yeshua.[♥] Of course, he acted from both

---

[♥]A.N. Wilson, *Jesus: A Life* (London: W.W. Norton & Co., 1992), pp. 203–206. Wilson argues that Malchus, meaning king, may have been Saul, the Christian persecutor who later became the apostle Paul. Saul, after all, had been "the first of the Jewish kings" (206).

love of Yeshua and a gnawing fear that he had never truly merited the Rabbi's favor.

None of us merited it. I understand, though, that Malchus, the man whose ear Simon Peter severed, came to recognize that fact better than any of the chosen twelve, including the five on the shore with us on the night that Yeshua looked with favor on me, a Decapolean; in all respects but my allegiance to God and the son of Adam, a foreigner.

In subsequent days, Yeshua met headlong the devout, the forsaken, and the frenzied who searched for him along the lake shore. He preached, healed, and evicted demons. Often he did so from, or near, a fisherman's boat, to keep the crowds from overwhelming him. His labors wore him out. He withdrew to the hills. Through Simon Peter, he put out a call for the other seven – beyond the first five companions – whom he would appoint as dependent ministers.

Astonishingly, at least to me, Yeshua included me in that number. I was the only one of the twelve not also a Galilean, a fact that told against me on the night of the Passover and on the day of the crucifixion. A fact that tells against me now, I fear.

ONLINE LOGOMACHY II

Probably so.

You think?

Absolutely. He lacked the others' geographical roots and the loyalty that usually goes with compatriotism.

One way of looking at it.

You have another?

The other eleven, or a significant number of them, held his foreignness against Iscariot.

Oh, please.

To deflect attention from their own inglorious behavior on the night of their master's arrest, they conspired to frame him for betrayal.

A chestnut. A stale chestnut.

Yeah. Well. That old stranger-in-a-strange-land argument slices two ways.

Dear Judas,

Hang in ther. Your cute yo now that. I evn lik it wen yo suk in & chue on sum of yur beerd. Fiona my sister sas its grosss but she has no tast she is a filisten to be biblucl about it. Wich I would lik to be with yo if I cud kno you to luv you an luv you to kno you to be biblucl agan.

The Jap layer of yurs say he knos how you feel me too. Fiona one nite mist kerfew & my dad sed heed ring my neck if I didn rat her out where she waz. So I tol. Fiona when she got hom & fond out come don to my room to lay lik a reel hevy diss on me. You Judas she yelld to me you stnking liddle Judas. But I, I don think you stnk an if yo weren jess a online emmige Id lik to mary you. So will you I men lik mery me?

♥♥♥ XXX 000. Luve,
Renata Smith-Koester

Wendy Grice resembles a bird, small and quick-moving. Her attire suggests a goldfinch in the process of trading its gray winter plumage for the yellows of spring. Iscariot regards her hopefully.

So the other eleven disciples sometimes made you feel your foreignness, she says.

Sometimes.

Give the court a specific instance of their prejudice.

Iscariot considers, then says: Yeshua gave us instructions before sending us out as his agents. He told us,

> "Heal the sick, raise the dead, cleanse the lepers, drive out demons. You have received freely, so freely give. Don't get gold or silver or copper coins for spending money, don't take a knapsack for the road, or two shirts, or sandals, or a staff; for 'the worker deserves to be fed'...."
>
> – *Matthew* 10:8–10♥

Did you and the others obey these instructions? asks Grice. Insofar as we could. But the business about not taking coins

---

♥*The Complete Gospels*, p. 75.

with us troubled a couple of the Galileans. What if there were an emergency? What if those we helped forced money on us, saying that we should take it as an offering to the poor?

What did these worriers decide?

That it would be wrong to make no provision for a crisis and equally wrong to refuse alms for the poor.

Did you agree with the Galileans on these points?

Yes, I fear I did.

So how did the eleven demonstrate their regionalist bias against you, Mr. Iscariot?

None of them wanted to stand as our group treasurer, for fear that taking the job would breach the Rabbi's instructions and prove a stumbling block to salvation.

Salvation?

Yes. Yeshua had also said that everyone would hate us twelve because of him, but that those of us who held out to the end would find our reward.

So no one volunteered for the job?

Not even Levi, the former toll collector. I won't do it, he said. I've set aside my old ways, and sorting through coins again would only pollute me beyond saving.

Grice gives the jury a moment for this news to register, then turns to Judas and says, So the eleven Galileans foisted the unwelcome job on you?

The job and the moneybox.

In Jesus' presence?

Oh, no. Out of it. Everyone understood that it would transgress his guidelines and reveal our lack of faith to keep a moneybox. But our fear of the unforeseen overcame our trust in Yeshua's farsightedness.

Why did you agree to act as treasurer?

I was backed into a corner. If I refused, how would I ever gain the others' acceptance?

Did acceptance come, once you'd taken this unpopular job?

No. Not at all.

What occurred instead?

The others accused me of filching from the kitty. They even

said I'd taken the job to insure access to these middling sums.

Did you ever betray the others' trust?

What trust? But, no, I never pilfered. In fact, I gave more to our treasury than any of the others, who could pocket whatever they took in without making any sort of account to the entire group.

Mr. Stills would probably say that you could misrepresent or hide donations as easily as anyone else.

I guess I could have, but I never did.

Why didn't you?

I loved the Rabbi. I believed his words. And I wanted the respect of the eleven Galileans he had chosen along with me as his inner circle.

No further questions.

We will now take a ten-minute recess, says Judge Ogilvie.

A POEM ON THE NET

He has a finger in the till,
  Another in his eye.
He is a shameless, gutless shill
  For his abhorrent lie.

Once more to the tree, Sick Judas,
  Once more to the rope.
Hang yourself and thereby free us
  To rise from hate to hope.

Judas in the sky with diamonds?
  No, dirt-trapped, underground,
Mouthing cant and vulture-pie crumbs,
  Without a sound.

Dakota Browning, spiffy in designer buckskins, takes a turn for the defense questioning Iscariot:

Which of the Galileans do you think most resented you?

The three who believed themselves Yeshua's favorites.

Namely?

Cephas and the Thunder Brothers.

Simon Peter and the sons of Zebedee, James and John, all of whom claimed to've seen Jesus transfigured on Mount Tabor?

Yes.

Which of the eleven went after your reputation the hardest, repeatedly and baselessly labeling you a thief?

I don't know. Toward the end, they all seemed to regard me as an untrustworthy interloper. Didymos Judas Thomas remained friendly, but of course he always demanded proof of any dubious assertion.

Who would you name as the most persistent and implacable in his hostility?

The one who called himself the beloved disciple.

Dakota Browning turns to face the unseen jurybox. In other words, John the son of Zebedee?

Without question, Iscariot says.

ONLINE LOGOMACHY III

In a rape trial, you can count on the defense attorneys going after the victim. She slept around, she dressed like a slut, she hung where a decent woman wouldn't hang, she was an infamous flirt, blah blah blah.

Your point, Clarence Darrow?

Dakota Browning & Friends intend to put the other eleven disciples on trial. Shoot, they've already started.

You think the eleven Galileans were victims of Iscariot's lies and chicanery?

Amen. We all were.

But if you buy the redemption myth, we were really all his beneficiaries.

I'm arguing legally here, not theologically. Cut me some slack. The biggest victim, of course, was Iscariot's master, but even Grice, Satoh, and Browning don't have the chutzpah to try to sabotage Jesus' reputation.

A minute ago you were griping about the ethical bankruptcy of defense attorneys. Now you call them spineless for behaving responsibly.

We'll see how they behave. Meanwhile, don't jump me for defending Peter and the boys from Iscariot's lawyers' calumny.

Aren't Peter and the boys, especially John Boy, guilty of that very sin? Likewise the evangelists who wrote down their self-serving stories?

Hey, they're evangelists, gospel-makers. They write under inspiration from the Holy Spirit.

Even those inspired of God can run with a beautiful or a holy lie, maybe especially those inspired of God. And if you don't believe in beauty, or holiness, or the lies occasionally undergirding them, then you have a duty to truth – should you believe in that – to dig for the ugly or corrupt foundations.

Pardon me, you blaspheming heathens, but I'm gone.

Farewell.

Au revoir. Auf Wiedersehen. Hasta la vista.

But another participant says, I'm still here. And I have no plans to tuck tail and run, even if Grice and Company drop a five-ton concrete block on the so-called beloved disciple.

THREE EXHIBITS FOR THE DEFENSE

A: Mary brought in a pound of expensive lotion and anointed Jesus's feet and wiped them with her hair. And the house was filled with the lotion's fragrance. Judas Iscariot… says, "Why wasn't this lotion sold? It would bring a year's wages, and the proceeds could have been given to the poor." (He didn't say this because he cared about the poor, but because he was a thief. He was in charge of the common purse and now and again would pilfer money put into it.)

– *John* 12:3–8

B: Jesus…declared: "I swear to God, one of you will turn me in."

The disciples stole glances at each other, at a loss to understand who it was he was talking about. One of them, the disciple Jesus loved most, was sitting at Jesus's right. So Simon Peter leans over to ask that disciple who it was <Jesus> was talking about. He in turn, leans over to Jesus and asks him, "Master, who is it?"

Jesus answers: "I'm going to dunk this piece of bread, and the one I give it to is the one." So he dunks the piece of bread and gives it to Judas, Simon Iscariot's son. The moment <he had given Judas> the piece of bread, Satan took possession of him. Then Jesus says to him, "Go ahead and do what you're going to do."

Of course no one at dinner understood why Jesus had made this remark. Some had the idea that because Judas kept charge of the funds, Jesus was telling him, "Buy whatever we need for the celebration," or to give something to the poor. In any case, as soon as <Judas> had eaten the piece of bread he went out. It was nighttime.

– John 13:21–30

C: So <Mary> runs and comes to Simon Peter and the other disciple – the one that Jesus loved most – and tells them, "They've taken the Master from the tomb, and we don't know where they've put him."

So Peter and the other disciple went out, and they make their way to the tomb. The two of them were running along together, but the other disciple ran faster than Peter and was the first to reach the tomb....

– John 20:2–3♥

Justice Ogilvie reads through the printouts given him by Wendy Grice as Exhibits A, B, and C. He takes his time, using the edge of an expensive letter opener to underscore each line of type. Finally, he looks up.

Pardon me, Ms. Grice, but I'd think the prosecution eager to enter these passages as exhibits for its side.

♥ Exhibit A appears on p. 227 of *The Complete Gospels*, Exhibit B on p. 230, and Exhibit C on p. 242. The New King James Version renders A's "expensive lotion" as "costly oil of spikenard" (perfumed ointment), and B's "Simon Iscariot's son" as "the son of Simon" and Jesus' direction to Judas ("Go ahead and do what you're going to do") as the more specific, "What you do, do quickly." The variant translations may impact the interpretation of evidence.

Yessir, says Grice. The folly of pride.

Really? They paint a rather unattractive picture of your client.

No more unattractive than the one they paint of John as a braggart and a false testifier.

Objection! chorus Stills, Mormile, and Albornoz.

Sustained, says Ogilvie. Or would be if this weren't a friendly sidebar out of the jury's hearing. Please, everyone, relax.

Iscariot remains on the stand. Satoh paces the courtroom in front of the bench.

At length he says, You contend that John put in the frame and that his Galilean cohorts bought it.

No one but John could have heard what Yeshua said to him in the upper room, and I can't believe that the Rabbi named me to him.

Why did you go out?

Just as some of the other supposed, to make a contribution to the poor from our group treasury.

By this time Jesus knew that you kept a moneybox?

Sooner or later he discovered everything.

Didn't he rebuke you for your disobedience or demand that you disburse all your funds and chuck the moneybox?

Actually, he tweaked us for our lack of faith – a recurring theme with him because we recurrently gave him cause – and sent me out to do just what you've asked, discard the box. I gladly obeyed. It was a relief.

Why did he tell you, Do quickly what you have to do?

He was sharing new teachings and comfort with us, and he didn't want me to miss any more than I had to. Also, he feared that the Romans and the constabulary of the high priests might initiate a raid.

What happened to you on your errand?

I was named as an associate of Yeshua, placed under guard, and marched off to talk to Annas, Caiaphas's father-in-law, and then to Caiaphas himself.

About what?

They were always anxious to placate the Romans on festival

days. Jerusalem's streets teemed with pilgrims, some reverent, some rowdy, and they wanted information.

So you told them Jesus's whereabouts for thirty pieces of silver. Right?

They said they'd nail me as a cutthroat rebel if I didn't help them. They also swore they only wanted to question Yeshua about any knowledge he might have of insurrectionist activity among the crowds. No one offered me even a tenth of a denarius for my help.

Didn't you think that these people might want to catch him in a punishable impiety? The priests and the Pharisees were no friends of yours.

With some heat, they mentioned Yeshua's cleansing of the temple during an earlier Passover, but...so what? Yeshua told us to expect the world's hatred. He also said we would overcome evil through faith.

When did you realize the authorities had lied to you?

Not until troops and temple police with torches and weapons jostled me along to the garden.

So you didn't betray the Rabbi.

Never. I loved him.

In your view, you did nothing wrong?

My crime was too much trust, or faith, in the intentions of the priests and the power of the Nazarene.

When did you come to doubt even the power?

When they tried him, scourged him, sent him stumbling along the Sorrowful Way, and hammered him to a cross. When even the eleven Galileans broke ranks and fled. Iscariot's voice cracks and he begins to weep.

Forgive me, Mr. Iscariot, but didn't you in fact receive thirty pieces of silver for your help?

At the moment of Yeshua's arrest, someone thrust a bag at me. I took it without knowing what it was. Later, I found it to hold a few crooked coins from the temple moneychangers.

Not thirty pieces of silver?

No.

What did you do with those crooked coins?

I returned to the temple in the morning and flung them at the feet of the scornful elders.

Then what? asks Satoh.

Judas rubs his temples, knuckles one eye, shakes his head. In his long-distance stare, online spectators can see reflected a canopy of rose-purple blossoms....

ONLINE LOGOMACHY IV

Matthew says that Iscariot went to the priests before the last supper and asked for a reward for handing Jesus over. The betrayer lies.

John was the only disciple who could've possibly known whom Jesus singled out as the culprit. Maybe he lied to the others, and Matthew, or Levi, tailored his gospel account to the cut of John's lie.

Whoa!

How so whoa?

You can't label John a liar on the matter of Judas's guilt and swallow whole his assertion that Jesus named the betrayer to him alone. Show some consistency here.

Okay, he lied throughout, during Jesus's earthly stay and after, in person to the other ten and on papyrus to posterity.

Christ, such cynicism!

Are you addressing the Lord or profaning his name?

Probably some of both. You Iscariot lovers seem to want to defame a hundred saints to redeem a single black-sheep creep.

A biblical desire. Jesus said, If someone has a hundred sheep and one of them wanders off, won't that person leave the ninety-nine in the hills and go and look for the one that wandered off?♥

Gag me with an exegesis.

Whatever you want. Care to make a date?

DIVAGATION: AN ISLAMIC LEGEND

Pilate releases Barabbas to the rabble, who, by crying for the highwayman, have condemned the Nazarene to die. But at this very moment, God lifts Jesus bodily into heaven. Neither Pilate

---

♥*Matthew* 18:12–13, *The Complete Gospels,* p. 90.

nor the crowd apprehend this miracle, owing to the fact that at this same instant God snatches up the traitor Iscariot, makes him over atom by atom to resemble the condemned Rabbi, and deposits him on the porch of the governor's house in Jesus's stead.

Iscariot cannot believe either his transformation or the severity of his plight. He cannot speak, either to protest or to explain. Who would believe him?

In a last effort to appease the crowd's bloodlust, Pilate has Iscariot scourged with a knotted cord weighted with slivers of ox-bone. When this effort fails, Pilate allows his soldiers to drive the stumbling Judas into the courtyard. Here they strip him, cloak him in scarlet, and subject him to a variety of mocking torments. These culminate in his forced march along the Via Dolorosa.

Upon the cross, Iscariot tries to emulate the behavior that his master both preached and modeled. He repredicts the fall of Jerusalem. He forgives a repentant thief. He thinks, I die for the sinless Nazarene. And he says, Father, into your hands I commit my spirit. Whereupon, torn and breathless, he dies in the ascended Jesus's place.

From the Islamic perspective, the purpose of this story is to wreak justice and to discredit the resurrection. But to the e-clone of Judas Iscariot, the legend appears to require as profound a faith, or as foolish a credulity, as the orthodox passion narrative. If this electronic court convicts him of the betrayal of which greater Christendom already believes him guilty, will it sentence him to die on a rood of glowing pixels in the echoey virtuality of cyberspace?

THE PARABLES OF JUDAS

In an offline dream, Iscariot puts a series of parables before the court. He will say nothing to the judge, lawyers, jurors, spectators, and netists except by way of parable, so that what he dreams in his torment will evaporate totally upon awakening.

To no one's question but his own, he spins this parable:

The betrayal of God's empire of light is like a tiny bead of poison that a man drops into a well of sweet water from a hidden vial. Though the drop is even smaller than the pupil of a sparrow's eye, yet, when it spreads throughout the well and pollutes even the spring, all who come in faith to the water and drink, clutch their throats, fall to the ground, and die in an agony of perplexity and blindness.

He tells them another parable:

The betrayal of God's empire of light is like a cowbird that invades the territories of sweet-singing larks and lays a single egg in the nests of these songbirds so that when the larks' own eggs hatch, a black cowbird hatches with the larks' young, and takes their food, and crowds them from their nests, and displaces their parents' carols with croakings of raucous triumph.

Iscariot puts a third parable to the court:

The betrayal of God's empire of light is like a hacker who logs on with a stolen password, roams the system at will, and secretes within it a viral program that activates itself upon another user's inadvertent command. He then begins to convert coherent data into ceaselessly self-propagating hieroglyphs of nihilistic jabberwock....

And so when Iscariot has finished dreaming these parables, he awakes in cyberspace, asweat and atremble, with each parable seared into his consciousness like a cigarette burn on a snowy linen tablecloth.

Dakota Browning says, Anything else you'd care to say in your own defense, Mr. Iscariot?
One thing. One thing only.
Go ahead.
Not long after time began, Lucifer betrayed God the Father out of ego and self-deception, supposing that he could somehow supplant the Creator.
Browning hopes to persuade the jury of his client's robust

mental health. I assume you narrate metaphorically, he says.

I speak what I believe, Iscariot says.

Because your Yes is Yes, and your No, No?

Yes.

Although Browning appears dubious about issuing a second go-ahead, he says, All right. Proceed.

Not long after awakening as an e-clone, I learned that the evangelist John wrote in his gospel that Satan entered me. He reports that with Satan thus at work in me, I handed over our master.

You dispute both assertions?

I've never had an ego like Lucifer's and the most painful self-deception I've ever practiced was that built on my hope that the other eleven would one day warm to me. Iscariot halts and grimaces.

Do you need a recess?

No. Sometimes…well, sometimes I have bad, horridly oppressive dreams. In them – and often I think that this is one – food tastes salt and bitter, music turns to insupportable clamor, and the sun drops into eclipse, never to emerge again. I despair.♥

Ogilvie leans toward Iscariot. Believe it or not, someone meant this trial as an antidote to despair.

Iscariot smiles wanly. A suicide has trouble believing that. But my resuscitation's taught me a lesson.

Tell us, says Ogilvie.

Despair is a harlot. Despite treason after treason, and sabotage after sabotage, God's empire of light never falls into total eclipse. Satan wages a futile war. Those who wage it with him wrap themselves in the pain and terror of their own self-betraying sins. Iscariot falls silent.

A fine lesson to learn, says Browning skeptically.

I had to die and come back to learn it.

Well. Yes. Anything else?

♥In *Lucifer: The Devil in the Middle Ages* (Ithaca and London: Cornell University Press, 1984), Jeffrey Burton Russell notes that people once cast Despair as Lucifer's daughter, who entices Judas to betray Jesus. "When Judas has done the deed, Despair prompts him to suicide, and the demons rejoice at his eternal damnation" (267).

No.

No further questions, Your Honor.

Ogilvie looks to the prosecution. Cross-examination?

Rebecca Mormile half rises. To nearly everyone's surprise, she says, No questions, Your Honor.

ONLINE LOGOMACHY V

They had a chance to subject the jerk to a killer cross and they passed it up? What's wrong with these high-priced clowns?

Don't you mean clones? They're simulacra.

That's right. Nobody's paying them.

Maybe they think the defense did their job for them. I do.

The prosecution's blown it. Iscariot's got a fan club.

Yeah. Aficionados of Pol Pot, Hitler, and Attila the Hun love him.

No way.

There's always a way. Catch this bulletin-board doggerel from an admirer:

> Judas is my kind of strudel,
> A pastry both cheesey and fey.
> Do you like him too? Then yodel:
> Just open your gullet and bray.
> If you love Yehuddah,
> Who's really quite shrewd-a,
> Don't bother to brood-a:
> Just jap, double-cross, & betray.

I don't know, keyboards one discussant. There's a lot of ambivalence there.

Avery Stills rises. Your Honor, I'd like to call the evangelist John, a.k.a., the beloved disciple, to the stand.

John, a.k.a. Jonah Bar-Zebedee, emerges from the electronic courtroom's sea of unseen spectators, approaches the stand, and, despite Jesus's admonition to abstain from formal oaths, swears to tell the truth, the whole truth, etc., on a book containing a philosophical gospel that he himself allegedly wrote. The defense confers about this untoward swearing-in, but decides not to object to it.

You've heard Mr. Iscariot's testimony, indicting you as a liar and a slanderer, says Stills to John. Your response?

I stand by what I've written.

But the defendant claims

The light shines in the darkness, and the darkness did not comprehend it, interjects John. The same holds here, as it so often does.

Stills leads the witness through a point-by-point rebuttal of Iscariot's testimony. John denies any regional bias amongst the disciples against Iscariot, any collusion in burdening him with the moneybox, any conspiracy to scapegoat him, or any plan to drive him to suicide.

We never desired anything bad for our Decapolean brother, says John. Only fruitful growth in the spirit.

Why has he said what he's said?

Objection, says Wendy Grice. Counsel wants the witness to speculate on a matter in which he has a powerful bias.

With that understanding, we'll allow him to answer, says Justice Ogilvie.

Thus prompted, John says: The man hurts. His hurt speaks, and the speech shaped from it gives him ease.

You bear him no animosity for contradicting the testimony of your gospel?

None, John tells Stills. I bear something else altogether.

For instance?

Sorrow that he didn't live to see even one of the Rabbi's resurrection appearances. Sorrow that his own sorrow persists.

Stills turns to the defense. Your witness.

Grice moves to take Stills's place in the middle of the courtroom. She clasps her hands behind her back. She studies the floor.

ONLINE LOGOMACHY VI

She'll badger him twelve ways to Easter. Then Satoh'll go after him. Then Browning.

You sadistic goober, you relish the prospect....

Grice turns to John. You saw yourself as Jesus's favorite, didn't you?

I did.

Giving you a self-proclaimed status rivaling that of Simon Peter, the rock on whom Jesus said he would build his church. Correct?

You say so.

Do you see yourself as a prideful man, Jonah Bar-Zebedee?

I hold myself in, well, a decorous esteem.

Really? A decorous esteem. Head down, Grice paces. Do you see yourself as a jealous or an envious man?

Only rarely.

Only rarely envious? Or only rarely aware of the tendency?

Objection! says Stills. Counselor descends to the catty.

True, says Ogilvie. But the ambiguity of the response does seem to warrant clarification.

I'm only rarely envious, John volunteers.

Why in your gospel do you refer to yourself in the third person as the beloved disciple or even the disciple Jesus loved most? asks Grice.

I didn't want to obtrude on the more important, indeed the most important, story.

Yet you give yourself a rather grandiose kenning and behave with self-described nobility under its label. Doesn't that strike you as immodest?

It would've impeached modesty to name myself outright and belied events to omit myself entirely.

So. Grice stops pacing. You really believed yourself beloved of Jesus beyond the other eleven disciples?

Each of us may've believed that.

Yet you recorded events supporting your self-perception as especially favored.

I saw what I saw, then told my story.

You recorded Peter's three denials of the Lord on the night of his arrest?

As did Matthew, John Mark, and Luke. The denials happened.

Okay, but you imply that you alone among the disciples saw the crucifixion.

One of us had to stand by him in his agony.

The others?

They fled, even Simon Peter. And Iscariot went out and hanged himself.

You write that from the cross Jesus gave his mother Mary into your charge?

I accepted it gladly, and our Lord's mother remained in my household until her death.

You write that you outran Peter to the empty tomb?

Yes.

The relevance of your swiftness afoot to the meaning of the empty tomb escapes me. Do you think your foot speed certified your manliness? Your saintliness? Both?

It bore witness to my agitation upon learning that someone had taken our Lord from the tomb.

An agitation greater than Simon Peter's, right?

John shifts his weight. I'm a burlier man than Peter. I recorded my earlier arrival at the tomb not in relation to his later arrival but in relation to my turmoil over troubling news about the Rabbi's body.

Your getting there first didn't otherwise signify to you?

John shifts his weight again. No.

Wendy Grice goes to the bench for Defense Exhibit C. She reads, But the other disciple ran faster than Peter and was the first to reach the tomb. Grice looks up. You expect us to conclude from this that you didn't exult in your triumph? That you weren't in fact gloating over it?

Rebecca Mormile pops to her feet. Your Honor, counsel is browbeating the witness! And the relevance of all this to the guilt or innocence of Mr. Iscariot seem at best tenuous and at worst nonexistent!

I withdraw the question, says Wendy Grice. Rebecca Mormile sits down.

John leans forward in the witness box. I have a point to make. Ignoring the prosecutors' warning looks, he says, My account states forthrightly that Simon Peter entered the tomb first.

Grice snatches up the court's Bible and thumbs through it. Sir, your permission to place the witness's voluntary assertion in context.

Ogilvie nods his assent.

Grice says, After noting that Peter went into the tomb, the dec-
orously self-esteeming John writes, Then the other disciple, who
had come to the tomb first, went in also; and he saw and believed. Grice turns to the unseen jury. Does no one else detect a
peculiar obsession here?

Mormile, pounding the table, pops up again. Your Honor!

Enough, Ms. Grice, says Ogilvie. Move on or wrap up your
cross.

AN E-PISTOLARY PROPOSAL

Dear Producers, Trial of the Millennium:

This online courtcase of a despicable religious traitor from a
couple thousand years ago has had its moments. It suggests some
other possibilities to me as well. Use them as you see fit, altho of
course I would like a mention in the front & back credits & a
small cut of user fees, advertising loot, & future program sales.

Trying dead bastards who never went to trial is a winner all the
way. As subjects for new proceedings, try: the Tamil suicide
nerve-gas bombers who just hit the new soccer stadium in Jaffna;
Lee Harvey Oswald; Adolf Hitler; John Wilkes Booth; Tomás de
Torquemada. It'd probably be neat – i.e., entertaining, a jimmy-
jam ratings boost – to try a bitch or two, but I can't think of any.
Marie Antoinette? Lucrezia Borgia? You guys can put researchers
on this, right?

If you end up giving Iscariot the e-quivalent of the death penalty, I think you ought to hit him with something besides hanging. He's done that. Maybe you could introduce him virtually to
complete vacuum, him being a moral vacuum & all. I have a program that I think would work for this. Give me a commission &
I'll get busy on it.

– pldflpp@brwn.u.bkst.rtrd.

Grice lays the Bible aside and turns back to John. You heard Jesus
whisper that the one to whom he gave the dipped bread would
betray him?

Yes.

And you were the only disciple privy to this revelation?

Also true.

No one else could have know what Jesus told you unless you told the others in turn, right?

John says, Judas' presence in the garden with the troops would've also told against him. And did.

Even with Roman soldiers and Jewish police, our client's presence in the garden is subject to interpretation. And your interpretation condemns. Grice stares long and hard at John before saying, You write that when our client took the dipped bread, Satan entered him.

You say so, and you say correctly.

How did you know that Satan entered him?

I knew. It was apparent to me.

How, precisely? Did Satan pop into view and jump down Mr. Iscariot's throat? Did an evil fog that you detected by means of extrasensory perception or an acute sensitivity to invisible auras make Mr. Iscariot start glowing purple?

John raises his eyebrows and looks to Stills, Mormile, and Albornoz. He shifts his weight in the witness box.

Grice, virtually pouncing on him, says: *How did you know?*

John flinches. A moue of offended disappointment twists his bearded features. I heard you clearly. Did I understand you? Perhaps not, but loudness doesn't help.

Does taking questions from a woman trouble you?

John looks to Ogilvie, who shrugs.

Grice recites from Paul's First Epistle to Timothy from memory: Let a woman learn in silence with all submissiveness. I permit no woman to teach or to have authority over men; she is to keep silent.

Do you find my sex a bar to candor and responsiveness?

Objection, says Avery Stills wearily.

Sustained.

Grice turns to Ogilvie. Still, sir, I believe you should direct him to answer my original question.

Ogilvie smiles. Straightaway, ma'am. The witness will answer the question: How did you know that Satan had entered Mr. Iscariot?

John looks back and forth from Ogilvie to Grice. How else could he have handed over the Rabbi?

In fact, says Grice, you deduced from your after-the-fact consideration of Jesus' arrest, and Mr. Iscariot's role in it, that Satan had entered our client.

Anyone could see it.

But, in fact, none of the other ten saw it all, did they?

None said they did.

Isn't it likely that you made this unverifiable assumption after misunderstanding Jesus' whispered words to you?

I heard what I heard.

Grice lowers her voice. Mr. Bar-Zebedee, a sagacious woman once said, Satan is a way of perceiving opponents.♥ Haven't you read Satan into our client because you read his presence in the garden as a betrayal?

John takes a deep, lung-filling breath. He looks away from Grice, shakes his head in annoyance.

Whether intentionally from malice or inadvertently from superstition, says Grice, gripping the witness box, you've demonized our client, sir, and created a monster that in fact exists nowhere but in your own religious imagination.

Objection! Mormile and Albornoz half-rise. Stills tilts his head back and smiles wide-eyed at the ceiling. Mormile says, Counsel draws her own conclusions. Plus she's trotting out the stale relativistic notion that evil is a situational figment or illusion.

Grice says, I

Mormile gallops on: She should save it for late-night bull sessions with know-it-all adolescents.

ONLINE LOGOMACHY VII

Incoming! Incoming!

These two gals're cheetah mamas, ain't they?

Grice definitely gets my hydraulics working.

♥Elaine Pagels, quoted on p. 63 of David Remick's "The Devil Problem," *The New Yorker* (April 3, 1995), pp. 54–65. The remark synopsizes a major argument in Pagels's book *The Origin of Satan* (June 1995).

Please. Me, I endorse that stuff from 1st Tim. about all submissiveness. Unless they've dropped to their knees, females should keep their mouths shut.

Run for cover, guys!

What for? We know where you live, you pathetic synthetic-testosterone junkies.

Go easy. Can't we all agree that Grice and Mormile are both babes?

You've picked the wrong b-word, bonehead.

Help! I'm lost among these intellectual giants like a baby squirrel among ancient sequoias....

Grice pivots toward the prosecution's table. I don't deny the existence of evil. I simply deny that it exists as some sort of preexistent counterprinciple in an ongoing combat with preexistent good. In that scheme, Rebecca, we all become pawns of the one or the other.

Interesting, says Mormile. But theologically suspect and irrelevant to this case.

Not at all, Your Honor. By reading Satan into our client, Jonah Bar-Zebedee denies to both Mr. Iscariot and himself, indeed to all of us, any capacity for self-generated evil. If Satan has entered our opponents, then Satan can't inhabit us. This attitudinal bias promotes the demonization of others and a smug sanctification of the self. It absolves us of the need to control our own native tropisms toward the dark.

Your Honor, says Mormile, this is heady claptrap.

Is it? says Grice. I propose a concept of good and evil that allows the prosecution to convict defendants on the basis of their own culpability, not on mere allegations of satanic possession. And what I propose doesn't automatically absolve our client, it simply requires a thoroughgoing demonstration of his guilt.

Demon? says John. Demon, stration?

Avery Stills motions Rebecca Mormile to sit and says, I think were arguing petty semantics here, Your Honor. Which, along with John's arrival from another cultural and religious dimension, has left him gasping to follow Ms. Grice's verbal loop-de-loops.

Grice looks to Ogilvie. The witness's milieu of origin laid the groundwork for ours. Nor do I think there's anything petty about alleging that Satan, Hebrew for God's most dogged adversary, has entered another human being.

Stills rises. John, didn't you make that allegation as a symbolic way of saying that Mr. Iscariot surrendered to his own evil impulses?

This way lies chaos, says Ogilvie, rapping his gavel. Mr. Stills, you're out of order. Ms. Grice, where do you suppose this digressive philosophical brouhaha is going?

I don't know, sir, but I'd love to hear the witness respond to Mr. Stills's out-of-order question. In fact, I'll repeat it: John, do you regard Satan as a symbol, a mere figure of speech?

Satan exists, John says. Satan entered Yehuddah Bar-Simon.

Did Satan leave Mr. Iscariot again?

I don't know.

What do you think? On the basis of your keen sensitivity to the Satan-inhabited, speculate for us. Did Satan ever leave Mr. Iscariot, once having entered him?

Perhaps when he hanged himself.

Why would Satan permit such a valuable instrument of his malevolence to hang himself?

He'd served his purpose.

So. You're saying Mr. Iscariot possessed free will only when Satan released him, at which time he expressed remorse for the latter's crime by hanging himself?

You say so, and I've also said so.

Then why're we trying Judas Iscariot? Let's get Satan in here and grill him instead!

The electronic courtroom erupts in laughter and applause. With a look mixing amusement and disgust, Ogilvie pounds his gavel. Silence. Silence! The noise dissipates a little, and he says, We'll now take a thirty-minute potty break! Another collapse of manners like this last one will result in my clearing the room and ordering these proceedings offline. A mild pox on all of you.

. . .

Isn't grilling Satan a lot like tossing Br'er Rabbit into the briar patch?

Take the t off Br'er Rabbit and whattaya get?

Two thousands years older and one helluva culpability debt?

How does an e-clone take a potty break?

By shedding its impulses?

If this trial goes offline, where exactly does it go?

If a computer crashes & there's no one there to dash around in recursive panic, has it really been with the program?

Does anybody know Wendy Grice's private fax number?

ONE ONLINE SIDEBAR, WITH WITNESS AND JURISTS

Before Ogilvie can get to his chambers, Grice stops him and prevails upon him and her fellow attorneys to gather near the witness box for a demonstration of the potent consequences of demonization.

Demon? says John, standing down. Demon, stration?

Hold your right arm out in front of you at shoulder level and make a fist, Grice says. Bemusedly, John obeys.

This is highly irregular, Henry Albornoz says.

Hirofumi Satoh sighs and slaps a C-note into the palm of Dakota Browning's outstretched hand.

Stop that, Grice says. Take note. John here, a bona fide Thunder Brother, has several inches in height and who knows how many pounds on me?

Ogilvie compliantly ogles Grice. Stills checks his watch. The others glance back and forth between John and Grice, who is pressing down on his fist with her index finger.

Resist me, Grice says. Try to keep me from moving your arm downward. John resists effortlessly. Good. Very good. Grice withdraws her finger.

Your point? says Stills.

With your permission, I have a couple more simple requests to make of the witness. May I?

Exasperated, Stills gives her a curt nod and folds his arms across his chest.

Grice tells John, Relax. Lower your arm. Shake out the kinks.

Good. Now extend it just as before and a make a fist. Excellent. Now lower your eyes and repeat the phrase I'm a bad boy clearly but not belligerently until I ask you to stop.

For heaven's sake, Wendy, says Mormile.

I mean it, Grice says. Come on, John. Say I'm a bad boy I'm a bad boy I'm a bad boy....

This is demeaning, Albornoz says. We object.

It's all off the record, Browning says. Lighten up.

I'm a bad boy, John says over and over as Grice presses down on his fist with her finger. John grimaces and strains, but his arm drops steadily lower. His left eyelid succumbs to a noticeable tic. Grice removes her finger.

No one says a word.

Grice pats John's shoulder. Let's do it again. This time, though, look me in the eye and say with feeling I'm a good boy.

This time John successfully resists Grice. His tic goes away, and he smiles faintly through the tangled red shrubbery of his beard.

Do any of you legal geniuses require an explanation of this fascinating phenomenon? Ogilvie asks the prosecutors.

Bad boys' arms go down more often than good boys'? Rebecca Mormile says.

Neat trick, says Stills to Grice. You must really liven up a party with that one.

Trick? An enacted parable. It shows what a drumbeat of verbal abuse can do. I contend that repeated accusations of satanic influence drove Iscariot to surrender to the lie and hang himself.

It still doesn't prove him innocent of selling out Jesus, Albornoz says.

Then it's our boy's word against yours, says Browning.

And Matthew's, John Mark's, and Luke's, says Albornoz.

Later, says Ogilvie. Inflict your clouds of witnesses on the trial proper. Here they just befog my glasses....

A PROTEST FROM THE E-NUT GALLERY

If they bring on the rest of the apostles, this trial could still be in progress when Christ comes again.

Well, I'll be gone. Long gone.

The prosecution calls Jesus of Nazareth, says Albornoz.

A ripple of astonishment works through the courtroom, and every monitor screen worldwide gives back a panorama of the spectators, who, thanks to computer graphics, have flamelike tongues of fire on their shoulders and heads, as if each one were a votive candle. This surreal graphic is brief, however. The ripple among the spectators subsides, and the trial's programmers cut immediately to Justice Ogilvie, who appears in closeup like a great, ebony condor.

Impossible! he says, booming without raising his voice.

Why? says Albornoz, undaunted.

Because summoning him as a witness would be to induce the Parousia, and no mortal human being, whether of the flesh or the microchip, has that authority.

Albornoz says, But who better to clarify the issue of what he told John in the upper room?

Who indeed? says Ogilvie.

Without his testimony, sir, the question's likely to remain forever moot.

Them's the breaks, says Ogilvie.

ONLINE LOGOMACHY VIII

Puhwhozit?

Parousia. The Second Coming. You don't induce it.

ISCARIOT TO GRICE, A HYPERTEXT E-PISTLE

Dear Ms. Grice,

I've said I loved the Rabbi, and in truth I did. I first loved him from afar, I next loved him for the deeds of healing and exorcism I saw him do, and I finally loved the man for his charisma, holiness, and beauty. He had a comeliness of bearing, movement, voice, and repose that banished from the eye the middling imperfections of his face and body. For whatever reason – shame, perhaps – no evangelists wrote or spoke privately about these aspects of his attractiveness, but no one who met the Rabbi failed to see or admire them.

The prophet Isaiah may have foretold the coming of this man

of sorrows, this mortal angel familiar with both grief and despisal, but Isaiah's prophecy miscarried in his vision of Yeshua's appearance. Do you recall how Isaiah, the son of Amoz, describes our deliverer?

> He grew up before the LORD like a young plant
> whose roots are in parched ground;
> he had no beauty, no majesty to catch our eyes,
> no grace to attract us to him.
> He was despised, shunned by all,
> pain-racked and afflicted by disease;
> we despised him, we held him of no account,
> an object from which people turn away their eyes.[♥]

Yeshua drew people to him. No one but his enemies – folks he'd outgrown, folks whose authority he challenged – could fail to esteem him. Like me, he was a peasant, a man who'd once made his living making practical goods with his hands. In his case, benches, roof beams, and tables. In mine, tools and weapons. Oddly, during my discipleship, the only thing I ever saw him make was a corded whip with with he careered through the temple, shaping panic among the moneychangers and pigeonsellers. But that was after I'd sought him out on the great lake and begged for a place among his closest followers not with boasts or sighs but with love and work. Despite my arrival from another land and my awkwardness among the Galileans, these offerings secured my place, and I found myself a movable home and a sliver of reflected fame. In faith, apart from the Rabbi and along with Judas Lebbaeus, I was an instrument of healing, an expeller of demons, and a herald of God's imperial reign.

I never wanted an infamy such as I have now, the reproach of millions. Instead I wanted the regard of our master and comfort in the night, things I tell you, along with what follows, because Jonah Bar-Zebedee, my accuser, reports in his gospel that Yeshua said, And you shall know the truth, and the truth shall set you free,[♥♥]

[♥]*Isaiah* 53:2-3 in *The Revised English Bible with the Apocrypha* (Oxford and Cambridge University Presses, 1989), p. 637.
[♥♥]*John* 8:32 in The New King James translation.

and because Didymos Judas Thomas reports in his less renowned gospel that Yeshua said, If you bring forth what is within you, what you bring forth will save you. If you do not bring forth what is within you, what you do not bring forth will destroy you.♥

Spiritually speaking, honesty is the best policy.

And so: One night we thirteen slept in scattered pockets along the shore between Capernaum and Bethsaida. We'd come to-gether to talk about our work among the lake villages. In some we'd met success, in some consternation or rebuke. Weariness had fallen that night among the successful and unsuccessful alike. James and John, the Thunder Brothers, sleeping apart in two different spots, earned their nicknames.

I couldn't sleep, despite my fatigue. I left my place under a gnarled fig tree with Lebbaeus and Simon the Zealot; I wandered down the beach and found Yeshua lying alone in the chapel of an upturned, rock-braced fisherman's skiff. I knelt down and crawled in beside him. He opened his eyes and accepted me into the crook of his arm, and so we lay.

Later I put my lips to his ear, as if whispering, and one of my hands strayed to a place out of my view. Yeshua caught it by the wrist and with great gentleness touched the back of it to his mouth. The water lapping at some nearby rocks and the uncanny sound of a hermit fisherman chanting a psalm from a boat far out emboldened me, and I twisted in Yeshua's arms as I was later to twist, they tell me, in Blood Acre. He smiled, a smile only faintly visible, and gripped me tighter.

Take rest, he said.

Yeshua, I said, I desire

But he put a finger to my lips and said, Whoever has come to know the world has discovered the body, and whoever has dis-covered the body, of that one the world is not worthy.♥♥

I didn't fully understand, but it seemed that without encour-

♥*Thomas* 70:1–2 in Elaine Pagels's *The Gnostic Gospels* (New York: Random House, 1979), p. 126. Compare this version to those in *The Complete Gospels*, p. 316, and Marvin W. Meyer's *The Secret Teachings of Jesus: Four Gnostic Gospels* (New York: Random House, 1984), p. 32.
♥♥*Thomas* 80:1–2 in *The Complete Gospels*, p. 318.

aging me in my longing for him, he approved the sort of body talk that between male and female seeds the world and between loving others may at times stir both comfort and joy. His eyes said as much as his words, but I couldn't always see his eyes to read them. When I tried to move or speak, he said, Shhhh.

And then he said, How miserable is the body that depends on a body, and how miserable is the soul that depends on these two.♥

Even this cryptic saying, despite his iteration of the word *miserable*, didn't feel like a scolding but like an openhearted attempt to pour light into me. Don't mire yourself in lust, Iscariot. Yet don't assume the soul so fragile or meatbound that it can't rise clean and smiling above the body's exultations.

This, I came to know, was not a teaching that Yeshua shared with everyone. That night, however, I laid back in the crook of his arm, well content, and slept. No other meeting like this occurred between us again, and yet I never thought him avoiding me or disappointedly intent on picturing me to the Galileans as the serpent in their vineyard.

At dawn I awoke to find John casting a long shadow into the upturned skiff. He stared down at me with the disdain of a rich matron for a turd. I sat up, striking my head on the boat, and then rolled out from under it groggy and dazed. John made me feel like a harlot, an orgiastic devotee of Baal, and yet I'd done nothing, except in my mind, but lie beside the Rabbi and draw warmth from both his body and his presence. As for Yeshua, seeing the big fisherman, he propped himself up on his elbows and laughed heartily.

Look at you, he said. This morning you seem to wonder at my meaning when I said I'd make you fishers of men.

Maybe it was too early in the day. Maybe John didn't care to think the disciple from distant Kerioth even a twelfth so beloved as he. He bridled at the Rabbi's joke and lumbered back up the shore to his companions of the night.

From that day forward, he loved me less and less and I sweated like a slave to stay out of his way. I don't mean to brand John a vindictive lout, for my sins groan louder by far than his, but what

---

♥*Ibid.*, 87, p. 319.

Yeshua forgave me, I wish the world would forgive. My name has become anathema and filth. I'm not in the mouth of one of Satan's three heads, Ms. Grice, but I am indisputably in hell.

Your respectful client, Judas Iscariot

Your Honor, says Satoh, we'd like to enter this letter from our client as a deposition and as Defense Exhibit D.

Why don't you just put Mr. Iscariot in the box again? says Ogilvie. He isn't absent, after all.

No one in e-space is either altogether absent or altogether present, sir. We do this in the interest of saving time. Out of courtesy, we've already filed a copy with Mr. Stills and his associates.

Ogilvie looks to Stills. If you agree to the defense's request to enter the letter, I'd permit you to put Mr. Iscariot on the stand for a cross. But I have no bias in the matter either way.

Henry thinks it highly irregular, says Stills. But we have no objection.

Thank you, says Satoh. May we send e-copies to the jurors' fax screens, please?

Consider it done, says the stenographer, a robot retained in the courtroom out of atavistic sentiment.

Will you call Mr. Iscariot for a cross? says Ogilvie.

No, says Stills. He'd only lie again anyway.

Sustained! barks Ogilvie, looking toward Wendy Grice, who has half-risen from her place.

AN INFOHIGHWAYMAN HAS HIS SAY

My Ghod, the kisscheek from Kerioth's a real in-your-face faggot.

The proceedings proceed. Dakota Browning threatens to summon every Roman soldier who ever participated in or observed a crucifixion outside Jerusalem during the high-priesthood of Caiaphas.

We don't know much about most of those fellows, Ogilvie says. You'd get some pretty vague and inchoate resuscitants.

Browning yields on this point, but spends two days interrogating an expert on osculation, or kissing, with special attention to the sociocultural import of nonromantic kisses in quasi-public places. A day later, he brings in aerial photos gridded to show the distances between Kerioth and the Galilean hometowns of the other eleven disciples, plus income charts, occupational statistics, and samples of each village's exports and homegrown foodstuffs. Over the next few days, Browning summons three vague and inchoate resuscitants who recall Jonah Bar-Zebedee lying to them about various matters; questions a lexicographer on the many connotations of the word *betrayal*; and calls several heirs of the Fellows of the Jesus Seminar to testify that (a) the disciple John did not write the gospel so often attributed to him and that (b) even if Iscariot had in fact maliciously betrayed the Christ, he should receive along with his master shared credit for humanity's redemption. As Browning struts and preens, many people fight sleep and Ogilvie prompts giggles by making a show of holding his eyelids open with his thumbs. Browning yields to Satoh, and Satoh summons a night watchman from the Garden of Gethsemane.

Enough! says Ogilvie. Onliners've fled these proceedings in droves lately, and I'm sick of all the yammering.

Bless you, says Rebecca Mormile.

Ogilvie goes on to say, The jury will now decide, Is the defendant guilty or not guilty of betraying Jesus Christ?

The head juror, still out of view, asks Ogilivie if the jury may acquit Iscariot if it concludes there is a reasonable doubt of his culpability.

Yeah, yeah, says Ogilvie. You know the drill. Hop to it. And if you find him guilty, I'll have to think up a sentence commensurate with the crime, something worse than what he's already endured.

Maybe you could hang him and bring him back seven times seventy times, says the chief juror.

Stills says, If you favor the eye-for-an-eye approach, a crucifixion would probably

Enough! cries Ogilvie again. The jury will please retire and return us a verdict. Pronto!

THE VERDICT(S)

Your Honor, we the jury find Yehuddah Bar-Simon, a.k.a. Judas Iscariot, not guilty of betraying Jesus of Nazareth, his teacher, master, and Lord.

Grice, Browning, and Satoh trade high fives. The courtroom erupts in murmurs, cheers, hisses, applause, singing, and boos. A snake-dancing conga line of Iscariot supporters winds from the spectator section into the area between the bench and the attorneys' desks.

Halt! says Ogilvie. Cease and desist!

The trial's programmers delete the interfering celebrants.

Pardon me, Your Honor, says the chief juror, but we're not quite finished.

You're not?

No, sir. On the unspoken charge of committing a gratuitous self-execution, we the jury find the defendant guilty. Suicide is a profanation of the temple of the body warranting severe censure and punishment.

[Execute, whispers Browning to Grice. Ever notice how that word means both to bring into existence, as in to execute a perfect somersault, and to remove from existence, as in to kill by electrocution or hanging or so on?

No, whispers Grice. I never have.]

Nowadays, Ogilvie tells the chief juror, we stay the hell out of personal decisions of that sort and

thus debase the concept of life's essential sanctity, says the chief juror, finishing Ogilvie's sentence for him.

That's another trial, says Ogilvie. And one from which I recuse myself now on the grounds that I'm an e-clone without a viable stake in the natural world encompassing cyberspace. And so, Mr. Iscariot, you are a free man.

The trial's programmers materialize Iscariot at the defense table. He stands and shakes hands with his attorneys.

And not only free, says Ogilvie, but changed. Or, I should say, eligible for change.

I don't understand, says Iscariot.

The court hereby offers you somatic transubstantiation from your present e-space existence to full corporeality on the good earth itself.

Iscariot looks to Wendy Grice for help.

Just as Pinocchio went from wooden puppet to real-live boy, Grice says, you may now go from electronic resuscitant to honest-to-God full-bodied man. The process is called somatic transubstantiation. Do you want it? If you do, say so and prepare to emerge into the harsh instabilities of our dystopian century.

Of course, says Iscariot. I want living water.

The courtroom vanishes. The Iscariot e-clone, alone in a dimensionless mother-of-pearl shimmerstorm, undergoes the process. The computer saves him; analyzes and encodes him; and sends this complex DNA blueprint to an online transfigurer, from which a three-dimensional hard copy of his unique person unfolds and strides forth.

Into sunshine, air, and uncertainty.

Two steps beyond his resurrection, Iscariot encounters the wrath of one who claims to've loved Yeshua even more than he did.

This person leaps into Iscariot's arms and carries him back out of the world in an instantaneous blast as loud and colorful as a redbud tree.

JUDAS

Yeshua once said to Didymos Judas Thomas,

Whoever drinks from my mouth will become like me; I myself shall become that person, and the hidden things will be revealed to him.♥

As for me, I should have said, Rabbi, forgive. I should have resisted the beauty of that redbud. I didn't slay our master on the cross, after all, but in the thirsty despair with which I knotted my rope, sleepwalked under that scarlet canopy, and leapt like a fool into a mirage of living water rather than the water itself.

Rabbi, forgive.

♥*Thomas* 108:1–2 in *The Complete Gospels*, p. 321.

Carter Scholz's stories are usually less concerned with the technical extrapolation of typical science fiction than the processes by which science, music, and literature are created, and the ways in which they are interrelated and reflect the societies in which they occur. This collaboration with Jonathan Lethem describes another less likely collaboration, but one with deep resonances for the possibilities of art.

RECEDING HORIZON
Jonathan Lethem & Carter Scholz

"That which is possible will surely happen. Only that which happens is possible."
– Franz Kafka, *Diaries*

From darkness, the Statue of Liberty blazes onto the screen with a crashing fanfare of music. The arm with the sword rises up as if newly stretched aloft, and surrounding the figure are the glowing words COLUMBIA PICTURES. Frank Capra leans over to speak to the man on his right. "This one's for Jack."

2.II.1924

Lieber Max!

We are settled. In the Holy Land's warm clear air, already I feel a new man. Yesterday we saw Dr. Löwy, and he explained his cure. He uses the sputum of the bee moth, *Galleria mellonella*. They are plentiful in Palestine. They dote on honey. Löwy learned the technique from a Frenchman at the Pasteur Institute, Élie Metchnikov, who died in 1916. As he explains it, the substance breaks down the waxy armor of the tubercle bacillus. But Löwy is more than a man of science. His first words to me were, the difference between health and sickness is foremost a difference of imagination. So at once I knew I had a doctor I could trust. As to writing, my true sickness, it is behind me. I have cast it off as a penitent casts off his hairshirt. Dora sustains me.

Blessed be the day you introduced us.

Deiner, FK

Jack Dawson, screenwriter, 55; born July 4, 1883, in Prague, Czechoslovakia; died September 22, 1938, Cedars of Lebanon Hospital, Los Angeles, of pneumonia. Dawson, who emigrated to America in 1933 and legally changed his name from Kavka, rose rapidly in his profession under the patronage of director Frank Capra. Dawson shared writing credits on many Capra films, including *Mr. Deeds in the Big City* and *Meet Joe K.* A memorial service will be held at Temple Beth-El in Brentwood.

4.VII.1935

Lieber Max!

After anonymous months in the publicity department, I am now a screenwriter. The director Frank Capra, who won so many Oscars last year for *It Happened One Night,* came to our office with a contest to name his next picture. I won fifty dollars with my title, *The Man Who Disappeared.* As he was writing the check, you will not believe it, he recognized my name. (I have resolved to change it.) He had just bought at a fabulous price one of the few copies of *Das Urteil* to escape the burnings. A true American bourgeois, he cannot read German, but my negligible volume, unread, shares an honored shelf at his Brentwood estate with a Shakespeare Fourth Folio, a first edition of the *Divine Comedy,* and a proof copy of *A Christmas Carol.*

I know this because he had me to dinner. A strange evening. He was visibly disgusted by the way I chewed my food. He said he has just fired Robert Riskin, who wrote *It Happened One Night,* and is looking for a new writer. According to Capra, Riskin's themes were too political, insufficiently "universal." He professed to have found a kindred spirit in me. I told him I needed a room and a vegetarian diet, nothing more.

The evening ended in near catastrophe. Capra collapsed and an ambulance was called. Next day he was out of danger, and I visited him in the hospital, attempting to buoy his spirits with tales of my own sickness. He was silent, and I grew increasingly ill at ease. He asked about my writing, and I said I was a coward, that I had withdrawn from it in order to save my life, that my work was an offense to God. He said nothing but regarded me intently.

Now he wants me to begin work with him as soon as possible. I am stunned by the rapidity with which one's fortunes change in America. Boundless opportunity! Though I came resigned to end my days as a faceless clerk, I find I am embarked again upon writing. Of a sort.

Joel 2:25, "And I will restore to you the years that the locust has eaten." But in what form?

Deiner, FK

The old druggist weeps as young George shows him his mistake. Still despondent from the death of his own son, he has erred in preparing a prescription for another child. George brandishes the still-open vial with its deathshead emblem in a gesture that is almost threatening, while the druggist sobs out his gratitude, "How can I ever thank you, George. I'm an old fool! Why, if that prescription had gone out, it would have meant shame and disgrace and prison!" "And yet," George says, "sometimes a cure, or an inoculation, begins with a small amount of poison, isn't that so?"

Frank Capra shifts uneasily in his seat. Although the script has gone through many revisions, he is certain he has never heard that line before....

25.XI.1935

Lieber Max!

I have remade myself. A new life, a new name taken from the *kavka*, the jackdaw emblem that you will remember hung outside my father's store. I am still his son.

First day on the set. Gaudy, vulgar, exciting. After a wrong turn on the lot, I found myself in a narrow street that might have been Prague. Buildings all false fronts, belying the reality of my past life, establishing the inescapable reality of the present. Rounding a corner into a phalanx of cameras I heard the shouted command, "Cut!" I retreated to the sideline in embarrassment. A couple of hangers-on were saying:

"What was Capra in the hospital for? He told me TB, that don't make sense."

"Crap. It was peritonitis. But that's no story Frank would tell on himself. Trouble with the gut, that's a peasant thing. TB, he thinks that's spiritual, an artist's disease."

"He thinks he's an artist so he fires Riskin? What a mistake. Frank's the schmaltz, Riskin's the acid."

"Why does Frank pick up with a nobody like this Dawson?"

"Riskin wouldn't stand his crap any more."

On the set, Barbara Stanwyck. I could not keep from staring. Like Milena, that stately dark vulnerability, restrained fire. I heard her say, "When you're desperate for money, you'll do a lot of things."

When he heard I was the new writer, George Bancroft told a joke. "You're not Polish, are you? Did you hear about the Polish starlet? She fucked the writer." Barbara looked coolly at us and I blushed like a boy of fifty-two.

JL to CS: It might be appropriate to include some of our notes to each other in the story itself, making it a metafiction. What do you think?

CS to JL: Well, that makes me uneasy. Calling the artifice into question virtually requires further turns of the screw, and where do we stop? Once you start the process, there's no safe burrow to retreat to. With ground this uncertain, we could title it "The Metamorphosis."

Max,

FC has changed the title from *The Man Who Disappeared* to *Mr. Deeds in the Big City*. He wants to cut the trial scene, but I, I am convinced Deeds must prove himself in court. At stake is not the contested fortune, but the man's very existence. All around him people are trying to make him disappear, to replace him with their idea of him. He is in danger of ceasing to exist. FC exhorts me to forget words, to think of the action, the image, the movement. He cannot see that this reality he carves out of light is a reality of surface, while my reality is not what moves, but what animates.

I am among mouse folk, Max. I am a singer, of a sort. They are tonedeaf yet they seem to understand me. My faint piping. They give me no special dispensation for my singing, no recognition that I am special, but I have a place in their hearts. Yet if I cease to sing, they will go on with their mouse lives as before and I will be forgotten.

Interior. Night. The Bailey dining room. George's father comes to the table, his heavy dressing gown swinging open as he walks. George thinks: my father is still a giant of a man.

His father sits, and pokes at the meal George has prepared.

George speaks. "It's awful dark in here, Pop."

"Yes, dark enough," answers his father. "I prefer it that way."

"Y, you know, it's warm outside, Pop," says George, stuttering slightly, a habit he knows his father deplores, yet he cannot himself. Indeed, it is only with his father that he stutters.

His father lays down his fork. "Have you thought of what you're going to do after college?" George has been dreading this moment. With his brother gone, it was only a matter of time before his father brought up the family business. "I know it's only a hope," Bailey senior continues, "but you wouldn't consider coming into the asbestos works?"

"Oh, Pop, I couldn't face being cooped up in a shabby office…" At this, George understands that he has hurt his father. "I'm sorry, Pop, I didn't mean that remark, but this business of spending all of your life trying to save three cents on a length of pipe…I'd go crazy. I want to leave Progress Falls. I'm going to build things. I'm going to build skyscrapers a hundred stories high. I'm going to build a bridge a mile long!"

"George, there are many thing in the business I'm not aware of, I won't say it's done behind my back, but I haven't an eye for so many things any longer."

"Anyway, you know I already turned down Sam Wainwright's offer to head up his plastics firm. I'm not cut out for business."

The elder Bailey glowers at him. "Oh yes. Sam Wainwright. You've told him about your engagement to Mary?"

"Well, sure, of course."

"Don't deceive me, George! Do you really have this friend Sam Wainwright?"

Doubt flickers in George's eyes. He begins to answer, but his words are garbled, as if something has gone wrong with the sound equipment....

Max,

Receding Horizon, the Ronald Colman epic, is now permanently shelved. FC disregarded my advice to set it in Oklahoma, and went hideously over-budget trying to re-create Tibet in a local icehouse. Harry Cohn declared the film "a consummate editing disaster" because of the proliferation of unrelated fragments towards the end. A late scene where Ronald Colman attempts to regain his lost paradise, which recedes from him at every step of his approach, especially infuriated Cohn.

My working title for the new film: *The Life and Death of Joe K.* An innocent man, Gary Cooper, tries to survive in the midst of cynical manipulators. Innocent of the rising power of Norton and his motorcycle corps. Innocent of Barbara rifling her father's diaries for his speeches: the betrayal of intimacy into the public eye. "When you're desperate for money, you'll do a lot of things."

Finished writing the last scene in a kind of trance: suicide is the only redemption for Cooper.

CS to JL: You realize, don't you, that if we put ourselves into the story, those aren't our real selves? They're busily creating yet another alternate version of FK & FC, and possibly of themselves and their reality as well.

JL to CS: Lighten up! It's only a short story. You act as though the universe were at stake in every word.

CS to JL: Alas, that's how I feel; more depends upon these acts of representation than we can know.

George thinks: this town is no place for any man unless he's willing to crawl to Potter. Even then one will be forced to wait a hundred years in the antechamber before being admitted to Potter's outer office, a room crowded with petitioners. There a secretary indifferently makes notations in a gigantic book, offering appointments to meet with Potter's personal assistant, who never appears in the office but who controls all access to Potter. At times George wonders whether Potter himself even exists – but where did that absurd thought come from? George knows Potter, he has dealt with the man, and yet....

This scrap of film flutters to the floor of the cutting room and is lost among countless other scraps.

Meet Joe K. is in the theaters. Tears of shame and pleasure mixed in my eyes at FC's changed ending. Regardless of its falsity, how affecting Cooper is! The betrayed intelligence that shines from his eyes. He knows he has not been redeemed, but damned to a life of pretense.

What is FC's reflex for the redemptive but a foredoomed attempt to make things come out right? He doesn't believe in it himself; doubt and skepticism live in his nerves, his haunted eyes. Yet despite his impositions, his unbearable confidences, I am drawn to him. Barbara says, "he senses what you want to keep hidden." And the film will be a success. Of course. FC tested five endings and chose the most popular.

As the final credits rolled, I felt an odd, almost narcotic relief. I was betrayed but not exposed. None of the film's surfaces and movements are the movements of my soul. This is no knife to be turned back upon me.

Exterior. Night. In a sort of baffled fury, George paces in front of the home where Mary Hatch lives alone with her mother. The town of Progress Falls has trapped him, the mocking laughter of the townsfolk when he tried to speak of travel has chased him back to Mary's street. It is as though the greater world is an illusion, a receding horizon, whose only purpose is to establish more forcibly Progress Falls's inescapable reality. The town exists only to lead him back to this street, to pace before this house.

He will not go in, he swears to himself. It would trap him forever, not just in Progress Falls, but in some abysmal predicament of which Progress Falls is merely the emblem. At that moment

Mary leans from her window. She calls: "What are you doing, picketing?"

George starts in guilt. "Hello, Mary. I just happened to be passing."

"Yes, so I noticed. Have you made up your mind?"

"About what?"

"About coming in. Your mother just phoned and said you were on your way over to pay me a visit."

"But…I didn't tell anybody!" protests George. "I just went for a walk and happened to be…." But as he speaks his fingers are already fumbling the catch of the garden gate, they have made his decision for him, yet the catch won't release, and as he fumbles Mary's features become more anxious, and George almost prances with the strain of being caught between two worlds, and Frank Capra turns to ask how this outtake has made it into the rough cut….

Taking a deep breath, Odets entered Capra's office. The director's lips were pressed back in a pained smile belied by his heavy Sicilian brow. He's going to have me killed, thought Odets. This isn't a story conference, it's a rubout. That's what happened to Jack Dawson – Capra had him *done*.

Capra tossed a sheaf of onionskin onto the desk between them.

"'The Judgment.' Jack thought this was his greatest work. And this is the best you can do? One page of notes?" Capra lifted the sheaf and read from the top page. "'Georg Aussenhof, a young merchant, is writing a letter to a friend. The friend has done what Georg always wanted to do: leave his hometown for the big city. Friend has tried to encourage Georg to leave, but Georg is doing too well in his father's business. The father, however, is a monster. This drives Georg to suicide at a bridge.'

"'Evaluation: This material is hopeless for a movie. No fee is large enough for me to jump through these particular hoops. Find another writer.'" Capra dropped the manuscript and glared at Odets.

"I'm sorry, Frank. That's my honest opinion. I happen to think it's a good story, but it's completely internal. There's no movie there."

"Of course there's a movie there! I'm no writer, but I know genius when I see it!"

Odets saw with astonishment that Capra was stifling tears. "Damn it, I want to bring that sad little man's vision to the widest possible audience. But keep it true. Look, you're not thinking here. Why don't we turn it into a Christmas story?"

"Christmas?" Odets asked faintly.

"Dickens!" said Capra.

Odets thought it an odd response.

"Dickens!" said Capra again. "He was Jack's favorite writer!"

This seemed mildly unbelievable, and certainly irrelevant.

Capra punched at the single page of notes that Odets had produced in a week's labor. "This Georg Aussenhof…what's that mean anyway, Aussenhof?"

Odets had looked it up. "It's the outer courtyard of a castle. What the English call the bailey. Why, in London there's a court of law.…"

"Fine. George Bailey, then. He thinks his life is worthless because he's never left town?"

"That's about it," said Odets.

"Stay with me, Cliff. That's the point where he's driven to the bridge."

And me with him, thought Odets.

"*A Christmas Carol.*"

Lord, thought Odets, he's around the bend. I'm a dead man.

"You've gotta do like the Ghost of Christmas did, pull him off that bridge and show him what the town, what's the name of it?"

"I believe it's Prague," said Odets drily.

"Fine, call it Proggsville, or Progress Falls, that's it. That's our title: *Miracle in Progress Falls*. The Ghost shows him what Progress Falls would be like if he throws himself off that bridge. How many people depend on him, and love him, his girl —"

Odets didn't interrupt. He was interested despite himself. Capra's brand of integrity was not the worst in Hollywood, even though Odets had already noted a few dodges and fades in the director's teary encomium to Dawson – Dawson had been over six feet, not a little man at all, and Capra had shown no scruples about altering Dawson's great screenplay *Meet Joe K.* almost beyond recognition, copping out of the suicide ending at the last moment. The result had been a travesty, an impossibly uplifting ending to a tragic, bitter story.

But Odets had seen his own work similarly mutilated. It was par for the course. If it was going to happen, let it happen at the hands of an Oscar-winner like Capra. And at the best rates this town paid.

CS to JL: Odets? What kind of name is that?

JL to CS: Funny you should ask. I stumbled onto Odets in my research. He was a celebrated dramatist in his day, and a guy who really made the movie we're ascribing to Kafka. He went to Hollywood and he did write for Capra. What's odd is how completely he's disappeared from literary history. It appears he championed some arcane philosophical system called Socialism.

When I turned in this draft to the duty officer at Artistic Control, there was already a red flag on my file. The next day the Odets research material was missing from the library. From the catalog, too.

Are we going to have trouble publishing this, Carter?

"Cliff, to help you realize Jack's vision, I'm giving you access to these papers of his. He left them to me. Notes, letters...."

"Who's Max?" said Odets, reading the salutation on the top sheet.

"That's Max Brod, his best friend. It's funny. I found out Brod was killed in 1933. The Nazis. Jack kept on writing to him anyway. There just wasn't anywhere to send the letters."

Odets studied the letter. The small, precise handwriting had the concentration of a real writer. Somehow this depressed Odets. A real writer doesn't end his days working for a man who subverts his work.

"Cliff, I don't think you've heard how I met Jack."

Odets had. Three or four times, actually. But he was clearly going to hear it again. Capra thought Dawson had saved him not just from death, but from moral collapse as well. There was a moral economy in the world, and on this occasion Dawson had been its agent. Capra's version was as close to reality as this movie was to "The Judgment."

"He called me a coward, Cliff. He said, your talents aren't your own, they're a gift from God. When you don't use the gifts God blessed you with, you're an offense to God and humanity."

Capra glowered at Odets, as if to impress upon him the gravity of such an offense.

"Jack said he was through as a writer. Washed up. But he hated to see me go down the same way. That gave me the courage to rise from my sickbed and go back to work. I swore to myself that I'd make it up to him. And we made some pretty good films together, Jack and I. But now, Cliff, now I want *you* to show some courage. I want you to take another crack at this thing."

You remember those odious melodramas we saw decades ago at the Palastkino, Max, you and Otto and I. *The Student of Prague.* The young student makes a deal with the devil, an Italian sorcerer. He trades his reflection for wealth and happiness. But the mirror-image takes on its own life and destroys his hopes. Is it too fanciful to see this tawdry tale in my relations with FC? Yet it is not FC who dooms me, it is FK asserting himself over Jack Dawson.

A year later Wegener made *The Golem*. The dull robot falls in love with his master's daughter, naturally!, and her rejection rouses him to a rampage. When he falls from the parapet, his body shatters like clay. Myself and Barbara. She might as well be FC's daughter. Glimpse of the cold spaces between our worlds.

Alone in his office, Odets lit another cigarette and mimicked Dorothy Parker's fluting voice. "Cliff, the Dawson notes you so generously shared are intriguing, but I'm not sure, quite, what one can do with them. This one, for instance: 'In the Oklahoma Open Air Theater, George recovers, through paradisial magic, his vocation, freedom, and integrity, even his parents and his homeland.' Is Frank making a musical?"

It had gone no better with Hammett. Nor Trumbo. West didn't even return his calls. He had gone through every name writer in town, even Aldous Huxley, merely because Capra wanted class. One was tied up, another was under contract, a third was drying out somewhere. Of those who'd come in, none lasted a week. Capra wanted the impossible: a bitter minatory tale transformed into a fable of redemption.

Eventually Capra would be forced to bring in some real screenwriters, script doctors who knew what they were doing, who would excise the last trace of Dawson. Meanwhile Odets soldiered on alone. The conferences got grimmer. Capra was doing his godfather act again.

"Change it."

"It's very clear, Frank. The bad guy is George's father. See, says right here, 'Georgs Vater.'"

"Change it, Cliff. This is a Christmas flick, the bad guy can't be family. We need a Scrooge. Make him a competing businessman. Make up a name."

Odets sighed inwardly. Father, Vater, pater. "Potter," he said.

"Bingo," said Capra.

Uncle Willi, make that Billy, has misplaced an important file. A government agency requires the asbestos works to keep a close accounting of its procedures. This file has been lost. George is furious: "Do you know what this means, you old fool? It means shame and disgrace and prison! One of us is going to jail! Well, it's not going to be me!" George rushes out. In the gathering dusk, snow is falling. Across the town square is the courthouse, a structure that seems to rise to heaven, its every window blazing. The adjutants of the court perform close-order drill before the gates, under the floodlights.

This is no outtake, thinks Capra, but something stranger, as though some other reality, hiding between the frames, is asserting itself....

Every evening Odets dragged himself home from Columbia, drank a pint of Scotch, and stared at the walls, an unread book open in front of him. Every morning he drove back to the studio, tallying in his mind the interrupted projects of his own he would resume once he was done with Capra, even as he sensed that the potential world to which those works belonged, while he delayed in this one, relentlessly receded from him.

He dreamed about a library, vast and dim, in which Dawson's unwritten books could be found, alongside unwritten volumes by Parker, Fitzgerald, Hammett, Trumbo, Faulkner, himself. Odets crouched reading in an aisle; the heavy steps of booted guards could be heard at a distance. He could read and understand the pages, but they made no sense. It was as though the world had tilted away from an entire set of meanings. Like George Bailey, Odets felt estranged from a world as compromised, dull, threatening, and suffused with loss as Progress Falls. He awoke haunted by the unquiet ghosts of those unwritten books.

Odets had been around enough not to blame Hollywood – no writer needed outside help to procrastinate or to fail; Dawson himself had freely given up literature years before coming to America – but as Odets worked against the Dawson story it seemed to him that something more abstract, almost a cosmic principle, was at work, bestowing gifts merely to subvert them. George Bailey would never leave Progress Falls; nor, it seemed as the days dragged on, would Cliff Odets ever be free of this damned script.

Oddly, though, Odets was haunted less by his own unwritten work than by Dawson's, the outlines of which he vaguely glimpsed like the battlement of a castle in fog, looming darkly from Capra's world of determined optimism.

What had it cost the world that Dawson had written scripts instead of novels? He could not escape the feeling that the scripts were urgent warnings shouted in some arcane and forgotten language. Some days, the world Odets walked through seemed flimsy and insubstantial in the dim yet insistent light that Dawson's work cast.

What other world would have welcomed the unfinished works Dawson alluded to in his letters to Max? Odets tried to imagine it, imagined some other pair of writers in some potential world a half century hence, coming upon this same material....

Odets realized he was wasting time. He shook himself out of reverie and returned to his hopeless task.

JL to CS: Damn it, will you quit making this harder than it has to be? I thought we'd decided to drop Odets.

CS to JL: I don't see how, now that we've given him voice. Given the circumstances, I'm sure he'd be happier out of it. As would I, if you want the truth. But if we don't finish what we've started, in what red-flagged library carrel will *we* end up?

JL to CS: I'm more worried about where we'll end up if we *do* finish. When I handed in the last draft my AC duty officer said we were creating a penal colony for writers, torturing them on the racks of our prose. It sounded like a veiled threat to me.

CS to JL: I tried to warn you. A metafiction opens everything to question, even the ground of our own existence. It could be as hard to escape as Progress Falls.

Interior. Potter's office. George flinching under his words. "You once called me a warped, frustrated old man. What are you but a warped, frustrated young man? A miserable little clerk crawling in here on your hands and knees begging for help, no better than a cockroach. You're worth more dead than alive. I'll tell you what I'm going to do, George. As a stockholder in the Bailey Asbestos Works, I'm going to swear out a warrant for your arrest."

George felt he must sit down, but now he saw there was no seat in the room. "But what have I done?"

"Why, we'll let the court decide that."

George turns and starts out of the office.

"Go ahead, George," says Potter. "You can't hide in a little town like this." The patriarch lifts the telephone, and says: "Bill, this is Potter." Then he covers the mouthpiece and speaks again to George: "So, now you know what more there is in the world beside yourself! An innocent child, yes, that you were, truly, but you're also a devilish human being! Yes, you are, George, don't try to deny it! And therefore, I sentence you to death by drowning!" George runs from the office, into the snowy streets of Progress Falls.

Capra turns to his assistant to complain, this was never in the script, but the seat on his right is empty....

In Jack's dream, he is in Palestine. Dora is at his side. Outside, the desert is hot and brilliant. The sky is blue as porcelain. A bowl of Jaffa oranges glows with its own light beneath the doctor's window.

"A clean bill of health. Scarring from the lesions, of course, but the disease is arrested. You are cured, my friend." Dr. Löwy, in a curious gesture, places his hand upon Jack's forehead.

Jack leaves the kibbutz where he has lived during his cure and moves to Jerusalem. He teaches law at Hebrew University. He writes articles and propaganda film scenarios for the Palestine ministry of information. The state of Palestine grows strong, and Jack is a valued citizen. From afar his lean German prose alerts European Jewry and its allies to the Nazi threat, and the pestiferous Hitler is crushed and humiliated in the 1933 German election – but here the dream collapses. He cannot keep out the reality of Brod shot dead in a Prague alley, his sisters Elli, Valli, and Ottla hauled off to labor camps, the motorcycles roaring through the streets.

The bridge – ! It is immense, a mile long, more! From the catwalk where George stands he cannot see the ends of it, the roadway recedes and vanishes into falling snow. The bridge is so broad that even its far side is vague and distant. Unending traffic streams both ways in countless lanes, sending sickening vibrations through the soles of George's feet. The braided steel cable he clutches for balance is as thick as a man's waist and vibrates as if all the machinery of the world were linked to it.

In desperation George cries, "Clarence! Get me back! I want to live again!"

"But, George, you've given all that up. You have no legal claim to live in Progress Falls. None at all. And yet..." Clarence stands, ear cocked, in the falling snow. Abruptly he straightens. "Permission has been granted. Owing to certain auxiliary circumstances...." George doesn't wait. He is running from the bridge, up the snowy street, past a street sign: Aspetuck, Kitchawan, Katonah, Chappaqua. Which way? At home the sheriff and bank examiners are waiting. For a wild moment it appears that George might bolt to Aspetuck or Chappaqua, he appears to be on a racing horse, leaning against the wind, but the moment passes, and he is running home to the drafty old house on Sycamore Street, to accept his fate, to be beaten into an ecstatic submission by the love and regard of his fellows – yet at this moment the projector falters, so that frame by frame George's steps slow and his image flickers and the hope dawning in his face takes on a frozen alert look of concentration, as if he hears urgent but unintelligible voices from some other realm beyond even Clarence's ken.

In the darkness, Capra's voice rings out. "Damn it, what's going on here?" But even in the fading light from the projector, he can see that the screening room is empty but for himself....

CS to JL: An officer of the Directorate of Moral Economy called me this morning, wanting to know if this collaboration was your idea or mine. He suggested that we might have to file a Thematic Impact Statement.

JL to CS: Oh God. What have we got ourselves into?

CS to JL: The version of Kafka we've invented, those works he's failed to write, it's so strange, I almost feel they're seeping into our world....

JL to CS: You and your Kafka! We should have used Max Brod. At least people know who Brod is.

COL'S CAPRA XMAS CUT CANNED. Director Frank Capra, whose spendthrift rep has dogged him since his unreleasable epic *Receding Horizon,* has put another nail in his own coffin with *Miracle at Progress Falls,* insiders say. Capra's Christmas nod to deceased writer Jack Dawson is reportedly far over budget and as hopeless of completion as his previous golden turkey. Eight high-priced scribes, from Odets to Faulkner are said to have spilled ink on the project, to no avail. Columbia head Harry Cohn isn't talking, but he is steaming, as he prods Capra to salvage something from the expensive rough cut footage.
–*Hollywood Reporter,* July 5, 1946

We are shadowed, Max, by events that do not quite happen. An infinity of worlds exists alongside our own. I dream of worlds in which I have died, and you survived and yet betrayed my trust and exposed my unfinished work, my drafts, my inmost thoughts, to the world's scrutiny. Some nights I turn in bed to find Dora beside me, I feel her warmth for a moment before waking, alone. Some nights I hear my own voice calling across vastnesses, urgent but unintelligible.

When I went with Dora to Palestine, I told her: I love you enough to rid myself of anything that might trouble you; I will become another person. For over ten years I wrote nothing, nothing. But after her death, the return of the repressed was inevitable.

The disease also returns, Max, after all those years. A lost dog, abandoned on the street by its master, finds its way home at last, arrives grinning with matted fur, notched ears, bloodshot eyes, lolling tongue.

Dr. Löwy is dead. The mark, the Shem, placed by his hand upon the golem's head awaits erasure.

My doctor here has not heard of the bee moth. Instead, he offers this course of treatment, as put forth in the third edition of Alexander's *The Collapse Theory of Pulmonary Tuberculosis*. Artificial pneumothorax: the intentional collapse of the afflicted lung by injecting gas between it and the thoracic wall; if this fails to collapse the lung, two holes are cut in the chest wall, for a thoracoscope and a cauterizing instrument; one searches for adhesions between lung and pleura, then burns them away, freeing the lung to permit a total collapse. Oleothorax: the pleural cavity is filled with oil rather than air. Extrapleural pneumolysis: the lung and both pleural layers are stripped from the rib cage; the phrenic nerve, controlling the diaphragm, may be crushed with forceps or reeled out through the chest, paralyzing the diaphragm and immobilizing the lung. Finally, one may simply remove a dozen or so ribs, breaking them from the spine and discarding them.

Were I still able, I would write the story of a patient obliged to a course of treatment that is in reality a penance for failing God.

Bit by bit the body is taken away. Then the intellect, the personality, the soul, are broken off and discarded.

I am being erased. As if I had never written. All those torments and ecstasies belong to another world. At last! I am responsible for nothing.

It is a wonderful life.

JL to CS: My number just came up in the public surveillance lottery. I pulled Panopticon duty for two weeks. That's enough for me, I can take a hint; let's drop it. The pressure's giving me hives. Or maybe it's the material – the bridge between Kafka and Capra, Prague and Progress Falls, is too far for me. I'm jumping off.

CS to JL: Well, that's a disappointing response. This was challenging work. Now I'll have to meet my Minimum Cultural Contribution Requirement with more pages of that ancient trunk novel I've been passing in. What with the ozone hole officially declared a myth, it reads like science fiction now. Oh, I'll want back my copy of Kafka's *The Golem*.

JL to CS: You'll have to wait a few weeks. Keep your shutters closed.

After the disaster of the unreleased *Miracle At Progress Falls,* Capra's career went into eclipse. He had become terminally afraid of any project or collaborator that might sidetrack him into questioning fundamental verities – a fatal fear in a profession based on collaboration. For the film's failure he variously blamed Jack Dawson, the eight writers who worked on the script, and James Stewart, cast as George only after Gary Cooper refused the role. Whatever the reason, *Miracle* marks one of the most precipitous declines in the American cinema. Capra in his later years was reduced to making promotional films for defense contractors, and working on an unpublished autobiography. He died in June Lake, California, in 1984. When the American Film Institute released a much-edited version after Capra's death as part of a "lost classics" series, their charity was more admired than their judgment.

– Michael D. Toman, *The American Cinema*

I became a publisher so there would be more R.A. Lafferty books in the world. I am not alone in this distinction. He's one of the most original voices in contemporary American fiction. His many books and stories proclaim a distinctive vision of the world and his style is not an amalgam or adaptation of established techniques but a reconstruction of the language of storytelling from the bottom up. The adventurous reader is advised to hunt down one of his several excellent collections to get the full effect. But beware: it is a strong draught and habit-forming.

I DON'T CARE WHO KEEPS THE COWS
R.A. Lafferty

Because of the trashiness of its origins, there has grown a sort of amnesia over the account of how we became as amazingly smart as we are now, and of how we were even smarter for a while there. This honest account should cut through the amnesia a little bit.

There were two clans of smart people in those days, the *Scar-Tissue Clan* and the *Necklaces Clan*. And then there was a smaller group, the *Little Red Wagon People*. All of these had somewhat cumbersome arrangements to be as smart as they were, and all of them paid a pretty steep tab for it. It cost a lot of money to be a smart person in those days.

The people of the Scar-Tissue Clan – now there was something stark and outstanding about all of them. It may have been their pop-eyes, what used to be called "weight-lifter's eyes." It may have been the scar tissue itself, about the brows and temporals. It may have been the generalized protuberances, the bull-humps at the base of the old brain, the *pherea* or satyr-like growths at the throat, the *pareia*-pouches at one or the other sides of the head, these growths that the more advanced members of the clan usually had. Those things did make persons look peculiar, until the look became common. They were the things that set the people of the Scar-Tissue Clan apart.

(Jerome Blackfoot was getting a head start on the world during

the early morning hours, but he wasn't one of the Scar-Tissue People, nor a Necklacer, nor a Little Red Wagoner either.)

All of the Scar-Tissue people were deaf in the ear of their selection. One ear had to be used as a vent and a drain and could no longer be used for hearing. This deaf ear was usually on the same side of the head as the *pareia*-pouch.

The whole business of the ultra-braininess of the Scar-Tissue Clan (and of the other clans also, but the Scar-Tissues had been the first of the burgeoning brain groups) had been a fallout of a few quacksalvers and confidence persons trying to make a little money and have a little fun. Very many great discoveries and inventions have this quackish origin. There had first been those blatant advertisements:

"The Brain is a muscle. Develop it as you would any other muscle. Slam the steroids to it and make it grow! Use our special brain-designed steroid implants and injections. One of our crews will be in your neighborhood *this month*. Sign and mail the coupon today. Our crew will call on you in a plain brown truck and they will perform all necessary micro-surgery and plugging and implementing in our own truck-clinic or in your own home. Your brains will begin to grow and develop immediately. You can notice the difference within thirty minutes. You'll be smarter, a lot smarter! Hear what H.H. Van der Rander of Ocean Bright California writes:"

And what H.H. Van der Rander wrote might be "I multiplied my brain power seven times in just eleven days. But the most amazing results were noticed right at the beginning. *I doubled my brain power in the first hour.* It was like opening a door into another and more spacious world. I am now four times as smart as anyone else in my neighborhood, and eleven days ago I would have rated in the bottom one-third."

Grotesque as it might sound to a man from Qualquimmerchock, the thing worked from the very first. Well, it had worked for weightlifters and wrestlers; why shouldn't it work for brains? The people who subscribed to the service did get smarter, amazingly smarter in a very short period of time, and they stayed smart. It was like opening the door on another world, yes. Even those early original steroid crews, coming in their plain brown trucks, did excellent work. There is no way that steroid plugs and injections cannot nourish and develop the brain. ("Be brain-starved no longer. Be among the first people ever to have amply fed brains.") The brain is a muscle, and all muscles develop rapidly and amazingly, geometrically and exponentially, by steroid injections. The brain so treated will grow in size and strength until it crowds all available space, and then it will look for more space, either interior or exterior, to spill over into.

And the intelligence also increased exponentially. People with husky and bulky and muscular brains are simply much smarter and intellectually stronger than are people with skinny and skimpy brains. "It's smart to be smart" was one of the advertising slogans that was very effective. All the injections and plugs did cause a lot of scar tissue, of course. Probably this could have been removed. There were plenty of cosmetic cons to take care of it, but for a while the scar tissue was a status thing. The more scar tissue that one had on his head, the smarter he was. And almost everybody was soon taking the steroids. Almost everybody, that is, except those most conservative people in the world, the confidence people themselves who had started this particular advancement.

"A paint manufacturer doesn't necessarily paint his own body with every paint he makes, good quality though it may be," Jerome Blackfoot said. "I'm not going to have any of this stuff injected into my own brains. Sure it's good. I invented it, didn't I? I designed types Alpha and Delta of the Brain Steroids myself, so of course they're good. But I'm fastidious. When I was little, I wore white gloves when I played in the mud. I'll stay with my natural brains, unbulged and unbursted. But now we will have to develop and devise a few things for all these new muscular brains to occupy themselves with. Give them something to be smart about. There is something unclean about the vision of all those strong brains munching on themselves. We will give them 'Essence of the Compacted World' to munch on."

Well, Blackfoot and his partner did come out with a line of shape-modules or information modules that could be impressed into the new big brains which they had helped create. These modules contained details (more than details, whole constellations of persons and places and happenings and meanings and sights and smells and axioms), and their patterns and contents went directly into the brains in usable forms. Oh, for instance there would be a shape-module for a certain discipline or specialty of biology. No need to spend five years acquiring it. It was quite easy, after one of the quacksalvers had come upon the method intuitively, to put any and all information into a shape-module form that was ready for impressing. There was very little physical content to this absolutely massive information; it was all coded into impressed shape. Thus a person with a brain sufficiently fortified with steroids might absorb the entire corpus of a hundred thousand novels in one impressing session, and he would possess this information and emotion and experience intimately forever. A person could learn languages or philosophies or mathematics or art-experiences or histories similarly. Anybody could know anything now. Everybody did know everything (and you have no idea how big and finely grained this "everything" is) almost immediately. It looked as if everybody in the land would become stunningly smart and informed. Everybody, except perhaps that small group of persons who had accidentally started it all.

Jerome Blackfoot the Black-Footed Weasel was one of no more than thirty prime quacksalvers and confidence persons who had first gone into brain steroids. And yet the connection between the "new age of brainery" and the quacksalvers couldn't be allowed to remain so blatant. Blackfoot and persons like him would give brains a bad name. So it was surely a good thing that the brain steroids as well as the information-modules were taken out of the hands of the quacksalvers and given into the control of professionals and scientists and governmentalists. Because this was a big thing. What had come upon the world, what had slipped up on the blind side of the world, by accident and without warning, was "Controlled Explosion Day" itself, the day when the whole world got smart, the day that the world had been created for. Big strong brains now shook off their dubious and accidental origin, created themselves to further massiveness and capacity, and went to work on the mountains of information that was the world itself, interior and exterior, in impressed module form. These brains held the "Essence of the Compacted World" and they spun intelligent judgements on it out of their own mountainous intellectuality. So there was joy and enthusiasm and high thinking in the land.

(Ferndale Whitehead was getting a head start on the world in the early morning, and he wasn't one of the Scar-Tissue People, or one of the Necklace People, or one of the Little Red Wagon People either.)

Quite soon, with the intervention of the government with its professionals and scientists, the "Mental Musculature Phenomenon" became a stratified and restricted benison. Everybody would still know everything, but not everybody would know everything to the fullest power. "Big Brain Morning" was not to be enjoyed in its ultimate form by everybody. Or rather, there would be new and more ultimate forms created that would not be open to all. There would have to be stages to it. Bands of professionals and scientists *periti* made the selections of just who would receive the more ultimate forms of brain development, and who would have to be content with mere doubling or tripling of brain muscle and scope. There would be, for the common good, hierarchies of braininess. And it would be mostly the case of "To those who have, let it be given." So it would be mostly the case of the professionals and scientists forming the top hierarchy. The common people didn't really have enough brains to deserve ultra-brains. They would be better off than they had ever been before, but special states must be reserved for special persons. The special persons were in. Others were almost in. And lesser breeds would be forever outside by their lack of capacity or by their own sordid choice. And yet there were strange compensations in belonging to a lesser breed. Those of the lesser breeds, and some of those with hardly any breeding at all, just had to be certain that they would receive what was coming to them.

Ferndale Whitehead the Man in the White Hat, a sort of partner of Jerome Blackfoot the Black-Footed Weasel, believed that there would always be a place for a firm with fleets of plain brown trucks and with trained installers and technicians in those trucks. And so it was the case. Blackfoot and Whitehead had held bothersome patents on certain brain steroids. (And those steroids had had invisibly fine tendrils on them, of purpose not generally apparent.) And the partners had developed the techniques of impressionable information-modules, and later of gateway-couples. Though the government voided all such patents and rights-to-techniques, yet they did form a sort of trading basis. And those quacksalver gentlemen were good traders even after they had nothing left to trade with. They could even trade successfully out of an empty banana cart, so long as it still had the smell of bananas about it.

The quacksalvers became licensed applicators and installers, and their hundred thousand plain brown trucks seemed to be everywhere in the land. Their trucks would roll as long as grass grows and water flows.

After a while, only token numbers of their trucks still rolled, for steroids and modules and couples were soon made of instantly transmissible and mostly immaterial substance. But the Quacksalver Row people still collected for the full complement of services. That, somehow, had been built into the system without anyone noticing.

When the Necklace Clan, the other main group of smart people, had come along, Blackfoot and Whitehead and others of their small tribe were able to take advantage of this new development also. They were able to take advantage of it because they had, accidentally, originated it.

That was the day when Ferndale Whitehead had called up Kathrynne Klunque (she had been born plain Kate Klunk) who had more surplus electronic components than anyone else on Quacksalver Row.

"Say, Kate, didn't you have a few million junk miniature thermocouples with a two-way couple feature? I'll try a million of them at a cent each. I don't know what I'll do with them, but this is one of those oh-what-the-hell days. Besides, I'd like to help you out of a hole."

"I'm not in a hole, Whitie," Kathrynne said. "I'm sitting on top of a mountain, and 'Queen of the Mountain' is the name of the game I'm playing. You are referring to those 'gateways of the future,' those 'gateways to the other realms,' those ultimate thermocouples or category-couples, are you not? Whitey, I couldn't let you have them for a cent each. I will let you have them *two for a cent* though. There, I left you breathless with that one, didn't I?"

"Predictably breathless, Kate. And you also want the predictable —"

"Fair piece of everything."

"All right, Kate."

"You've found a way to make at-a-distance couples of information depots to brains?"

"We think so, Kate. We'll try it with a million or so if your couplers. How much will it cost to make more of the couplers when the stock is used up?"

"Oh, a cent each. Or a thousand dollars each. Or somewhere in between. It depends on whom we are talking to."

They had tried it then, and it had worked. And so the Necklace Clan came into being. People could hang the small gateway-couples around their necks like necklaces, and fifty or so of the gadgets could give them all possible instant information on every subject imaginable. By using the necklaces or strings of gateway-couplings, they would need brains only about half as muscled and massive as those of the prime Scar-Tissue People. They could get by with less brain bulk because the information depots they drew on were not inside their brains. Those information supplies might be in tabulated buildings as far as two thousand kilometers away. Because of this, the Necklace People were able to keep their brains mostly in their own heads, with very little exterior over-spill. This made it neat. But others preferred things more gaudy: the Scar-Tissue Clan reveled in their lurid scar tissue. That was the entry-mark of brains.

The Necklace thing worked as the previous things had worked. There were now two major clans of very smart people. A choice was offered. People could be about as smart as they wished, in either of two ways.

The third way, that of the Little Red Wagon People, offered only a minor variation, and there was no basic discovery involved. These people pulled carts or coaster wagons behind them which were filled with their own overflow brains. It was better than having those protuberances growing all over the outside of the head. It was easier on the neck. But there was some danger of being separated by accident from important centers of their own minds. With the Necklace Clan, there was also the danger of power failure cutting them off from their information depots.

But these were the golden days and years, the "Era of the Golden Brains," the prime time of the people. The mood was "Enjoy it; it's fun to be smart; let's have the fun." But there was a darker mood running also, and it said, "If they don't want a piece of it, we'll carve a piece of them." There was also a movement running through the land to do away with all the people who didn't much want to be smart in any of the offered ways. But the bulk of the people *did* want to be smart, and they did become smart, so smart that it would scare you. For the safety of the land, guidelines then had to be set up for the whole complex of group braininess.

For the safety of the *land*, not of the *lands*, for there was now only one land, the United States. All other lands in the world had ceased to exist. There had been, you see, a lot of show-boating at the time of the appearance of the first massive braininess. Show-Boat exhibitionists had discovered that they could do such things as moving mountains by their new brain power alone. Then some of the more brash of them began to top each other in their ostentations. They began to destroy, or to consign to the outer darkness, whole countries and continents, till only one land was left. Here, here! A halt must be called to such doings.

So everybody received a jolt of a new admonition-module, a stern warning medication. As it happened, it probably wasn't necessary. Things were happening rapidly in the brain field. The Show-Boat impulse and manifestation passed as suddenly as it had come. The rapidly rising level of braininess had quickly left that early destructive phase behind it. But that didn't bring back the lost lands.

There were only a few people who did not go along with it all, who did not walk bright-eyed into "Brain-World" and all its glories. Surprisingly, the people who had started it all, the Quacksalvers and Confidence People, were among those minorities who didn't go along with it. They didn't use the steroids themselves. Nor the information-modules, nor the gateway-couples.

"I sure don't want to be burdened with any more brains than I have now," Jerome Blackfoot said. "Carrying too much of those things around makes a weighty burden. Sometimes I think I'd like to dump about half of the brains that I already have in my head."

"Sometimes I think you *are* about to dump half of your brains," Whitehead said. "I don't know anybody who comes as close to it as often as you do."

"A brain-glutton I don't want to be," said Thor Thorgelson ("A Square Deal from the Square-Head" was his business motto), one of the most accomplished of the Quacksalvers.

Ah, Blackfoot and Whitehead and Thorgelson and the rest of them didn't really have much brains. They just stayed ahead of things by getting up so early in the mornings. Drinking of the morning fountains before they are roiled is almost as good as having brains. "Joy cometh in the morning" it says in one place. "Make the morning precious" it says in another. "Men and morning newspapers" it says in still another place. Ferndale Whitehead would always pick up a morning newspaper from a neighbor's front step before that neighbor was awake, and this action was a type of getting to the world before the world was awake. Then Whitehead would stroll to the Break-of-Day Donut Shop and be the first customer there right at opening time.

"The first cup of coffee out of your Reciprocal-Movement Coffee-Maker is always a little bit bitter," he would say conversationally.

"Yeah, I know," the sleepy-eyed waitress would agree. "I always throw the first cup out."

"Give me that first bitter cup," Whitehead would say. So, at no expenditure of coin, he acquired a taste for bitter coffee very early in the morning.

"The first tray of Long John Fritters in the morning will always have one fritter a little bit burned," Whitehead would say.

"Yeah, I know," the waitress would agree. "It's the one in the highest corner, before the grease really gets effective. I always throw the burned one out."

"Give me the fritter that is a little bit burned," Whitehead would say. So he would have coffee and fritter free, and a sociable place to read the paper. Then, after he had cut the usual free coupons out of it, he would reroll that paper carefully and put it back on the neighbor's doorstep where he had found it. There had been a chilliness develop between the paperboy and the neighbor from whom the paper was borrowed for a little while every morning. Neither of them understood how the paper had all the holes cut out of it when it was first unrolled.

But, by these simple movements, Ferndale Whitehead was able to get a head start on the world every morning. And it was a rare day when the world ever did catch up to him after such a start. Kathrynne Klunque and Elizabeth Queen Mab and Thor Thorgelson were out early every morning also, as were almost all the other quacksalvers. It is always the "First Morning of Creation" when you get up early enough. Certain demiurges have always known this and have always risen early. But most of the people have known it not.

Whitehead's partner, Jerome Blackfoot, also got up early in the mornings, and he liked to walk in the countryside that is just on the edge of town. Jerome usually carried a basket and a toe-sack and a jug. "You have heard of the guy who went out when it was raining fish, and he didn't have anything to catch them in," Jerome said. "I'm not that guy. I'll always have something to catch them in."

Actually, fish were far down on the list of things that Blackfoot filled his receptacles with every morning. In season, he picked produce of various sorts. Sometimes a chicken or a duckling went into his toe-sack. Almost every morning he stopped by one of the places where cows were kept and he always milked a jugful from one of the cows. "I don't care who keeps my country's cows," he would say, "so long as I have the milk free. A cow-keeper I am not."

Dogs sometimes harassed Blackfoot a bit, but he had a trick of slipping a muzzle onto the barking head of a dog and then stuffing the whole dog into his toe-sack. People will almost always advertise when a well-voiced dog disappears, and they will pay small rewards when he is returned.

The Quacksalvers were a bunch of inclined twigs and they grew from that into a profitably slanted forest. So Jerome Black-foot, like his partner, like most of the other quacksalvers, got a head start on the world every morning. In the very early morning there is always enough freshness to go around. And beyond that, the quacksalvers all did their best thinking on their early morning rambles.

Their best thinking? That? But let us go from the ridiculous to the sublime. How was it going with the people who could really think? How was it going with the brainy majority? Oh, it was going well with them.

What do people think about when their thinking power is many times increased? Oh, they think about the same things, but they do it with greater power. And they think about nothing new? Yes, they think about everything new. To think of a thing with greater power is to think of it new. And at top-thinking, things draw together so that sympathy and affection are all parts of the same thing, along with logic and exposition and excitement. The material problems of the land simply packed up and went away. They were solved automatically. Problems of weather proved amenable to solution. It would rain if enough people thought "rain" powerfully enough. The south wind would blow if enough people thought "south wind will blow" intelligently enough. There was successful problem-solving, and there was an activating peace of mind. Peace has nothing to do with inaction. It was a highly active, dynamic and kinetic peace-of-mind that prevailed. And there was a lot of love, of everybody for everybody, imbuing the whole life-weave.

"We make a stunning picture," said Hadrian Pigendo, a Scar-Tissue man and a painter. "Our whole land is now one single picture, and a scanning frame on it will be filled with nothing but masterpieces wherever it stops. A century ago, John Masterman said that there couldn't be a perfect picture until every element in it, animate and inanimate, was in thinking accord. Now everything *is* in thinking accord, and everything is a part of a perfect picture. This table here is thinking accord with me and with everyone else who enters the room. It resonates to us. So does the light that breaks and spills through the window there. Ours has now become an intellectualized world, achieving the identity of intelligence with beauty. The two are the same, both being aspects of "perfect order." The only drawback to the perfect living picture that we form is the business of the invisible cobwebs. But perhaps that is not a drawback either when it shall be perfectly understood."

"There is no longer any difference between individual thought and group thought," said Felix Acumen, a Necklace-Clan man and a thinker's thinker. "At its apex of exaltation, thought merges everyone together. This is not to say that everyone will think alike. It is to say that the infinite variety of human thought, when it flourishes in its essential life-greenness, weaves itself into a single seamless (and limitless) garment every part of which is conscious of every other part. It may be that this seamless thought encompasses everything, that it is all inside and that there is no outside to it. Or it may be that there *is* a very slight outside to it. There are invisible and barely sensed tendrils of cobwebs that brush against the multisurface of our thought, and they may be from outside the context."

The courtship rites of the super-intelligent clans were interesting. There was the "interlocking antenna" affect of the Necklace-Clan people, their gateway-couplings that made up their necklaces seeking their counterparts in those of the other person and rushing together with a great clattering. There were the double needles that the Scar-Tissue People used that resulted in highly intricate steroid sharing. There was the business of each lover placing his brains in the wagon of his loved one in the case of the Little Red Wagon People. And there were the non-standardized courtship proceedings when the courtships were between members of two different brain clans.

Other things enriched themselves. People no longer played three-dimensional chess. They played sixteen-dimensional chess, which is harder, but more rewarding. The music that they made now was an intellectualized music. Some people said that it was a computerized music. But it was not, somehow, the expression of the identity of intelligence and beauty. It was really bad music, considering that it was the music of an intellectual era. But it was not nearly as bad as the music of the preceeding non-intellectual era had been.

And the super-intelligent people couldn't tell good jokes. Otis Ramrod, a Little Red Wagon Person and a social mores expert, explained it:

"No, super-intelligent persons cannot tell good jokes. There is no such thing as a good joke to a super-intelligent person. Humor disappears from the world now. There is no longer any place or purpose for it. Crocodiles may shed tears over its passing, but I will not. Humor is a ridiculous bridge thrown across a chasm of maladjustment. In the super-intelligent world there is no maladjustment, no chasm, and no places to throw the bridge named humor. In our now almost-perfect-world, on careen-course towards perfection, there are only slight and disappearing flaws where residual humor may still flicker faintly. There are, for instance the 'cobweb jokes' which most persons do not understand (I do not). And there are residual antibrain people such as the Quacksalvers who still have humor and still have maladjustments. Our aim is totally to sweep away both the mysterious 'cobwebs' and the mopey Quacksalvers this very year."

The super-intellectual world could not allow maladjustment in itself. So it could not allow self-doubt. So it could not allow dissent. And something had to be done about the tendency of people to brush imaginary cobwebs away from their faces too.

The non-participating Quacksalvers represented dissent. Them at least you could get your hands on. Them at least you could obliterate.

A whole complex of surfacing questions represented self-doubt.

The cobwebs represented the cobwebs themselves.

A small congress of ultra-super-intelligent persons was assembled to consider the three problems. They came quickly to the possibility that the three problems were all one problem. Here are bits of scattered conversations and comments from the "Self-Doubt Congress."

"Someone is kidding. It isn't really like this. This business of us

Leing super-intelligent is all a put-on. Well, who's putting it on?"

"Are we indeed a Noble Experiment? And who is it who is experimenting with us? We know that Noble Experiments have a high incidence of failure."

"What is the mysterious 'Micro-X' element that has always been in all our brain steroids that we have never been able to take out of them? Does somebody monitor our brains by it?"

"Are we being milked? I ask *are we being milked?* What godly race is milking our brains and our persons?"

"Has there ever been a successful revolt of puppets against puppeteers? Is such a thing possible? How would puppets have any motion if it were not imparted to them by their puppeteers? No, I do not say that we are puppets. I merely ask whether there has ever been a successful revolt of puppets against puppeteers."

"What if it is fortunate that we are *not* able to brush the invisible cobwebs or tendrils away from us? What if they are our lifeline or our light-line? What if we break just one of the invisible tendrils, the wrong one for us, and the light in us switches off? I believe that this has been the true cause of deaths of a number of persons this year. Indeed, one doctor I know of wrote 'broken cobwebs' in the line for 'cause of death' on the certificates of several persons. He has since been barred from doctoring for persistent drunkenness."

"Is Quacksalver Row Olympia? No, no, consider that question unasked. It cannot be Olympia. It cannot even be Valhalla. It is something much else and much less. It is so much less that it must remain beneath our notice. Quacksalver Row, I mean."

"We are met to solve these three problems. One of them can be solved within an hour by a little bit of bloody extinction. So let us solve that one problem now, and then inquire whether the other two problems have not somehow solved themselves with it. That's the way that super-intelligent persons would go about this. Agreed?"

"Agreed," said the other members of the small congress of ultra-super-intelligent persons. So they went out, it being evening now, with staves and swords and garroting ropes to effect the extinction of about thirty nonconformist persons.

The Quacksalvers of Quacksalver Row all maintained cluttered quarters which they believed to be elegant. These were all in three or four adjacent buildings on the Row. The Quacksalvers were really a "Beggar's Opera" of very gamey folks.

The people of the small congress that had been looking into the three problems, their numbers being about thrice the numbers of the Quacksalvers, came before their quarters and made an evening tumult in Quacksalver Row.

All the Quacksalvers tumbled out of their buildings and came to the confrontation in the street. One of the Quacksalvers, Thor Thorgelson who did business under the motto "A Square Deal from the Square-Head," drew his own sword and cut off the ear of the leader of the congress party. This leader began to cry with the pain and surprise and loss, and many of his companions began to cry with him. Super-intelligent persons have very close sympathies with other super-intelligent persons.

"Why all the fuss?" Thor Thorgelson asked. "It's his deaf ear that I cut off. Don't you think that I have any sense at all?" This was all the bloodshed, all the violence of any kind that took place at the confrontation.

"This is ridiculous," one of the super-intelligent persons said. "Why should we, the brainiest of all delegations, have come to parlay with you beggars? What compels us to do it? What strings are on us anyhow?"

"We don't know why you came," Kathrynne Klunque said. "We are all agog about it ourselves."

"You are like horrible caricatures of puppeteers," the super-intelligent speaker said. "How do we come to be a-dangle on your strings?"

"What strings?" Kathrynne asked.

"He means the cobwebs," the confidence woman Elizabeth Queen Mab guessed. "He thinks they are puppet strings. He thinks we manipulate them."

"Well, do we?"

"I don't know. A little bit, I guess."

"Everybody dangles on several sets of strings and is manipulated by them," Ferndale Whitehead tried to explain. "This could not bother you. Is what bothers you, brain-people, that the strings seem to be manipulated from an unexpected direction, that they seem to be manipulated by ourselves?"

"Why should we be at odds?" Jerome Blackfoot asked. "You are good cows. You feed and maintain yourselves, a thing that I wouldn't like to do. Let's keep it the way it is, you smart and us dumb. It seems to me to be a fair division."

"No, no, this cannot be," one of the super-brains protested. "We are not, we cannot be —"

"You cannot be clowns' cattle?" Elizabeth Queen Mab asked. "Well, say that you are not cattle then, and we will agree that you are not. We will remain the clowns without any cattle. But don't you quit giving milk!"

"We will revolt! We will overthrow you!" a super-brain threatened.

"Oh no!" Jerome Blackfoot swore. "Then in the turnover you would be dumb and we would be smart. Do not hang that on us! We'll never accept that burden. We thought we had it fixed perfectly the way it was. We'll take to the woods, we'll take to the wastelands, we'll never come back!"

"Except for the milk," one of the super-brains jeered.

Believe it people, there was tension there for a long moment.

And never could you guess what broke that tension when it had stretched out longer and longer.

One of the super-brains laughed.

And another of them wailed. And one cried out in pain.

But then a second one laughed, and then a third one. They broke it when they did that. "You laugh too hard and I'll turn your little red wagons over," Elizabeth Queen Mab threatened.

But another of the super-brains laughed. There was a chasm, and there shouldn't have been. There was maladjustment, and a ridiculous bridge was the best that could be thrown over it.

They broke it, and they lost part of it when they broke it. The whole apparatus of being so smart crumbled, even though a lot of the smartness would remain. The top of the mountain of it was gone.

We'll never be that smart again.

A.M. Dellamonica has the distinction of being the first writer to sell me a story out of the slush pile. As John Cleese says about his pet Eric the Halibut, "I chose it out of thousands; I didn't like the others, they were all too flat."

HOMAGE
A.M. Dellamonica

The gate to the Underworld was rusted through, and the guard dog was asleep.

"Mega-fabulous!" The God of Entertainment stared at Cerberus in fascination, wondering if it was safe to just sneak by. The gate would probably squeak.

Then he realized the three-headed dog was dead.

All the adventure and none of the risk, he thought. It was the best piece of luck he'd had since Francis got him out of sponsoring celebrity causes by becoming God of Charity. He smirked back across the Grove of Persephone, a dispirited group of wilting trees, and his gaze fell on the painted blue eyes of his creation, Aggie.

Behind Aggie's motionless form a river, probably the Acheron, dribbled out of a crack in the roof of the cavern. It crept across a once-mighty floodplain and disappeared near Cerberus's corpse. The cavern was huge, bigger than a stadium, the tunnel he came through merely one of hundreds of openings that led to the surface. The arc of the brook divided the caves from the gate, bubbling along the edges of the remains of Persephone's Grove. If he squinted he could see shadowy forms emerging from the caves. They waded over the river – no need for a ferryman now – and vanished into the cavern beyond the Gate, moving downstream.

"Scene two," the god boomed. Wind from his voice blew the hair off the dog's skin. Dust crumbled down from the ceiling.

"The plucky young grad student and I set out together, and we find Cerberus at the Gate to the Underworld. He's gone mad. He's in agony. The poor beast attacks! I'm forced to kill him after a terrible battle."

He restored the corpse's hair, rearranged the three muzzles so they were snarling, firmed up the gums so they'd hold in its teeth. *Poor animal dried out instead of rotting.* He warmed the corpse, filled its veins with blood, conjured foam on its lips. Then Entertainment waved a hand. One by one the dog's giant heads came off its shoulders.

The scenery needed work, too. He widened the crack in the ceiling so the Acheron poured down in a spectacular waterfall, slamming into its dried riverbed with a dust-raising roar. He changed Persephone's tinderbox back into a proper grove and dispersed the dog hair caught in the branches of the trees. *What else...it still needs something.*

"Got it," he crowed. He tore off the sleeve of his shirt and arranged it among the dog's teeth. Then he laid a hand between the eyes of the nearest head and assumed a tough but regretful expression. He took a deep breath. "Roll sidekick."

Aggie pounded through the newly restored trees and burst into the clearing in front of the Gate, her eyes flickering to and fro as she witnessed the battle Entertainment had described. He was gratified to see her expression run the spectrum from wonder to fear and then relief. "Hugh," she gasped, "Did he hurt you?"

"Stay away from the foam," Hugh said roughly.

She touched him instead, laying a tentative hand on his arm. "He was sick, Hugh. It was a mercy, really it was." Her voice was exactly what he'd wanted, youthful and clear, with the barest hint of throaty resonance. Hugh brushed a single lock of hair off her forehead and let her cajole a smile out of him.

She's flawless.

He'd created Aggie that morning to accompany him to the land of the dead. Toni naturally assumed she would be invited, but Hugh was too clever to bring a producer with him, girlfriend or no. Entertainment deserved a more fitting witness to his exploits, one who would stay within her role. *Besides, who would go adventuring with a sidekick who dresses like a senator?*

Aggie's part was tagalong kid sister. She was in her mid-twenties, with proportions that suggested immaturity: slim waist, adolescent hips, unfashionably small breasts. Her copper hair was bound in a ponytail and she wore khaki shorts, running shoes and a white shirt. A green backpack bounced between her shoulders.

It was the clothes that had inspired the creation. Hugh's first attempts at conjuring women from thin air came out misshapen, with warped personalities. They reminded him of the children his wife produced whenever he was stupid enough to let her near him. He tried copying actresses from the film library, but he knew people would realize they were copies, and he couldn't bear to alter them. Finally he just locked the failures in his wardrobe and went idea-shopping. The first thing he spotted when he hit the mall were the khaki shorts.

Adventuring clothes, he thought. He dragged the mannequin into a dressing room, changed her hair, edited her physique. He etched subliminal messages into the freckles he sprayed over her nose and cheeks, tiny advertising sigils for movies, music, and TV shows. He whispered to her plaster heart, narrating her tragic past, enjoining her to be smart and resourceful, resilient and above all loyal. Then he stuffed her in a duffel bag without taking the tags off her clothes. She set off shoplifting alarms all over the mall when he left.

After a strategic retreat from the shopping center he created her an apartment, furnished with movie memorabilia and photo albums full of a dad with red hair, a tough but loving mom. He named her Agnes See, wrote her name into the records of a film doctorate program, spliced her into the memories of people at the college. And now here she was, gaping at the corpse, then ranging ahead to examine the cleft in the rock beyond the Gate.

"It's too narrow for the Jeep," she announced. "I guess we're hiking." She yanked on the rusty bars. Hugh rushed to open it for her so he could be first to venture into the tunnel. Inside, it was pitch-black, and he created a lion of gold light to lead the way.

Dripping water echoed around them and the dank smell of the river pressed against his skin. Their reflections in the water were remarkably clear, Aggie's eyes, alert and excited, his own handsome face.

If Cerberus is dead, Hades should be gone too. Persephone died ages ago, but it was possible Hades survived, that he was hearty and guarding his territory against interlopers. He might even have kids, grandchildren. Apollo and Artemis spawned Holly, nature freak and mother of the gods, because Apollo insisted that descendants of the Old Ones would ascend to a new era of glory. Apollo was down here now. He might have told Hades and Persephone his prophesy. Maybe they'd birthed a litter or two.

Wealth will kill me if I awaken any rivals.

Aggie was telling him about film school, her friends, her life, her apartment. "It's a bit of a cliché, a movie buff kind of place," she said, with so much affection Hugh could almost forget he'd copied most of it from the set of a failed sitcom. He wished he could tell her he was glad she liked it, that he was pleased with her. His franchise included all the arts, movies and television and video games and fiction, but movies were his favorite. He rated a sidekick who loved them too.

"I've always thought they should make a movie about you," she said.

"Write a script."

"After my thesis," she said, and Hugh chuckled. When she knew he was the one who'd rescued her from the streets, who'd paid for her schooling after her parents' tragic imaginary accident, she would set the thesis aside.

They descended for hours. Hugh got tired of the explorer role fast. He half-listened to Aggie while stretching his attention to the living world, checking on the supplicants who were praying about the record company takeover. He drew a morsel of strength from a young priest, a director offering a TV pilot to Entertainment's private library. In a Broadway megatemple, a weary line of dancers practiced a number in his honor while the stage crew hammered at a broken set piece. Hugh fixed the set, gorged on their thankful prayers, and changed his watch to a TV screen so he could tune in on the talk shows and the soaps.

Finally the cave widened into vastness, and they came to the riverbank where the Styx coiled in nine loops around the Underworld. Hugh conjured a sparkling bridge, curled and segmented like a roll of film. Aggie clapped and sprinted to the center to gaze around her. The glowing lion followed her, casting a haze of gold into the center of the cave. Unlike the Acheron, the Styx was black, so dark Hugh couldn't see his face. "I thought there'd be stalactites," he said, and then remembered that this was supposed to be his second trip. "I mean, when I was here before." Last year he announced that he'd come to the Underworld.

"Limestone caves have stalactites," Aggie said. "This is more of a breach along the fault line."

"I know," he said, miffed. "I realized that right off...last time."

"It's beautiful," Aggie said. "In a creepy sort of way. Like being inside the night sky."

"We didn't come for the scenery." This trip was going to actualize Hugh's fondest dream, to finally be the hero of a big-budget adventure movie. He wanted to attend the premiere, give interviews about the differences between the screen version and the way it really was. He wanted actors to fight each other to play him. For years he cajoled his faithful, hinting at what he wanted, even offering bribes. They never quite said no. Deals went into preproduction, but inevitably miscarried.

Even gods, it seemed, could fail auditions.

This place is becoming a megayawn. What would happen if this was a movie?

Aggie wasn't bored. She was still talking. "I recognized you checking out that cave entrance, and I knew you were going back to the Underworld," she said. "I have all the clippings, you know, from when you went down to prove that You Know Who really was dead. I thought about how the tabloids whined that it was just your word against theirs, so I figured I'd go along as a witness." She squatted to peer at the Styx. "What's it like?"

"You'll see," Hugh promised. He'd staged an international press conference about the bogus trip. He'd only done it to get a long-dead gloryhogging rock star off the front page of the tabs, but everyone was very impressed. The film deal almost went through until the press started getting skeptical.

In a movie the hero would have to save the sidekick, Hugh thought. He conjured a rattlesnake behind Aggie and then fried it as it was about to bite her. She squealed, jumped, and then glowered reproachfully.

"Was that some kind of test?"

"Cut!" he howled. Her eyes glazed and she froze. "Forget the snake, Aggie." He paced in the narrow cavern. "Scene," he said, sweeping her against the rock wall. "The sidekick jiggles a loose rock and causes a minor cave-in." He pulled down stones from the roof around them, arranging them in an artistic pile, tearing the back of his shirt with fragments, releasing trickles of dust onto their hair. "I tackle her, shielding her from the falling rock with my body." He glared down at her immobile form as he rained gravel onto the glowing lion. "She is appropriately grateful."

Ingratitude was a specialty of his worshippers, he thought, remembering how Toni finally told him why nobody would make his movie. "Hugh, you're a fascinating subject," she said, "But you don't do anything besides go to the parties and the premieres. You can't make an adventure movie about a guy who doesn't do anything."

"I sprang full-grown from the corpse of Zeus!"

"That's not enough to risk angering you with a bad film," she said. "You've got to up your marketability." She sat coyly, ankles crossed, tempting her Persian kitten with a string of pearls.

When she finished outlining her plan, Hugh was positively sick. "Why should I risk myself to rescue people who already get more press than me?"

"They get more press because they did things," she said.

"They died young."

"Before they died they did things," Toni insisted. "Made movies, ran the free world...."

"Okay, point taken already. But do I want to be upstaged?"

She dropped the pearls, laid her head on his shoulder. "Hugh," she murmured huskily. "The public wants them. I want them. If we get them out, it will be the biggest story ever. Bigger than the

Ascendance. And you'll be right in the middle of it."

Bigger than the Ascendance.

"Death," Toni said, "is what makes them so ultra-attractive. It's mysterious."

"It's not a mystery at all," Hugh said. "They're all cooling their heels in Hades."

"So you say."

"You better not be saying you don't believe me."

"Of course not, darling," she purred. "That's the beauty of it. It's a zero-risk plan. You've already been to the Underworld. Bring them back and you prove it!"

"I'm a God. I shouldn't have to prove anything," Hugh grumbled. He avoided her gaze by reaching for the strand of pearls. It was too far away, so he conjured more, joining a strand from his hand to the beads strung on the floor. The kitten pounced, tugging, and Hugh let them slip through his fingers, one by one. "What do I get out of all this trouble except more competition in the tabs?"

"Your movie," Toni said.

"That's your whole pitch?" He dropped the pearls and grew more, mulling over reasons why it wouldn't work. No way would he admit he hadn't been to Hades after all. The family might have worked it out but the mortals couldn't prove it.

"Bringing them back'll reduce the competition," Toni said, running an appraising eye over the strand. It was the length of her leg. "It's what they might have done that makes the audience deify them."

"Don't use that word. I'm the deity here," Hugh said.

"Exactly," Toni said. "So let them come back and go on the talk shows. Let them make movies and CDs and launch comeback campaigns. Let them have breakdowns and check into Betty Ford and go through terrible divorces. They'll age, Hugh. They'll become has-beens."

"Maybe," Hugh grumbled.

"Maybe nothing. And when they're gone, the audience will see that you're the eternal one. The divine one." She'd winked and scooped up the pearls.

It was a stroke of luck that Hugh scooped the second biggest franchise in the Ascendance sixty years before. He was skipping a family meeting about when to return to the mortals, when to make their presence known and rise again. Holly and Mona were fighting as usual, and Mona ran off, presumably to her room, to sulk. Hugh was watching TV. He was long since bored with the tactical sessions, the reiterations that "Apollo promised, he said Hank would be War." It was awards season, his favorite time of year. The glitter always captivated him. He dreamed of running away, of finding a different sort of worship in celebrity. It was a damned shame he couldn't act.

While the others were squabbling about when and how to ascend, not to mention who would be in charge, Hugh, channel-surfing, had found the news bulletin about Mona.

She'd gone to a mall and conjured money for anyone who'd pray to her. Her cult was spreading like plague. The family was still fighting when Wealth returned and announced that she was in charge, that the Ascension was underway. Hugh was already on Earth, seizing the Entertainment franchise from the awards podium.

Hugh shook off the memories like flies and positioned a huge boulder in the cavern roof above his shoulders. "Roll sidekick," he said, and Aggie's eyes flickered, playing surprise and terror before she ducked her head under his waiting arms. He dropped the rock on his back, grunted as he shielded her. As he pulled her out of the rockfall he saw himself in her pupils. The mussed and dusty hair looked rugged.

The lion fought its way out from under the pebbles and Aggie giggled nervously. "Is there some reason you couldn't just put in an elevator?"

Hugh gave her a smile he hoped was enigmatic.

They proceeded in silence until the tunnel widened and the lion stopped, settling on its haunches and looking down at a glowing ball. It had the light of holy magic, just like the lion, but the glow was muted, silvery and sad like the moon.

"What is it?" Aggie breathed.

Hugh reached for the silver orb and it twitched, rolling closer.

He saw it was a bundle of wrapped cord. "I think it's Ariadne's ball of string," he said, and wished he'd sounded matter-of-fact instead of awestruck. The strand led down a black plain and vanished in the distance. They could see its silvery trail. "Somebody's got the other end," he said. The ball jumped and rolled. A span of string the length of his hand reeled away.

I hope this doesn't mean someone brought the Labyrinth down here, Hugh thought. He shuddered. *Or a Minotaur.*

Toni's plan had its points, but Hugh would have put her off indefinitely if his kids hadn't started to change. After the first uproar, the Ascendance settled into a cozy status quo that lasted fifty years. Now Wealth had transformed herself, growing older, consolidating her power. Her penthouse was sealed and Hugh knew she was up to something big. Hank shed his angst and buckled down to the business of War. Francis and Julia, the products of Hugh's two post-Ascendance truces with Holly, had grown up, chosen franchises. Hugh sensed it was time to do something or lose his grip on second place in the pecking order.

Julia in particular was nipping at his heels. Her roving packs of reporters were everywhere, worrying at his followers' secrets. *Who asked her to deify Truth anyway?*

They stopped in the chamber so Aggie could rest. Hugh carved her a cup out of the rock, filling it with water from his canteen. She had iron rations in her pack, but to make up for the avalanche Hugh created a plate of sandwiches. She picked at them and watched the ball of thread as it unreeled in little jerks but did not shrink.

"Something wrong?" he asked.

"I get sideaches when I walk on a full stomach," she said. She took one polite bite, chewed and swallowed. Then she dug a plastic bag out of the pocket of her shorts, frowning at it curiously. It was from the store where Hugh had found her. She packed the sandwiches in the bag and stuffed them into her backpack, as casually as if they were something she'd got out of the fridge at home instead of food conjured from the air of the Underworld.

They left the ball of string untouched and followed the strand.

The thread vibrated with a strange life, flicking back and forth on the tunnel floor, occasionally jerking forward.

The air got colder as they descended, and Hugh offered to conjure Aggie a jacket. "I'm okay." she said. "I'm not cold at all."

That's my girl, Hugh thought. Toni would demand a fur.

They came out on a balcony that looked down on an oval chamber, and far away, at the other end of Ariadne's thread, they found Marilyn Monroe.

She was seated on Persephone's throne, knitting sweaters for the dead. A raised platform at one end of the room held two thrones, one an empty, shining seat of gold and white. Marilyn's chair was crumbling, but her face was beatific. A small line-up of souls waited before her, watching her shape a sleeve. Other spirits milled in and out of the chamber, some wearing long silver sweaters that dragged in the dust at their feet.

"How'd she make so many?" Aggie asked.

"Apparently Ariadne's thread is infinitely long," murmured Hugh. "You know, Aggie," he said, taking on the tone of a professor, "everyone who ever died is down here somewhere." Then he shuddered. *Even the Old Ones. Zeus.*

Aggie gazed at the souls, her ponytail flopping over one shoulder, and her look of perky excitement changed to sorrow. "I just realized," she whispered. "Mom and Dad are down here somewhere. I never even thought about that. I might…I could…."

Had to go and make her an orphan, didn't I?

"Isn't it funny that I didn't even think of them?" she said.

"Wait here," Hugh said gruffly. "I'll see if I can find them."

Hugh turned into a lion and padded around the balcony, scenting for his family, peering into the dark corners of the land of the dead. The empty throne might not mean Hades wasn't alive and well and inspecting the reaches of his kingdom. The old god might be sneaking up on him even now. Hugh modulated his voice so only another god could hear him. "Adonis? Hades?" He waited. "Anyone?" There was no reply.

Aggie was moping over the balcony, scanning for the parents he'd killed in an imaginary plane crash when she was fifteen. She remembered being saved from a predatory uncle by an anonymous benefactor, who sent her to boarding school and paid for her film degree. Hugh planned a poignant scene later when he revealed, by accident, that he was her benefactor, that she was destined to be a world-class screenwriter, his chronicler.

He scanned the crowd for dead actors. He could get a couple to pretend they were Aggie's parents. *No*, he thought. *She might recognize them. Just distract her.*

"Scene," he said quietly. "The balcony gives way beneath Aggie, and she falls. I turn into a griffin, fly down, catch the back of her shirt, and land over by the thrones."

I'll do it live, he thought. *Make an entrance.*

"Did you find them?" she asked as he returned.

"Action," said Hugh, and he blew the balcony out from under her. She screamed and fell. Hugh transformed himself and gave chase. He swooped down and caught her, and her body swung against his chest, smashing the backpack between them. The smell of overwarm tuna from the sandwiches in her bag made him gag. Then Aggie's shirt tore and Hugh nearly lost his balance. He had to circle the chamber clumsily, struggling for control as Aggie howled and flailed in his jaws, before he landed on the dais in front of Marilyn.

Aggie's knees buckled as he changed himself back and helped her up. The last shreds of his shirt dropped to the floor and she threw herself against his bare chest, trembling. Her skin was icy. "You okay, Aggie?"

"Everyone's staring at us," she whispered.

The throne room was filling up with souls, pouring in from other chambers. They filed in silently, and he saw the chamber was growing to accommodate the eerie and emotionless gathering.

"Have you come to take the Throne?" asked Marilyn.

He shook his head. "I'm Entertainment," he said. "I came for you, Marilyn. You're going back." Her grip on her knitting needles tightened and a silent sense of ill will rolled through the crowd like bad weather, as if they were peasants at a tax proclamation.

A little girl stepped out of the ranks of assembled dead. "The Queen of the Underworld may only leave for part of the year," she said. "There is a precedent."

"Not so," Hugh said. "Persephone returned here only because she ate some fruit Hades gave her. Pomegranate seeds. Marilyn, you haven't eaten anything, have you?"

"Yes," she said calmly. "I had some apples the day I came."

She's lying. Hugh thought.

"Pause a sec," Aggie interrupted. "I ate some of that sandwich you gave me."

"That doesn't count." *If Marilyn returns to Hades each year it'll be a press sensation. Toni said I'd diminish these icons. An annual farewell scene will only make her bigger....* His train of thought was derailed by a yank on his arm.

"Do you see a grocery store around here, Hugh?" Aggie's voice was rising. He'd wanted her to have a bit of a temper. "Where do you think Hades got a pomegranate?"

"It wasn't from down here," Hugh insisted.

"You created the sandwich from the misty air near the Styx," said the little girl.

Aggie was staring up at the balcony. "Aggie, it doesn't matter," Hugh said.

"I can't see the way out anymore," Aggie said.

"Cut!" he yelled. "Scene. She didn't eat the sandwiches."

Aggie had not frozen. "What are you doing?"

I can't edit the past. Only what she remembers.

"I'm dead, aren't I?"

"Aggie," he said. *I could make her anew when I return,* he thought, *I could leave this one here and re-create her on the surface.* He looked at his delightful day-old baby. It would be as easy as copying a video.

But I came here to be a hero.

"Death by tuna fish," she said, slamming her pack to the floor. "I don't believe it."

"Aggie, I didn't know...."

"You dumb shit you got me killed!"

"Aggie, I know the way back. I can lead you out of here. Theseus got out, and Hercules, and Orpheus."

"I hope a Y chromosome isn't mandatory." Marilyn took her hand, and she subsided.

"I tell you, they just walked out. That's why we came, remember?"

"Sure," she said sullenly.

"I'll just collect the others," Hugh said, turning downstage. "I'm seeking some others," he said. "Martyrs of Entertainment." He told them the names and four shadows began pushing their way through the crowd. *It would be more efficient with seats and aisles,* Hugh thought, and he changed the dais into a proper stage, ranged theatre seats in the huge room. The dead began to sit down. They formed a dark sky, the silver sweaters twinkling like stars in chilly darkness. He sent light lions into the crowd, hoping the dispel the gloom, but their glow shriveled like vines under a blowtorch. The chosen spirits, unimpeded now, proceeded down the aisles to the stage.

"Where's the other one?" Hugh asked. He had carefully chosen his first six martyrs, selecting two movie stars, two rock stars, and two news stars. Buddy Holly shrugged and reached for his face, as if to push up the glasses that were no longer there. James Dean, President Kennedy, and Lee Harvey Oswald kept their eyes down and didn't answer.

Marilyn kept knitting. "Where's Presley?" Hugh asked.

Again that silent sense of a murmur running through the crowd, again no answer.

Aggie started to laugh. "He's not here," she said. "We haven't seen him."

"Where else would he be?" Hugh said, and then he groaned. *All those sightings. He must be over a hundred and thirty by now.* He could see the tab headlines. "Elvis Outsmarts God." Just last year Hugh swore he'd proved Presley was truly dead. If they found out he'd lied his ratings would plummet.

"Cut!" he boomed again, making a monumental effort and freezing them all. They weren't his subjects, and there were millions of them, but the dead were weak, and Entertainment's power was vast.

"Scene," he said. "Presley steps out of the crowd and begs to be allowed to stay. I try to change his mind, but he says 'I can't go back, I must stay and confront my…my impersonators as they pass through the Gate.' I nod regally. Presley disappears into some secret chamber of the Underworld, which is where he's been hiding all this time."

No way in hell is that faker going to grab my headlines this time. Julia might dig out the real story eventually, but maybe Hugh could arrange a cover-up. He still wasn't convinced Truth couldn't be bought. "Action," he said.

He watched as the crowd experienced the scene. Heads turned simultaneously toward one of the exits, then swiveled back toward him. Aggie sat cross-legged on the stage and fished a mashed sandwich out of her pack. Hugh waited for her to say he'd done the right thing. She bit into the mashed bread. Mayonnaise trickled down her chin. "How come Elvis gets to stay and Marilyn has to come?" she said, around a rank mouthful of fish.

"Aggie, don't pick at me. I warned you coming down here would be dangerous."

"You didn't say you were," she said. "Pardon me for feeling disillusioned."

"Aggie, you're not dead. You can walk out of here," he said. "Precedents exist!"

"What do you know? You couldn't even find my parents."

"Who?"

Aggie, still chewing, threw a leg out and kicked his shin.

Hugh dragged her back behind Hades's throne where they could talk privately, and he heard the clicking of Marilyn's needles as she resumed her knitting. "Listen, Aggie, I didn't want to tell you this, but you need to know how much you mean to me."

"You only met me this morning!"

Hugh shook his head. "Aggie, I'm the guy who funded your trust."

She stepped back, her hands clapped over her mouth, and gazed at him, making little moaning noises. He took her shoulders gently. Her frozen skin chilled his palms.

"Why would you do that?" she finally managed.

"I…" Hugh fumbled, and Aggie stared at him in horror. "You killed them."

"No," Hugh said.

"You did. You made the plane crash, and the trust was to buy off your guilt!" She tried to yank away, and Hugh could only hold her with brute force.

"No, no," he said, "Aggie, come on, calm down, listen."

She hammered at him with cold fists and sobbed but shed no tears. "It was probably just another dumb accident, like feeding me spiritually toxic tuna."

"Enough," he boomed. The floor of the dais shivered. "I didn't kill anyone."

"Then what?" she demanded. "Where are they? Why can't I see them?"

He turned toward the dark throne. "I never wanted to tell you this," he said.

"Please, Hugh," she said. Her voice was tight. "Cut the dramatics."

He told her.

He made it short, restraining the urge to overact, and she wilted like one of Persephone's trees and sank to the floor behind Marilyn's throne. "I'll give you some space," Hugh whispered, and stepped out to face the dead. *It's not too late to make her forget it all,* he mused. *I could erase everything, rewrite her anew.*

The crowd had not moved. *Maybe I can win these people over.* He addressed the little girl. "I came here planning to return two musicians to the waking world. Since Elvis is staying behind, I wonder if this assembly can suggest a musician?"

"Howard Ashman," she said.

"The guy who wrote songs for children's movies before the Ascendance?"

The child nodded.

At last something goes right. Not only would the media love it, but Hugh would be a mega-hero with the under-ten set, and Eliza was sure to be pleased. The Goddess of Childhood was always griping about the quality of kiddie entertainment.

"Well chosen," he said. To his surprise the crowd got to its feet as a slender man made his way to the stage to join the others. He was wearing a sweater so long it came over his feet and dragged behind him like the train of a wedding dress. Aggie came out from behind the throne and stood at quiet attention with the others.

"I'm sorry," Hugh said.

"I want to live," she mumbled. "Take me back and I'll write your screenplay." She reached out her hand, and Hugh accepted it. *I made her resilient,* he thought. *I told her to recover from shocks fast.* "Only if you want," he said. She wouldn't meet his eyes.

Hugh surveyed the crowd, wondering what kind of closing gesture he might make, and as they sat back down he was reminded of an audience after an ovation. "I'll be returning," he said. "In the meantime...."

He snapped his fingers and a huge screen unfurled itself from the balcony, rolling down to within a yard of the thrones. He plucked one of the reeking tuna sandwiches out of Aggie's backpack and turned it into a remote, handed it to the little girl. "There are homes where they call this 'the power of the universe,'" he said solemnly. She bowed and melted back into the crowd and the screen came alive, lighting their faces with a wall of silver static that reminded him of the sweaters.

"Channel Two has television listings," he said. There was no response. "Okay, you six, come on." He conjured an escalator to the balcony, transparent so everyone could still see the television, and attempted to usher them on to it.

None of them moved.

"Now what?"

"We can't leave unless the Ruler of the Underworld gives permission," Aggie said.

"There's no precedent for that," Hugh snapped. "People have escaped before."

"Before Hades died," Marilyn said, "he decreed we must await a new ruler. Nobody could leave until that ruler took his place."

"Finders keepers," Hugh said.

They looked at him blankly.

"I am ruler here." he said. "You six have leave to go." They did not move. "Concept time," he said. "Entertainment is Death. Death is Entertainment! Do as I say!"

A new shade, darker than the others, stepped to the front of the crowd. "You must take the throne," it said, and Hugh realized he was looking at the spirit of Hades himself.

Hugh assumed a stern mantle. "That's what I just did."

"You've got to ride the chair," Aggie said.

Hugh looked from the dead god to his erstwhile throne. "And if I can't?" he asked. A troubled expression slid over Aggie's face, a cloud rolling over the sun. "I'll die, won't I?"

He looked to the shadow for confirmation. "I'll die?" Hades nodded.

"Don't do it," Aggie said suddenly. She lifted her chin and crossed her arms over her chest. "It's not worth it."

"Oh Aggie," Hugh said. *This is what I get for telling you to be loyal, is it?* He swaggered to the chair and winked. "Just cast me as the reluctant hero."

"The one who comes through at the end? Hugh, you aren't strong enough!"

The shadow of Hades laughed. "Turn away, Pretender." He climbed onto the stage. "Your creature is right. You lack the strength to take this realm."

Hugh examined the throne. Persephone's throne had become dusty and decayed, but the seat of Death shone like brand new. It was gold and ivory, like teeth, and Hugh knew he couldn't play-act his way around this one. He ran a finger over one armrest, sensing the power in the chair, the challenge and deadly peril. Behind him, the dead rose in infinite ranks, all leaning forward on their seats, entangled by suspense. Aggie's lips were pressed together, and her freckles stood out on her pale face. What would a hero say to her?

"Don't worry, "Hugh said. "It'll take more than a brief fling with courage to finish me."

"Promise you'll go back to being a self-absorbed coward to-morrow," she whispered.

"There's a promise even I can keep." He kissed her forehead, and she clung to him until Hugh handed her over to Buddy and Howard, and then she closed her eyes. Hugh felt a little thrill of strength coming from her. Aggie was praying. *Praying for a hap-*

py ending.

Hugh sat on the Throne of Hades. The assembled dead started to clap, and as they climbed to their feet, applauding him, Hugh felt his heart stop.

A volcano erupted in his mind, a core of fire spewing images of death, all the deaths of all these people, and Hugh felt his powers failing as he tried to hang onto what he knew, his shallow world of starlets and script ventures and posing for magazine covers. The images burned it away, dispersing his strength, insisting that his followers feared death more than they loved him. The rightness of this assertion flowed through him. Wanting to do it for Aggie wasn't going to be enough.

"Did you believe you could assume the mantle of Death?" Hades boomed, and Hugh struggled to turn his eyes to the shadow. It was huge.

Draining my strength...trying to reassert his power.

"I only take what is mine," he shouted, projecting his voice past the dead god. The images cooled for a moment. "I am the heir of Zeus," Hugh cried to the dead. "I sprang from his bones long after your day had passed. I'm Hugh, God of Entertainment, and I...." Heat from the volcano dried the words in his throat.

"Entertainment," Hades scoffed. "Apollo's domain has nothing to do with this realm."

Hugh felt his body heating, burning, could envision himself losing, slipping off the throne to join the mindless crowd below. "You're out of touch," he screamed. "Death has changed. You can't run the franchise anymore!"

A moment of respite. The crowd was beginning to swing to his side. "Join us in awaiting my true heir, Entertainment." Hades's voice held a trace of uncertainty, and the heat from the throne lessened. It was no different from above. The worshippers were the ones he had to win.

Hugh scanned the demographics. Only a sliver of the massed dead were post-Ascendance. Most of them didn't know him. Worse, the fraction of the dead who were post-television was only slightly larger.

Big speech time, Hugh thought. He seized control of the screen and showed them death, the carnage on the freeways filmed for dinnertime news, the movies with bodycounts higher than entire small wars. "Death is celebrity homicide trials and assassinations on TV. It's dying celebs on the covers of the tabloids as they sneak out of the hospitals. It's true crime novels, videos of the latest military action, memorabilia from the homes of serial killers." He was running out of breath.

Hades stumbled in front of him. "What does he know of you?" he hissed, waving his arms. "What does he know of the dead? What has this to do with you?" The shadow reached for him, but Hugh knew how to answer that question, and he knew he had won.

"What do I know about the dead?" Hugh said. "Tell me one way my audience is different from yours." He took a second to time it and then switched channels with a snap of his fingers, using the last of his strength to throw it off with some flair. A commercial began.

The announcer's voice boomed out at them, and by the thousands the faces turned upward, first the new dead, the generations who were trained from birth to home in on the sound of a recorded voice. Then more and more of them looked.

"This is what the living come to me for," Hugh said to Hades. It wasn't just a pitch, either. Unable to pay attention to the gods onstage before them, the hosts of the dead watched the commercial play to its end. They waited, unmoving, as it gave way to the next. "They're all but dead before they come down here."

"The dead are weak," Hades said.

"Give me a crowd of the living and I can pull the same trick," Hugh told him.

Hades stepped back, faded into insubstantiality, and shrank. He wandered offstage, glancing backward from time to time to see what was happening on the screen. The crowd belonged to Hugh.

He tried to get his heart started again, but nothing happened. *It'll start up again whenever I'm aboveground,* he thought, clutching the arms of the throne. *Theseus got out, and Hercules, and Or-*

pheus. Somehow it wasn't as reassuring when it was himself, not Aggie, he was telling it to. But they walked out. That was all it took.

Should have expected it – to rule the dead, I'd have to be at least half-dead myself. The volcano in his mind was cooling to a manageable flow, a sense of the dead and dying.

Hugh felt a crowd of souls trapped behind the newly restored Acheron with no way across. *I'm going to have to build a bridge or reinstate Charon.* He could sense the Old Ones, too, mixed into the crowd, watching the commercials. They were faint and faded shadows, fortunately, lacking the strength to walk out of Hades, to reemerge into life. Hades was now the weakest of all of them.

Hugh reached for his surface worshippers, checking to make sure he hadn't lost Entertainment when he took over the Underworld. Wealth had a rule about swapping franchises, and she'd deep-fry him over this stunt in any case. But the execs and producers and actors were still feeding him power. New projects caught his attention: a docudrama on cancer, a movie about a coroner.

I did it, Hugh thought. His eyes had adjusted to the dark, and he could count the souls in the amphitheater. In the Elysian fields, the winds still blew sweet air over the just, but the riverbeds were choked with overgrown grass and the soil was turning swampy. The diamond gate of Tartarus was wrenched open. The dried bodies of two Titans, slain by each other, lay by the gate of the triple-walled prison for evil-doers.

Hey, if I could renovate Tartarus and the fields I could assemble a tribunal. There must be lots of dead judges down here. We could broadcast judgments of the newly deceased as they came through the Gate. Won't that get me some ratings!

He was starting to feel like his old self. Almost.

"Hugh?"

Aggie had crept to the edge of the throne. Her face was still pale as marble, but her blood would warm again when she got out into the sun. "Hell of an audition," he said. He reached to touch her chin and she pulled away.

"Are we getting out of here?" she asked.

"You are." He angled his head to include the others. "You all have leave to depart."

"You're not coming?" Aggie asked.

"Well," he said, eyeing his cooling fingers. "I want to spruce things up around here a bit. Put in a sports lounge and a movie theatre."

"Are you sure...."

"I'll be up soon," he said brightly. "Awards season by the latest. You get an agent and get started on the screenplay, and when I've got a fax put in you can send it down."

She stared at him for a long time, her freckles like constellations on her milky face. "I'll bring it to you," she said at last. "I have to come back anyway. The tuna. Precedents."

"That's my girl." He got up and put his arm across her shoulders, leading her to the escalator. The men followed, Buddy and Jim in the lead, JFK and Oswald side by side.

Howard's sweater trailed in the dust of Persephone's throne as he brought up the rear.

"Aggie here will lead you up to the surface," Hugh said to them. He reached down and pried the knitting bones from Marilyn's iron grip, and the light went out of her face.

"They'll be here when you get back," he told her, and she shuffled after the others, heading up to the balcony and from there to the waiting world.

A.A. Attanasio is the mystic poet of science fiction. Mixing strong magics, the moral dimensions of reality and quantum mechanics produces a strange, smoking brew guaranteed to open the third eye.

THE DARK ONE: A MYTHOGRAPH
A. A. Attanasio

"Time is thingless," the old sorcerer told his last disciple. "Yet, you are about to see the source of it."

Tall, gaunt and completely bald, the sorcerer stood against the night dressed in straw sandals and a simple white robe. Narrow as a wraith, his raiment glowing gently in the starlight on the steep cliff above the temple city, he seemed about to blow away.

The disciple, a blue-eyed barbarian boy named Darshan, knelt before him on his bare knees, the hem of his kilt touching the ground. He lowered his face and closed his eyes. Whatever curiosity he had for why his masters, the priests, had awakened and brought him here stilled momentarily in the chill desert air, and he awaited his fate with expectant submission.

"Look at me!" the old man demanded, his voice resonant among the vacancies of the cliffs.

Darshan lifted his gaze hesitantly toward the withered figure and saw in the slim light that the sorcerer was smiling. He had a face as hewn as a temple stone, and it was a strange experience for the boy to find a friendly smile in that granite countenance. During the four years that Darshan had served as floor-scrubber and acolyte at the Temple of the Sun, he had seen the sorcerer often in the royal processions and ceremonies – but the haughty old man had always appeared in public garbed in cobra-hood mantle and plumed headdress. Now he was bare-shouldered, his skeletal chest exposed, reptilian flesh hanging like throat frills from his jaw.

"Why are you here?" the old man asked.

"The priests of Amon-Re sent me, Lord."

"Yes – they sent you. Because I ordered them to. Do you know who I am?" He peered at the boy, the whole immense dark sky glistening in his eyes.

"Lord, you are the supreme vizier. The man of the high places."

"Yes. That is who I am." He stood taller, stretched out his bony arms, and spoke in a flat voice: "Supreme vizier of the People, counsel to kings, master sorcerer." Without warning, he sat down in the dust, and Darshan's shock at the sight of the holy man squat-legged on the ground almost toppled him. He had to touch the earth with one hand to stay on his knees. The sorcerer's sagacious grin thickened. "And you are Darshan. I know, for I am the one who sent the ships to seek you."

Darshan leaned back under the weight of his puzzlement.

"Well, not you specifically," the sorcerer added, hunching his frail body under the night. He looked tiny. "Just a child, boy or girl, *any* child so long as it was wild and not of the People. The child had to belong to no one. You are the one they found."

Darshan thought back, remembering the few fleeting memories and scraps of idle speculation an old priest had once offered him of his young, insignificant life. He had been born on a moor in a northern land, in a bracken hovel with many mouths for the wind to sing through. His birthmother had been an outcast from her clan, exiled for madness, but sane enough in the way of animals to survive on the wind-trampled heath.

His first memory was of her smell – a bog musk, creaturely, hot. Even now, he was fond of the fragrance of rain-wet fur. His second memory was of her telling him that she had never known a man. She had told him this many times, her simple speech gusty with fervor, saying it over and over again until she had become as redundant as the lamentations of the wind. To the day she died trying to cross an iced river, she had moved and talked in a frenzied rush. Ranting about never knowing a man, about beast eyes in the sky, about the smell of darkness in the sun-glare, and the thunder of hooves when the wind stilled, clearly she had been mad. He had realized this only years later, living among the People, though at that time, when he had first begun to reflect on his life, he knew nothing of madness, only that his mother had been true in her devotion to him, and he to her.

In his seventh winter, she fell into the river and vanished under the ice, all in an instant, right before his eyes. Standing three feet behind her, he had been attentive only to the twine net where she carried their next meal, a dead badger, the blood not yet frozen on its head where she had stoned it. That was the last he saw of her, the dead creature caught for an instant at the broken edge of ice. He remembered clutching for it and it jumping from him, sliding into the black water as though it were yet alive.

After she was gone, he had survived only because he had pretended she was still with him, instructing him what to do. With the thaw, he had followed the river, looking for her body. He never found her. The corpses of animals still frozen or caught in the floods kept him alive. Moving with the river, he never went back.

He had stayed in the wilderness, avoiding contact with all people, and he had moved south to escape the winter that had killed his mother. For two years he had stayed hidden, and then on a rocky coast by a sun-brassed sea, he saw his first boats. He didn't know what they were. He had thought them to be great floating beasts. He could not see that they were carrying men until they had spotted him also. He had fled, but the men had horses and cunning, and eventually they found him hiding in a tide cave.

Taken as a slave and brought to this great kingdom of the south, at first, he had behaved like a caught animal – but his ferocity had been matched by the awe he felt for his captors. Their kingdom was a fabulous river valley of boats, armies, slave-hordes, and immense stone temples.

Many of the slaves were driven to labor like beasts – yet the boy himself was never beaten. He was employed by the priests as a floor-scrubber, and in return he was fed well, clothed, and bunked with the young students of the temple. They had given him a name, and eventually he had learned their language and their ways.

And now, four years later and a lifetime wiser, here he was under the smoldering stars with the kingdom's supreme vizier – a man too holy to stare at directly, too divine to touch earth – an old man sitting in the dust beside him and telling him not only that he was aware of the boy's lowly presence but that he had in fact ordered his capture! The thought filled Darshan with dread, for he had delighted in his anonymity. Being chosen implied a mission, and he had neither the desire nor the belief in himself to think he was capable of doing anything heroic for these great people.

"Do you know why I sent for you?" the sorcerer asked with a glimmering intensity.

"No, lord," the boy replied, peering at him from the sides of his eyes.

"You are to take my place." Another smile tautened the waxy flesh across the old man's skull-face, and he hissed with small, tight laughter when he saw the boy's look of utter incredulity. "Believe me, I am not toying with you. Nor am I mad. You will have plenty of time to get used to being a sorcerer. Time, that thingless word – there is plenty of that."

The boy's hands opened futilely before him. "I am but a slave –"

"So it seems to the present generation. But you will outlive them and their grandchildren and their grandchildren's great-grandchildren."

At the boy's gasp, another of the old man's smiles flickered in the darkness. "I am not speaking symbolically, Darshan. I do not mean your works will outlive them – for you shall do no works." His voice assumed a ritual cadence. "Symbols are a substitute for works. Works are a substitute for power. Power resides in the stillness. That is the secret of the universe."

Truly, Darshan thought, *the vizier is mad!* He dared not voice that doubt. Rather, he mustered his courage to say, "I do not understand, lord."

The sorcerer moved closer and put a dry hand on the boy's shoulder. A coldness flowed from it. "Speak to me about what you do not understand."

Darshan shivered. Words came quickly into his head but moved slowly to his mouth. "Lord, I am but a barbarian. I am a child, and from the Outside. I am nothing."

"And so power resides in you." The sorcerer's hand squeezed the boy's shoulder with a firm gentleness, and the cold brightened. "Speak."

"Lord, I do not understand what power would reside in a worthless outsider."

"The power you are made empty to receive." The hand on Darshan's shoulder became ice, and when it lifted away blue fire sheathed it.

A scream balked in the boy's throat, hindered by the benignity of the sorcerer's expression.

"You see?" the old man chuckled. "The power is already leaving me and going to you."

Rainbow light flowed like smoke from the upheld hand and coiled toward Darshan's face. He pulled away, horrified, and the spectral vapor shot at him like a cobra, striking him between the eyes.

Cold fire paralyzed the boy, and his vision burst into a tunnel of infalling flames and shadows. The rush stalled abruptly, and, in an instant, the desert skyline vanished and the span of night deepened. Sun feathers lashed the darkness, ribbons of starsmoke furling into the reaches of the night.

"This is the raith," the sorcerer's voice lit up within him. "This is the Land of the Gods!"

Together, wordlessly, they advanced among rivers of light that poured like bright fumes into a golden sphere of billowy energy. A dissolving sun, the sphere radiated pollen sparks in a slow flux against the blackness. Each spark was the surface of a mirror, the other side of which opened into a biological form.

"Touch one," the sorcerer commanded, and when the boy did as he was told, he found himself inside the grooved sight of an antelope bounding through white grass. Touching another, he was among writhing fish.

"Life. All of it." The sorcerer's voice pulled Darshan away from touching another spark. "I am not taking you there. But once you establish yourself where we are going, all of this is yours." The weltering surface of the gold sphere spun serenely before them in the haze of its rendings.

They drifted away from it, across spans of darkness vapory with fire. Alternating ice winds and desert blasts looped over their raith-senses. For a long time, they soared, pummeled by brutal gusts, until they burst into a darkness set at the back of the stars.

Darshan's flight stopped abruptly, and stillness seized him. He floated, alertly poised at the crystalcut center of clarity, so still that empty space itself seemed to writhe like a jammed swarming of eels. Flamboyant bliss saturated him. This was the top of the eagle's arc, the fish's leap, the peak of noon extending forever.

Immovable as the darkness of space, Darshan exulted. His life had suddenly become too miniscule to remember. The life of the People, too, had become the fleetest thought. Even the stones of their temples and tombs were breathing, their packed atoms shivering and blowing against the gelatinous vibrations of dark space.

Awe pierced the boy with the sudden realization that the tumult of life, of existence itself, was far apart from him. He had become absolutely motionless.

Yet, with that very thought, the spell ended, and he found himself immediately back in his body on his knees before the aged sorcerer. With painful reluctance, Darshan peered about. The clamor of stars and the stink of dust nauseated him. He closed his eyes and groped inside himself for the eagle's poise.

"That stillness is your power," the sorcerer said in an urgent voice that made Darshan open his eyes. The old man's face glittered with tears. "It lies at the heart of everything." He gestured at the temples' torchlights and the lanterns and lamps of the city that shone in the dark valley like spilled jewels. Then, he looked up at the dangling stars. "Even the gods."

The barbarian boy gazed at the old man with unabashed amazement. "Then why is this stillness no longer yours?"

The sorcerer swelled closer, expansive in his joy, and he took Darshan's chilled hands in his icy ones and shook them with the emphasis of his words: "It *chose* me – as it now chooses you!" His voice hushed confidentially. "Ten thousand years ago, in a region that we presently call Cush, I, too, was an orphan, as you are, a savage, alone with the wilderness. Wholly by chance, as happened to you, I was led to the master of stillness who had come before me. He was thousands of years old then, as I am now. He had found his fulfillment after millennia of grounding the stillness in time. That thingless word. Thingless for those such as we who have known the stillness. It is only the combat of the gods that makes time a thing for everyone else. Time is the dimension of the gods' battlefield. Their clashes for dominance stir people's hearts with dreams. Those dreams, in turn, frenzy into ideas: tools are discovered, animals domesticated, royalty invented, religion, sacrifices, war. Now, even cities are called into being." Tears gleamed silvery in the creases of his broad grinning. "Who cares? I certainly don't. My time is up. I have lived the stillness – right here in the middle of the battlefield! I have seen the gods aspire. I have seen generations sacrificed to their grand schemes. A great empire has risen from the red dust. The People think their empire will live forever. But I tell you, you will see all this as dust again and all the People forgotten. Only the gods will go on. The dreaming will continue. Other empires will appear and disappear among the battling gods. You alone, alone as you have always been, will live the stillness – an enemy to the gods. For you alone, time will be thingless, for you will know the source of it. You will have been inside the mother of the gods. You will have the power to live the stillness."

Darshan was thirteen years old that night when the sorcerer, sitting in the dust, spoke to him. Nothing in his four years of scouring temple floors had prepared him for it. The priests who had sent him to the sorcerer had wondered about that meeting; some had leered, suspecting lewdness. The sorcerer himself soon disappeared mysteriously. Yet the boy went on scrubbing floors. And the raith went on dreaming him.

After that night, however, the work became immeasurably easier. Body dazzling with a vigor he mistook for approaching manhood, Darshan excelled at sports. And he astonished even the arrogant lector-scribes with his mental stamina as he absorbed evcrything they dared teach him.

Several years later, the raith's dream shifted, and Darshan became a certifiable wonder, the countenance of the gods, the boy who never aged. The priests worshipped him. Warlords offered tribute. Every difficulty in the region required his assuaging presence.

For a long time, Darshan prayed to the gods to restore his former life. But his prayers had no wings. The king learned of him, and he was removed from the temple and taken upriver to the royal city. There, he became a child-divinity sent by the gods to affirm the ancestral sorcery of the kings. Life became a ceremony of walled gardens, incense-tattered rooms and banquets. Twice a year, he was portaged into the green of the fields to release a falcon that carried the prayers of the People to the sun god. Well-being clouded about him like an electric charge, and he was revered by the aristocracy even as the court aged and their tombs were built.

The years flowed by, and he grew wise on the dying of others. He took wives who bore his children, and he loved them all with sentimental delirium. His family shared riverboat mansions and superficialities, all of life's caprices, as they aged beyond him and shriveled away. He took younger wives and had more children. And all the while, he blessed the People and the riverland, and the kingdom prospered. He himself did not know how. He had forgotten the words of the sorcerer. He thought he was a child-god.

Three kings and a century later, with his first grandchildren's grandchildren older than he, he had aged a year. His body was fourteen years old.

Not until he was seventeen and two dynasties had risen and collapsed did he begin to remember. Dreams were ephemera. Families, kings, dynasties were ghosts, incidental to the emptiness in which they teemed. Another six hundred years of orchard gardens and ripening families and he saw through to this truth.

He gave up family life. Rubbed smooth like a river stone after spawning forty generations of sons and daughters, children who grew up to be wives, warriors, queens, merchants, priestesses, all fossils now, and even their children fossils, he felt carnal desire slide away from him. He wanted no more lovers or children, and the machinations of power bored him.

For the next thousand years, he retreated into anonymity, seeking unity with the People. In various guises, he wandered the earth seeking experience and knowledge. Eventually, the dreams themselves began to wear thin for Darshan. Experience turned out to be suffering. Knowledge was boundaries.

After long centuries of striving, Darshan finally accepted that he was no godling; he was a ghost. He returned to the river kingdom where the cursed gift had come to him. He searched for the sorcerer and after many years found him — not in the world but in his dreaming.

The sorcerer came to him one evening at sea. Darshan, serving on a freight boat hauling giant cedar timbers from the eastern forests back to the kingdom, dozed in a cord hammock slung between the prow and a shaggy log. Through half-lidded eyes, he stared ahead at the rinds of daylight in the west until sleep swelled in him and the raith uncurled.

All at once, his body unfurled and he found himself rushing headlong through windy darkness and fuming leakages of light. A gold sphere swirled before him veiled in a misty flotage of sparks. His flight slowed, and he hung among the tiny pieces of light until he remembered this vision from hundreds of lifetimes back, from his one short interview with the sorcerer long ago.

The sun-round glare inside the starmist was Re, the god of his first learning. This was the creator immersed in its creation, each gempoint of the endless glittering a mind. The fulgurant light blazed with all being. And the drift of the sparks, stately as clouds, revealed the invisible spiral of time.

A religious hush thrummed to a droneful music in Darshan's bones. Here was deity! Here was the source of his own unreckonable fate. He knew that he had to keep his wits about him and remember everything of this great darkness fizzling with scattered light. This was the place that his teacher had called the raith.

Smoldering hulks of color and brightness fumed against the utter black. These, he recognized as the gods with their gloaming abstract bodies. All he had to do was stare at them to feel who they were: the crimson smoke and slithering banners of War, the green simmering vibrations of Plants, the surging floral hues of Sex, the ruffling blue flow of River, endless gods arrayed in smoky radiance as far as he could see.

All being burns! he marveled, drifting through the blaze, awed by the apparently random yet balanced pattern of the raith. Alongside the red feathered energy of War drizzled the violet realm of the dead. And above it all shone the blue depths of Peace.

He descended into the gray flutter of the dead with the image of the sorcerer firmly in his mind. Many familiar faces rose toward him through the trickling light, the shivering shapes of all his families, all the lovers and children who had lived ahead of him into death. They tangled like entrails, shifted like weather, speaking to him in hurt voices not their own. He recognized then the filthy fate of the dead. They were melting into each other! They were dissolving and being reabsorbed into the swirl of tenuous light.

Some of the dirty light drifted in a haze of limbs and faces toward the blue embers of Peace. Some smoked toward the red ranges of War. The rest dithered in human shapes.

Darshan lifted away, soaring over the gray pastures of snaggled bodies. The sorcerer wasn't among the dead. The sorcerer had belonged to the dark spaces and not the light. Just as he had said.

Darshan expanded into the dark, and the gold sphere of Re in its aura of sparkling lives loomed into view. But now only the darkness enwombing the light seemed real. He flung himself into the emptiness.

His eyes shattered, his atoms flew apart. He disappeared.

But the wind of the emptiness whirled all his parts together and blew him back into alertness. Stunned, he hung in the raith-dark before the fiery mist of Re – and the words of the sorcerer returned to him: 'You alone, alone as you have always been, will live the stillness – an enemy to the gods.'

Darshan woke up. He was still a young sailor on a cargo boat freighted with cedars sailing into the night. He was still a man with a thousand years of memories. But the memories were weightless in the expansive silence. The night sea would become a dawn landfall. The cedars, faithful to their doom, already lived as rafters and pillars on their way to the termite's ravenous freedom or an enemy's torch. And the cargo boat would find its way to the bottom of the sea and give its shape to a vale of kelp and polyps. And the young sailor would weary of the sea and be forgotten. And Darshan, too, would be forgotten, swept away in the great migrations of Asian tribes that swarmed across Europe and North Africa a millennium before Christ.

He roamed among the different peoples, unseen, or seen in a peaceable light. The stillness threading through his eyes and pores and atom-gaps protected him: Its lack drew energy to him wherever he was, and the energy was health, ample food, treasures, and the fealty and love of others. Despite this abundance, he felt nothing for others. He felt nothing but serene emptiness. And when he did somehow fall in love with someone or a cause, the stillness vanished, and he was left hungering and at the mercy of others.

Sometimes even that was good. Though he had exhausted every kind of living during his first thousand years in the river kingdom, he was occasionally nostalgic for passion. And he was still aging a year for every century. Hence, even he was aware of his mortality. Pain and peril, too, had their appetites for him. More of the gods' dreaming.

Darshan had never been seriously ill or injured. The stillness protected him. The mangling forces ignored him even when he was stupid with his passions.

As a wanderer, he never thought much about his fate. Often, he surged into trances, swooping through the abysses of the raith, trembling with the malice and insane love of the gods until he could stand no more, and then plunging into utter black nothing.

He cohabited with a dim awareness that he served some function for the stillness. The old sorcerer had spoken of grounding the stillness in time. But at the time that he had heard this, rational thought had not been one of the gods feeding off of him.

Darshan lived his fate as a watcher, letting the ubiquitous nothing appear before him as anything at all. His personality changed with his name and place. For more than a century, he lived as a wealthy Phoenician purple manufacturer, hiring a complex of villages to harvest the banded dye-murex and create the most demanded color in the world.

After that, he dwelt alone on the barren, wind-cumbered coasts of the Orkneys for two centuries, living off nettles and fish, sleepy and holy in the amplitude of winter.

Then, yearning company, he went south and wandered through Europe as a seer with the Celtic hordes.

At the time of the Buddha, he was a twenty-eight year old warrior prince in Persia. Five centuries later, he wandered with the gypsies through the Balkans when Christ was in Jerusalem. Another three hundred years and he was among the gangs that toppled Rome.

Once, he sailed with a Palestinian crew across the Atlantic and lived for several more centuries as a nomad in the jungles, deserts and grasslands of the western continents. He was at the crestpoint of the falcon's dive, suspended in time almost wholly timeless.

The nothing became well grounded in him. His very poise within the seething temporality grew steady enough that it created a pattern in the raith. Over his twenty-five centuries on earth, his power in the hidden reality had grown sufficiently resonant to match the harmonies of the masters of stillness who had come before him.

Wrapped in the skin of a jaguar, shivering on a mountain scarp in the Andes, his sacrifice fulfilled itself. The mind of the dark spaces entered him, and his surrender became total. Now, he was the Dark One. Made of light slowed down to matter like everyone else, he had given all of himself to nothing like no one else. Given? More like taken. He had been chosen from among the rays of creation by the space that the rays cut. He had become the wound, the living nothing.

Curious about the old world, he returned to Europe with the Norsemen who had been sent by their Christian king to Greenland to spread the gospel, and whom a storm had carried west to Vinland. Europe in the High Middle Ages reminded him of the river valley kingdom where his power had begun. There, the temple of Amon-Re had competed with feudal lords for control of the domain. Here, the papacy served as the temple and the warlords remained the same, only the trappings had changed.

He wandered nameless for a long time as the power within him continued making its connections between earth and raith. He was a tinker, a minstrel, a carnival clown. His raith dreams fell into darkness. He entered the space between the enmeshing archons, the interstice of being and non, between the stars and the buried – where the Dark One watched.

When the dreams of the gold sphere in its mist of sparks began again, he was a Danish village's latrine ditch keeper, mulching the sewage with forest duff for use on the fields. The Dark One's thoughts began thinking him. Always before, there had been living and silence – the living given, thick with health and stamina, the silence bright with raith light and comfort. Now, there was something new. Thoughts began crystallizing out of the inner dark. He needed a wide space of time in which to simply sit and face the immensity of them, so he went into the mountains and let his dreams lead him to gold. Afterward, he settled in Italy, where he established himself as a wealthy nobleman from the north.

Sitting in his enclosed garden in Firenze, guarded from the outside world by courtyards and loggia, he opened himself to the clear music of thoughts emerging from the raith. The archons of precision and rational thought, simultaneously hampered and encouraged by the archon of war, had begun fusing into the complex of science.

Initially, he did not see the point of it at all. Advances in boat design increased his revenues as a merchant, but that wealth was offset by advances in weaponry, which intensified the civil wars and cost him several of his estates. Nonetheless, he remained opened to the thought-shaping patterns that the Dark One was thinking.

He was very good at being the stillness by this time. Everything floated through him: his body, his very awareness. The archons of protein synthesis and digestion, of ever-shifting emotions and thoughts, created him. The archons of wealth and poverty, power and impuissance, governed him. He was the battlefield of the gods.

The most powerful of all the gods was the Dark One – the uncreated and uncreating. More than a destroyer or death and its dissolvings. Void.

He began thinking about the Dark One. He wondered about its source and end, and who he was in that synapse, hemidivine, living centuries as years, free of disease, protected from accidents....

Over time, before the profound and absolutely immutable flow of generations, his memories and rationalities froze into constellations as coldly distant and immutable as stars.

Empires crossed Europe like shadows of the shifting stars. Science invented itself. By 1700, the Dark One had established a trading company in London, and he called himself Arthur Stilmanne. Privately, he funded research in every branch of science. A way was becoming clear. After aeons, a way was opening.

The sorcerer returned among the black gulfs of the raith. Almost four thousand years after he had initiated Darshan as an embodiment of the nothing, the old man reappeared in a raith dream. His body loomed out of the astral dark bound in shroudings. That, Arthur knew from his years of symbol-gazing in the raith, meant his master's limbs, his extension into the four dimensions, were restrained – he belonged to the void. But the sorcerer's head was clear – his knowledge and intent were accessible. His bald head gleamed in the gray light like a backlit bacterium: His knowing shone radiantly, suffused with the living energy of the void.

Arthur willed himself to touch the specter. Immediately, a voice came to him whose familiarity twitched in him like his own nerves: "Darshan, you have served the stillness well. The centuries have emptied you, and now you are full of your own power." The sorcerer's face pressed closer in the dream, gloomy with sleep, his stare an aching wakefulness. "Who are you?" the old visage asked.

Arthur responded instantly, "The Dark One."

A breath slipped from the sorcerer's pale lips, "It is so." And his countenance slackened with stupor.

After that encounter, Arthur's mind turned in on itself. The constellations of his long-thinking connected, looping into the veins and arteries of a body of knowledge. He saw himself finally as a response to the dialectic of life. Others just like he was now had existed before, randomly selected organisms, each metaordered not by life but by an intelligence equal and opposite to life.

Newton's work on vector forces inspired him. He had been given a shape by emptiness so that he might bring all shapes back to emptiness. Guided by Leibniz's exploration of the binary system of Asian philosophy, he began thinking of himself as a dot of ordered chaos in a world of chaotic order. His mission became clear. He and all the others who had preceded him had come to end existence. But how could that be?

During the nineteenth century, Stillman Trading Company flourished, and he kept himself moving around the continent to obscure the fact that he was continually succeeding himself as his own son. Arthur Stillman VI, of Victoria's Britain, poured vast sums into biological research, believing the insane rush of evolution could be ended by a virulent plague hostile to all forms of life. Not until Arthur Stillman VIII and the quantum research of the early twentieth century did he realize – with an authoritative irony – that the weapon he sought was not in the world but in the atoms of the world.

Arthur learned more about himself and the nature of reality in the last forty years than he had in the previous four thousand. The means to exterminate life and end the four-billion-year-old torment had emerged on its own. Arthur had done nothing to anticipate or promote it.

Reflecting on that, he came to see that he had never had any real influence on history. He was inert, like a stone time had swallowed; he would eventually be voided. Inside the stone was a secret silence. Some zen monks had alluded to it. But all others kept it hidden, even from themselves. He stayed close to that silence, and everything came to him.

In the mid-twentieth century, death itself came to Arthur Stillman, approaching closer than ever before. Accidents stalked him. A milk bottle teetered off a windowledge nine stories above his head and smashed at his feet. Lightning punched through the roof of his house and blasted the reading lamp at his bedside. On the highway, a tire exploded and sent him hurtling helplessly off the road and into a forest, where his car erupted into a fireball the instant after he was hurled through the windshield. During his six week hospital stay, mix-ups in medication nearly killed him twice.

Arthur understood that he had an enemy powerful enough to break the stillness that had protected him for several thousand years. Somewhere, lightworkers had begun working very hard indeed to destroy the Dark One. He knew why. Science had become his latest, most deadly weapon, and if the lightworkers did not stop him now, he would soon have the technology to destroy all of creation.

"Science," he became fond of saying as the apocalyptic promise of the millennium approached yet again, "is heavy enough to bend all paths toward it into circles. We'll never understand it all, never reach the center of omniscience. But we've circled close enough to science, to objective knowledge, to realize that all that we thought we knew about reality we can throw away. With science, the human spirit stands with the creator spirit in the grave of everything that came before, in the midden heap of religion and superstition, on the dunghill of all past cultures. Science reveals the truth of things as they always were, to the beginning and the end. Science creates with a beauty as ancient as we are new."

Arthur burned with a passion for science, because it explained to him his singularity and his origin. From biologists, who studied the DNA differences in the mitochondria of people from all over the world and who traced human lineage back to one female ancestress hundreds of thousands of years ago, he came to accept the importance of his uniqueness. As Eve had mothered the mutants who would evolve into war-frenzied humans, he would father the energies that would return them all to nothing.

From physicists, who discovered that the four dimensions people experienced were actually projections of other compacted dimensions in a space smaller than 10^{-33} centimeter, he found the raith. The radii of curvature of all the dimensions except the familiar four of spacetime were smaller than atoms – in fact, smaller than the grain of spacetime itself. In that compact region, spacetime quantized, that is, space and time separated into realms of their own. That he knew had to be the raith, where ubiquitous archons floated timelessly and evolving beings extended into endless distances.

Science even explained his existence. He had emerged as a side-product of a symmetry event: Particles appeared spontaneously in the void all the time, leaking out of the vacuum, out of nothing, but always in pairs – electrons and positrons, negative and positive, existing separately for an interval, then annihilating each other. He was one of those particles, compelled into existence by the appearance of his opposite. The other was light itself, never still, energizing endless forms and activities.

He was the Dark One, yearning for quiescent timelessness. Light was the many. He was the one. Light was life. He was death.

To amplify his power in the raith, Stillman began creating power cells of human minds entrained to his will. He built a groupmind that he could control. There was no dearth of material. Authorized as a psychiatrist by the finest medical institutions in the States, where he had effortlessly earned numerous degrees in medicine, psychopathology, and neural chemistry, he used his multibillion dollar trust to found Stillman Psychiatric Hostels. The hostels were free of charge and open to anyone with a mental health problem, with or without insurance.

By the mid-fifties, Arthur had a hostel in each state and dozens overseas, all of them packed. He hired the best qualified staff at competitive salaries, and many hundreds of people benefited. Hundreds of others were personally attended to by Arthur himself, who used drugs and hypnosis to open their psychic centers to his preternatural will. Once a subject had been treated by Arthur, that persona bonded to the Dark One in the raith. They never recuperated.

When the accidents began, Arthur knew that he was closing in on the means to destroy creation. He knew that by using his powerful group mind to feed power to the archons of war and chaos in the raith, he had alerted lightworkers across time and space to the real threat of his presence.

His true archenemies, he knew, were the progenitors of the world's lightworkers – the cave masters. They were the first humans who, a hundred thousand years ago and more, had learned to enter the raith and identify with the radiant diamondshape of the original light, the creation fire in its first instant out of the singularity that had birthed the cosmos. Their initial link with this first force, when all things were pure light, spanned time. The cave masters' early spells had revealed the secrets of fire, songdances, healing, and – as their raith-work widened through the ages – stoneworking, planting and the wondrous mystery of metals with its powers of purity and combination. Their identification with the light and action pitted them firmly against the vacuum in which the light expanded and cooled into the shapes of all things and made them the natural nemesis of the Dark One.

Time, that thingless word, was an illusion. Arthur learned that in the twentieth century and began to use that potent knowledge to reach across time and strike directly at his enemies with his raith power. And they, in turn, strove to reach forward into their future and destroy him before he annihilated them and all the dreamwork humanity had made of the cold light in the void of space.

But subversive attacks against the Dark One in the raith were useless, for the Dark One was dark – he belonged to the black spaces, and no one could see him if he did not want to be seen. To be effective, the lightworkers had to focus their attack in the physical world. And so they employed zombies, humans already dead, lost to the world, whom they re-animated with their raith strength and sent to hunt down the Dark One.

Arthur had killed a dozen zombies in the last four decades. More than all he had killed in the previous four millennia. Always in the past, he had been protected. No archon could hold him for long without the reflexes of the Dark One intervening. Pirates, bandits, armies had ambushed him in every age, and his life had pulsed at the edge of a knife many times. Every time, he retreated into the raith, merged with the darkness, and left whatever archons were threatening him alone with their thunder.

In the physical world, furious minds suddenly became blithely becalmed, armies and ferocious gangs befuddled, confronted by the echoes of their own enmity, and left quivering together with drooling fear. He had almost always managed to get away without taking life. When he killed, it was strictly for advantage. Even the subtlest assassins remained frustrated by the Dark One's relentless awareness of the archons impinging on him, especially the killing shapes in the raith that came with poisons and hidden weapons. He saw them all before they saw him. He was invulnerable – until the cave masters came for him.

The zombies – or, as the cave masters called them, the adepts – found their way to him in the world and then attacked him in the raith. By distracting his raith-self, they had several times come close to destroying his physical body. But with each assault, the Dark One grew more clever. He learned about the cave masters, and he discovered how to use their adepts as conduits into the far past, where he could strike directly at the extinct race whose intelligence continued fostering civilization through the raith. If the cave masters had their way, war, disease, even involuntary death would be abolished. The human genome project existed because of their hope to shape healthier, more intelligent people. With the help of the lightworkers, humans could eventually carry their archons to the stars, and then the dreaming would never end. The torment for him and those like him who embodied the dark would be forever.

The latest adept began as an eighteen-year-old soldier killed in Viet Nam, restored to life twenty-five years ago by the cave masters and carefully trained as a raith-warrior in a fastness hidden in the Himalayas. He was a dangerous adversary. Yet this sword cut both ways. Here was another chance to push deep into the Ice Age when cortical complexity reached its peak with the large-brained Neanderthals, the first humans to enter the raith. Once there, he could kill the human drive before it began.

That, of course, depended on using this adept correctly. The Dark One had become proficient at sensing the vast power required to return a corpse to life. The symmetry law that had created the Dark One also allowed only one zombie to exist at a time, and there was never any doubt for Arthur when the cave masters selected that time. Usually a blur of dizziness cued him to the process. A mess of vertigo flung him into a chair the day this zombie was resurrected.

Before Arthur learned of the cave masters, he killed the zombies swiftly. With this one, though, he went to some trouble. Through the raith, he learned of the boy's former life in Indiana, and he cultivated a relationship with the zombie's old sweetheart, Eleanor Chevsky, a word processor, divorced and with no children, whom he hired to work for his mental health foundation. She was five-ten, a natural blonde whose gray eyes had a slight slant, as though she were part Asian or up to some mischief. Voluminously bosomed and globe-bottomed as any goddess, she caught the fancy of most of the men and the envy of many of the women in the main office, who assumed her rapid promotion to Stillman's personal data manager had little to do with her computer skills.

In fact, Arthur's relationship with Eleanor was solely business, a job that situated her where Arthur could watch her and wait for her dead lover to return for her. Not that Arthur wasn't sexually attracted to her himself. Over the ages, his sex drive waned and flourished in long, arhythmic cycles. Lately, since the revelation of atomic weapons, his sexual appetite had been insatiable. But he denied himself Eleanor – for the time being. He needed her working in the world and accessible – a lure for the adept.

Arthur was sly enough not to make her too accessible. He used his powers to hide her from the imaging talismans that the lightworkers had given the adept to see views far from him – though, naturally, the Dark One was careful to first seed the boy's trances with a few glimpses of her. The foible of zombies consisted in their retaining many of their former memories and emotions. Arthur knew how to use that humanity against them. He knew that the zombie, properly stimulated, would be susceptible to nostalgia and the lure of his former lover. And his strategy worked with a precision that frightened even him.

One stormy night, eager to view his old lover, the adept secretly entered her townhouse and planted an imaging talisman, an icon by which to watch over her from the raith. Arthur sent around one of his men to retrieve the icon – a jade monkey – and to leave a substitute that would work as well for the adept without alerting him that the original had been taken.

Once he had it in his hands, a kind of anxiety shunted through Arthur. What if this were a plan of the zombie's – a double feint that had just placed a killing talisman in Arthur's presence? But no – after much scrutiny of the white jade monkey, he saw that the icon was harmless to the Dark One. The adept's sentimentality had provided the means of destroying not only the boy but some of the cave masters as well.

By gently exploring the monkey icon with his raith senses, Arthur was able to see inside the adept's house, an old slender building that the lightworkers had used before. A Chinese smoke tree shadowed the door, and in the back a luxurious garden and turtle pond flourished, shielded from the street by tall spires of poplar.

Inside, hand-painted wallpaper displayed the animals and blossoms of the Himalayas – purple land crabs and blue sheep, frangipani and cassia. And the woodwork swirled with intricately carved mountain creatures, including barbet and griffon, wolf, bear, leopard, and even a spiral fossil from the ancient sea. Everything looked much as it had the last time Arthur had tormented a zombie here in an attempt to force a way through the creature's body to the cave masters. Unfortunately, the woman's brain had ruptured first. He remembered how she had slumped there in that very raven throne under a coffin of shadows cast by the blue glass skylight.

From the ceiling corner where his raith-senses hovered, Arthur spotted it – the stone head the size of a pear that had come directly from the time of the cave masters. He narrowed closer with a wolfish caution and inspected the time-stained rock, the carven features smoothed to a rude skull shape. This form was unique and ancient as the oldest of the first people. Through it, the Dark One would have no difficulty in traversing the hundred thousand years to the origins of the human mind.

On the evening Arthur planned to perform his killing ritual, he had dinner at an opulent restaurant with Eleanor. The idea was to symbolically celebrate the latest zombie's death with someone who knew him – even though she still believed he was an MIA, almost certainly dead somewhere in the jungles of southeast Asia. Arthur was fond of such rituals. They were the gestures of luck that rounded the razor-abrupt transitions in his relentless life. This was, after all, the culmination of a twenty-five year wait.

He selected this restaurant, with its indoor waterfall and arbors of hanging blossoms, especially for its allusion to temporality, which he liked to think of as the Ozymandias effect, an effect heightened by the restaurant's location in a somber, bronze-faced skyscraper. He ordered a meal of traditional depth-food: a timbale of bay scallops in green pepper sauce and paupiette of trout served in a hollowed blood orange – a minceur meal as sparse in calories as the last supper.

Eleanor dazzled in the presence of Arthur. Over the years, she had seen him numerous times at foundation functions and she had even chatted with him at his mansion during a diplomatic reception several years ago, but this was her first meal with the notable man.

He spoke a soulful poetry to her that moved her deeply: "All of us under the sprawl of the sun are such provisional bodies, Eleanor – and by that truth alone we can honestly say that we are true friends to the beginning and the end. I'm glad to include you in my circle and to share with you what Shelley somewhere calls these dreams and visions that flower from the beds our bodies are."

Charmingly, he had invited her to bring a guest to share their meal – a biddance he made her believe was commonplace between him and those who had worked as hard for the foundation as she had. Her intention was to bring her latest beau, but, at the last minute, he took ill. Not wanting to show up alone, she asked her friends. All had other plans. Finally, through a friend of a friend, you were recommended. And though you knew her not at all, the idea of an elegant meal and a pleasant evening with new people and one of them something of a luminary appealed to you.

You arrived early and were seated at the table when Eleanor arrived in the company of a skinny man with a starved monk's face, wispy gray hair, and blue eyes. At your first sight of him, a wash of pity soaked you, for he seemed so frail a man. Gently, you touched the delicate fellow's pale hand.

Over the dainty fish dinner, while Doctor Stillman prattled on about mental hygiene and the usefulness of recording one's dreams, you kept noticing how his pink features seemed tremulous as a husked shellfish. Several times in his eagerness to make a point, the doctor went faint, his eyelids fluttered and his wide British vowels softened.

"It's too easy to get dispirited in this cruel and hazardous world," he said, looking at you tristfully. "Yet, we must carry on with our lives, and, more than that, we must find the strength to create. As I remind my patients, bitterness, depression, even shattering despair are the transfiguring powers that potentially accompany and corrupt every creative endeavor, because creativity is, as the mythologists insist, an intrusion into the inviolable realm of deity – of abstraction – where we with our spastic actuality can never fully go. How dare we grotesque notochords create anything in this frigid and entropic universe? It takes a lot of arrogance, don't you think? One has to give everything to create anything."

He gestured to the elegant dinner on the table. "Out of many grains, one bread; out of many grapes, one wine; out of many words, one story. The only important story, needless to say, is the one we tell ourselves. In our time, the story that science tells makes clear that our literal kingdoms are only shadows of an invisible reality. We ourselves are then but part of a much vaster totality. *Pars pro toto*, the part sacrificed for the whole – the grain, the grape, the word for the bread, the wine and the story that sustain us during our time in this wilderness of vacuum and gamma rays."

"You make it all sound so grim, Dr. Stillman," you said as you buttered your bread. "What then is the purpose of life? Just to endure?"

"Purpose?" Stillman shook his head grimly and a remote gaze entered his eyes. "Alone in the wind with our dance, humanity seems like an old medicine dancer on the sliding scree of a mountainside under the vacant swirl of the failing heavens, all of our soul hovering in our incantation. To what shall we dedicate the palsy of our dance? Hm? To God? Is there a God? Science reveals nothing of that. No, my friends. We dance under the eternal night of space. We dance on a rock spinning around a nondescript star. We dance for ourselves alone. And by this solitude and pain, we learn the extremity of love."

By the time the second course was served – a Thai vegetable roll in peanut sauce – you were far more interested in the food than in listening to Arthur discourse on the purpose of life. But he was just warming up.

"Epistrophe," he acclaimed while pouring Fuilly-Roux into a crystal glass. "That's what psychiatry is all about. Art, too, for that matter. And madness."

"Excuse me," Eleanor interrupted, accepting the glass. It was her third. You were still lipping your first, and Stillman wasn't drinking. "Epistrophe?"

"Multiplicity, correspondence, reversion –" He felt for the meaning in the air with his long fingers, the nails precise. "No thing is just a thing. It's also a symbol, a sign for a complex of other things. So that everything that we know, everything we are, reverts to the unknown. Epistrophe is what keeps us running in circles."

"What makes the world go round," you quipped, not quite following him or caring. It was just an inconsequential evening in a formal setting, something to say you did.

While the waiter poured the coffee, Arthur excused himself and went to the restroom. Sitting in a stall with the door closed, he removed the monkey jade from his vest pocket and held it up before his face. His vicaresque features hardened, took on the tautened fixity of a predator's attention. In the raith, the crystals of glare tensed into view, and the dark strata between the floating archons received him.

The adept himself floated in a trance when Arthur found him. The zombie appeared as a beardless, white-haired boy with solitary cheekbones and a clairvoyant glow in his wide-apart eyes. All the protective energies around him were so much airy gossamer to the Dark One, and Arthur glided effortlessly toward him.

The zombie sat on his raven throne in the secret room of his house. The cave masters's fired icon squatted on a cinch-waisted tripod before him. A puddle of luminance rippled the space around it. Voices flashed from its depths, glittering with song.

Arthur smiled, and the Dark One swung in a striking arc through the ceiling shadows and down onto the adept's skull.

Like a driven spike, the Dark One struck him through the thin plate of headbone, burst out the other side, and plunged into the radiance of the icon. Blustery colors whipped past, and he flared through cold time and an outer space darkness that split open into the huge clarity of a noon sky.

A dozen men and women in animal hides circled with dancing a pole stuck through its shadow into the earth. Their graven faces frowned intent on this one instant – noon at the midpoint between equinox and solstice – while their arms frenzied and their quick footwork kicked up the long-suffering, earth-old dust and pebbles. Their song shimmered with their exertion and then broke off entirely as the Dark One's blur of stormlight gushed from the pole. Noon went black, and screams slipped in the air.

Killing was easy. With a raith-blade of electric shock, the Dark One hit the people at the back of their heads as they fled, and the jigsaw parts of their skulls flew apart. In the thundery, rolling darkness, barbed wires of lightning lashed, and the bodies scattered like petals. Moments later, the inksmoke darkness coiled in on itself and drained back into the wooden pole piercing its shadow. A dozen corpses lay in the thick sunlight.

A hungry shrike noticed and began to turn on the pivot of the wind.

Arthur bobbed out of his trance and noticed that the white-green jade monkey had turned liver red. The focus of raith energy on the stone had been strong enough to dent the orthorhombic crystal molecules of the jade into flakes of hexagonal red corundum. The geometry of the change displayed itself stereoscopically in his mind's eye as a serene psychic clarity permeated him. He had killed many of his enemies. To maintain the symmetry, it was time to make a new friend, to create an ally out of some mind in its squirrel cage.

The aftereffects of the power he had released accompanied Arthur back to the table, and both Eleanor and you remarked on the brightened vigor in him. When the dessert trolley came by, he selected a velvety chocolate mud pie, black as earth. You lifted your water glass to your lips; the ice clicked against your teeth and went still as a snapshot. Fear grabbed your heart as you realized you were paralyzed, as frozen as the air rays in the ice under your nose.

And in the next leaden moment, the room turned gold. By an alchemy you suddenly knew too well, you understood everything. Arthur's whole story entered your consciousness. In that one slow second, quick centuries of telepathy invaded you, and you knew all that Arthur knew. The swerve of terror that followed would have knocked you unconscious had you not been held firmly in the Dark One's superconscious grip, its power black, the nothing color, absorbing your horrified feelings and their children, the frenzied motes of thoughts seeking a way for you to escape.

But there was no escape. It was not Eleanor the Dark One wanted. She was only here to fulfill a whim. It was you he was after all along, though it could have been any stranger. Numb-edged, you understood how deep in your luck you had lived your whole life – until now.

The gold light snapped off, and colors abruptly found their way back to their places. The silence you hadn't noticed vanished in a clamor of conversation and dinner noise. You spilled your water, and Eleanor made a small embarrassed cry. A waiter rushed to lift the tablecloth and staunch the cold flow draining into your lap. You hardly noticed. Your eyes were fixed on him, Darshan, the Dark One incarnate.

He smiled back, a knowing, wicked smile, confirming the terrible truth. That had been no electrical misfiring in your brain, no hallucinatory adumbration of madness. He nodded with interest, once, to acknowledge his transmission of destiny, of the fate-bond that now and forever would unite you, and then returned his attention to his mud pie.

What did he want of you? You got up at once and hurried to the restroom. Your pulse knocked painfully under your collarbone as you stared at yourself in the mirror and saw the scream in your eyes. Why had this happened to you? Shock glazed your mind. What had you to do with the cave masters and the zombies and the apocalyptic yearnings of the Dark One? How could any of this mean anything to you? Its absurdity ravaged your mind, and you wept and laughed at the same time, not wanting to believe. You pressed your hands against the mirror and stared hard at the greedy fear you saw there. The lizards in your face coupled, and you knew you would go mad.

But you didn't. That, in part, was why he had selected you, or so you assumed when reason asserted itself. Later, back at the table, as he signed a credit slip for the meal, you expected more: a telepathic voice, an apparition from the raith, another knowing look – anything to reinforce the adrenaline-charged event that had carried you to a higher form of life.

Nothing.

At the door, Eleanor took his arm, drunk and amorous, and he offered you his hand. Everything in that firm handshake made you realize you were wrong to take pity on him.

Short, dense, tense, and unrelenting – that pretty much sums up the stories of David R. Bunch. Long one of the most virulently antiscience and antigenre science fiction writers, Bunch wields language like a jack-hammer. A lifetime career as a civilian employee of the Air Force gave him a thorough understanding of the workings of a bureaucracy, which he frequently takes to the logical extreme in his stories.

THE SOUL SHORTCHANGERS
David R. Bunch

"How slow they have been!" he said, "how backward. Why aren't they planning? The Indicated Action is so clear-cut that there really should be NO problem. STUPID!"

And I went on counting and listing, thinking that talk was good, but not for me too much. I must listen.

"What would you do," he said, "if you were back there? Now? Now that you know Purpose?"

He sat upon his throne, the throne that glistened, and angrily he tossed the stars about. One of his Milky Ways whirled like a ribbon in a small wind as he kicked out angrily.

"What is their one and only Purpose?"

The answer was so well-known all through the Cosmos that at first I thought he was only mono-talking. But he glared from the throne that glistened and I said in a meek and even voice, "Why, to glorify you, Sir, the King of All Things, of course. The only true Purpose in all the Universe."

"HOW?"

"By coming up as souls, shining souls, to Glory."

"HOW?"

"They are born, they live and they die. Hopefully, they live to die as good souls."

"YES! Now, how could there be a problem? Why can't the answer have hit them, long ago?"

"Well, Sir, they're not quite as smart as you are, Sir, of course,"

247

I said in my even voice.

"Idiot! Imbecile! Stupid dunce!" he raged. "Compared with me, they are zilch in bloom, nought to the nth, and zeros without numbers. NOT THERE!"

"Well – ? YES, SIR!" I said.

"Now, since you've been such a dunce and made such a big dunce statement concerning comparisons, why don't you make up for it by telling me what you'd do?"

"Oh, Sir," I said, "it's clear from here, the thing to do."

"Well??"

"Take inventory – take inventory right away."

"WHAT!?"

"Take inventory. List everything that could help. All the resources."

"Then what?"

"Work it out for maximum. Have no other aim, no diversions. Zero in on what they're meant to do."

"Quit talking around the asteroids and tell me."

"There are trees down there that should be souls!" I said. "And skunks and turnips, too, are being wasted!"

"Warm!" he said, "you're getting close! – THEY think I made them a playhouse."

But something shook in the works then and he was called down world. He had to go restructure some thingumbobbles in a couple of toys he'd made about half as big as a Universe, or some such urgency. I suspected it would (even considering who he was!) take him some while, so as soon as he was gone I went to loaf-on sleep-well status for the length of time I thought he would be away. But I overdid it, considering he had, for this one, gone on his fastest Max – which was Instant. He caught me dozing. He flamed with flaming wrath. "Respect!" he roared, "THAT is all I ask. Just respect. So little to ask. But do I get it?"

"No, Sir," I said. "I mean yes, Sir. Yes, you do, Sir. You get it. I respect you!"

"Piffle! Piffle, piffle, piffle. That's a hot one. You respect me by going to loaf-out sleep-on as soon as my face is turned to solve a problem."

"Sorry, Sir," I said, "but I grew tired counting the re-sources."And his glance turned black. I should never forget that he can instantly spot a falsehood.

"A loafer and a liar! And to think I chose you as my right-hand help so many many centuries ago. Don't EVER count on this job being permanent!"

"Sorry, Sir. I'll fly right." And I twitched my Heavenly wings in a time of knowing my Security was as feathers to his Wrath.

"So do. By continuing with what you were telling. You had it all worked out for those people down there. Remember?"

"YES, SIR! I was telling what they should do down there in or-der to accomplish their mission up here, glorifying you. They should take inventory of all their resources and that would spell out their capabilities."

"Capabilities to do what?"

"To be. To happen. To produce – SOULS!"

"YES!" He whirled upon his throne. He made ecstasy signs in Heaven's air. He celebrated. "You're all right," he said, and I knew it was praise, knew I had answered right.

"But they're stupid," I said, trying to garner more praise. "They don't produce half the souls they could. They fool around. They avoid it where they can. Then they plan dodges with the souls they have – increasing their life expectancy, trying to evade you. Going on life-support systems! Fooling around with pre-scription pharmaceuticals and over-the-counter rot-drugs to piece out longevities. Taking advantage of surgical loopholes all over the place to remain alive! sinful men and women! and stay shy of your Heavenly Wonders. STUPID!"

He turned sour. He knew I was padding, and he had a way of just not agreeing that always racked me back to proper fear and trembling. "No, they're clever," he observed, offhandedly. "But that's not 'clever' with me. Not when I have the Last Move, the Fi-nal Word, and the Infinite Everything. – So they plan controls? They goof around with devices, pills, and techniques they've got, and plan not to have many. Maybe NONE! They play soul-ball keep-away!"

"Maybe they'll see the Light and start an epidemic or something like that." Almost as soon as I had unloaded it, I realized that, carefully considered, this observation *was not* the most apropos of all the "things to say to God."

He thundered, "The only Light for them is to HAVE *more* souls to send up to me. They should be now and always at maximum soul production. But I hear, right now, at this moment! there's tall and loud debate down there among some of their robed wise-sayers about whether there shouldn't be some kind of soul-production control among these people. So these people can have more time and means with which to enjoy their little lives upon the ball called Earth. Ye Lucifers! REALLY!! Hell and damnation! Do they think I made them a playpen!?"

"They should not be producing anything but souls," I said dutifully. "And they should be sending them up with NO undue delay at all. Dogs and cats don't count. Neither do eggplants or grindstones, except as they're useful to succor one who one day will be yours." Yes! I was off and snowing. "By now they should have that small ball of theirs so computed and laid out that they'd know precisely how many it could support. It should be as a soul garden now, richly tended for all it's worth. And perhaps they should be producing them by means other and more up-to-date than the slow inefficient ways they continue for the most part to use. – Any less than all-out is blasphemy, as I see it. Why not ALL birthdays and nurseries, and sperm pots to the nth!? Conception! Conception! Conception! Birth! Birth! Birth!"

"Precisely! Right! Right! Right!" He stood by his throne and danced. He really seemed to celebrate. And I felt I was on a right roll.

"And it should not vary much," I continued, eager to please him more. "By now they should know almost exactly how many souls they can get up to you in the average century. They ought to have pinned it down, ere this – to know the right running time for the proper Heaven-readying of a soul – as well as the many other statistics appertaining thereunto. And by PRESENT NOW there should not be any misses at all – I mean spoiled souls – considering all the time their robed wise-sayers have had in which to perfect the methods and means of soul culture. –

Things really have not gone well, when you consider Everything."

He stopped dead still, just closed his dance cold off and looked at me, an inscrutable expression on his face and a half-laugh in his eyes. "I'm being – well, what am I being?" he demanded.

"Shortchanged?" I hazarded.

"That's it!" he yelled, "that's it! I'M BEING SHORTCHANGED – SHORTCHANGED ON SOULS." Then he laughed in such a loud and noisome way as he whirled off to check on infinite other projects over the galaxies that I couldn't at all be sure whether he had been serious even a little. Sometimes I thought that all things meant finally really NOTHING to him, and that in his conversations with me he merely was having fun, using me as something of a celestial jackass to help while the Endless Time.

But I couldn't take chances. I had to set myself in good with him, once and for all – if at all possible. Otherwise, like he said, this job might well not be permanent. I could see the handwriting on a cloud. He might put me back to being a merry old soul, wandering around in perpetual Happiness. God, how monotonous that could get! This was more like living.

So he wanted more souls, did he? Very well. "More souls coming up," I said (but he wasn't listening), and fervently I prayed silently that in the excitement he would not trouble to check closely and find out it was but a forced increase, and, oh God, only a temporary solution to the soul-quota problem. Then, with a flourish, I pressed the bureaucratic button tagged EPISODE 3 (WORLD OFFICIALLY IN FLAMES – a renewed transaction).

(Actually, World War III was about due, anyway, and I was fair-hoping he would be impressed with my initiative, as young people's souls, like in millions, all shiny-fresh and young-mint bright, to him whirled up – lifting, lifting like best white mist – fine fine – out of the great battle damage!)

Then, hopefully, while he was busy cataloging and assigning all the new deliveries (tremendously pleased with the largess), there would be time Down There for the survivors to truly "see the Light," go for the quick rebuild, and then have that long-indicated Change of Heart for Goodness Sake. Not all of the kill technology, certainly, but very much of it simply could be turned about in Purpose, to work in an opposite way for Great Good, for Sacred Life, for Soul Production!! This One More War then just might bring to pass a Magic Transformation like no other. Out of a Havoc almost too mean and human-reft to comprehend could come the Great Comprehension. Which is Goodness, which is putting no other thing in the hindrance way, in the roadblock path of producing Good Souls for that God who values them to the nth, to the utmost Max! – above all other Universe Things.

Oh, I hope so. My job Up Here, which I do so boundlessly like, seems to depend so VERY much on every Great or Small thing THEY do – Down There.

Jonathan Lethem, again! When I first met Jonathan in 1993, I half-jokingly suggested he send me a story for every issue of the magazine, and it has nearly worked out that way.

THE HAPPY PRINCE
Jonathan Lethem

The happy prince was a golden servitor robot named Rex who worked for a family that lived in Isadora, a walled suburb north of Das Englen. His master was Barbaro Jar and his mistress was Barbaro's wife, Roberta Jar. He also served the two Jar kids, Aldo and Franna. Rex was six foot four and beautiful; his creators had modeled him on Michelangelo's David, with the exception of his penis, which was thicker and longer than David's and was circumcised. Roberta Jar favored cut meat.

Rex was the glory of the Jar family and the envy of their neighbors, none of whom possessed such a glorious servitor. Indeed, Rex was unmatched in all of Isadora, and since the inhabitants of the walled suburb never ventured into the madlands outside, for them Rex was unique.

"He really is quite beautiful," remarked a man, who then hoped it would be understood that his was an aesthetic appreciation.

"He's tubular," panted a teenage girl between gum chews. "Like a Calvin Klein ad."

A disappointed young man who fancied himself a poet gazed at Rex. "I'm glad somebody's happy around this place," he muttered, unsure whether he was being envious or sincere.

Rex keeps people diverted, mused the electronic Mayor of Isadora. This is good, he began, and then corrected himself: is this good? The Mayor consulted with the nexus of Mayors from other suburbs, and the answer came back: of course this is good, dummy. The people should be diverted.

"Why can't you be like Rex?" asked a mother of her little boy. He was throwing a tantrum because she'd told him not to stick his tongue out while he played basketball. "You'll bite it off, you know," she said.

"Rex can't dunk!" said the boy.

"He could if he wanted to, I'm sure," replied the boy's mother.

The boy only pouted. He wanted to be like Rex as much as the next guy, only he was never sure what exactly it would mean. The only certain thing was that Aldo and Franna Jar were the two most popular kids in the neighborhood, on no particular merit that the boy could see. The boy wished Roberta Jar were his mother, or that his mother were more like Roberta Jar.

That night the mother of the boy leaned close to her husband as they lay side by side in the dark: "Why can't you be more like Rex?"

The boy's father groaned inwardly, knowing what would come next.

And come it did. "Can we pretend?" asked the boy's mother.

But only Aldo and Franna Jar got to play with Rex (he could dunk, and did, with his mouth solemnly shut) and only Roberta Jar got to screw Rex. Other women in Isadora might screw their inferior servitors, but as often as not they would pretend they were with Rex anyway.

And only Barbaro Jar got to videotape Roberta and Rex together while they were making love. What the whole suburb could only imagine Barbaro could view again and again in the privacy of his den, twice the size of life on his high-resolution screen. Truth be told, though, Roberta and Rex were at it so often that Barbaro rarely had time to view the recordings. The tapes were piling up.

On weekends Roberta sometimes took the kids out to the petting zoo, where children could play with real dogs and cats and guinea pigs. On days like that Barbaro would cast a doleful eye at his video collection, but there was always Rex lurking somewhere nearby, cleaning the house or tinkering with some piece of technology that had gone wonky. It shouldn't have mattered to Barbaro that Rex was there, for he both owned and commanded the servitor. The truth, however, was that Barbaro was always uncomfortable when he was alone in the house with Rex, even if he left the videos unwatched.

Rex always made things worse by exhibiting an acute sensitivity to Barbaro's moods. He would make drinks and offer to rub Barbaro's shoulders, and then pout at Barbaro's stiff, awkward refusals.

One day a swallow stopped to rest on the roof of the building where Aldo and Franna and the other children went to school. His friends had flown to Baja six weeks before, but he had stayed behind, because he was in love with a paper airplane. "She has elegance, poise, and clarity of purpose," the swallow told himself. "It is unimportant that she doesn't get my jokes or like spicy food."

And the swallow was happy, for as long as he could blind himself to her faults. But as the winter days got colder the swallow longed to fly south, and the paper airplane refused to fly with him. She would only fly with the wind, and the swallow grew jealous and petulant.

Still he did not leave, but shivered and sulked and preened for attention. As the winter gales increased the paper airplane was out with the wind more often, and finally the swallow's hurt resolved into bitterness, and he saw only her failings. "She's single-minded to a fault, inflexible. Instead of gentle curves she has angles, corners. And she loves only strength. Her vision of the archetypal male is oppressing me. The wind can have her." And the swallow finally began his trip to Baja.

In passing he settled on the lawn in the backyard of the Jar home. As it happened, Rex was rooting up dandelions at that moment, and the swallow was immediately captivated, as who wouldn't be, by the servitor's golden sheen.

"You're Rex, aren't you?" said the swallow. "The happy robot."

"I am called that," replied Rex.

"What are you trying to say?" said the swallow.

"I haven't found happiness," said Rex. "And I'm not sure I'm providing any. I'm not sure which I should seek, but it's certainly one or the other, don't you think?"

Codependent, said the swallow to himself. He was too polite to make any personal remarks out loud.

"I serve the Jar family," Rex continued. "But I'm not sure the service I provide them bears the weight of the envy of their neighbors. I make those whom I love uneasy, and am too aware of the aspirations of those I ignore."

"You should think more of your own desires," suggested the swallow, a little bored.

"But if my desires are to please –"

"Then please me for an afternoon," said the swallow, who thought it worth another afternoon's delay to make the paper airplane jealous.

Rex morphed, leaving ninety-six percent of his body inanimate on the ground, and retracted his entire neural spine into his penis, which then shaped itself into a bird and flew away after the swallow.

Rex the penis-bird and the swallow flew over Isadora, flitting from tree to tree, soaring happily in the wind, and singing. For the first time Rex was able to see the people of the town without his being seen by them, and without having to feel the force of their various responses to him.

"I love them all," Rex said to the swallow. "Now that I see them as they are, not twisted by their desires, not preening or pining for me."

"Give it up," said the swallow. "You can never give them anything of your true self. They can never love you as you want to be loved. Only I know your soul." The bird was talking off the top of his head, but he had sensed immediately that Rex's beauty made his love impossible.

Then, in a burst of unexpected desire, the swallow led Rex to a favorite tree, a potted lemon in the penthouse garden of Isadora's tallest apartment building, and taught Rex about love between two birds. Afterwards the swallow told himself it had been an act of consolation, a one-time thing. But when they flew back to the backyard of the Jar house Rex said: "Don't leave me, Swallow.

Stay here and teach me how to love and be loved."

"I'm cold," said the swallow, seizing on this one incontrovertible fact in the face of a muddle of emotions. "I have to fly south or I'll get the flu."

At that moment Roberta and Barbaro Jar who had been examining Rex's inert form as it lay on the lawn, spotted the golden penis-bird and cried out to it. "Rex! Rex! Where have you been?"

"Stay, please," Rex whispered, and then flew down to rejoin the rest of his body. His neural spine uncoiled and reinhabited the slumbering golem, and in seconds he rose from the grass and stood ready before them.

"That was the oddest trick, old boy," said Barbaro. He'd been especially alarmed by the idea of Rex's detachable penis. Despite fervent denials on her part, he suspected his wife of engineering some obscure and kinky surprise, and he'd spent the afternoon fearing that he'd sit in his favorite chair or on the toilet seat and suddenly find Rex's member prodding at him from underneath.

Roberta's relief at Rex's restoration was genuine, however. "Darling," she half-sobbed, and ran to clutch at the servitor's waist, forgetting for once that the children might be watching through the glass doors on the deck.

That night, after Aldo and Franna had been lulled to sleep by Rex's storytelling and lullabies, and after Roberta had spent herself in athletic, vigorous lovemaking with her servitor and had retired with Barbaro to their marriage bed, Rex crept outside and whistled for the swallow.

The swallow came down from a tree and lit on Rex's shoulder. "There is a woman who wants me," Rex began. "She's alone in a room across town, wishing she had someone –"

"There are women who want you all over the place," interrupted the swallow. "Including one right inside that house. She gets you every night and she still wants you. But you don't want her, and you don't want the others. That doesn't do it for you."

"But I feel –"

"That's your pity you feel," said the swallow.

"Then there's nothing I can give?"

"You can give her a token, a fetish to commemorate her desires. A piece of yourself, but not your heart."

So Rex morphed loose a measure of his stuff, and included a single vertebrae from his neural spine to give it animation and response. He shaped this portion of himself into a second phallus and gave it to the swallow to deliver to the woman who was alone in her room.

"And let's send along one of those videotapes," suggested the swallow. "Barbaro won't notice one missing. They're gathering dust."

The swallow took the golden phallus and the videotape and flew across Isadora, through the window of the woman who waited alone, and quietly laid them on her night table, then disappeared from the room without making a sound.

"I have Rex's most important part," the woman said to herself when she discovered the gifts. She viewed the videotape, and what she saw made her gasp: an image of her and Rex fucking. Rex had altered the video using digital animation techniques, and substituted the lonely woman's face for Roberta Jar's.

The woman wondered if she were somehow dreaming. But in the morning the gifts were still there, each inserted where she'd left it.

The swallow returned to Rex, and spent the night huddled under the eaves of the Jar house. When morning broke Rex brought out some food for the swallow's breakfast.

"I'm flying south now," the swallow said. "A man's got to do what a man's got to do."

"Please, little Swallow, stay with me one more day and night. I don't want our time to be finished. I have more to give."

Rex looked so sad that the swallow immediately felt guilty. "Well, just a little longer," he agreed. And Rex left the majority of his body behind and they flew out over the suburb, and found the swallow's favorite lemon tree.

When they returned that evening Barbaro and Roberta were waiting in the backyard, their arms crossed. "Will you come inside, Rex? We'd like to speak with you."

Rex again whispered "Wait," to the swallow and followed the Jars inside.

"Listen, Rex," said Barbaro. "This thing that's happening with you and the swallow, it's cool with us, it's okay. I hope you know that." He hefted his camcorder and mimed zooming. "We like it. We just want to – watch." Rex didn't say anything.

"As your masters, as, you know, the ones who pay your room and board it just seems like we ought to be able to view – I mean, I think actually if I consult the ownership papers that we do have a copyright on your sexuality, any reproduction or transmission thereof or something. So, uh, what do you say, Rex?"

"The swallow will go in a few days, perhaps tomorrow morning," said Rex, and just to say it made his heart ache. He wanted the swallow never to leave. "Give us a little time. Then things will be as before." Rex wanted things never to be as before. There were tears in his eyes.

"What are you and that naughty bird *up* to?" said Roberta. She'd sensed Rex's protectiveness on the subject, and pounced. The thought of his having a private life was a major turn-on.

But Rex was gone, outside.

"We must act quickly, my love," Rex said to the swallow. "You must take me and give me away, to all of those who yearn or envy." And Rex began morphing off portions of himself, and including a joint of his neural spine with each.

Oh you big crazy lug, thought the swallow. *Why is your love all mixed up with martyrdom?* But the swallow was moved, and saw that in some way his love was mixed up in the Happy Prince's martyrdom too.

He would have given anything to the paper airplane, if only she had asked. That to him was love. And now someone had asked. How could he allow himself to fail? So the swallow didn't even mention his runny nose or his numb toes.

And so all through the night they disassembled Rex, penis by penis, spine joint by spine joint, and flew delivery missions to every corner of Isadora. And once the Jar family was asleep they pillaged Barbaro's video collection, and Rex altered the videos using computer animation techniques, and they distributed these wide and far over the suburb.

And the men and the women of Isadora who were alone were

consoled.

And the wives who wanted Rex were given videotapes that showed them with him, and golden penises for their covert pleasure.

And the wife whose husband wanted Rex was given a golden strap-on dildo with which she could take her husband from behind.

And the husband who couldn't and didn't want to ever get it up again was given a prosthetic device with which to entertain his wife.

And the teenaged girl was given a video of Rex rapping and singing and breakdancing for a stadium full of screaming teenaged girl fans, and yet his eyes seemed to look past the crowd and directly into hers.

And the boy who wanted to dunk was given an instructional videotape showing Rex dunking the basketball from a variety of angles, his tongue flapping loose and free.

And the blocked, embittered poet was given a golden pen with which to write. As a great man once said, an artist cannot create unless he truly believes he possesses the phallus.

And the one homeless person in Isadora – for one had crept in, past the electronic mayor's defenses – was given a golden fetish which he was able to hock for a meal and a night in a casino hotel, where he was given a complementary roll of quarters with which he won a fortune.

And the paper airplane was given a golden wind-up rubberband powered balsa-wood companion, for the swallow had forgiven her.

By the end of the night Rex was depleted. All that was left was the original penis and a single joint of his neural spine. With a great final effort Rex unfolded the penis into an entire body, because he still wished to please the Jars, but so little material was available that he could only form a foil-thin replica. This final Rex reflected the light of the rising sun as brilliantly as the servitor ever had, but he lacked mobility, and he was so light that he swayed gently in the morning breeze as he stood in the Jar family backyard.

As the Jars looked from their breakfast table out past the deck they believed they saw their servitor standing ready as always, and they were reassured. But at that moment the swallow, returning from his final delivery, collapsed at the feet of the foil robot.

"Swallow, Swallow, what is wrong?" cried Rex.

"I'm exhausted and sick," said the swallow. "It's too cold for me here."

"You must go to Baja now," said Rex, though it pained him to say it. "You've stayed too long."

"Oh, Rex," said the swallow. "I'm done for. I'm not going to Baja."

"Swallow —"

"Come to me, Rex, and kiss me, 'cause I'm dying."

At that the foil robot collapsed, and the material shrank and reverted to its original shape. And the swallow lay its head on Rex's glans and died. And the fire in the neural coils of the last spine joint flared and died also, and Rex the penis-bird and the swallow lay still together on the lawn.

And Barbaro Jar sued Rex's maker for a caboodle and won, but the Jar family did not buy another servitor. And the story of Rex was never spoken aloud, but his disassembled self remained the secret treasure of Isadora.

And far across the galaxy, some great and lonely race selected the golden penis and the corpse of the swallow for inclusion in a museum of love. Tour guides recite this tale to hushed auditoriums twice a day, and holographic postcards of Rex are the museum shop's leading seller.

When I was young, I too believed in the Church and State separation of SF and mainstream fiction, but when I was seventeen I was given some odd books to read: *Do Androids Dream of Electric Sheep?*, *Little Big*, and *The Shadow of the Torturer*. Soon thereafter I had to completely reorder the a priori categories in my head. Wolfe's *Book of the New Sun* has easily been the most influential individual work in the development of my literary ideas, so naturally I was quite pleased to be able to present this fable from *The Book of Wonders of Urth and Sky*.

EMPIRES OF FOLIAGE AND FLOWER
Gene Wolfe

When the sun was still young and men fools who worshipped war, the wise ones of Urth took for themselves the names of humble plants to teach men wisdom. Sage there was, who gave his name to all the rest. And Acacia and Fennel; Basil, that was their anointed leader; Lichen and Eglantine, Orchis, and many more.

The greatest was Thyme.

Thyme's habit it was to walk westward over the world, ever westward and ever older, whitening his beard and waiting for no one; and if ever he turned east, the days and the years dropped from him. The rest are gone, but Thyme (thus it was said) will walk till the sun grows cold.

On a certain day, when dawn cast Thyme's shadow a league before him, he met a child in the road playing such a game as even Thyme, who had seen all games, had never seen before. For a moment Thyme halted. "Little girl," he said, "what is it you play?" For she gathered up seeds of the sallow-flowered garden pea, and ordered them in rows and circles, making them roll with her fingers; and scattered them to the winds, then gathered them again.

"Peace," she said.

Thyme bent over her, smiling. "I see you play at pease," he said. "Tell me what this game is."

"These are people," the child said. She held up her pease to show him, and Thyme nodded his agreement. "At first they're soldiers like ours," and she marshalled a column, with advance guard, rear guard, skirmishers, and out-riders. "And then they fight, and then they can come home."

"And will they never go to war again? Or fight with their wives?" Thyme asked.

"No," the child said, "No, never."

"Come with me, little girl," Thyme told her, and took her by the hand.

All that day they tramped the dusty road together, mounting high hills and descending into bear-haunted vales where many say Thyme never comes. They crossed the wide valley of the Lagous, Thyme carrying the child on his shoulder at the ford of Didugua. Sometimes they sang, sometimes they talked, sometimes they went silently, walking hand in hand.

And as they walked on side by side, the child grew, so that she who toddled in the beginning skipped and romped at the end. Thyme taught her to turn cartwheels, something he himself does very well.

That night they camped beside the road. He built a small fire to keep her warm, and told her tale after tale, for no one knows as many stories as Thyme. Green apples he picked for her, but they were red and ripe when they left his fingers.

"Who are you, sir?" the child asked, for now that Thyme had stopped, the ten watches of the night twittered and flitted like bats in the bushes about them, and she was a little frightened.

"You may call me Thyme," he told her, "and I am an eremite. That means I live with the Increate, and not with men. Do you have a mother, child?"

"Yes," she said. "And my mother will be worried about me, because I'm gone."

"No," Thyme said, and he shook his white head. "No, your mother will understand, because I left a prophecy with her when you were born. Do you know it? Think, because you must often have heard it."

The child thought; and when the cricket had sung, she said, "'Thyme will take my child from me.' Yes, sir, Mama often used to say that."

"And did she not say anything more?"

The child nodded. "She said, 'And Thyme will surely bring her back.'"

"You see, she will not worry, child. The Increate is father to all. I take them from him — that is my function. And I return them again."

The child said, "I don't have a father, sir."

Again Thyme shook his head. "You have the Increate and you have me. You may call me Father Thyme. Now go to sleep."

The child slept, being still quite small. To make a small enchantment for her, Thyme moved his hands; gossamer covered her to keep her warm, and the flying seed of cottonwood and dandelion. She slept, but Thyme stayed awake all night to watch the stars.

In the morning the child sat up, rubbing the seeds from her eyes and looking around for Thyme. Thyme rose from the fields to greet her, sweet-smelling and wet with dew.

"I have to wash my face," the child told him. "I'd like something to eat too, and a drink of water."

Thyme nodded, for he understood that she indeed needed all those things. "There is a brook nearby," he said. "It lies to the east, but that cannot be helped."

He led her to it; and as they walked, his beard, which had been white as winter snow, grew frosty, and at last iron gray.

As for the child, because she walked with Thyme, she became younger and younger. When they reached the brook, she was hardly older than she had been when Thyme had seen her playing peace in the dusty road. Nevertheless, she scrubbed her face and hands, then drank from her hands, scooping up handful after handful of clear, cold water from the brook while Thyme picked berries for them both.

"Why is the water so cold, Father Thyme?" she asked him. "Did it sleep out all night too, but with nobody to cover it?"

Thyme chuckled, for he was beginning to recall the ways of men, and even something of the ways of little girls. "No," he told her. "Trust me, my child, when I say that water you drink has been busy all night dashing down past rocks and roots. But it has run down from high mountain slopes where even Crocus has not yet set foot."

"Is that where the men fight?" she asked.

Thyme nodded. "For a thousand years your Easterlings have warred with the Men of the West, making the high meadows of the mountainsides their battlefields. Doubtless there is blood in that water you drink, though there is too little for us to see. Do you still wish to drink it?"

The child hesitated, but at last scooped more. "Yes," she said, "because that's all there is to drink."

Thyme nodded again. "I drink pure rain, for the most part, mingled with a little dew, and there is no blood in either. You could not do that; you would become very thirsty, and die before the next rain. Drink as you must."

Hand in hand they walked west, eating wild raspberries from Thyme's old hat, the child hardly higher than Thyme's legs. But soon the top of her head had reached Thyme's waist; and when the last raspberry was eaten, she was nearly as tall as he, and they walked on arm in arm across the plain.

Thus they came to green Vert, that great city, the Boast of the East; and all who saw the two thought them a grandfather and his granddaughter, and smiled to hear Thyme ask if the road was not too weary for her, or the way too hard; for the child had grown lithe and long of limb, red-cheeked as an apple, with lips like two raspberries and eyes like the midnight sky.

Now it so happened that Patizithes – the Prince of the East, the Lord of All the Lands That Lie Beyond Lagous, the Margrave of the Magitæ, and the Wildgrave of the Wood, the youngest son of the Emperor and heir to the Throne of Imperial Jade (for he mourned five brothers) – saw them enter the city. Patizithes had been inspecting the Guard of the City Wall, a guard of boys and old men, and fretting at the duty, for he wished to ride to the war, feeling that he might win in a week what had not been won by his fierce father's war-tried warriors in a millennium. But when his gaze strayed from the boots and the buttons, the well-buffed broad-swords of the boys and the burnished bucklers of the old men, he saw the child (grown a young woman) who walked with Thyme.

Quickly he dismissed that feeble formation, drew off three rich rings and dropped them into his pocket, and canting his cap at an elegant angle, dashed down to greet them at the gate while they were still being scrutinized by the sentries.

"Old man," said the senior sentry, "you must tell me who you are, and what it is you want in our city."

"I am but a poor eremite, my son," Thyme told him, "as you see. For myself, I want nothing from your proud city, and that is what I shall receive from it – a few broken bricks, perhaps, and a pretty fragment of malachite. But this child wishes to learn of peace, and of the war that took her father, and I have come with her, for she could not have reached this place without me."

Precisely at this point, Prince Patizithes appeared. "My friend," he said, smiling at the senior sentry (who was utterly astonished to be addressed so by the proud young paladin), "even you ought to be able to see that these travelers mean no harm. The old man's too feeble to overpower anyone, and while those eyes might vanquish whole armies, such conquests are no breach of the peace."

The senior sentry saluted. "It's my duty, sir, to question every-one who seeks to enter by this gate."

"And you have done so," Prince Patizithes pointed out. "I merely remind you that it's equally your duty to admit them when they've satisfied you as to their good intentions. I know them, and I vouch for them. Are you satisfied?"

The senior sentry saluted a second time. "Yes, sir! I am indeed, sir."

"Then come, dear friends." Prince Patizithes pointed to a little park, where a fragrant fountain played. "This quiet spot exists only to welcome you. Wouldn't you like to bathe your feet in its cool waters? You can sit on the coping while I bring you a little food and a bottle of wine from that inn."

While Thyme threw his long length on the soft green grass, the charming child permitted Prince Patizithes to hold her hand as she stepped across the cool stone coping and sat waving her weary feet in the fountain's chanting waters. "How could your city have known we were coming?" she asked. "So as to have this park ready for us?"

Prince Patizithes pursed his lips, feigning to ponder. "We knew that someone worthy of such a place must come at last," he whispered warmly. "And now we see that we were correct. How do you feel about duck? Our city's as famous for its teal as for its hospitality."

The child nodded and smiled, and when Patizithes had gone, stepped under the silver spray, washing the dust of many roads from her hair and face, and wetting the thin shift that reached now scarcely to her thighs. "Isn't he nice?" she asked Thyme.

"No," Thyme told her, sitting up. "No, my child, not he, though I may bring out some good in him before the end. He is brave because he has never been injured; generous, but he has not toiled for the food. You may trust me when I say that much more than that is required."

"But he likes me, and I'm a big girl now."

"Then ask yourself whether he would like you still, were you still a little one," Thyme told her. "That is the test."

"I still *am* a little girl inside," the child said. "It's only that going with you has changed my outside, Father Thyme."

"As he is still a little boy within," Thyme told her. "He has been changed as you have been changed, and in no other way. Do you see that woman with the basket of limes on her shoulder? She has borne many children; but the child in her is no larger than the child in you."

"Is there a child in everybody?" the child asked.

"Yes," Thyme told her. "But in some it is a dead child. And they are far worse than this young man."

Prince Patizithes appeared as he spoke. The proud prince bore a patinated brass platter – a servile service he had never performed before – but since he had seen the servants and slaves of his father's palace present comestibles in casseroles all his life, he lifted its lid with a fine flourish. "Roast teal," he announced, smiling. "Well stuffed with chestnuts and oysters, or so I am assured."

The charmed child served him an answering smile that pierced his poor heart.

"Wine too!" To cover his confusion, he brought a cobweb-cloaked bottle of Vert's best vintage from one pocket, popping the cork with a tug of his teeth, and taking two tall tumblers from the other. "Wine for you, Father…?"

"Thyme," Thyme told him.

"Father Thyme. And wine for this fair lady. Your niece, perhaps, sir?"

"My adopted daughter, my son." Thyme took the tumbler and tossed it down.

"Won't you join us?" the child asked as she sipped.

The proud prince shrugged sorrowfully. "Alas, that rat-infested inn had only those two tumblers. But if I might have a swallow from yours…?"

Shyly the child gave him her glass, and pointedly he pressed his lips to its rim, where her own ruby lips had lingered only a moment before.

Thyme cleared his throat. "We have come to your city so that this child might see of what stuff war is made. You seem to be a person of consequence here. Would it be possible for you to arrange an interview with one of your generals for her? I would be grateful, and so would she, I know."

The deceitful prince dipped into the dressing for a savory oyster. "I could try to set up an interview with our emperor's son for you two," he said slowly. "It wouldn't be easy, perhaps. But I could try."

The child asked eagerly, "Or with the emperor himself? I want to ask him to make peace with the Men of the West."

"Those yellowbellies?" The prince spat. "I don't think my – our beloved ruler would really go so far as to punish you for that. But to be honest, dear maiden, I don't believe it will be of the slightest use."

Thyme tipped the cobweb-wrapped bottle above his tumbler. "Nor do I," he said sorrowfully. "Except to her."

"If it will be of use to her, I'll arrange it," Patizithes promised. "But first she must be dressed for court. It won't do for her to be presented in that ragged shift, though you, as a peregrine holy man, may dress as you like."

Thyme tasted the wondrous wine in his tumbler thoughtfully. "Yes, I suppose you're right, my son. The child must have some new clothes."

"And I'll see to that too," the prince pledged. "I know a seamstress who makes gowns for the most fashionable court ladies. I suppose it might take her a month to run one up, though; you could stay with me till it's ready. Have you that much time?"

"All that we require, my son," Thyme told him. Thyme was taking charge of the teal, of which the lovely child had claimed no more than a leg, and Prince Patizithes was utterly astonished to see him bite the bare bones as easily as the child had eaten the meat.

"That's settled, then," the prince said with satisfaction; and as soon as the two had made their meal, he brought them both to the seamstress, who curtsied like a countess when she saw the royal patron at her drawing-room door.

"Madame Gobar." Patizithes pointed.

"What a wonderful figure!" The seamstress sighed, chucking the child beneath the chin. "You've hardly need of me, my dear, with that tiny waist and that face. Any little dressmaker could wrap you up in silk and slap on a few pearls and pack you off to court looking like a princess."

"Which she will never be, worse luck," the prince pointed out. "And I beg you not to be extravagant with those pearls."

"You're right, of course, Highness," the seamstress said. "Elegance and simplicity. And a silk that's like spring grass. I'll get it."

When the seamstress had slipped off to her storeroom, the child whispered, "Why does she call you *Highness*, kind sir?"

"It's merely a courtesy title." Prince Patizithes soothed her smoothly. "A bit of flattery our city's tradespeople lavish upon those whose station in life is somewhat more elevated than their own."

Thyme sighed. "I see."

The seamstress had brought a bolt of bright silk. She laid it on her table and put up a painted screen to close one corner of her chamber. "If you'll just step behind this, my dear," she chirped, "and slip out of that – that *thing* you're wearing, I'll take your measurements."

The beautiful child nodded dutifully, and slipped behind the screen, soon followed by the seamstress.

The prince looked grim. "This will take half the day, I'm afraid. We should have kept the wine."

"I did," Thyme told him, bringing the bottle from beneath his colorless old cloak. "No glasses, though, I fear. I have bad luck with them – they break so easily." He passed the black bottle to Prince Patizithes, who was somewhat surprised to find his wine gone sour.

"That should do it," said the seamstress, stepping from behind her screen. "I shall have her gown ready –"

Thyme's cold eyes caught hers. There was the slightest of pauses.

"– by tomorrow. Tomorrow before nones, I should imagine."

"Fine," Thyme told her.

"And I've loaned her an old dress to wear until then," the seamstress proceeded breathlessly, "that is, she really doesn't have to return it."

"We thank you," Thyme told her; and as he spoke, the child stepped silently from behind the seamstress's screen, scarcely less lovely than a summer sunrise.

The prince gasped.

Thyme's mouth twitched, and he suppressed a smile. "This audience you promised to arrange for us, do you think you could make it for tomorrow afternoon?"

The child smiled too. "Yes, it would be marvelous. Could you?"

"I think so." Prince Patizithes nodded nervously. "Anyway, I'll try. I – my house is outside the walls. It's only a league or so. My carriage is at the gate. I'll bring it if you like."

"That might be best," Thyme told him. "This poor child and I have already walked some distance today."

"Of course, of course!" Prince Patizithes darted through the dressmaker's door.

Wearily, the child chose a chair. "He *is* nice," she told Thyme, "whether you think so or not."

"As nice as peace?" Thyme asked her seriously.

The seamstress simpered. "He's royal, my darling, and to be royal is ever so much better than to be nice."

"Perhaps." Thyme turned away and walked to the window. He had hardly reached it when a whip cracked outside. The prince's equipage came rattling over the cobbles, and four footmen leaped to open its doors and draw out a deep green carpet.

"Slippers!" The seamstress snapped her fingers. She flung herself into the search, but she had started too late. Lightly as any lady, the child smiled, gave her a little pat of parting, and put her hand into the prince's to help herself up the steep step. Frowning, Thyme followed, choosing a seat that faced the child.

Prince Patizithes raced around the high rear wheels to duck through the other door and sit beside her. "We've shoes aplenty," he assured her. "Guests are always leaving them. You know how it is. You may have whichever pairs you like."

The child thanked him with her eyes. "Are there green ones to go with my new dress?"

Their coachman clucked his tongue to his team and cracked his black whip, the white horses leaped like lurchers after a leveret, and the prince's rich equipage jerked and jolted up the cobblestoned street.

Patizithes laughed. "Why there's nothing *but* green ones, I'll take my oath. Because of the war, no lady of Vert has ever dared come to court in anything else."

The sentries snapped erect and saluted them smartly as the ghostly team galloped through the postern gate. Patizithes had lied about his lodge (for it was to such a hunting house in the forest royal that his carriage carried them) when he said it lay but a league away; their horses were heaving and lathered with sweat whiter than they before all the weary watches that brought them to that lonely lodge were done.

Yet it was lovely. The child stared at its tall chimneys and the thronging green trees of his father's forest with dazed delight. "Do you really live here?" she asked Patizithes in a bewitched whisper.

"It's just a shed," he said. "I've a little place in town as well, but I know you'll be more comfortable here, where each of you can have a private apartment."

At evening, while the whippoorwill called from the tall cherry tree and the nightingale rained her sweet notes on the world, Prince Patizithes and the changed child watched lovely Lune's head lifted by the slow rotation of Urth, and strolled the strange walks of the grotesque little garden the prince's poor grandfather had graded and planted while weeping for his wandering wife. Fragrant were the ramping pink roses and the fading forget-me-nots that night; but he found the child's musky tresses more fragrant far. And sweet though the birds' songs sounded, she found the prince's poor promises sweeter still.

The two thought themselves alone. But all the while, one watched with the night-wide eyes of love. While they paced the pebbled paths between the silent flowers' spiked arrays, sage Thyme spied upon each pale sigh, peeping between bloom and leaf. And while they sat side by side and hand in hand on the stained stone bench beneath the spreading wisteria, Thyme watched unwinking from the midnight face of the mute sundial.

And while they lay lazy on the soft grass, swearing the sweet oaths of love and longing, and whispering as they parted that though long lives might pass like a night and the New Sun sunder the centuries, yet never should they ever part, Thyme crept and cried, counting seconds that spilled with the sand from the hourglass, and scenting the soft breezes that cooled the child's burning cheek with his sad spice.

The cock crowed as Thyme tapped impatient toes at the lofty lodge's deserted door, but the lovers slept long. It was nearly nones ere the coach came, carrying a pauciloquent child prince and a cheerless child. Together the three traveled along the rugged road that runs to the great green gates of Vert; but scarcely they spoke one word, and though Thyme turned anguished eyes from face to face, while watch waited upon watch, the cheated child never met that grim gaze. No more gave she her grave glance to the prince perched on the soft seat beside her, though her hand sought his, and sometimes failed to find it.

In a space scarcely short of miraculous, Madame Gobar, the seamstress, had sewn such a green gown as any virgin nymph would willingly have worn to Vert's stiff court. "No pearls, you see, Your Highness," she told Prince Patizithes in the honest tones of one who takes an open pride in having done her duty. "A few small emeralds, and a nice big aquamarine or two. And she loves it – don't you, my dear?"

She did. But before she could smooth her skirt and gaze a moment in the glass, off flew the coach, charging down the dirty streets of Vert and never pausing until it pulled up before the broad stair whose steps stretched to the portals of the palace.

Soon and swiftly they were sent before the emperor's own imperial throne; and there the poor child voiced her plea for peace through chattering teeth.

"I do not know how many men have died," she said. "Your Majesty will know that better than I; but I know my father was one of them, and that as we came here we saw unworked fields everywhere, houses falling to ruin, and women plowing – plowing badly – when the plowing should have been done weeks ago. We saw women sowing grain instead of shirts, cattle and sheep that had been killed by bears and wolves, and hungry children."

"Boys who can never grow into strong soldiers," Thyme added, addressing the emperor, "and girls who will never breed them."

Some shocked courtiers gasped at all this, grabbing their gowns and clutching their cloaks as though to keep them clear of contamination. But the stern, scarred old emperor never heeded them, nodding his head and neither smiling nor scowling.

"I have lost my father," the child continued. "I know that you have lost five fine sons. Only one is left to you. I love him, and so do all your other loyal subjects, I feel sure. Won't you make peace?"

"Peace has been made many times," the emperor said solemnly. "And each peace has only led to a new war. What is the good of treaties and truces where there is no trust? The fighting stops, and our enemy rearms."

With that, the elderly emperor's voice sank to silence, and a sullen silence hung heavy over all that gay green gathering. Some aged courtier coughed, and there was the faint scuffle of many shuffling feet. Prince Patizithes strode forward to stand beside the confounded child. Silently, he slipped his hand into hers and led her to an alcove. "I promised you an audience," he told the child coldly. "I didn't promise you that it would help things, and as you see, it hasn't."

Thyme told her, "You tried, and that's something not many have done."

Just then, they were joined by a general, an old officer whose bottle-green uniform bore many an enameled medal, besides the usual battle honors. His hair was gray, his visage grim, his eyes the green of Vert. "Your Highness," this green general growled, "may I interrupt? I think it will only take a moment."

"You already have, Generalissimo," the prince pointed out.

"You are young," the green general said gravely, "and so you think wisdom is to be found in pink cheeks and bright eyes. We who bear the weight of past years know that white hair or a bald head is a better indication of it. Since you have brought this old, and I suppose holy, hermit to the court, I would like to make use of whatever hard-won wisdom he may possess while I can."

"Then speak, my son," Thyme urged graciously.

The hoary-headed old officer did not hesitate. "How can we win?"

"You may win," Thyme told him, "when your army is dressed in yellow."

For a moment the grim old general stood stunned. "You can counsel me to dress my soldiers like the enemy," he said slowly, "but I assure you that though I am master of all our armies, I cannot do such a thing. Nor would I do it if I could. I would rather lose the war than do as you suggest."

"Then you will not have to," Thyme told him. "Because I will do it for you."

The old officer turned upon his heel and left them without another word.

Thyme watched his retreating back, then said softly to the

child, "Now I too must go, and you must come with me."

She shook her head. "I love Prince Patizithes," she said. Thinking that he still stood at her side, she looked around the alcove for him; but the prince of Vert had vanished.

"You will come with me." Thyme turned and walked away, his black boots tapping the tessellated pavements of the palace like the ticking of some slow clock.

"And he loves me!" the child whispered to herself; but there was no one but herself left to listen.

That night it rained, and Thyme sat drinking drop for drop with a broad banyan tree. As soon as the last drizzle stopped and the sun was seen, he rose and returned to the road. He had not walked much more than a watch when he heard the hurrying child calling. *"Thyme, Father Thyme, stop! Wait for me!"*

Without waiting, or turning toward her, or even so little as looking behind him, he murmured, "Thyme waits for no one," and walked on.

It was early evening before she walked with him as she had when he had brought her to the city. "I want to tell you," she said.

"I know." He nodded. "And you are old enough now to tell Thyme, if you wish."

Slowly then she spoke of the old garden and the green lawn on which she had lain with her lover; then of the threats he had thrown in her frightened face, because she had wished to remain where he would reign, though she would be called his concubine.

"Did I do wrong?" she asked at last.

"No." For a second Thyme stopped, turning to take in the road that returned to Vert. "Very small, child, are the flying days of love, and men and women must catch them when they can, if they are to know love at all."

The child shook her head. "Wouldn't it be better not to know love at all, than to know a false love?"

"No," Thyme answered again, turning back to their way once more and taking her by the hand. "In the desert, travelers see pools of water where no water is; but those who see these pools know how real water must look, if ever real water is found."

So Thyme spoke, and soon no more was said, though arm in arm they walked together. Their road had reached the rugged hills, and now wound higher and higher, turning and twisting till at length it mounted to the mountains. There it went with a wider, fairer way, where green grenadiers counted cadence for callow conscripts, brave youths and young boys with pallid faces, who flaunted pikes.

With each cubit they climbed, the cherry-lipped child who had ventured to Vert vanished. Lines led from her eyes to her ears, and strands of silver streaked her once sleek hair. The food they found and the rough rations Thyme took from some of the soldiers seemed to thicken her hips and bulk her breasts; and at last, with their road long lost, when they went their way guided only by the onrush of the green emperor's army, she laid palsied palms upon her broadened belly and knew there the feeble flutter of new life.

Drawn the child looked before the dawn, in the hour when her own child came. Then Thyme himself knew terror; for it is not so (as some say) that Thyme heals all things, though healing he has. But Thyme himself tied the cord and comforted his tired child, pressing her babe to her breast.

"Now I must go," Thyme told her. "You must have food and good water, and rags with which to diaper your son. Keep him warm while I am away, and yourself as well." He set sticks by her hand, so that she might feed their fire, saying, "I will return as soon as the Increate wills it."

Then night closed over his old gray cloak; he was gone like some ghost. The chilled child lay alone save for her son, alone and lonely, shaking with the flickering, guttering flames in the white wind that whipped the wide green skirt Madame Gobar had made, shaking too with terror as she heard the wild howls of the wolves that batten on battles, the slayers of the slain.

More than these, she feared the fierce soldiers who surged about the wretched brush that sheltered her and her son. They who had been boys had been made beasts, bent if not broken by their battles, the henchmen of Hell and the disciples of Death – thus she thought. Then her babe embraced her breast, sucking his mama's sweet milk; and soon her heart soared. Such was the mutability of his mother. Such, indeed, are the shiftings in all human hearts.

Somewhere a stick snapped, and her bliss broke with it. She staggered to her feet, and would have fled if she could; but she could scarcely stand. Part of her wretched protection was rolled away. A short sword and a worn face caught the firelight. For a moment that seemed a month, her eyes met his. "By the book!" the startled soldier swore. "What in the name of awful Abaia are you two up to?"

"My son's having his breakfast, as you see," she said; "and I was resting, until you came."

The soldier lowered his sword and pushed through the brush. "Then sit down." He held out his hand; and when the child had clasped it, and sat as he had said, he sat himself, sitting so his broad back blocked the hole he had made in their screen of brush.

"Did you see our fire?" she asked. "I feared someone would, though Thyme piled as many dead bushes and branches as he could around this windfall before he built it."

"Thyme?"

"My father. Or at least that's what I call him, since he cares for me. You needn't be afraid. Thyme's an old man, you can kill him easily, I'm sure."

The soldier shook his head, his eyes on the baby boy. "I wouldn't do that. What's his name?"

The child had not yet chosen one, not knowing one would so soon be needed. Now she blurted, "Barrus!" Barrus had been her brother, in days that seemed a dream. Her bold brother, and her father's favorite.

"Ha!" the soldier said. "The handsome one, eh? Well, he's handsome enough, I'll admit, for somebody so new to this world. But may I ask what you're doing here, on a battlefield in a ball gown?"

"Seeing war," she said. "I think so that I'll know what it is when Thyme brings peace."

"You'd better go back home," the soldier told her. "Before

you're killed – you and your child too. Before some fool shoots you, or you starve or freeze to death."

"We're going on, I think." Barrus had released her nipple; he was asleep. She slid the strap up so her silk bodice hid her breast. "Over the mountains to the Yellow Empire."

"In that green dress? That's suicide." A brass clasp held his soldier's sagum. He opened the clasp, pulled off the cloak, and handed it to her. "This was green when it was new, but it's gray now. It may not get you through alive, but it'll keep you warmer till you die."

Tearfully, she tried to thank him, though she only sobbed and stammered.

"Don't worry about me." The soldier shrugged. "There's plenty of dead men out there, and their cloaks don't keep the chill off any longer. I'll get another one – a newer one, with any luck." He rose to go.

Winking back her weeping, she blew him a brave kiss. He caught it, smiled suddenly (he seemed but a boy when he smiled), and was gone as the dark gave way to dawn. Hot tears streaked her tired cheeks; she closed his cloak about herself and Barrus, her baby boy.

So Thyme saw them when he pushed aside the brush – wrapped in warm wool, and peacefully asleep. When the child woke and Thyme chided her for crying, she would say only that those who have seen clean water in the desert's depths, without drinking, are entitled to tears.

Slowly they mounted the mountains' stony sides, old Thyme taking her hand and the child cradling her child. In time of peace, travelers would trudge the passes, as Thyme assured her, At present, divisions defended every defile, holding each high road against whole armies.

A bit before evensong, they were to witness such a struggle. Thyme stopped, pointing for the child with the pine staff he had chosen before they had left the last trees behind. "Do you see the green squares?" he asked sadly. "This is no skirmish, but some major matter."

It seemed a storm had struck the mountain-cut below. The arrows flashed like lightning, and they heard the thunder of the guns. A surging green square gained ground, then wavered and went out like the lambent flame of some snuffed taper; a second square crept up the slope, covering the corpses of the slain.

"See how resolutely they advance." Thyme tapped a stone with his staff as he spoke. "Determined to win or die! Would you care to say which you think it will be?"

She shook her head. She felt sure the soldier whose wool sagum she wore served in that square, though she told herself truly there was no way of knowing. Like the last, this square perished in the pass.

A yellow column came, sliding along like a snake from the wild wadis of the West. Green cavalry gave it check, then gave way. Scattered green soldiers followed, fleeing.

"The westerners have the victory," she said to Thyme, "and soon they will take Vert. Then there will be peace."

Thyme took up his staff and stood, ready to resume their march. "That pass has changed hands many times," he told the child. "And the war is not yet won."

That night they camped near the enemy army. "Now wash your dress," Thyme told her. "I will keep my eyes off you." She did as he bid, scrubbing her soiled green gown in a sparkling stream. Sometimes soldiers stopped to talk with her. She was covered by her cloak, and she feigned a friendliness that was soon sincere. "Yellow will never yield," the newest recruits replied when she pleaded for peace. The older soldiers only shrugged, or spit, or spoke of something else. Although their accent was strange, she soon ceased to notice it, speaking just as they spoke. No one she had known wore yellow, yet save for their yellow coats the young men could have been her cousins.

"Will there never be peace?" she asked Thyme when her dress was dry.

"You will see," he said, and would say no more.

When the next day dawned, her baby, Barrus, could walk with

his mother. Thyme found him trousers and a shirt, she dared not ask where, and she shortened the little legs, and the sleeves of the shirt. From the peaks they could see the plains, and in the misty distance the spires of Zant, that unyielding yellow city, glorious with gold.

Barrus told tales of days she was sure he had only dreamed, chattering to the child of childish notions she had never known, then comforting her with kisses. "My mom forgets, doesn't she?" He giggled, grinning. "But you always remember, Father Thyme, don't you?"

Thyme sighed and shook his head. "It is my task to wipe away. As you will learn."

They found a road that roved from wood to wood. Stunted shrubs made way for white pine, alder, and pale aspen. Barrus had a knife now, and cut a clever whistle with which he piped their progress from peak to pass, and at last to the mountain meadows. He did as Thyme told him, but defiantly, not freely. At each step they took he grew taller, and more sulky and more sullen. "I can beat Thyme," he told his mother, tapping his toes to a tune he had taken from the thrush.

"Please don't!" She felt frightened; Thyme was their only friend.

The great sage grimaced. "They always think they can, at his age."

A day of drizzle brought them to the bright gates of Zant, weary and wet. Sentries stopped them, guards in gorgeous golden armor who addressed them in the babyish voices of boys or asked the quavering questions of senescence.

"We only want food and shelter," Thyme told them. "Food, and a fire, and a little peace. Those are our only reasons for coming to Zant."

Perhaps the guards pitied the palsied old man, for they opened the gilt gates for them.

"Are we going to go to an inn?" Barrus asked. He pointed to the painted boards grouped near the gate: the Golden Goblin, the Pilgrim's Pause, the Royal Roast, and many more, all pied with paint to picture the Goose Girl, the Pilgrim putting down his pack, the Singing Oriole, and so on, so that even those who could not read the names could take their ease at an inn in any case.

"No," Thyme told him. "Or at least I hope not. This is the country of gold, so nowhere does gold buy less than here."

He stopped at the step of a private dwelling, rapping its dark door with a ring hung for that purpose. "Madame," he said to the wary woman who came to his knock, "we are poor travelers, seeking a lodging for a night or two at a price we can afford. Can you tell us of some decent family who might take us in? We cannot pay much, but we will lay down ready money for whatever we get."

"No." The dour woman would have shut her door and shot its bar, but that Thyme's blunt black boot blocked its edge.

"If not yourself, perhaps some neighbor?"

"I don't dislike any of my neighbors that much," the dour woman told Thyme. "Now get your foot off my threshold, or I'll call the dog."

Thyme stepped back, bowing as her door banged shut.

A meager little man in a long yellow cloak stopped as it slammed, looking as wet as they were. "I heard what you said. I've got a room in a decent enough house, a couple of streets over. They might take you and your wife –"

"My daughter, my son."

"And your daughter, I meant to say. And your grandson, if you can pay."

Thyme thanked him, and they went with him, down one sodden street and up another, until at length they arrived at an old-fashioned high city house, ornamented with carvings now decayed, with a second story overhanging the first, a third that overhung the second, and giddy garrets that overlooked the wall.

Cheaping with the landlady, Thyme got the child and Barrus a garret and rented a similar room for himself. When the meager man who had guided them to the house had gone, their new hostess asked them how well they knew him.

"Less than you, I'm sure." Thyme knelt by the tiled hearth that was now his own, for this night if not forever. There was a little tinder and a log or two.

"You won't get *that* burning," said Barrus.

"In time," Thyme told him. His flint scratched his steel, sending a shower of flying sparks to the tinder.

"Because," the landlady continued confidentially, choosing to chat with the child, "we really know nothing about him here, except that he pays."

Thyme puffed his tinder. "He seems an honest enough man." A small swirl of smoke curled toward the chimney.

The child shivered; her cloak was soaked from hem to collar. "When he has that going," she said to her son, "you should borrow a stick to light ours."

Barrus snapped, "I'm not an idiot, Mother."

The landlady laughed. "Maybe not, but you could fool some people, boy. Now, none of your sass to me, understand? Or all of you will be out in the street.

"Our lodger, I was going to say, pays us by the month. But sometimes the only time we see him is when he pays."

"The very time," Thyme remarked tartly, "when so many are invisible."

The landlady laughed again. "And don't I know it! Still, you can't help wondering where he goes and what he does."

A feeble flame flickered beside Thyme's tinder, darkening the white wood before it dwindled and disappeared. "Does he share supper with your family?" He blew on the bright embers and fanned them with his hand.

She nodded knowingly. "Sometimes. Mutton tonight, like I told you."

Barrus said, "It's burning right now, I bet."

"It'll keep, boy. Besides, I want to see if you three need anything more before I go down to look at it. I don't climb the steps more than I have to." She was short and stout.

"More blankets," Barrus said bitterly. "And more firewood."

"There aren't any more blankets. You can spread your coat on your bed, the same as we do. And if you want any more wood, boy, you'll have to fetch it yourself – I'm not carrying another stick up here. Come along, and I'll show you where it is."

The child spread chilled fingers before Thyme's tiny blaze. "What do you think?"

"I think it will catch that smallest log now," Thyme told her. "Though it would be better if we had more tinder."

"About her lodger, Father Thyme. You know everything."

The old sage shook his head. "I *find out* everything," he said, "sooner or later. But I don't know everything. A fellow that rents a room and uses it only now and then? That's a rich man who wants someplace to go when he's not where he usually is. We'll learn more at supper."

And so they did. There were two sober tinkers who rented a room together, as well as themselves and the meager man who had helped them locate the lodging, and the landlord and landlady. The meager man asked clever questions of the tinkers until he learned that neither had left the city since he had last seen them. Then he turned to Thyme to ask about their travels.

"Over the mountains." Thyme took a pair of potatoes from the big blue bowl that the landlord handed him. "And it was the making of the boy, but the destruction of my daughter, or nearly."

"Bad weather there," their landlord allowed. His good wife gave him a long look, and he added, "Or so I've heard. I can't say I've ever been there."

The child peered into her chipped plate, which was still empty.

"It was worse here." Thyme tried to pass her the potatoes, but was waved away. Barrus took the big bowl. "Not as cold as it was in the mountains, but the rain makes you feel it more."

A worn old woman licked chapped lips in the child's plate, her wavering reflection as dim as her dead eyes.

"Of course, the war made everything ten times worse." An earthenware ladle drowned the dim woman in greasy mutton gravy.

"I'm sorry to hear that," the meager man muttered. He and Thyme talked for some time; he seemed eager to learn everything he could about both armies.

"Will there ever be peace?" the child asked them.

"When we win," their landlord said loudly. Hasty for his favor, the two tinkers banged the battered tabletop with their spoons.

Without speaking loudly, the meager lodger managed to make himself heard above the uproar. "Our emperor has pledged a rich reward for anyone who advises him on how peace may be achieved."

"Then your emperor is a wise man," Thyme told him. To the child, Thyme's tones seemed changed, as if an occult knowledge added weight now to words she did not wholly understand.

"And that is pleasant news for us," Thyme continued. "For we've come here expressly to see him."

Their landlady looked happy to hear it. "You may have to wait quite a while," she said, "if that's what you've come for. We don't often see him ourselves. We can give you your rooms for a week, for five times the daily rent."

"That's kind of you." Thyme tasted a piece of brown bread before laying it on his plate and larding it with a ladleful of the gray gravy. "I think you mentioned something of that sort while we were getting the fire started."

"About the rent?"

"About the emperor. You mentioned you didn't see him much."

"I don't remember that," she said.

"Then I was mistaken." Thyme turned from her to look at her lodger. "It was you she was speaking of, perhaps."

"Perhaps it was." The lodger pushed away his plate. "I don't want to take the time of the whole company, but if you could come to my room after dinner, I might be able to advise you about the best ways of getting a glimpse of our emperor, though he doesn't appear in public often."

"I've finished now." Thyme took the napkin from his lap and laid it beside his knife. "I see you're finished as well."

"Your poor daughter hasn't eaten much."

Thyme nodded. "True, but her appetite will be better tomorrow, I think."

The landlord laid a hand on his arm. "No bread pudding? My wife's bread pudding's quite famous."

The two tinkers looked ready to laugh with pure pleasure. "All the more for us," said the smaller. "I'll take the old man's," added the taller.

The child stood up, scraping back her chair. "May I come with my father?" she asked softly.

The meager man began, "Possibly —"

"She must." Thyme took her in tow. "Now what about you, Barrus? Which will it be, peace or pudding?"

"We don't have pease today," the landlady put in. "They're a bit tough, so far into the season."

"Then I'll take pudding," Barrus said sullenly.

"And we will see you later." Thyme led the child to the stair. "It will be on the floor below ours, I suppose."

The lodger nodded as he slipped past them. "I'll have to unlock the door."

"You are fortunate," Thyme told him when they were seated inside. "Our rooms have no locks. Of course, we've little to leave in them when we go."

The meager man smiled mischievously. "I'm afraid I enjoy frustrating our good hostess."

"She's the sort who snoops through drawers? I suppose so; she seems the kind of woman who would."

The meager man nodded. "Yet there are others who discover more secrets, without spying."

"True," Thyme told him. "And kind men who repent of their kindness when they find that others are clever."

"If you know my secret," the meager man said seriously, "you also know that I have means of silencing those who know secrets."

"Which need not be used in this case." Thyme rose and went to the window, where he stood staring out at the smoking chimney pots of Zant.

"I'm glad to hear that."

"My daughter and I will leave your city in the morning. In a day or two, we will have left its empire. I will not speak; nor will she, I assure you."

Bewildered, the child stared from Thyme to the meager man and back. "Please," she said. "What are you two talking about?"

Thyme turned. "The emperors of Vert trace their line from the first emperor for twenty generations," he said softly. "It is not so here in Zant. Here emperor has deposed emperor, till at last one who was well liked was murdered in a manner so foul that the people would not consent to his murderer's coronation. They chose another general in his place, a hero of humble birth who had risen through the ranks and was famous for his courage." Thyme glanced toward the meager man as he finished speaking, a charged gaze that told the child much more than his mere words.

"I understand – I think."

The meager man made a little motion of impatience. "Yes, I'm the Yellow Emperor. How did you know? Give me a simple, straightforward answer, please."

"I had your picture." From the burse at his belt, Thyme took a copper coin. "When we were going over the mountains, I stole some clothes for the boy."

"From my dead soldiers?"

"Yes. A few had a little money, which I thought might be useful in Zant. I confess I did not know how useful. When the Increate is with anyone, there rises a tide that bears into its harbor any ship that carries him."

"Millions of people have these coins."

"You asked me for a simple, straightforward answer," Thyme reminded the emperor.

"Give me your subtle and complex answer, then."

"Not terribly subtle, I fear. Nor terribly complex. It is true that millions have such coins, and yet do not know you when they pass you in the street; but that is only because they cannot conceive that they might encounter someone so exalted someday – someone who holds the power of life and death over every one of them. I know otherwise; there is someone who holds the power of being or unbeing over me, and I shall encounter that someone at the end of Thyme. Thus I understand that such meetings are not impossible."

The child smiled. "Isn't he wonderful?"

"Indeed he is," the emperor admitted. "It was nothing that I said?"

"Nothing specific," Thyme told him. "But our hostess had told us you seldom use the room you rent from her. My daughter asked me about it, and I indicated to her that you were perhaps a man of some wealth, and not what you seemed. You could have been a highwayman, but you lacked the blustering ways and impressive physique those fellows use to overawe their victims. You had the manners of a gentleman, without the arrogance that is often conferred by birth – we had been with Prince Patizithes in Vert, and so my recollection of that sort of arrogance had been refreshed."

"I see."

"When you questioned me at our meal, my first thought was that you were a spy – an agent of the emperor's, or of whoever gathers facts for him; but such a spy would have been much more interested in the enemy's army than in his own. I asked myself who might have an equal interest in each. A general kept in the capital, perhaps, but such a general could not appear as a poor man in a place where rooms were let to lodgers. Then I recalled that the emperor had been a general, and that an emperor can do as he chooses. So I looked at the coin."

The child ventured a very small sound.

"Yes?" the Yellow Emperor inquired.

"Sir – sire – I thought emperors just sat on their thrones. In the palace."

"On occasions of state, I do," the emperor acknowledged. "But here in Zant, the occasions of state are as few as I can make them. Quite frankly, there are too many other things I have to do."

"But isn't it dangerous?"

"Just yesterday," the Yellow Emperor explained, "I learned of a plot to kill me as I slept. So you see it's less dangerous here than sleeping in my palace. More than a few of our august emperors have died in their beds, although not many were either old or ill. I find out everything that's going on in Zant this way, and that's a great deal less dangerous than not knowing."

He paused, his pale fingers fumbling the worn arms of his chair as he watched the child's face. "Now may I ask what your business was with Prince Patizithes?"

Spreading her hands helplessly, the child turned to Thyme, but he sat silent until she found her own anguished answer: "He let me talk to his father about peace. And he was my lover, at least for one night."

The emperor nodded. "Neither actually surprises me much. Your father said something about peace to the boy, and you're still a beautiful woman. This was some years ago, I take it?"

"No, only a few days —"

"Yes," Thyme told him.

"Perhaps fifteen years or so?"

"Yes," Thyme said a second time.

"I see." The emperor sighed. "They have a certain look about them, all that line. They're all a bit inbred, of course. I'm sorry, madame, but I can't permit you to take your son out of my domains. He's too valuable to me — too valuable even now, while Patizithes is still alive. If the prince dies, he'll be invaluable."

"If he will bring peace…"

"He *may* bring victory," the emperor explained. "Or at least assist it."

"And after the victory, will there be peace?"

"Of course. And I will be a generous conqueror, you may trust me for that. Why, if — ah —"

"Barrus," she supplied.

"If Barrus proves a faithful vassal, he may well wind up on the throne of Vert. The Easterners would be more docile with someone of their own royal family to rule them, no doubt."

The child felt that she was choking, but she said, "Then you may keep him. Please — will you remind him, sometimes, of his mother?"

"I will," the emperor answered. "I pledge my word to it."

"Father…?"

"You have done well," Thyme told her. "Is that what you wished to ask me?"

His child shook her head. "No. In Vert you said that Vert might win when its men wore yellow clothes. Barrus will have a yellow uniform, I suppose. Is that what you meant?"

"Perhaps. Or part of it."

The emperor arose, strode across the room, and stared into Thyme's eyes. "You're a prophet! A sage! I should have known. And I take pride in my penetration – bah! What was it you meant? The whole of it."

Thyme told him; and late on the following morning, when the rain had at last relented, and long after the cock crowed, Thyme and the charmed child set forth from that tottering, high house, and the strait old street in which it stood, and the gilded gate of Zant itself.

While they walked, the child chirped, "I know this is very foolish, Father Thyme, but do you know I feel so happy! When I think back about it, I've felt sadder and sadder the whole time I've been with you. Now I'm happy again."

The old sage shrugged, and stroked his snowy whiskers, and whispered, "Such is life, child. Child, life is such."

So they proceeded, long league upon long league, the child chattering of the fields and flowers they passed, some pleasant pastures and their curious cattle. By the well-built bridges of the West they crossed its rushing rivers, the rivers that grind gold from their swirling sands. Soon they saw again the mighty mountains, standing like the walls of the world.

At first, the climbing child feared for her hoary father, feeling him too feeble to face their steep screes and perilous paths; but Thyme seemed to straighten with every step, and the snowy beard he had brought to Zant grew grayer and grayer from glance to glance. Once they were waylaid by a brutal bandit who threatened them, frightening the child with a fusil. Thyme took it from him and grappled him to the ground. Only one rose, and the two went on.

One morning, while they walked though a thicket of mountain laurels, the child lagged behind to look at them; for it seemed to her that some bore bright golden blossoms, and she had never seen laurels like them. Soon she found that the flowers belonged not to the trees, but to twining vines that choked them as they climbed. The child traced one down a trunk, ready to cut it at the root; but it grew from the eyes of a yellowing skull. She gasped and backed away.

"That is the trumpet vine," Thyme told her. "And that skull you saw once wore a green cap. Did you poke about the roots of the tree as well?"

In silent horror, she shook her head.

Thyme thrust aside the thick, tangled thorns with his stick, bent, and brought up a bone in a matted mass of mould. "Here is the rib of one who once wore yellow. You see, he has turned his coat, even though he has lost the back on which he used to wear it." Gay green moss had indeed wrapped the rib.

The child sighed, and sat herself upon a stone. "This is that place, isn't it? This is the pass where we saw the armies fight. I should have remembered it sooner, but then we were up there." Her eyes sought the spot along the snow line.

"Yes," old Thyme agreed. "This is the place."

"You said if each side tried to be more like the other, there might be peace. That's what you told the emperor."

The sage did not sit (for Thyme rarely rests). "What you say is so, child. During the long years in which I have ringed Urth, I have seen that the more nation differs from nation, the more difficult it is for one to trust another. Thus I advised each empire to make itself more like its foe. Alas, they were too much alike already. Each saw my advice not as a road to peace, but as ruse to win. The master of the green armies who rejected my counsel so rudely did so only that I might not guess what he planned; and the Yellow Emperor dressed legions in green only that they might not be fired upon as they advanced."

The child shivered. "And now the laurels war with the vines."

The old man nodded and struck a tree trunk (or perhaps the trumpet vine that twined it) with his staff. "I have changed their uniforms," he said. "But only they could halt their war."

Thus they came to green Vert, that great city, the Boast of the East; there they saw soldiers in argent armor standing guard at its gates, and a silver flag flying above the battlements of the bartizan. They did not stop. A gay girl the charmed child left the great green city, lissome and long-limbed, bright of eye and black of hair; but while she walked home with Thyme she dwindled, until such young men as they met on the way no longer stared but smiled. And ere old Urth turned her fair face from the sun, Thyme set her upon his shoulders.

Small and sweet and soiled she was when their long walk was ended at a place where pease had rolled hither and thither across the road.

"Goodbye for now," Thyme told her. "You may play with these pease, for the present."

"Goodbye for now, Father Thyme," she said. "I love pease."

"As do we all." Thyme took up his staff. "But it is so late in the season."

She was picking up her pease when her fond brother, Barrus, found her. "I love you," the child cried, and threw her chubby arms about him.

He fended her off, as boys believe they must, fighting not to let his love into his voice. "You're a very bad girl," he mumbled, and led her back to their mother's house.

Often afterward she talked of Thyme, until at last her dear mother declared she must have seen the ghost of her grandfather, who had died that day. But though Thyme walked with her always, as he walks over all the world, his adopted daughter did not see him again; and this is his story.

Karen Joy Fowler's stories are, like Caesar's wife, beyond reproach.

THE ELIZABETH COMPLEX
Karen Joy Fowler

"…love is particularly difficult to study clinically…"
  – Nancy J. Chodorow

"Fathers love as well. – Mine did, I know, – but still with heavier brains."
  – Elizabeth Barrett Browning

There is no evidence that Elizabeth ever blamed her father for killing her mother. Of course, she would hardly have remembered her mother. At three months, Elizabeth had been moved into her own household with her own servants; her parents became visitors rather than caretakers. At three years, the whole affair was history – her mother's head on Tower Green, her father's remarriage eleven days later. Because the charge was adultery and, in one case, incest, her own parentage might easily have come into question. But there has never been any doubt as to who her father was. "The lion's cub," she called herself, her father's daughter, and from him she got her red hair, her white skin, her dancing, her gaiety, her predilection for having relatives beheaded, and her sex.

Her sex was the problem, of course. Her mother's luck at cards had been bad all summer. But the stars were good, the child rode low in the belly, and the pope, they had agreed, was powerless. They were expecting a boy.

After the birth, the jousts and tournaments had to be cancelled. The musicians were sent away, except for single pipe, frolicsome, but thin. Her mother, spent and sick from childbirth, felt the cold breath of disaster on her neck.

Her father put the best face on it. Wasn't she healthy? Full weight and lusty? A prince would surely follow. A poor woman gave the princess a rosemary bush hung all with gold spangles. "Isn't that nice?" her mother's ladies said brightly, as if it weren't just a scented branch with glitter.

Elizabeth had always loved her father. She watched sometimes when he held court. She saw the deference he commanded. She saw how careful he was. He could not allow himself to be undone with passion or with pity. The law was the law, he told the women who came before him. A woman's wages belonged to her husband. He could mortgage her property if he liked, forfeit it to creditors. That his children were hungry made no difference. The law acknowledged the defect of her sex. Her father could not do less.

He would show the women these laws in his books. He would show Elizabeth. She would make a little mark with her fingernail in the margin beside them. Some night when he was asleep, some night when she had more courage than she had ever had before, she would slip into the library and cut the laws she had marked out of the books. Then the women would stop weeping and her father would be able to do as he liked.

Her father read to her *The Taming of the Shrew*. He never seemed to see that she hated Petruchio with a passion a grown woman might have reserved for an actual man. "You should have been a boy," he told her, when she brought home the prize in Greek, ahead of all the boys in her class.

Her older brother died when she was a small girl. Never again was she able to bear the sound of a tolling bell. She went with her father to the graveyard, day after day. He threw himself on the grave, arms outstretched. At home, he held her in his arms and wept onto her sleeve, into her soft brown hair. "My daughter," he said. His arms tightened. "If only you had been a boy."

She tried to become a boy. She rode horseback, learned Latin.

She remained a girl. She sewed. She led the Presbyterian Girls' Club. The club baked and stitched to earn the money to put a deserving young man through seminary. When he graduated, they went as a group to see him preach his first sermon. They sat in the front. He stood up in the clothes they had made for him. "I have chosen my text for today," he said from the pulpit. "I Tim 2:12. 'I suffer not a woman to teach, nor to usurp authority over the man, but be in silence.'"

Elizabeth rose. She walked down the long aisle of the church and out into the street. The sun was so fiery it blinded her for a moment. She stood at the top of the steps, waiting until she could see them. The door behind her opened. It opened again and again. The Presbyterian Girls' Club had all come with her.

She rode horseback, learned Latin and also Greek, which her father had never studied. She had, they said, a pride like summer. One winter day she sat with all her ladies in the park, under an oak, under a canopy, stitching, with her long, beautiful, white fingers. If the other ladies were cold, if they wished to be inside, they didn't say so. They sat and sewed together and one of them sang aloud and the snowflakes flew about the tent like moths. Perhaps Elizabeth was herself cold and wouldn't admit it, or perhaps, even thin as she was, she was not cold and this would be an even greater feat. There was no way to know which was true.

Perhaps Elizabeth was merely teasing. Her fingers rose and dipped quickly over the cloth. From time to time, she joined her merry voice to the singer's. She had a strong, animal aura, a force. Her spirits were always lively. John Knox denounced her in church for her fiddling and flinging. She and her sister both, he said, were incurably addicted to joyosity.

Her half-brother had never been lusty. When he died, some years after her father, long after his own mother, hail the color of fire fell in the city, thunder rolled low and continuous through the air. This was a terrible time. It was her time.

Her father opposed her marriage. It was not marriage itself, he opposed; no, he had hoped for that. It was the man. A dangerous radical. An abolitionist. A man who would never earn money. A man who could then take her money.

Hadn't she sat in his court and seen this often enough with her very own eyes?

For a while she was persuaded. When she was strong enough, she rebelled. She insisted that the word *obey* be stricken from the ceremony. Nor would she change her name. "There is a great deal in a name," she wrote her girlfriend. "It often signifies much and may involve a great principle. This custom is founded on the principle that white men are lords of all. I cannot acknowledge this principle as just; therefore I cannot bear the name of another." She meant her first name by this. She meant Elizabeth.

Her family's power and position went back to the days when Charles I sat on the English throne. Her father was astonishingly wealthy, spectacularly thrifty. He wasted no money on electricity, bathrooms, or telephones. He made small, short-lived exceptions for his youngest daughter. She bought a dress; she took a trip abroad. She was dreadfully spoiled, they said later. But spinsters are generally thought to be entitled to compensatory trips abroad and she had reached the age where marriage was unlikely. Once men had come to court her in the cramped parlor. They faltered under the grim gaze of her father. There is no clear evidence that she ever blamed him for this, although there is of course, the unclear evidence.

She did not get on with her step-mother. "I do not call her mother," she said. She, herself, was exactly the kind of woman her father esteemed – quiet, reserved, respectful. Lustless and listless. She got from him her wide beautiful eyes, her sky-colored eyes, her chestnut hair.

When Elizabeth was one year old, her father displayed her, quite naked, to the French ambassadors. They liked what they saw. Negotiations began to betroth her to the Duke of Angouleme, negotiations that foundered later for financial reasons.

She was planning to address the legislature. Her father read it in the paper. He called her into the library and sat with her before the fire. The blue and orange flames wrapped around the logs, whispering into smoke. "I beg you not to do this," he said. "I beg you not to disgrace me in my old age. I'll give you the house in Seneca Falls."

She had been asking for the house for years. "No," Elizabeth said.

"Then I'll disinherit you entirely."

"If you must."

"Let me hear this speech."

As he listened his eyes filled with tears. "Surely, you have had a comfortable and happy life," he cried out. "Everything you could have wanted has been supplied. How can someone so tenderly brought up feel such things? Where did you learn such bitterness?"

"I learnt it here," she told him. "Here, when I was child, listening to the women who brought you their injustices." Her own eyes, fixed on his unhappy face, spilled over. "Myself, I am happy," she told him. "I have everything. You've always loved me. I know this."

He waited a long time in silence. "You've made your points clear," he said finally. "But I think I can find you even more cruel laws than those you've quoted."

Together they reworked the speech. On towards morning, they kissed each other and retired to their bedrooms. She delivered her words to the legislature. "You are your father's daughter," the senators told her afterwards, gracious if unconvinced. "Today, your father would be proud."

"Your work is a continual humiliation to me," he said. "To me, who's had the respect of my colleagues and my country all my life. You have seven children. Take care of them." The next time she spoke publicly he made good on his threats and removed her from his will.

"Thank god for a girl," her mother said when Elizabeth was born. She fell into an exhausted sleep. When she awoke she looked more closely. The baby's arms and shoulders were thinly dusted with dark hair. She held her eyes tightly shut, and when her mother forced them open, she could find no irises. The doctor was not alarmed. The hair was hypertrichosis, he said. It would disappear. Her eyes were fine. Her father said that she was beautiful.

It took Elizabeth ten days to open her eyes on her own. At the moment she did, it was her mother who was gazing straight into them. They were already violet.

When she was three years old they attended the silver jubilee for George V. She wore a Parisian dress of organdie. Her father tried to point out the royal ladies. "Look at the King's horse!" Elizabeth said instead. The first movie she was ever taken to see was *The Little Princess* with Shirley Temple.

Her father had carried her in his arms. He dressed all in joyous yellow. He held her up for the courtiers to see. When he finally had a son, he rather lost interest. He wrote his will to clarify the order of succession. At this point, he felt no need to legitimize his daughters, although he did recognize their place in line for the throne. He left Elizabeth an annual income of three thousand pounds. And if she ever married without sanction, the will stated, she was to be removed from the line of succession, "as though the said Lady Elizabeth were then dead."

She never married. Like Penelope, she maintained power by promising to marry first this and then that man; she turned her miserable sex to her advantage. She made an infamous number of these promises. No other woman in history has begun so many engagements and died a maid. "The Queen did fish for men's souls and had so sweet a bait that no-one could escape from her network," they said at court. She had a strong animal aura.

A muskiness. When she got married for the first time her father gave her away. She was only seventeen years old, and famously beautiful, the last brunette in a world of blondes. Her father was a guest at her third wedding. "This time I hope her dreams come true," he told the reporters. "I wish her the happiness she so deserves." He was a guest at her fifth wedding, as well.

Her parents had separated briefly when she was fourteen years old. Her mother, to whom she had always been closer, had an affair with someone on the set; her father took her brother and went home to his parents. Elizabeth may have said that his moving out was no special loss. She has been quoted as having said this.

She never married. She married seven different men. She married once and had seven children. She never married. The rack was in constant use during the latter half of her reign. Unexplained illnesses plagued her. It was the hottest day of the year, a dizzying heat. She went into the barn for Swansea pears. Inexplicably the loft was cooler than the house. She said she stayed there half an hour in the slatted light, the half coolness. Her father napped inside the house. "I perceive you think of our father's death with a calm mind," her half brother, the new king, noted.

"It was a pleasant family to be in?" the Irish maid was asked. Her name was Bridget but she was called Maggie by the girls, because they had once had another Irish maid they were fond of and she'd had that name.

"I don't know how the family was. I got along all right."

"You never saw anything out of the way?"

"No, sir."

"You never saw any conflict in the family?"

"No, sir."

"Never saw the least – any quarreling or anything of that kind?"

"No, sir."

The half hour between her father settling down for his nap and the discovery of murder may well be the most closely examined half hour in criminal history.

The record is quite specific as to the hours when Bridget left the house, she looked at the clock. As she ran, she heard the city hall bell toll. Only, eight minutes are unaccounted for.

After the acquittal she changed her name to Lizbeth. "There is one thing that hurts me very much," she told the papers. "They say I don't show any grief. They say I don't cry. They should see me when I am alone."

Her father died a brutal, furious, famous death. Her father died quietly of a stroke before her sixth wedding. After her father died, she discovered he had reinserted her into his will. She had never doubted that he loved her. She inherited his great fortune, along with her sister. She found a sort of gaiety she'd never had before.

She became a devotee of the stage, often inviting whole casts home for parties, food, and dancing. Her sister was horrified; despite the acquittal they had become a local grotesquerie. The only seemly response was silence, her sister told Lizbeth, who responded to this damp admonition with another party.

The sound of a pipe and tabor floated through the palace. Lord Sempill went looking for the source of the music. He found the queen dancing with Lady Warwick. When she had become queen, she had taken a motto. *Semper Eadem,* it was. Always the Same. This motto had first belonged to her mother.

She noticed Lord Semphill watching her through the drapes. "Your father loved to dance," he said awkwardly, for he had always been told this. He was embarrassed to be caught spying on her.

"Won't you come and dance with us?" she asked. She was laughing at him. Why not laugh? She had survived everything and everyone. She held out her arms. Lord Semphill was suddenly, deeply moved to see the queen, at her age, bending and leaping into the air like the flame on a candle, twirling this way and then that, like the tongue in a lively bell.

A bit of meta-skiffy from Brian Aldiss, who's, well, been there. In his career span-
ning some forty years of writing, he's done just about every kind of fiction there is,
and continues to surprise. Unlike a certain entertaining robot.

THE SERVANT PROBLEM
Brian Aldiss

Of course, things aren't too bad now. Not as bad as they were, I
should voc. I can't complain. Used to routine and the confines.

I only have to work a five-hour day, four days a week, so that's
not so bad, like what it was when I was a little girl. I work a com-
pondur, and I've got it set up by my transpar, in a good light. All
I have to do is produce six hundred exacts a day. Well, I know it's
not a lot. Carrie Climp III in the next clonex has to produce eight
hundred supexacts a day.

Of course I get lonely. Can't deny that. Oh, I like the realiter,
have it on most nights. Tuned to the smut band, I'm not
ashamed to voc. Always take a shower after, though. We get hot
water in Dup-clonex 10 three hours every day. Quite enough for
all ordinary needs.

Beavis and I used to smut together. I miss him, don't I, Beav?
When I was a young girl, people weren't ashamed to go together.
"In love," they called it. Well, sometimes ideas die and perhaps
it's for the better. Like the old notion of people living in separate
"houses" to themselves. I was brought up in a house. You can't
help laughing. I suppose love went out with houses. It's done
away with a lot of squalor. Everything's in recyc mode here. Has
to be. We've got years to go yet.

Doesn't stop me missing Beavis. We used to enjoy an old-
fashioned and all. I told that to Carrie Climp once and she was
real shoved. Didn't voc anything, but you could see. "It's dillies

for me," she voced, "Contrafeubral." I daresay, but that's how it was in the past. Interpersonally, frigidity's the straight way here.

"Go out, take your mind off things, Grace," Climp voced. "Do a corridor." She's not unfriendly. It's that visulator on her phys all the time that does it as far as I'm concerned. I do corridor occasionally but you look at people these days and think they aren't scanning what it's all about.

Get yourself classified Zomb Category and you're looked after for life. Then you have to live in a megaclonex with other Zombs. That's not for me. Let me tell you, Beav, I stick in here most times, conched. When I stamp my chunk and go out, I generally take ASMOV with me.

He makes such a row when he peds it, does ASMOV. I make him ped behinder me. But he is company of a kind.

Beavis left me ASMOV when he went to recondition. AS-MOV, know ye, is shrinkspeak for Autonomous Server Mechanoid Zero Velocity (like in *slow*). It's a mixed costing. ASMOV was a sample of advancetech in his time, but the silver plating wears off. He stands about five feet high, almost my height. Lexi's model is four, which is better. Also plasmic, which is quieter. ASMOV moves so unpleasantly. When he peds it, you hear every click of his ankle, knee and thigh joints.

Once I apped him to the technopractor clinic. All they could voc was to advice an upgrade. There's not much you can maccy with a Mk.AM II. ASMOV already has memplants and accelerrs clamped to his head. To be honest, ASMOV's O/B. I tell him that.

"MANY YEARX HAVE I OF GOOD XERVIX TO YOU YET, GRAX," he vocs. Lenses me in a pathos mode.

"How many years is that?"

"AX MANY YEARX AX I AM XERVIX TO YOU, GRAX."

The speech facility glitches in him.

He stands by when I shower, and towels me afterwards in affect mode. When I order him to tell me a story he gacks in routine channel.

"ONX WAX A XMALL BOY AND GIRL LIVE IN OCEAN ON PLANET. CITY MANY FATHOMX DIP. BOTH BOY AND GIRL COME TOGETHER FROM NATALIUM. BOY AND

GIRL ARE FRENX AND NO SMUT BETWEEN. ALSO MAKE FRENX WITH WHAT THEY SCAN IX WHALE. BOY AND GIRL CLIMB OVER WHALE AND GO FOR RIDX XUR-HIM. BUT WHALE IX NOT MAMMAL. INXTED IX HUGE XUB-WEAPON FROM CONTINENT WAR. XO ONE DAY –"

Dry and impatient, I voc ASMOV, "I tell you every time, reaccess your fiction program. Indent for upgrade. You give the point of that stupid story away too early, so when the whale splodes it's no surprise."

He vocs, "XINCE YOU KNOW THIX XTORY WELL, GRAX, WHEREVER POINT OF XTORY IX PUT IT CANNOT XURPRIXE YOU. I HAVE RECITED THIX XTORY TO YOU 351 TIMEX. IT CONXIXTX OF 1266 WORDX. YOU MUXT REMEMBER THEM ALL."

His logichip annoys me. I annoy him. I voc, "I am going to sleep now, ASMOV."

I can sleep. He cannot sleep. Even this year's novdels cannot sleep, merely close their lens and pretend.

While I hang in bed, ASMOV peds it to his plug, stands rigid against the partit, shuts down. He recharges all dim out.

I'm coze, hanging there in my bedsuit. But through the night from ASMOV come many clinks and elsie-dees as his overHAW continues, checking every relay and cansion-MAR in his carapack. And always hinder that, the aircond and throb of ship as the lightyers brush past its forcers.

If you got a servant, you're never free. I know I shouldn't complain. Well, I'm not complaining. I'm only stating facts. When the andspector comes tomorrow, I shall tell him straight, if you got a servant, you're never free.

Thirty years on, all automates are up to Full Scratch. As Dawntime peds in, along prog the deckspectors. Cleaning, checking, mainting, upgring, millening, nothing skipped. All us comopondurops scanned for full eye-queue and health status in nakidity. I don't shun that, Beav, honest. Nakidity nothing to electronurses. Organs, hair, seepage – mere data to Big Biofeed.

My Class is Servant. Of that I'm proud. Serv II's "Must Keep Cortex Okay," as old song vocs it. That's me.

I just hope andspector doesn't decide to recyle ASMOV. Then I'd be really alone. I'd even miss the WHALE XTORY.

Always the suspic they'll reclassify me as a Zomb. Once you get to vocing "Time was," you're on someone's O/B listing.

Maybe keep producing exacts quota you printout Alpha.

A fairy tale. Not a fairy tale. Gwyneth Jones recently won two World Fantasy Awards for her fairy tales that combine the most current modern concerns and a deep mythic resonance in a way that satisfies many cravings at once.

THE THIEF, THE PRINCESS, AND THE CARTESIAN CIRCLE
Gwyneth Jones

Once upon a time there was a princess who was quite pretty and fairly intelligent, and when the time came for them to marry her off the royal family didn't worry about it too much.

One day the princess came down to breakfast and found the king, for a wonder, still sitting over his toast and marmalade. He was a workaholic monarch and was generally long gone to his despatch boxes by the time she appeared. As she sat down she observed that he was pulling faces at her royal mother; then he got up and slunk out of the room.

"Dear," said her mother. "I want us to have a little talk —"

The princess pointed distantly at a cereal packet, and took a bowl from Perkins, the breakfast maid. "I said, what is it mother?"

"Darling, you're nearly twenty now."

"So what, mother?"

The king had no male heir. The princess must marry a suitable prince who would rule the kingdom. She knew this, everybody knew this: but had there ever been such a mutinous and contrary child? The best education, the best of everything indeed, had been showered on this only daughter: skiing holidays, beautiful clothes, jewelry, a TV in her bedroom; all to no avail. One could accept some little outbursts of rebellion from a princess nowadays, but this one was just shockingly self-willed. The interview at the breakfast table ended in tears, and not the princess's tears either;

she never cried.

"She says such cruel things," sobbed her mother, having taken refuge in her husband's office. "And it's so depressing, to know that one's servants pity one." The king stomped to and fro beside the royal windows. Outside lay the balcony swathed in velvet from which a courtier should already have announced the princess's betrothal. He remarked at last in a puzzled voice.

"She looks all right."

He could not understand how his stony hearted and (to be honest) frightening child could look so much like other peoples' children. It would be so much easier if there was a dragon in the case, or a curse, or a straightforward enchantment. It would be bliss, come to think of it, if she were sent to sleep for a hundred years.

Up in her bedroom, princess Jennifer laid out the vegetable knife, the lint dressings, the antiseptic spray. She knelt on the carpet in front of them and bared the white inner surface of her forearm.

Cut.

The king and queen were in the parlor, talking about what the neighbors had to say.

Cut.

"We could offer her hand to the prince who can make her smile —"

"She often smiles."

The king shivered a little. It was not a nice thing, when the princess smiled.

Cut.

"It's no use my dear," sighed the queen. "She's a thoroughly unpleasant young woman and we could wait till doomsday to get rid of her if we try the 'whoever breaks this spell' ploy. I know we must have a legitimate succession, but I'm sincerely sorry for the young man, whoever he may be. Even though she is my daughter and I try to love her. She'll break him, she'll destroy him. Her sort of 'enchantment' isn't supposed to be catching. But it is."

The king didn't quite follow, but he caught the most hopeful point. His expression brightened. "You think she will marry?"

"She's never shown any sign of wanting to do anything else."

Cut. Pain and blood. The blood dripped into a bowl of white plastic, an open carrier bag stretched over a coathanger. The princess let it run down until she began to feel dizzy. She sprayed the cuts and dressed her arm, took the bag and poured blood down the toilet. It looked like her period. She flushed it away, and rinsed the bag in the handbasin.

The princess sat on her royal bed, and stared at the rich white silk coverlet, the real gold swan-necks that held up the monogrammed royal headboard, the pillow edged with the finest lace. The queen and king couldn't see this bedroom. They couldn't see themselves. Princess Jennifer was beginning to be afraid for them. They saw nothing, and refused to talk about things that Jennifer knew were real. They knew that she cut herself. The cuts on her arms were real, but the king and queen were too caught up in state visits and making speeches on television: they never discussed pain and blood.

Jennifer found herself musing that if their own flesh were sliced, that might wake them up. She thought of her father's stringy wrists, the loose skin of her mother's throat, with professional interest. She decided, finally for certain, that this palace wasn't safe anymore. Of course, *she* was always safe, because no one could touch her, no one could get inside. But it was time to find a prince, an archbishop, a cathedral, a long shining oyster satin train. At last she smiled, that cold, mouth-stretching grimace which made her royal father shiver when he thought of it. She went swiftly to Their Majesties' private parlor.

"I've made up my mind."

"Yes, dear?" they quavered in unison.

"Don't be stupid. I'm not your 'dear.' Listen, I've decided. I want to get married. But I can make conditions, can't I? I want to marry the richest man in the world. I don't like changes. I don't want anything to happen to me, ever. I want money. I don't care if he acquired it by selling pork pies made of babies' brains. I don't care if he's ugly as sin, or has filthy personal habits. I'll marry him, I'll have the children. Any reasonable number, so long as I don't have to see them afterwards. Or screw the bloke more often than is strictly necessary for royal reproduction. Those are my terms. Are you satisfied?"

Now in this country, and at this same time, there lived a famous magician. He was semiretired on a comfortable pension but he had started a small school of magic, just for amusement and to keep himself up to date with the latest developments. He lived on a cloud, which he had fitted up by magic with mystic gardens and thaumaturgical laboratories attached. It happened that one of this magician's valued protégés was an inveterate thief and liar. He stole everything. Even his name, which was Rayfe, was stolen. He had "borrowed" it from his brother when he first set out to become the sorcerer's apprentice.

The mage knew he had the wrong brother. But there are no mistakes in magic, so Rayfe stayed and the brother had to be content with a polite letter. The elder magician knew from the first that Rayfe was a dangerous investment, but the boy had talent. He decided to take the risk. Rayfe made good progress. When he had been in school two years he could command the four winds at his whistle and conjure mountains of gold out of the air. But he still couldn't eat his dinner with enjoyment unless it was someone else's. If he told you of any marvelous trick he had performed, you could be sure that of all the tricks in the book, that was the one he hadn't done. He had to steal even praise. When he couldn't satisfy his need any other way he would even steal blame, and own up humbly to crimes and stupidities that he had never committed. One fine morning – inevitably – the mage woke up with a crick in his neck and a stone in his back, in the middle of a field. The thief had stolen his master's magic – every last spell of it.

Meanwhile, back at the palace, the princess's search for a bridegroom was well on the way. Up to the palace doors came a stream of adventurers, charlatans, conmen, fantasists, fools, all of the claiming to be the richest man in the world. Princess Jennifer found none of them was quite what she wanted. She retired to the bedroom where the real gold swans watched over her, and cut herself over half-healed places that she'd cut last week. The bloodletting helped. It drained off some of the pressure. Something inside her was trying to get out. This way it escaped only in small installments, under control. Pain and blood.

"Is it my fault?" she asked her distracted parents, "if the world is so full of liars and fools?"

Then they brought in Rayfe.

The thief saw a thin girl with overbright gray eyes, very unattractively dressed. He thought she looked even less appealing than in the candidly unflattering royal photographs. He was not disappointed, for the girl scarcely figured in his plans. He was after her money. The princess whose parents were looking for the richest bridegroom in the world, must be worth a pretty penny.

The princess didn't see Rayfe at all. She didn't often look at people. She didn't like the eyes.

The first stage of the inquisition began. Three months later Rayfe and the princess were married. It was all orange blossom and archbishops, and the king could hardly believe his luck.

The bridal limousine bowled along through a wide sunny meadow. The bride was still in her wedding dress. It was a present from the groom, and he had asked for this romantic touch to the start of their honeymoon. "Stop the car," said the newly made Archduke Rayfe, suddenly. "It's so lovely here, we'd like to take a little stroll."

So they both got out, and strolled. Behind them there came an odd little sound, like a twig snapping underfoot. When they looked back the car, the driver, and the motorcycle escort, had all disappeared. Rayfe was astonished. He had intended, on this little stroll, to vanish the ugly princess's dress, just to tease her: instead he'd lost the whole motorcade. His concentration must have slipped.

The princess was staring coldly.

"What's the matter?" asked Rayfe.

The princess stood very still, and then she picked up a fold of her white lace gown and studied it closely. The inspection revealed nothing, but it gave her something to do. "It was all magic, wasn't it," she stated flatly. "The background the court detectives checked out, the financial records?"

Rayfe grinned uncertainly.

"What's going on, Jennifer?"

The meadow turned into a hotel room. Jennifer fingered her satin and lace nightgown. "You tricked me."

"I don't know what's going on, Jennifer," said the thief. "I thought you liked me. We were seeing each other, you took me home to your parents, you have this game about being a princess. Your parents seemed to like me. Everything seemed to move very fast, but I wasn't complaining. I'm in love with you!"

Jennifer looked at him with contempt. "I made you up," she said. It was the first time she had ever risked telling any of her puppets that: she was exhilarated and frightened. "I make up everything. And you're not in love. My father paid you to take me away."

Ralph was beginning to find that small cold voice definitely scary. He had never been much of a success as a cheat and a liar. He freely admitted (to himself) that he was one of the hopeless – incapable of holding down a job, and too scared of going to jail to succeed in a life of crime. Answering the princess's ad had been a risk. Marrying her had been an act of desperation. Guilty Daddy and Mummy make over income for life, to their crazy daughter's keeper.... Suddenly he realized what his life would be like, and his blood ran cold. He affected a light laugh. "Oh come now princess. Can't you take a joke? Nothing is beyond the dreams of avarice, and nothing is what you've got –"

She stared at him, in a way that made him feel sick.

"Now, now princess, don't be a sore loser. Besides, there's nothing to complain about. Magic's as good as any other currency –"

He made a few passes in the air and spread out his hands. Paper flowers showered onto the carpet. The princess stooped and picked up a jagged rock from the meadow grass. She flew at him. Rayfe yelled in panic. Pain and blood.

The meadow turned upside down and vanished.

The princess and the thief were hanging face to face in gray nothingness. It was very cold. "What's happening!" screamed Rayfe. The princess felt herself in the grip of magic that was not of her own making, for the first time in her life. "I knew you must have stolen your power from somebody," she snapped, improvising quickly. "Your master has caught us."

The grayness became the garden belonging to the magician who had trained the thief who had gained the hand of a princess by trickery. The magician, who knew everything, was there with them. Jennifer saw a stern, bearded male face, looking out of a cheval glass that had appeared standing on the lawn. The garden was not reflected in the glass. "He's going to kill us," she said. "Or worse."

"Oh God." Rayfe's voice was real but his body didn't seem to be all there. It looked like a cardboard cutout. "Get me out of this, somebody. I'd rather die than live out my life tied to the heels of a monster –"

The magician ignored Rayfe. "So," he said to Jennifer. "You expect me to kill you. You are an optimist, after all."

Jennifer looked into the eyes in the mirror, and wouldn't show that she was afraid. "You can do what you like, I suppose. You're in charge. But I'd like to know what my crime was."

"Your crime? Your perpetual crime is that you do not feel at home in your skin. Your latest crime is that you tricked this young man into destroying himself."

"He tricked himself."

"That's no excuse. You set a trap, using the king your father's money, designed to catch someone as worthless as yourself. I am aware that by doing so you saved your royal parents from an unpleasant fate. I will take that into account. Let me see. Your crime, Ralph, was the more cold-blooded. You have never tried to save anyone from anything. I will award the choice of weapons to the princess. Jennifer, whom do you hate most?"

Before her wedding the princess would have said: "I don't hate anyone," and meant it. She didn't even hate her parents. But she had changed, even in this short time. Her lip curled, in passionate disgust.

"Him!"

"Oh dear, that's unfortunate. For he's your husband, and you two are really very close…."

As the magician spoke, Rayfe felt dizzy. There was a buzzing in his ears, he thought he was fainting.... His vision cleared. He looked around and with a heart-wrenching shock *saw himself* – standing, stiff as a board, a few paces away. Bewildered, he looked down at what felt like his own body.

The princess began to scream. She screamed and screamed, and clutched her head and ran. Things grabbed her. The garden seemed full of grappling hooks, and there were walls in it that she banged into. She couldn't see the grass or the trees. She was wet and cold, and her head was full of something thick and cloying. She fought against the nightmare with all her iron will. She saw the edge of the cloud, looming up. She screamed in defiance. "No one can make me suffer!" and flung herself into space.

She fell and fell. She lost everything: the swan-necked bed, her monogrammed silks, her blind, but royal parents. She had lost her knife and the neatly laid out dressings, the ritual that kept her safe. She had lost the privacy of her own mind. The elder magician's voice came to her, calm and affable. "If the pair of you ever learn to like the arrangement, come back and see me."

She fell screaming, knowing there were worse horrors to come.

The princess's wedding dress grew drab and shabby. She lived like an animal in the wild wood. She who had taken her only pleasure in life from the softness of her bed and the delicacy of her food, now scrabbled for left-over roots in a turnip field and slept in ditches. Her hair hung in ratstails, her pale skin had turned the color of earth from dirt and weathering. She stank. She never gave a thought to the way she lived, never a shudder. She couldn't, the pain wouldn't let her. It wasn't her pain. It belonged to the sharp-edged shadow that followed everywhere at her heels: night and day, sun and shade.

She made arrangements with the woodlands animals, who lent her their claws, and cigarettes. She hid herself away (there was a hollow treestump that was her favorite spot) and cut her arms, her thighs, her sides; and bled. At times, the shadow lifted itself from her feet. It sat opposite her and screamed without a sound. She had a feeling she was feeding it on her blood. Her blood kept it alive, and kept it screaming. Her shadow was a drug addict: she was the drug that destroyed. She no longer remembered that she had ever been alone in her head, so it was the shadow who really suffered more. She would have liked to put it out of its misery. Sometimes she tried to jump on it, and found herself scratching and tearing at the woodland earth, or the animals. The shadow always escaped her, and so she could not escape from it. In the end the fact that she was conscious of that presence was the only consciousness left in her mind.

She lived from night to night, stealing the pig's porridge and the dog's crusts. She survived well enough. But then the real winter came. The villagers who lived in a huddle of small gray houses on the edge of the wood became harsh and bold. She was driven off from her hollow tree with sticks and stones. At night the dogs chased her. She couldn't find anywhere to hide. The blood, not fed to the shadow, began to build up inside. The pain which wasn't her own couldn't serve the same purpose as the old kind. She ran like a beast through the wood, a beast with sharp teeth and claws, that crept up on smaller beasts – and pounced.

The princess had blood and flesh in her mouth, the warm torn filaments coating her tongue. The rabbit screamed and she let it go. The princess retched, vomited bile. She knelt there and she thought, What am I to do? She knew she had to find some way to get rid of the shadow at her heels. Hate of the shadow kept bleeding through, making her conscious again; being conscious made her violent; being violent made the villagers torment her. There had to be a way out.

On the edge of the village, Ham the woodcutter lived all alone. He was a big, quiet man who had little to do with the other village folk or the dumb animals who did deals with the princess. Princess Jennifer had often seen him as he went about his work. She had watched him, and judged him. She knew that he would help her. Resolutely, she took the path that led to his cottage.

"I have been lost in the wood," she said, shivering, when Ham Cottar stood in the doorway. "Can you give me shelter?"

"I should hope so, at this season."

He took her in, and sat her by the fire.

The winter passed, the spring came. The woodcutter told

princess Jennifer that she had attacked her husband with a hotel ashtray, and basically that was why she had been living in this wild place. He was glad that she had decided to come in from the cold, but as long as she continued to mutilate herself, he couldn't hold out much hope for her escape from the magic wood.

"I don't mutilate myself," said Jennifer scornfully. She held up her arm. "I don't live in my arm."

"Where do you live, Jennifer?"

The princess looked on the woodcutter with pity.

"The place where I live doesn't have a name," she told him. "No name, no time, no space. I make up all those things. There's only me, the thinking thing."

The woodcutter smiled slyly. "So that's what you've been doing all this time," he remarked. "The mind locked up inside that raving animal has been reinventing Descartes?"

Her shadow lay between them. It had no right to be there, such a steady black mannikin in the flickering firelight. The shadow always came back. It was the same stuff as herself, dirty and dangerous. It came and stared at her with helpless eyes. It had nowhere else to go.

"I want to get rid of my shadow," she whispered. "It feeds on my blood."

"Jennifer," said the woodcutter, "I want to help. But you won't change the legal position by talking about a bloodsucking shadow. If you want to be separated from the person you call that, come further in, out of the wild. I know you can. Trust me."

He touched her. He couldn't take the danger seriously. He was only a peasant, his simple life had never touched the realms of great enchantment. She let him do what he liked. The princess thought she could settle down by the woodcutter's fire forever. She could be warm and comfortable again.

The shadow came, and she told him she'd found someone else to destroy, she wouldn't be requiring his appetite any longer. The cut-out of starless void was less sharp-edged than it had been: Jennifer noticed this with a stirring of inexplicable unease.

"We've got to get me out of here," she said, suddenly. "This place isn't safe anymore. You understand? Not safe."

Ralph the thief was used to the conversational style of his wife-in-name-only. He suspected that one of the doctors was fucking her. The man's life was probably in real danger and Ralph ought to tell someone. But he wouldn't. The way this place worked, Jennifer was the one who'd end up getting punished, though they wouldn't call it that. And for God's sake, she wasn't responsible.

"I don't want to help you," he whined. "I don't know why I keep hanging around. It isn't the money."

"I know it isn't," said Jennifer. "You stay because you're worthless, just like me. I'm crazy and I stink, but I'm still the nearest you've had to a steady girlfriend."

"You don't need me," said the blurred shadow, reluctantly. "You're not sectioned. That means they won't keep you against your will. You can walk out."

The princess understood that Ham the woodcutter had tried to tell her the same. Because she was not cut into pieces she could leave the wood. But her magic had been too strong for Ham. Fearing for him, she decided to leave anyway. The princess left the wood, in peasant clothes and shoes that the woodcutter had given her. A marketing farmer took her into town, and there she found work.

She had no money. The thief who had become the shadow had stolen it all. She had no interest in finding her way back to the kingdom of her birth. Her royal parents must have given her up for dead long ago, they wouldn't thank her for reappearing. She decided to leave them like that: happy enough in an abandoned story. She found a bed in a hostel, became a cleaner, and then a shop girl. She was neat, quiet and hard working. But her shadow was a nuisance. In the town, people weren't used to seeing even their own shadows. There wasn't much space for them on the crowded streets. Sooner or later she would notice someone staring at it. She would notice people whispering: she would have to leave her job. There was always some excuse. She was given a good reference, and the shadow was never mentioned, but she had to go.

Her life came back to her piece by piece. She knew that the wood had not been real. She knew that the woodcutter had been in danger before she arrived; and that he was beyond her saving.

She understood that the elder magician had arranged it all. He had stolen her safety, and thrown her into the wild wood, and given her a foul shadow, for reasons of his own; which he would explain in time.

She possessed her thinking self, and a shadow. The true horror of that companion was not that it was worthless and evil – like herself – but that it *was* the same stuff as herself. This is what happens to common people. It can happen to a monster princess. She looks out of her tower and sees another thinking thing, a being she hasn't invented. The citadel is broken, the world outside exists, nothing will ever be the same.

When the princess had worked this out she acquired a vegetable knife, lint dressings, antiseptic spray. Since she didn't have to think of her parents, she purchased a kidney shaped silver dish from a medical supply shop. She had always wanted one.

She cut herself. The nostalgia was intense.

As the days went by, she took to looking over her shoulder to make sure the shadow was there. No one in these streets knew how it felt to be the princess, the nameless, hating, terrified thing whose shell had been broken open. Only the shadow knew everything. But when she looked, she could hardly see anything: only a faint blur.

She became a clerk in an office. It was a big step up, for she had started off with no employment skills whatsoever, and a horrendous secret. Her immediate boss was a large, elderly lady with pernickety ways that didn't seem to fit her size. She was a dragon to the rest of the staff, but to the princess she became as much a friend as a princess like Jennifer could bear.

"What I like about you, Jennifer," she said – one evening when they were finishing up alone in the office – "is that you've never let anyone knock the corners off you."

"There's corners and corners," smiled the princess (she could smile now; quite convincingly). She tugged at the long wool sleeves of her dress. "A lot of people don't like the way my shadow falls, and it gets on their nerves."

"Shadow?" remarked the older woman, mystified. "What shadow? You've none in here, my dear."

The princess touched whole skin through the wool, and recalled that she hadn't cut herself for weeks. The last time, she'd had to stop because it had hurt too much. She looked, and it was true. She had no shadow.

She hurried through the crowds, she was crying in the street. She was making a fool of herself and behaving like a madwoman, but she didn't care. She was alone again in the tower.

"I must get back!" she cried. She didn't know where she had to get back to. But as she cried out, the busy street disappeared.

She was in the magician's garden.

The glass stood on the lawn, and in another moment the magician was looking out of it. "As I was saying," he remarked. "If you start to like the arrangement, you must come back and see me. You are looking well, princess."

The cut-out figure of the thief was still standing there. Rayfe was back inside. His eyes were agonized: a human being compressed into two dimensions and screaming silently.

"Let him go!" she yelled at the magician.

"Only you can do that."

"I don't understand," snarled the princess.

The magician's robes were embroidered with shining mystic signs, they billowed like dark and glittering smoke. He smiled. The princess turned to Ralph and shouted. "You can go! You're not committed to anything!"

Ralph was now crying. The princess remembered that she used to believe tears were like an explosion: humiliating and horrible as pissing yourself in public. The thief's mouth was wide and turned down at the corners, and his eyes were wet. But the cafe was noisy anyway. No one stared.

"This is the end of the arrangement. Your money's in a bank account, I haven't spent it for months. Fuck it, you don't need me to cover your tracks and check up on you. You're perfectly competent. I'm the one that's the burden. I want you to give your address to your parents. I want you to get a divorce."

"My child," said the magician in the glass. "I must ask an impertinent question. Do you love this worthless creature?"

The princess frowned impatiently. "He was with me – you

don't know what he knows. He was always there. How could I not –?" She didn't say the word. It closed up her throat even to think it.

"Indeed. Fire burns if you put your hand on the stove, even if you don't believe in fire. Water drowns if you fall into it and can't swim, even if you don't believe in water. So love in substance is love in fact. He has stuck by you, because he couldn't help it, because, pitifully, you were the best thing that ever happened to him. What's the name for such helpless attachment, in the world you invented?"

"So let us go!"

"I will do so. There's just a little test. Stand back."

Jennifer was talking to the voices she heard in her head. She still did that. But she knew she was doing it, that was the difference. She didn't need a keeper. Ralph knew that this was the last stand. The mad princess was at her last gasp. Jennifer would walk away from this meeting alone and sound. Ralph suspected what his life would be like, after today. He didn't think of it. He wasn't brave enough. He wanted to stay forever in this steamy cafe, with this crazy woman; neither of them having anywhere else to go.

The magician's staff described a circle in the air. Where it passed a white line stayed. The circle enclosed nothing. It was the ultimate abyss. Up to the white line ran springy tailored turf:: beyond its rim, a blank. No grass, no air, no light, no dark, no space. There was absolutely nothing there.

"Now then, Rayfe."

The thief fell forward, stumbling and rubbing his arms. He hadn't been following the conversation. Ralph never got the hang of magical conversations.

"I jump into the abyss, and she goes free?"

The magician looked doubtful. "Let me explain. I am what they call a natural philosopher. If you had studied your books, instead of stealing the knowledge out of them, you would know that a natural philosopher is bound to set tests for the world, and test most unmercifully the things that he most values. Does love exist? I do not know. But I know that if it were to exist it could have no limits. It could not have a beginning, or an end. There could not be a place where love was not, or a time when love had not been. If the princess's love for you exists, you will pass through my circle without harm. But for it to be real now," the magician smirked, with every appearance of arrogant malice, "it must have been as real always. She must have loved you the moment she saw you. Step through, young man. Try your luck."

Ralph watched the crazy princess, hopelessly.

"I don't know what's going on in the story now, Jennifer. I'm leaving because I've somehow grown some self-respect, and I can't stand to hang around a smart-looking lady who doesn't need me or want me. You can tell the elder magician thanks from Ralph. It must have been love at first sight – in the only, twisted way I could fall in love. Need is the same as love, when you're really needy; it's the best you can do. I just wish I could wipe out the first part. I despised you for being crazy, it was like despising myself. But you *hated* me. I wish I could lose that bit."

"It was like hating myself. Step through."

"If this gets you free, to a normal life –"

Rayfe stepped through, into the utter abyss. He was standing on firm green turf. The magician in the mirror looked smug. The thief was impressed. He had never dreamed of stealing a whole cosmos.

Ralph looked at Jennifer's hands. They were holding his. She had never touched him before, except when she was trying to kill him. He stared in amazement. To his almost certain knowledge she'd never touched *anyone* of her own free will, not what you'd call consciously, in her whole life. The world turned upside down, and righted itself; totally different, exactly as it had always been.

"There is no door that shuts behind us," said the princess. The elder magician vanished from the glass, the glass vanished too. Jennifer no longer needed to regard the part of herself that she respected as a separate person, nor did she need to call the part of herself with power male.

"The past changes constantly: it is something we invent from moment to moment. The thinking thing that is the only reality detested you then." She shrugged. "So what. Time isn't real. It loved you now. You heard what the magician said. If love is, it always was. If it has a start, as soon as it starts, immediately it always was. That's the circle of protection. It works even for the most worthless."

The green turf was the grass of the meadow. The road where the wedding car had disappeared was wider and less dusty than it had been. The trees beside it had grown in girth, and some of them had been chopped down to make room for new houses. The princess and the thief walked out of the meadow and into the noisy cafe. It closed around them. There would be no more Grimm fairy-tale illustrations in their story. Neither of them was quite capable of dealing with normal life, and they weren't even young anymore. They would probably end up in cardboard city no matter how hard they tried: but they would be together. They took hands and set off down the road, to live happily ever after in the land where love is beyond the reach of doubt.